LOS ANGELES NOIR

EDITED BY DENISE HAMILTON

AKASHIC BOOKS
NEW YORK

Published by Akashic Books
©2007 Akashic Books
Introduction ©2007 Denise Hamilton

Series concept by Tim McLoughlin and Johnny Temple
Los Angeles map by Sohrab Habibion

ISBN-13: 978-1-933354-22-4
ISBN-10: 1-933354-22-4
Library of Congress Control Number: 2006938153

First printing
Printed in Canada

Akashic Books
PO Box 1456
New York, NY 10009
info@akashicbooks.com
www.akashicbooks.com

LOS ANGELES NOIR

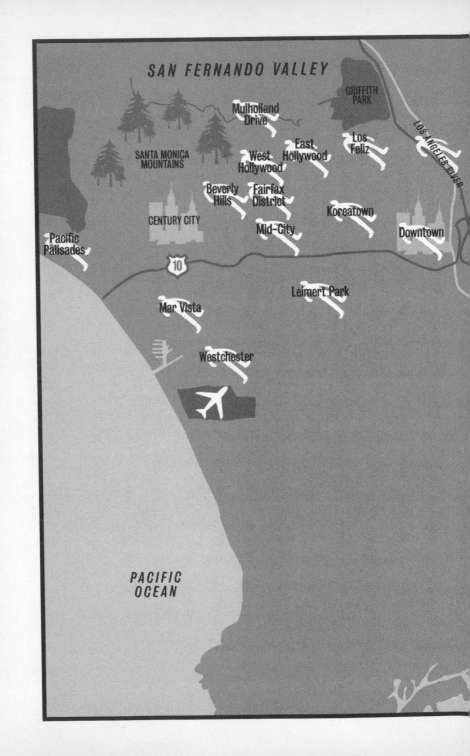

L.A. is epidemically everywhere and discernible only in glimpses.
—James Ellroy, "James Ellroy Comes Home," 2006

It occurs to her that what she most appreciates about this City of the Angels is that which is missing, the voids, the unstitched borders, the empty corridors, the not yet deciphered. She is grateful for the absence of history.
—Kate Braverman, *Palm Latitudes*, 1988

TABLE OF CONTENTS

13   *Introduction*

PART I: POLICE & THIEVES

21   **MICHAEL CONNELLY**   Mulholland Drive
       Mulholland Dive

39   **NAOMI HIRAHARA**   Koreatown
       Number 19

54   **EMORY HOLMES II**   Leimert Park
       Dangerous Days

85   **DENISE HAMILTON**   San Marino
       Midnight in Silicon Valley

PART II: HOLLYWOODLANDIA

97   **JANET FITCH**   Los Feliz
       The Method

122   **PATT MORRISON**   Beverly Hills
       Morocco Junction 90210

145   **CHRISTOPHER RICE**   West Hollywood
       Over Thirty

155   **HÉCTOR TOBAR**   East Hollywood
       Once More, Lazarus

PART III: EAST OF LA CIENEGA

179 **SUSAN STRAIGHT**   Downtown
     The Golden Gopher

209 **JIM PASCOE**   Los Angeles River
     The Kidnapper Bell

228 **NEAL POLLACK**   Commerce
     City of Commerce

242 **LIENNA SILVER**   Fairfax District
     Fish

264 **GARY PHILLIPS**   Mid-City
     Roger Crumbler Considered His Shave

PART IV: THE GOLD COAST

287 **SCOTT PHILLIPS**   Pacific Palisades
     The Girl Who Kissed Barnaby Jones

299 **BRIAN ASCALON ROLEY**   Mar Vista
     Kinship

318 **ROBERT FERRIGNO**   Belmont Shore
     The Hour When the Ship Comes In

330 **DIANA WAGMAN**   Westchester
     What You See

350 **About the Contributors**

INTRODUCTION
CITY OF ANGELS & DEMONS

I write crime novels now, but for a decade before that I was a reporter for the *Los Angeles Times*. Although I'm a native, there are still places I don't know and the landscape changes at such warp speed that it's impossible to keep up. Journalism gave me a passport to excavate the city's layers, nose behind the scenes, and interview everyone who wanted to talk and many who didn't.

Walking into the newsroom each morning, I never knew whether I'd face a triple homicide at South Pasadena High, a celebrity stalking in Malibu, or a brown bear that lumbered down from the San Gabriel Mountains to splash in someone's pool. The city was mythic and alive, pulsing with a thousand short stories unfolding all at once, tales of heartbreak and triumph, survival despite incredible odds and tragedy so horrifying it could have come straight from the ancient Greeks.

Each night when I got home, the voices of Los Angeles played like a broken tape loop in my brain. As time passed, I began to yearn to tell these stories unfettered by the constraints of journalism. Eventually I left the paper and started writing fiction. And if my books have a noir sensibility, well, it's a long and hallowed tradition among the city's writers. L.A.'s just a noir place.

So when Akashic Books publisher Johnny Temple asked if I'd be willing to edit an anthology of new fiction called *Los Angeles Noir* as part of the Akashic Noir Series, my first thought was that it was a great idea but surely someone had already done it. To my surprise, no one had. There's a tabloid photo book with that title and a noir cinema book. But what you hold in your hands is the first collection of Los Angeles noir fiction that we know of.

I think you'll agree that it's about time. Los Angeles is the birthplace of all things noir, starting with the Depression and World War II–era films that oozed an edgy fatalism and sexy recklessness mirroring the social anxiety of the times. Many of film noir's architects were refugees from Hitler's Europe, steeped in Expressionism and existential despair, and they brought that sensibility to the shadows, silhouettes, urban labyrinths, and hard-boiled plots of their movies. Over time, this narrative style infiltrated our waking lives and even our dreams, helping to define how we see the city and to shape the stories we tell about ourselves.

More than a half-century later, Hollywood continues to cast a giant shadow. Maybe it's the seductive blur of artifice and reality, the possibility of shucking off the past like last year's frock and reinventing yourself beyond your wildest dreams. Maybe it's the desperation that descends when the dream goes sour, the duplicity that lurks behind the beauty, the rot of the jungle flowers, the riptides off the sugar sand beaches that carry away the unwary.

Writers like James Cain, Dorothy B. Hughes, Nathanael West, Chester Himes, and Raymond Chandler understood both the hope and the terror that Los Angeles inspires, and they harnessed this duality to create their masterpieces. Hollywood, always a dowsing rod of the culture, reflected it back to the world through film. Even essayists from Carey McWilliams to Joan Didion to Mike Davis gave us prose about Los Angeles that's shot through with noir imagery.

When you consider the earthquakes, the fires, the mud slides, the riots, the poverty, the glamour, the wealth, the crime, the crackpots, the cults, the gangs, the scandals, perhaps it's inevitable.

Of course, Los Angeles has changed beyond recognition since Philip Marlowe stalked the mean streets. Today's suburbs were orange groves in Chandler's day, and many of the ethnic enclaves that make the city such a vibrant Pacific Rim megalopolis hadn't yet taken root. But the noir essence of Los Angeles never really went away, it just morphed into something more colorful and polyglot. Twenty-first-century L.A. is more noir than ever, a surreal sprawl where the First World and the Third World live cheek by jowl and people are connected across lines of race and class and geography, especially when crime, secrets, and passion intersect.

With *Los Angeles Noir*, we've brought you the ethos of Chandler and Cain filtered through a contemporary lens, showcasing some of the most innovative and celebrated writers working today. Open these pages and you'll embark on a literary travelogue that stretches from the mountains through the hardscrabble flats to the barrios and middle-class suburbs, the mansions of the wealthy, and the shores of the Pacific Ocean where we finally run out of continent. The breadth of talent on display is as exciting and diverse as the city itself.

We've got National Book Award finalist Susan Straight writing about a group of Rio Seco characters who wash up at a Downtown L.A. bar called the Golden Gopher. Janet Fitch takes us inside a Los Feliz love triangle that evokes the movie *Sunset Boulevard*, millennial style. Michael Connelly dreams up a classic noir story set on iconic Mulholland Drive, which "rode like a snake" along the city's backbone, and Robert

Ferrigno's Yancy delivers a soliloquy about a heist gone terribly wrong in Belmont Shore. Neal Pollack visits a gambling casino in the City of Commerce, where a mafioso and his thuggish bodyguards await the unlucky. *Los Angeles Noir* also marks the fiction debut of KPCC host, NPR commentator, and *L.A. Times* columnist Patt Morrison, who weighs in with a sly, Celia Brady–like romp through old Beverly Hills, where losing the best table at a top restaurant is akin to a dagger through the heart anywhere else.

There are newer talents as well, like Naomi Hirahara, whose tale of obsession set in a Koreatown day spa evokes Patricia Highsmith. Many of these stories overlap and layer like the city itself, ending, in true L.A. commuter style, far from where they began. The protagonist in Gary Phillips's story ticks off the changes in his neighborhood—a bar on Wilshire now engulfed by Koreatown, the Ambassador Hotel where Robert F. Kennedy was shot falling to the wrecker's ball, his own Mid-City streets invaded by cacti-planting, Southwest-decorating homeowners—as if to ground himself amidst an ever-shifting reality. Brian Ascalon Roley's working-class Mar Vista families watch uneasily as yuppies build three-story glass-and-steel lofts.

This anthology also conjures up fictional landmarks straight out of our collective unconsciousness. When Emory Holmes II describes the Château Rouge, a ten-story black marble curvilinear structure on Martin Luther King Jr. Boulevard built by L.A. architect Paul Williams that "looked like a fat stack of bop records ready to be played," we think, *Oh yeah, that place*. If it doesn't exist, it *should*.

But then, Los Angeles has never been defined by physical geography—it's a grab bag of ethnic clusters, neighborhoods, communities, subcultures. A state of mind. Lienna

Silver's world of Russian immigrants who carry memories of their homeland like a snail's shell and Christopher Rice's tale of two young gay men nearing the end of a relationship might take place on different planets instead of four miles apart. And Beverly Hills, West Hollywood, San Marino, Commerce, and Belmont Shores aren't even in L.A. proper, but they're part of the recombinant DNA that is helping Los Angeles evolve into something so new we can't even imagine what it will look like five years from now.

What we can be sure of is that it will remain a funhouse mirror reflecting back into infinity, and that we'll glimpse bits that look frighteningly familiar. Jack Nicholson's Jake Gittes wouldn't recognize the Chinatown of Jim Pascoe's story—whose tiny crooked alleys now house hipster bars and art galleries—but he'd sense the same edgy despair. Diana Wagman captures the eerie dislocation of Westchester, a 1950s model suburb under the shadow of LAX airport where body parts might rain from the sky. The detective in Héctor Tobar's story is obsessed with the damage done by kids with guns. Soon after Tobar turned in his story, a fourteen-year-old boy in L.A. shot and killed an eleven-year-old over a bike.

Tobar's story is set in working-class East Hollywood and his Armenian- and Mexican-American detective duo reminisce about the moldering movie star photos of famous alums at their alma mater, Hollywood High. When the authors in this collection write about The Industry, they refract it through an oblique angle—Janet Fitch's '70s actress hiding away in a decaying Los Feliz mansion; Scott Phillips's sexy Valley cocktail waitress whose claim to fame lies in the title, "The Girl Who Kissed Barnaby Jones"; Morrison's security chief for the studios who quashed the story about the producer bludgeoned by his own jewel-encrusted dildo.

These are stories that begin after the tourists go home and the klieg lights turn off. It's the city examining itself through a gritty, glamorous, tawdry, and desperate lens and finding grifters, gamblers, newly arrived immigrants, third-generation bluebloods, confused kids, millionaires, has-been actors, murderers, meth addicts, and traitors of the heart.

It's impossible to distill L.A. into one noir story. That's why we've brought you seventeen. *Los Angeles Noir* creates a kaleidescopic template for what it means to live and die in L.A. today. Read. Shudder. Enjoy.

Denise Hamilton
Los Angeles
March 2007

PART I

POLICE & THIEVES

MULHOLLAND DIVE

BY MICHAEL CONNELLY

Mulholland Drive

Burning flares and flashing red and blue lights ripped the night apart. Clewiston counted four black-and-whites pulled halfway off the roadway and as close to the upper embankment as was possible. In front of them was a firetruck and in front of that was a forensics van. There was a P-one standing in the middle of Mulholland Drive ready to hold up traffic or wave it into the one lane that they had open. With a fatality involved, they should have closed down both lanes of the road, but that would have meant closing Mulholland from Laurel Canyon on one side all the way to Coldwater Canyon on the other. That was too long a stretch. There would be consequences for that. The huge inconvenience of it would have brought complaints from the rich hillside homeowners trying to get home after another night of the good life. And nobody stuck on midnight shift wanted more complaints to deal with.

Clewiston had worked Mulholland fatals several times. He was the expert. He was the one they called in from home. He knew that whether the identity of the victim in this case demanded it or not, he'd have gotten the call. It was Mulholland, and the Mulholland calls all went to him.

But this one was special anyway. The victim was a name and the case was going five-by-five. That meant everything about it had to be squared away and done right. He had been thoroughly briefed over the phone by the watch commander about that.

He pulled in behind the last patrol car, put his flashers on, and got out of his unmarked car. On the way back to the trunk, he grabbed his badge from beneath his shirt and hung it out front. He was in civies, having been called in from off-duty, and it was prudent to make sure he announced he was a detective.

He used his key to open the trunk and began to gather the equipment he would need. The P-one left his post in the road and walked over.

"Where's the sergeant?" Clewiston asked.

"Up there. I think they're about to pull the car up. That's a hundred thousand dollars he went over the side with. Who are you?"

"Detective Clewiston. The reconstructionist. Sergeant Fairbanks is expecting me."

"Go on down and you'll find him by the— Whoa, what is that?"

Clewiston saw him looking at the face peering up from the trunk. The crash test dummy was partially hidden by all the equipment cluttering the trunk, but the face was clear and staring blankly up at them. His legs had been detached and were resting beneath the torso. It was the only way to fit the whole thing in the trunk.

"We call him Arty," Clewiston said. "He was made by a company called Accident Reconstruction Technologies."

"Looks sort of real at first," the patrol officer said. "Why's he in fatigues?"

Clewiston had to think about that to remember.

"Last time I used Arty, it was a crosswalk hit-and-run case. The vic was a marine up from El Toro. He was in his fatigues and there was a question about whether the hitter saw him." Clewiston slung the strap of his laptop bag over his shoulder. "He did. Thanks to Arty we made a case."

He took his clipboard out of the trunk and then a digital camera, his trusty measuring wheel, and an eight-battery Maglite. He closed the trunk and made sure it was locked.

"I'm going to head down and get this over with," he said. "I got called in from home."

"Yeah, I guess the faster you're done, the faster I can get back out on the road myself. Pretty boring just standing here."

"I know what you mean."

Clewiston headed down the westbound lane, which had been closed to traffic. There was a mist clinging in the dark to the tall brush that crowded the sides of the street. But he could still see the lights and glow of the city down to the south. The accident had occurred in one of the few spots along Mulholland where there were no homes. He knew that on the south side of the road the embankment dropped down to a public dog park. On the north side was Fryman Canyon and the embankment rose up to a point where one of the city's communication stations was located. There was a tower up there on the point that helped bounce communication signals over the mountains that cut the city in half.

Mulholland was literally the backbone of Los Angeles. It rode like a snake along the crest of the Santa Monica Mountains from one end of the city to the other. Clewiston knew of places where you could stand on the white stripe and look north across the vast San Fernando Valley and then turn around and look south and see across the west side and as far as the Pacific and Catalina Island. It all depended on whether the smog was cooperating or not. And if you knew the right spots to stop and look.

Mulholland had that top-of-the-world feel to it. It could make you feel like the prince of a city where the laws of nature and physics didn't apply. The foot came down heavy on the accelerator. That was the contradiction. Mulholland was built for speed but it couldn't handle it. Speed was a killer.

As he came around the bend, Clewiston saw another firetruck and a tow truck from the Van Nuys police garage. The tow truck was positioned sideways across the road. Its cable was down the embankment and stretched taut as it pulled the car up. For the moment, Mulholland was completely closed. Clewiston could hear the tow motor straining and the cracking and scraping as the unseen car was being pulled up through the brush. The tow truck shuddered as it labored.

Clewiston saw the man with sergeant's stripes on his uniform and moved next to him as he watched.

"Is he still in it?" he asked Fairbanks.

"No, he was transported to St. Joe's. But he was DOA. You're Clewiston, right? The reconstructionist."

"Yes."

"We've got to handle this thing right. Once the ID gets out, we'll have the media all over this."

"The captain told me."

"Yeah, well, I'm telling you too. In this department, the captains don't get blamed when things go sideways and off the road. It's always the sergeants and it ain't going to be me this time."

"I get it."

"You have any idea what this guy was worth? We're talking tens of millions, and on top of that he's supposedly in the middle of a divorce. So we go five by five by five on this thing. *Comprende*, reconstructionist?"

"It's Clewiston and I said I get it."

"Good. This is what we've got. Single car fatality. No witnesses. It appears the victim was heading eastbound when his vehicle, a two-month-old Porsche Carrera, came around that last curve there and for whatever reason didn't straighten out. We've got treads on the road you can take a look at. Anyway, he went straight off the side and then down, baby. Major head and torso injuries. Chest crushed. He pretty much drowned in his own blood before the FD could get down to him. They stretchered him out with a chopper and transported him anyway. Guess they didn't want any blowback either."

"They take blood at St. Joe's?"

Fairbanks, about forty and a lifer on patrol, nodded. "I am told it was clean."

There was a pause in the conversation at that point, suggesting that Clewiston could take whatever he wanted from the blood test. He could believe what Fairbanks was telling him or he could believe that the celebrity fix was already in.

The moonlight reflected off the dented silver skin of the Porsche as it was pulled up over the edge like a giant beautiful fish hauled into a boat. Clewiston walked over and Fairbanks followed. The first thing Clewiston saw was that it was a Carrera 4S. "Hmmmm," he mumbled.

"What?" Fairbanks said.

"It's one of the Porsches with four-wheel drive. Built for these sort of curves. Built for control."

"Well, not built good enough, obviously."

Clewiston put his equipment down on the hood of one of the patrol cars and took his Maglite over to the Porsche. He swept the beam over the front of the high-performance sports car. The car was heavily damaged in the crash and the front had taken the brunt of it. The molded body was badly distorted by repeated impacts as it had sledded down the steep embankment. He moved in close and squatted by the front cowling and the shattered passenger-side headlight assembly.

He could feel Fairbanks behind him, watching over his shoulder as he worked.

"If there were no witnesses, how did anybody know he'd gone over the side?" Clewiston asked.

"Somebody down below," Fairbanks answered. "There are houses down there. Lucky this guy didn't end up in somebody's living room. I've seen that before."

So had Clewiston. He stood up and walked to the edge and looked down. His light cut into the darkness of the brush. He saw the exposed pulp of the acacia trees and other foliage the car had torn through.

He returned to the car. The driver's door was sprung and Clewiston could see the pry marks left by the jaws used to extricate the driver. He pulled it open and leaned in with his light. There was a lot of blood on the wheel, dashboard, and center console. The driver's seat was wet with blood and urine.

The key was still in the ignition and turned to the on position. The dashboard lights were still on as well. Clewiston leaned further in and checked the mileage. The car had only 1,142 miles on the odometer.

Satisfied with his initial survey of the wreck, he went back to his equipment. He put the clipboard under his arm and picked up the measuring wheel. Fairbanks came over once again. "Anything?" he asked.

"Not yet, sergeant. I'm just starting."

He started sweeping the light over the roadway. He

picked up the skid marks and used the wheel to measure the distance of each one. There were four distinct marks, left as all four tires of the Porsche tried unsuccessfully to grip the asphalt. When he worked his way back to the starting point, he found scuff marks in a classic slalom pattern. They had been left on the asphalt when the car had turned sharply one way and then the other before going into the braking skid.

He wrote the measurements down on the clipboard. He then pointed the light into the brush on either side of the roadway where the scuff marks began. He knew the event had begun here and he was looking for indications of cause.

He noticed a small opening in the brush, a narrow pathway that continued on the other side of the road. It was a crossing. He stepped over and put the beam down on the brush and soil. After a few moments, he moved across the street and studied the path on the other side.

Satisfied with his site survey, he went back to the patrol car and opened his laptop. While it was booting up, Fairbanks came over once again.

"So, how'z it look?"

"I have to run the numbers."

"Those skids look pretty long to me. The guy must've been flying."

"You'd be surprised. Other things factor in. Brake efficiency, surface, and surface conditions—you see the mist moving in right now? Was it like this two hours ago when the guy went over the side?"

"Been like this since I got here. But the fire guys were here first. I'll get one up here."

Clewiston nodded. Fairbanks pulled his rover and told someone to send the first responders up to the crash site. He then looked back at Clewiston.

"On the way."

"Thanks. Does anybody know what this guy was doing up here?"

"Driving home, we assume. His house was in Coldwater and he was going home."

"From where?"

"That we don't know."

"Anybody make notification yet?"

"Not yet. We figure next of kin is the wife he's divorcing. But we're not sure where to find her. I sent a car to his house but there's no answer. We've got somebody at Parker Center trying to run her down—probably through her lawyer. There's also grown children from his first marriage. They're working on that too."

Two firefighters walked up and introduced themselves as Robards and Lopez. Clewiston questioned them on the weather and road conditions at the time they responded to the accident call. Both firefighters described the mist as heavy at the time. They were sure about this because the mist had hindered their ability to find the place where the vehicle had crashed through the brush and down the embankment.

"If we hadn't seen the skid marks, we would have driven right by," Lopez said.

Clewiston thanked them and turned back to his computer. He had everything he needed now. He opened the Accident Reconstruction Technologies program and went directly to the speed and distance calculator. He referred to his clipboard for the numbers he would need. He felt Fairbanks come up next to him.

"Computer, huh? That gives you all the answers?"

"Some of them."

"Whatever happened to experience and trusting hunches and gut instincts?"

It wasn't a question that was waiting for an answer. Clewiston added the lengths of the four skid marks he had measured and then divided by four, coming up with an average length of sixty-four feet. He entered the number into the calculator template.

"You said the vehicle is only two months old?" he asked Fairbanks.

"According to the registration. It's a lease he picked up in January. I guess he filed for divorce and went out and got the sports car to help him get back in the game."

Clewiston ignored the comment and typed *1.0* into a box marked *B.E.* on the template.

"What's that?" Fairbanks asked.

"Braking efficiency. One-oh is the highest efficiency. Things could change if somebody wants to take the brakes off the car and test them. But for now I am going with high efficiency because the vehicle is new and there's only twelve hundred miles on it."

"Sounds right to me."

Lastly, Clewiston typed *9.0* into the box marked *C.F.* This was the subjective part. He explained what he was doing to Fairbanks before the sergeant had to ask.

"This is coefficient of friction," he said. "It basically means surface conditions. Mulholland Drive is asphalt base, which is generally a high coefficient. And this stretch here was repaved about nine months ago—again, that leads to a high coefficient. But I'm knocking it down a point because of the moisture. That mist comes in and puts down a layer of moisture that mixes with the road oil and makes the asphalt slippery. The oil is heavier in new asphalt."

"I get it."

"Good. It's called trusting your gut instinct, sergeant."

Fairbanks nodded. He had been properly rebuked.

Clewiston clicked the enter button and the calculator came up with a projected speed based on the relationship between skid length, brake efficiency, and the surface conditions. It said the Porsche had been traveling at 41.569 miles per hour when it went into the skid.

"You're kidding me," Fairbanks said while looking at the screen. "The guy was barely speeding. How can that be?"

"Follow me, sergeant," Clewiston said.

Clewiston left the computer and the rest of his equipment, except for the flashlight. He led Fairbanks back to the point in the road where he had found the slalom scuffs and the originating point of the skid marks.

"Okay," he said. "The event started here. We have a single car accident. No alcohol known to be involved. No real speed involved. A car built for this sort of road is involved. What went wrong?"

"Exactly."

Clewiston put the light down on the scuff marks.

"Okay, you've got alternating scuff marks here before he goes into the skid."

"Okay."

"You have the tire cords indicating he jerked the wheel right initially and then jerked it left trying to straighten it out. We call it a SAM—a slalom avoidance maneuver."

"A SAM. Okay."

"He turned to avoid an impact of some kind, then overcorrected. He then panicked and did what most people do. He hit the brakes."

"Got it."

"The wheels locked up and he went into a skid. There was nothing he could do at that point. He had no control because the instinct is to press harder on the brakes, to push that pedal through the floor."

"And the brakes were what were taking away control."

"Exactly. He went over the side. The question is why. Why did he jerk the wheel in the first place? What preceded the event?"

"Another car?"

Clewiston nodded. "Could be. But no one stopped. No one called it in."

"Maybe . . ." Fairbanks spread his hands. He was drawing a blank.

"Take a look here," Clewiston said.

He walked Fairbanks over to the side of the road. He put the light on the pathway into the brush, drawing the sergeant's eyes back across Mulholland to the pathway on the opposite side. Fairbanks looked at him and then back at the path.

"What are you thinking?" Fairbanks asked.

"This is a coyote path," Clewiston said. "They come up through Fryman Canyon and cross Mulholland here. It takes them to the dog park. They probably wait in heavy brush for the dogs that stray out of the park."

"So your thinking is that our guy came around the curve and there was a coyote crossing the road."

Clewiston nodded. "That's what I'm thinking. He jerks the wheel to avoid the animal, then overcompensates, loses control. You have a slalom followed by a braking skid. He goes over the side."

"An accident, plain and simple." Fairbanks shook his head disappointedly. "Why couldn't it have been a DUI, something clear cut like that?" he asked. "Nobody's going to believe us on this one."

"That's not our problem. All the facts point to it being a driving mishap. An accident."

Fairbanks looked at the skid marks and nodded. "Then that's it, I guess."

"You'll get a second opinion from the insurance company anyway," Clewiston said. "They'll probably pull the brakes off the car and test them. An accident means double indemnity. But if they can shift the calculations and prove he was speeding or being reckless, it softens the impact. The payout becomes negotiable. But my guess is they'll see it the same way we do."

"I'll make sure forensics photographs everything. We'll document everything six ways from Sunday and the insurance people can take their best shot. When will I get a report from you?"

"I'll go down to Valley Traffic right now and write something up."

"Good. Get it to me. What else?"

Clewiston looked around to see if he was forgetting anything. He shook his head. "That's it. I need to take a few more measurements and some photos, then I'll head down to write it up. Then I'll get out of your way."

Clewiston left him and headed back up the road to get his camera. He had a small smile on his face that nobody noticed.

Clewiston headed west on Mulholland from the crash site. He planned to take Coldwater Canyon down into the Valley and over to the Traffic Division office. He waited until the flashing blue and red lights were small in his rearview mirror before flipping open his phone. He hoped he could get a signal on the cheap throwaway. Mulholland Drive wasn't always cooperative with cellular service.

He had a signal. He pulled to the side while he attached the digital recorder, then turned it on and made the call. She answered after one ring, as he was pulling back onto the road and up to speed.

"Where are you?" he asked.

"The apartment."

"They're looking for you. You're sure his attorney knows where you are?"

"He knows. Why? What's going on?"

"They want to tell you he's dead."

He heard her voice catch. He took the phone away from his ear so he could hold the wheel with two hands on one of the deep curves. He then brought it back.

"You there?" he asked.

"Yes, I'm here. I just can't believe it, that's all. I'm speechless. I didn't think it would really happen."

You may be speechless, but you're talking, Clewiston thought. *Keep it up.*

"You wanted it to happen, so it happened," he said. "I told you I would take care of it."

"What happened?"

"He went off the road on Mulholland. It's an accident and you're a rich lady now."

She said nothing.

"What else do you want to know?" he asked.

"I'm not sure. Maybe I shouldn't know anything. It will be better when they come here."

"You're an actress. You can handle it."

"Okay."

He waited for her to say more, glancing down at the recorder on the center console to see the red light still glowing. He was good.

"Was he in pain?" she asked.

"Hard to say. He was probably dead when they pried him out. From what I hear, it will be a closed casket. Why do you care?"

"I guess I don't. It's just sort of surreal that this is happening. Sometimes I wish you never came to me with the whole idea."

"You rather go back to being trailer park trash while he lives up on the hill?"

"No, it wouldn't be like that. My attorney says the prenup has holes in it."

Clewiston shook his head. Second guessers. They hire his services and then can't live with the consequences.

"What's done is done," he said. "This will be the last time we talk. When you get the chance, throw the phone you're talking on away like I told you."

"There won't be any records?"

"It's a throwaway. Like all the drug dealers use. Open it up, smash the chip, and throw it all away the next time you go to McDonald's."

"I don't go to McDonald's."

"Then throw it away at The Ivy. I don't give a shit. Just not at your house. Let things run their course. Soon you'll have all his money. And you double dip on the insurance because of the accident. You can thank me for that."

He was coming up to the hairpin turn that offered the best view of the Valley.

"How do we know that they think it was an accident?"

"Because I made them think that. I told you, I have

Mulholland wired. That's what you paid for. Nobody is going to second guess a goddamn thing. His insurance company will come in and sniff around, but they won't be able to change things. Just sit tight and stay cool. Say nothing. Offer nothing. Just like I told you."

The lights of the Valley spread out in front of him before the turn. He saw a car pulled over at the unofficial overlook. On any other night he'd stop and roust them—probably teenagers getting it on in the backseat. But not tonight. He had to get down to the traffic office and write up his report.

"This is the last time we talk," he said to her.

He looked down at the recorder. He knew it would be the last time they talked—until he needed more money from her.

"How did you get him to go off the road?" she asked.

He smiled. They always ask that. "My friend Arty did it."

"You brought a third party into this. Don't you see that—"

"Relax. Arty doesn't talk."

He started into the turn. He realized the phone had gone dead.

"Hello?" he said. "Hello?"

He looked at the screen. No signal. These cheap throwaways were about as reliable as the weather.

He felt his tires catch the edge of the roadway and looked up in time to pull the car back onto the road. As he came out of the turn, he checked the phone's screen one more time for the signal. He needed to call her back, let her know how it was going to be.

There was still no signal.

"Goddamnit!"

He slapped the phone closed on his thigh, then peered back at the road and froze as his eyes caught and held on two glowing eyes in the headlights. In a moment he broke free and jerked the wheel right to avoid the coyote. He corrected, but the wheels caught on the deep edge of the asphalt. He jerked harder and the front wheel broke free and back up on the road. But the back wheel slipped out and the car went into a slide.

Clewiston had an almost clinical knowledge of what was happening. It was as if he was watching one of the accident recreations he had prepared a hundred times for court hearings and prosecutions.

The car went into a sideways slide toward the precipice. He knew he would hit the wooden fence—chosen by the city for aesthetic reasons over function and safety—and that he would crash through. He knew at that moment that he was probably a dead man.

The car turned 180 degrees before blowing backwards through the safety fence. It then went airborne and arced down, trunk first. Clewiston gripped the steering wheel as if it was still the instrument of his control and destiny. But he knew there was nothing that could help him now. There was no control.

Looking through the windshield, he saw the beams of his headlights pointing into the night sky. Out loud, he said, "I'm dead."

The car plunged through a stand of trees, branches shearing off with a noise as loud as firecrackers. Clewiston closed his eyes for the final impact. There was a sharp roaring sound and a jarring crash. The airbag exploded from the steering wheel and snapped his neck back against his seat.

Clewiston opened his eyes and felt liquid surrounding him and rising up his chest. He thought he had momentarily blacked out or was hallucinating. But then the water reached his neck and it was cold and real. He could see only darkness. He was in black water and it was filling the car.

He reached down to the door and pulled on a handle but he couldn't get the door to open. He guessed the power locks had shorted out. He tried to bring his legs up so he could kick out one of the shattered windows but his seat belt held him in place. The water was up to his chin now and rising. He quickly unsnapped his belt and tried to move again but realized it hadn't been the impediment. His legs—both of them—were somehow pinned beneath the steering column, which had dropped down during the impact. He tried to raise it but couldn't get it to move an inch. He tried to squeeze out from beneath the weight but he was thoroughly pinned.

The water was over his mouth now. By leaning his head back and raising his chin up, he gained an inch, but that was rapidly erased by the rising tide. In less than thirty seconds the water was over him and he was holding his last breath.

He thought about the coyote that had sent him over the side. It didn't seem possible that what had happened had happened. A reverse cascade of bubbles leaked from his mouth and traveled upward as he cursed.

Suddenly everything was illuminated. A bright light glowed in front of him. He leaned forward and looked out through the windshield. He saw a robed figure above the light, arms at his side.

Clewiston knew that it was over. His lungs burned for release. It was his time. He let out all of his breath and took the water in. He journeyed toward the light.

James Crossley finished tying his robe and looked down into his backyard pool. It was as if the car had literally dropped from the heavens. The brick wall surrounding the pool was undisturbed. The car had to have come in over it and then landed perfectly in the middle of the pool. About a third of the water had slopped over the side with the impact. But the car was fully submerged except for the edge of the trunk lid, which had come open during the landing. Floating on the surface was a lifelike mannequin dressed in old jeans and a green military jacket. The scene was bizarre.

Crossley looked up toward the crestline to where he knew Mulholland Drive edged the hillside. He wondered if someone had pushed the car off the road, if this was some sort of prank.

He then looked back down into the pool. The surface was calming and he could see the car more clearly in the beam of the pool's light. And it was then that he thought he saw someone sitting unmoving behind the steering wheel.

Crossley ripped his robe off and dove naked into the pool.

NUMBER 19

BY NAOMI HIRAHARA

Koreatown

The Korean women, lined up in black bras and underpants, pushed and pulled the flesh on their individual tables as if they were kneading dough.

Ann watched for a moment and then dipped down into a steaming bath a few yards away. She was naked and unadorned, aside from a locker key dangling from a bright orange plastic bracelet around her wrist. She didn't know why she even bothered securing the locker. There wasn't much worth taking. Her beat-up jeans, size four, extra skinny, extra tall, and a simple T-shirt. A ratty bra with a rusty clasp and twisted underwire and matching panties. A fake leather hobo-style purse, bought at a discount store on Hollywood Boulevard, a couple of miles from her apartment. Platform shoes that stank of too much wear. She didn't have a car right now, so she traveled with a monthly bus pass. In her wallet was a fresh twenty—for the tip her coworker Marie told her to bring—and a couple of ones.

The spa had been expensive—a hundred dollars and then the twenty dollar tip—but Marie told Ann that she needed to treat herself when she was feeling down. "Who needs antidepressants?" she had said. "Just get a salt scrub in Koreatown." Marie was the only other waitress who bothered to speak to her at work. The other girls seemed scared of Ann, as if she had some kind of sickness that they were afraid to catch.

Ann lifted her face from the hot water and brushed away wet hair plastered on her forehead. She tried not to stare at the masseuses working in the open spa, but it was hard not to. Marie had forewarned her about their lack of clothing. "Only makes sense, you know? It's the same for the masseurs in the men's section. They scrub off your dead skin and then rinse you off. Everyone gets wet. If they're going to get soaked, they might as well wear bathing suits."

But these weren't swimsuits—at least it didn't look that way from the jacuzzi.

About every ten minutes, a masseuse would leave her station and call out an assigned number into the open spa. Ann's masseuse was Number 19, which was written and circled on the envelope she had received, along with two square pink washcloth mitts. The texture of the cloth was rough, like sandpaper. "You'll feel like you're getting rid of all of the asshole customers we had to deal with this past week," Marie had told her. "A little pain for pleasure."

Ann was all for pain. She preferred hot baths—scalding ones, in fact. Her fingers right now were becoming shriveled, to the point that the outside layer of skin was almost melting off.

"Nine-teen. Nine-teen." One of the masseuses called out. The slick plastic table next to her was empty.

Ann drew herself out of the tub. The tile floor was slippery and she clutched onto her washcloths and envelope while holding her thin cotton robe and towel over her bare front. The massage table area smelled dank and slightly syrupy—not a fragrance that she had ever encountered before.

Number 19, her black hair frizzed from a bad perm and held back with bobby pins, must have been in her mid-forties at least. The skin around her jowls, below her armpits, and around her belly seemed soft and pudgy. Ann had seen that look before. It was comforting, reassuring. She could imagine melting in those fleshy arms so that her body would no longer be floating without an anchor.

Number 19 took Ann's robe and towel and hung them on a hook beside a steaming barrel of water. The envelope went on a shelf. "Lie down." She nudged Ann toward the slippery plastic table. Even that gentle touch made Ann flinch—when was the last time someone had touched her bare back? Ann did as she was told, turning her head toward the left. She could see that the waistband of Number 19's black panties was torn. The masseuse took one of the pink wash-cloths and Ann heard her squirt liquid—the seaweed salt treatment, no doubt—onto the center of the mitt.

The slosh of water from the barrel came next. It was luke-warm, not hot like the jacuzzi's water.

Then Number 19 began scrubbing her shoulders, her backside, her legs. Ann now understood what Marie was talking about. All the bad residue from work seemed to be stripping away from her body, breaking up, disintegrating with each scrub and rinse of water.

Number 19 then tapped Ann on the shoulder and gestured for her to turn over.

Ann didn't have much breasts to speak of. It didn't bother her that they looked more like a chubby pubescent boy's chest, rather than a woman's. She had no desire to buy implants like a few of her coworkers. She remembered when her body was just developing and she was sitting in the back-yard with her mother, aunt, and a girl cousin about Ann's same age—maybe ten. Ann didn't know why, but all of sud-den her mother and aunt lifted up Ann and her cousin's cotton shirts and undershirts, revealing puffs of growing breasts. They each squeezed a breast as if they were testing rolls of bread in an oven. The two women then laughed and returned to their cigarettes and gossip. Ann and her cousin didn't know what all the fuss was about. Ann didn't feel violated or abused, just that she wasn't privy to a secret that her body apparently held.

After the washing came the massage. Number 19 twisted her fists and fingers into knots that had developed throughout Ann's back from carrying heavy trays of ceramic dishes. The pain shot down into the center of her lower body and even moved to her toes. Then came the slapping down her spine. The slapping made Ann feel delirious.

No one really talked in the spa, so there was no sound of voices or music, only the sloshing of water, slapping, and scrubbing. The spa took on a rhythm that was more felt than heard.

Ann herself wasn't the type to initiate conversation, but somehow the loosening of the knots in her shoulders made her more bold. "When did you come here? You know, to this country?" she asked in a low voice, while Number 19 slathered moisturizer on her back.

The masseuse paused for a moment. From the corner of her eye, Ann could see her frown and suck on the inside of her cheeks. It was as if Ann had accused her of doing something wrong.

She took a deep breath and whispered in Ann's ear, "Two year." Number 19's breath felt warm and actually smelled sweet, like fresh milk with sugar mixed in. She then did a last squeeze of Ann's shoulders. "Very tight," she said as Ann got up from the table.

Ann didn't know how to say *waitress* in Korean, so she mimed writing in an order pad.

"Oh, that's good job." Number 19's voice sounded sad, as

if she knew that her job—cleaning naked bodies in black underwear—was anything but good.

Ann attempted to correct the masseuse—she must have thought she was secretary or something—but Number 19 was already calling out into the open spa, "Nine-teen, nine-teen." Their session was officially over.

Ann returned to the locker room to retrieve her clothes. The dressing room had a couple of hair dryers but the vanity area was so crowded that Ann opted to just comb her wet hair and let it air dry.

When she went into the waiting room, the desk clerk and manager, a Korean woman with immaculate skin and over-sized glasses, explained the spa's tip policy. "Twenty dollars in envelope, and you put in here," she said, pointing to a locked wooden box. "Make sure number is on the envelope."

Ann did what she was told, but felt uneasy. Why had Number 19 hesitated before explaining when she had come to this country? Her arrival or stay may not have been through legal channels, Ann figured. And the silence in the massage room—it didn't seem to exist to promote relaxation, but to snuff out secrets. Would Number 19 get her twenty dollars? Ann wondered. She walked out the doors toward a driving range where golfers were hitting balls into a large green net, two stories high. Ann had learned to play golf when she was a teenager from one of her mother's boyfriends. "Never know when you'll need to know the game," he had told her. She watched the golfers for a few minutes, debating whether she should go back into the spa and make sure Number 19 received her tip. But she decided against it. Who was she, anyway? She was an outsider. She didn't understand the spa's ways.

That night Ann tossed and turned in her sleep. She had

a nightmare and woke up gasping for air as if someone was trying to keep her from breathing.

After that first time at the Korean spa, Ann knew that she had to feel the touch and hear the voice of Number 19 again. But it had taken her three months to save up that initial hundred and twenty-five dollars. If she wanted to go again, she would have to be more aggressive in placing money in her personal bank, an old pickle jar where she stuffed extra bills and change from her daily tips. She began collecting her neighbors' empty soda cans and walking to a recycling shack near the local supermarket and waiting alongside homeless junkies to exchange cans for coins. Three weeks later she rolled the quarters, dimes, nickels, and pennies on a TV tray. She came up with fifty dollars in change. With her five- and one-dollar bills in tips, she had enough to cover the spa.

This time she was more bold in her questions. "You have a car?"

"Bus. Two stops to Hobart."

Ann knew the bus line that traveled that route.

"What's your name?"

"No name. Only number."

Ann asked her questions while lying on the massage table. She noticed that the tear in Number 19's underpants was getting larger and wondered why she didn't use some of her tip money to buy a new pair. She ended up not asking her, but the question remained in her mind.

Before she left, the masseuse stared up at Ann's face.

"Nice," she said.

Ann furrowed her eyebrows.

Number 19 pointed to Ann's eyes. "Very pretty."

* * *

About two weeks later, Marie told her some bad news at work. "The bitch laid me off. Said I talk too much. I think it's just an excuse because business has been so slow." Marie ripped the apron from her waist and whirled the combination on her locker in the back room of the restaurant. "It's just as well. I'm sick of L.A. I'm going back home."

Ann couldn't remember where home was, but it was some state shaped like a rectangle in the middle of the U.S.

"You can get another job."

"Yeah, another one at a dump like this. It's not worth it anymore." Marie removed her purse from a hook in the locker and looped it through her arm. "You know, Ann, you might think of moving on too."

Ann was jumpy all day. She messed up two orders and accidentally broke a juice glass. She was relieved that she worked the day shift and had the evening to herself. When she got home, she noticed that the pickle jar was only half-full of change, not nearly enough for a full salt scrub, but enough for the use of the jacuzzi. At least she could see Number 19. It was early evening on Thursday, past 7:00, so maybe she would be on her last customer. They might even have time to go out, have a cup of coffee, thought Ann.

Number 19 was in the middle of a massage when she arrived. Her customer was a tall, thin woman, about Ann's size. Ann watched from the jacuzzi, her eyelashes clumping together in the steam. Two other women were in the tub; one had placed a wet towel over her forehead and had closed her eyes.

Number 19 seemed in an unusually good mood. She smiled a couple of times and dipped her head down to her customer's ear. And then—no, it couldn't be—it seemed that Number 19 was laughing. Ann wiped the sweat drops from her eyelashes. She stumbled out of the tub, her knees almost sliding on the tile. But Number 19 didn't bother looking her way.

Ann slipped on her clothes without properly drying her body, so the sleeves of her shirt clung awkwardly to her upper arms. She felt embarrassed about being so upset. This was Number 19's workplace, after all. She had to be friendly to all the other customers.

Ann left the massage room and crossed over to the driving range to hit a bucket of balls. Since she didn't have any clubs, she had to rent a nine iron too. She hadn't hit balls since her mother's ex-boyfriend had left them. Seven irons were the most versatile clubs, her mother's ex-boyfriend had said. If you had a decent swing, you could even tee off with a seven iron at a three-par course. You could never go wrong with that club.

She placed a ball on a one-inch plastic tube, a substitute tee, on the plastic grass pad. She then overswung three times, missing the ball completely. *Remember not to muscle the ball,* her mother's ex-boyfriend had said. *Don't force it. Just use the laws of nature and gravity.* Ann relaxed and slowed down. Soon she was in a groove and the ball was sailing past the hundred-foot marker.

"Hey, lady, you want more balls?" asked a teenager who was collecting the empty metal buckets at some point.

Ann looked down and saw her bucket was empty. How long had she been taking swings without the ball?

"It works better with balls, you know."

After the sun went down, Ann decided to return to the massage waiting room. The wooden box was unlocked and the desk clerk was slitting open the tip envelopes with a knife.

On top of the reception table were neat stacks of twenty-dollar bills.

"We closed," the clerk said, finally noticing Ann. She smiled as if she knew of an inside joke. Her magenta lipstick looked freshly applied.

Ann couldn't imagine why the clerk needed to looked well-groomed to count money. She figured the clerk must be a higher-up, maybe a manager. "You know that's their money, not yours."

"We pay them tomorrow. They will get their money, I assure you."

Once Ann returned to the apartment, she ate a bowl of tomato soup she had bought from the 99 cents store. It was a brand she had never heard of; the soup, which had the consistency of silt, was a strange crayon orange color. Marie had been right—business had slowed down considerably and now people were leaving their spare change instead of dollar bills for tips. Ann looked for Marie's cell phone number in her purse and dialed it. A man answered the phone.

"Is Marie there?"

"Huh? I think you got the wrong number."

Ann ended the call and tried again.

"I told you that you have the wrong number, okay?!" The man then cursed, warning Ann that there would be consequences if she called a third time.

That night Ann fell asleep to a repeat of a late-night talk show, voices laughing at jokes that didn't make much sense anymore.

The next evening, Ann returned to the block where the spa was located, but this time she waited at Number 19's bus stop. She didn't know if she would recognize the masseuse with her clothes on, but the minute she and another masseuse walked across the street, Ann got up from the bench.

"Did you get your tip money?" she asked.

The masseuse and her friend looked afraid.

"This is America. You have rights—it doesn't matter if you're illegal or not."

Just then, a bus roared to the stop and the two women rushed to get inside.

"Next time I'll give *you* the tip. Or give me your address. I'll send you the money," Ann said from the street. The doors folded together; the bus sighed before joining the lines of traffic.

"I'd like to see Number 19." Ann stood in front of the check-in desk of the spa on Friday. It was the same manager, only this time she was wearing tangerine lipstick instead of magenta.

"One hundred dollars."

Ann wasn't about to admit that she didn't have the money. "I just need to speak with her."

"Number 19 working."

A couple of other women in yoga pants entered the waiting room and the manager turned her attention to them. Ann kept her place at the front of the line, but the manager just moved over to the side to collect the women's money and give them their towels and robes.

"You bother our customers," the manager said after they left for the locker room.

"I need to talk with Number 19."

"Number 19 doesn't want to see you."

"You didn't even speak to her. You don't know."

The manager adjusted her glasses and pointed to a sign above a glass shelf that held beauty products. *WE RESERVE THE RIGHT TO REFUSE SERVICE TO ANYONE*, it read. Ann was very familiar with the sign. They had the same one at the restaurant.

"Listen," Ann said, raising her voice, "I can close this place down, you know."

"Yah, yah." The manager turned her back to Ann and rearranged some bottles of body scrub on the glass shelf.

"I'll tell immigration that you're using illegals."

The manager snapped her head back toward Ann. "What has Number 19 told you?"

Ann's stomach felt queasy. Maybe she had gone too far. The last thing that she wanted to do was get Number 19 in trouble with her boss. "Nothing," she said. "Just that you better watch out."

Ann walked out of the waiting room and went to the driving range to release some tension. This time she chose a spot on the far left side so she could keep an eye on the massage room door. One of her balls was sailing to the hundred-fifty-foot mark when she noticed someone leaving the massage room.

Number 19. By herself.

"Number 19!" she called out, and quickly walked over to face her.

The masseuse lowered her head, as if she was preparing to experience something distasteful. One of her bobby pins was coming loose, and Ann fought the urge to push it back in her hair.

"What's wrong? Did your manager do something to you? I tried to set her straight—that tip money is yours."

"Why you say anything? Not your business." Number 19 continued walking, and Ann pulled at her elbow.

Number 19 wrestled back her arm and Ann was surprised to experience her wrath. "I fire!"

Ann couldn't believe this news. "I was just trying to help you. You have to understand."

"No job. No money. How can I live? You understand?" Number 19 ran down the stairs and Ann, still carrying her nine iron, chased after her. But the masseuse knew the ins and outs of the building better than Ann, who lost track of her, then dashed outside and asked the security guard if he had seen the masseuse walking by. The security guard shook his head, so Ann headed to the bus stop to find Number 19. But there was no sign of her.

After an hour, Ann went to speak to the manager again. "You need to give Number 19 her job back."

"I need to do nothing." The wooden tip box was open again, the stacks of twenties lined up beside it. "Get out. You can't prove anything."

"I can get you in trouble."

"Who you? Poor nasty girl. Nobody going to listen to nasty girl."

"They'll listen," Ann said, fingering the grip of the nine iron. "You need to give Number 19 her job back."

"Number 19? You know numbers, but no name?" The manager threw her head back and laughed, her tangerine mouth resembling a demented clown's.

Ann held the golf club like a baseball bat and swung. A matte of hair flew off the manager's scalp and her body lurched backwards into the glass shelves, which shattered, spilling the bottles of beauty products onto the linoleum floor.

It was quiet for a moment, aside from the bottles rolling in the shards of glass. A bloody mass clung to the end of the club as Ann dropped it on the floor. She then walked over to the other side of the counter. The manager's face was contorted and her glasses had flown to the far corner of the reception area. There was a huge gash on the right side of her forehead and blood was pouring out, looking like a red dye soaking the roots of her hair.

On the floor was a light-blue Tiffany bag with Tupperware inside—the manager's lunch perhaps. Ann held it to the edge of the counter and scooped in the stacks of twenties. Next to the cash register was a taped work schedule. Ann pulled it off and then walked out.

When she reached the parking lot, her head was pulsating. She walked past the security guard again, even acknowledging him with a nod.

Ann reached a church, a traditional brick building with a cross. A canvas sign, all in Korean, was stretched above the double doors. There was a light above the cross and Ann sat on the stairs and studied the work schedule. On the left side was a list of Korean characters corresponding to addresses in English on the right-hand side. Two of the addresses were on Hobart Boulevard with the exact same number. It had to be Number 19's apartment.

Ann could have taken the bus, but opted to walk instead. She passed mini-malls with neon signs that she couldn't read, rows of multilevel apartments with fire escapes that didn't seem to lead anywhere, and another driving range. Adrenalin was pumping throughout her body and she couldn't stand still. Number 19's apartment building was much like hers, a dilapidated structure made of bricks that didn't seemed attached to one another, loose teeth in old gray gums. Sloped grass lawn full of weeds that could probably accommodate two parked Chryslers.

Ann climbed up the creaky wooden steps to Number 19's unit. She didn't bother to try the doorbell—they never seemed to work in these buildings. Instead she rapped the dark wooden door with the side of her bent index finger.

The door slowly opened, and Number 19 didn't seem surprised to see Ann standing outside her home. She looked shorter, plumper, and older in the doorway of her apartment.

"I need to talk to you. May I come in?"

Number 19 nodded, holding the door open for Ann. It was a one-bedroom apartment and it looked like somebody slept on the couch. Number 19 gestured toward the kitchen, which was connected to living room.

"I tried to get your job back, but I couldn't." Ann then dumped the contents of the Tiffany bag onto the kitchen table. The cash, mixed in with shards of glass, tumbled out, almost knocking over a plastic soy sauce bottle and a jar of chili paste. Last of all, the Tupperware container of the manager's half-eaten lunch slid on top of the bills. "Here's your money; it's all yours. You deserve it."

Number 19 looked at her, first with fear and then sadness. Her hands trembled as she touched one of the bills. Then the bedroom door burst open. Uniformed officers with guns yelled, "Police!"

Number 19 was crying now into her bare hands. Her roommate—Ann recognized the woman from the spa—emerged from the back bedroom and tried to console Number 19.

One of the officers pulled Ann's arms back and, while reciting her rights, secured her wrists in plastic ties.

After Ann was led out of the apartment, one of the police

detectives, a Korean American who spoke Korean, turned to the masseuse. "Did you have a relationship with that woman?" he asked.

The masseuse kept shaking her head as if she were trying to erase any thought of the girl from her mind. "Just a customer," she said. "She was no one special."

DANGEROUS DAYS
BY EMORY HOLMES II
Leimert Park

1.

Every Halloween, his birthday, John Hannibal "Quick" Cravitz liked to put aside his usual routine of chasing power and pleasure in the cloak-and-pistol world of private security and devote a day to rest and public service.

That Halloween eve, when the day's work was done, Betty Penny, his office manager, strung their offices with skulls and *calaveras*, crepe paper cats and autumn leaves. Some of the girls from Satin Dolls brought in champagne and gumbo. Cravitz gave everyone a pumpkin stuffed with treats and a hefty check *for the holiday.*

After his staff had gone home, he invoiced his latest gig. Four weeks of sold-out concerts at the Inglewood Forum. The Zulu Boyz, Priest KZ, and Th' Flava Foolz, the cream of L.A. bands, performed. His young firm, Universal Detection, furnished security and muscle. There had been no violence.

He was getting ready to call it a day when the buzzer rang.

The shadow on the screen flipping him the bird, putting on a show for the surveillance camera, was his old friend Ramon Yippie Calzone.

"This is a raid, you old ass mutherfucker! Come out with your hands up. I know you got bad Negroes up there."

Cravitz buzzed him up. When he opened the door, Yippie embraced Cravitz, who, at 6'5", was taller than him by a head. Then his friend strode past him into the office. "Okay, birthday boy, I got good news and bad. Which do you want first?"

The two men grinned at one another. With his black briefcase, and the hooch he carried in a brown paper bag, Yippie looked like a *cholo* Republican: He wore a black leather jacket, faded jeans, motorcycle boots, lumberjack shirt; his long, graying hair tied in a ponytail with a silver clasp; his handlebar moustache pepper-gray. A gold earring in the form of a crucifix dangled from his right ear. A tat of Montezuma with an Aztec princess peeked through the break in his shirt.

"Good news first," Cravitz said.

Yippie Calzone raised the hooch: "*Pulke,*" he said.

The two men drank in Cravitz's conference room overlooking 43rd. The potent cactus brew was thick and cool and sweet, and Cravitz was genuinely thrilled to have a taste of the fabled Mexican moonshine. Even more, he was happy to see his old *carnale,* Yippie Calzone. Yippie, a cop, had been a neighbor back in the old days of South L.A. Later, Yippie was Cravitz's mentor at the police academy. Cravitz got out after only three turbulent years on the force.

"I'm giving you Esmeralda," Yippie Calzone said abruptly.

"Pretty-ass Esmeralda? You nuts?" Cravitz asked, genuinely surprised.

Yippie Calzone opened his briefcase and pulled out Esmeralda—his custom-made service revolver, a snub-nosed Colt .45 Peacemaker—and carefully laid her on the table.

Cravitz stared down at the beauty. She gave off a brazen sparkle that seemed to bewitch the mind.

The piece was one of a matched pair that once belonged

to Jack Johnson, the Negro heavyweight champion, in 1908. Her grips were fashioned from Alaskan whale bone and her barrel and frame were forged with silver from Civil War–era coins. There was a flaw in her muzzle that gave her bullet-holes a distinctive teardrop shape.

"I've decided she's a cold-hearted bitch. I don't love her no more," Yippie said. "She'll listen to you; she'll take care of you."

Like most of his pals, inside the law and out, Cravitz had always had a hard-on for Esmeralda. The weapon had been a gift to Calzone from the City of Los Angeles for his years of courageous service—twenty years back.

In his lawless teenage years—when Cravitz was pursuing his ambition of becoming a criminal just like his big brother, Cash—he and Cash had once worked out an elaborate plan to steal the treasure. The scheme fell through when Cash was arrested for a shootout—at a goddamn crap game.

The arrest of his big brother turned out to be a boon. Good and thoughtful people—including his own folks—swept into the breech left by his thuggish brother. It would take a brutal stretch at Pelican Bay before ol' Cash saw the profit in pulling at least one of his feet out of the mire of everyday crime. Since the '92 riots, Cash had rehabilitated his reptilian image and remade the Château Rouge, the abandoned, rat-infested hotel he'd bought, into a hangout joint for politicos and big shots; all attracted like flies by the old G's deep greasy pockets and his doe-eyed and perfumed, big-titted bar girls.

"This feels like the bad-news part," Cravitz said.

"Well," Yippie said, "you do know I'm a killer."

"That was a good shooting," Cravitz said.

No one in the city could forget the time that Calzone fatally shot two boys during a drug sting in Midtown. The weapons the boys had leveled on Calzone and his partners turned out to be toys. Because Calzone was Chicano and the boys were black, the incident quickly took on a nasty racial tone.

There were at least ten reprisal shootings. Black kids shot up brown folk picnicking in the park; Chicano kids shot up black folk at bus stops.

"*Good shooting*," Yippie repeated with contempt. "Me, killing kids. Imagine."

"They were perps, homeboy," Cravitz said, pouring out two more glasses of *pulke*. "It was them or you."

The men drank again in silence and Cravitz could hear the bustle of traffic just outside the window.

"I have nightmares, Quick," Yippie said. "I can't get their faces out of my head. And those mothers—" After a moment, the old cop took out a pack of Camels, "I'm taking time off. I already spoke to Vargas."

"Nothin' wrong with that," Cravitz said. "Manny will bring you back into the fold."

Yippie lit a cigarette and took a short drag, then, as quickly, mashed it out in the ashtray. "I've made a will," he said. "I've been too lucky too long."

Yippie Calzone's face, covered over with pockmarks and scars, was not handsome. But there was something compelling about his sad, soulful eyes.

"I've always had death threats," Yippie said. "They come with the job. But the dreams . . ." Yippie said. "I dreamed someone is going to kill me before this week is done."

Cravitz got up from his chair and placed his big bony hand on Yippie's shoulder. "Dreams ain't real, homie. Get a grip."

"Never thought I'd be afraid of dying, Quick. But I am," Yippie said. "This was the week I killed those boys—five years ago tomorrow."

Cravitz drained his glass and set it on the table. "So what if you make it through the week? Maybe your dream killers will go away," he said, attempting a smile.

"Maybe," Yippie ventured.

"It's settled then," Cravitz said. He picked up a pad and scribbled. "Here," he tore off the note and handed it to his friend. Yippie's strong hands trembled as he took it. "I want you to go to this pad in La Caja."

"The canyon above Pacoima?"

"That's it. It's Cash's hideaway, but I'll make him give me the keys. You pack and stop by the Château Rouge tomorrow morning at 7. The place is a dump. No air-conditioning. But the toilet flushes and the power's still on. Lay low until the weekend is over."

"Your fuckin' brother hates me."

"Cash hates everybody," Cravitz said dryly. "But he's legit now. Even your boy the mayor likes him. There's hope for him yet."

Yippie smiled. "It might work. I'm not ready to die. I've still got work to do. I owe this city so much." He pushed Esmeralda slowly across the table. "Happy birthday, old friend."

Cravitz snapped up the pretty pistol. "I can't take away your baby. I'll have Cash lock her in the safe tomorrow. You can pick her up when all this bad business is past. She'll be safe at the Château Rouge. Ain't a hoodlum in the world crazy enough to try to jack Cash Cravitz."

"*Simone*," Yippie observed quietly—so true.

The two men stood up.

"You sure Cash is gonna be down with this?" Yippie said. "That mean ol' man will do anything I ask."

2.

He tipped Pauli, the parking valet, twenty bucks when he brought around the black Escalade. Cravitz jumped in and kicked Wilson Pickett's "In the Midnight Hour" on the box. He perused his pretty self in the mirror.

Cravitz's coal-black, bald, magnificent head was adorned with two small hoop earrings. His eyes were gray. Angular, muscular, and deliberate, his black silk Armani duds made him flash and shimmer like a blade. And on this eve of his twenty-ninth birthday, Cravitz felt like a man reborn. He'd helped his friend; now he would try to help others.

Cravitz paused to admire his neon sign blinking *Universal Detection*. He peeled off.

There were scores of revelers out in Leimert Park. Cravitz took Vernon to Angelus Vista and sped west, up the slopes home to View Park.

Cravitz rose at 4 a.m. on Saturday, Halloween day, and promptly got things going. Two hundred sit-ups, *zip, zip*. Then he put on John Coltrane and oiled his magnificent head with cocoa butter until it sparkled like obsidian. He scanned *Jet*, *Guns & Ammo*, and the *Wall Street Journal* on the john and concluded a leisurely toilette with a brisk wash-up, a vigorous flossing, and a shave.

He put on his robe and slippers and strode out into darkness of his rose garden. His rambling View Park home was situated along the ridgelines of the north-facing heights. He clambered to the garden summits.

As the sun rose, Cravitz touched his forehead reverently

against the earth and said a prayer to the awakening world and to his ancestors and vowed, as he had every year for a decade, to be a good man and do at least one good thing for someone more needy than himself. For twenty-four hours he'd drink only water and fast from his bad habits: gratuitous violence, pussy-chasing, wine, and greasy-ass food consumption.

Things were going swimmingly until Cash called.

"Happy Halloweeeeen, little brother," the old dude began.

Cravitz winced. His big brother Cash had burned up careers as a policy man, a dope man, a loan shark, and a hustler. He'd done time at Folsom, at Vacaville, and at Pelican Bay. For many of L.A.'s starry-eyed wannabes, he stank of money, power, and the streets. He was now in his fifties but still had the tastes and habits of a small-town hood.

"It's your world, *play-ah*. S'up?" Cravitz said not very convincingly.

"Naw, you d'play-a, *play-a*," Cash bellowed.

"What ya want?" Cravitz said.

"Y'boy Yip been here," Cash said.

"Already?"

"Yep, he ran by early this morning. I was just gettin' outta my breakfast meeting with Bennita and 'nem. The muthafucka was staring at Bennita like she was made outta cake."

"How did he look?"

"Skeerd as a cat."

"Scared?"

"Did I stutta?"

"You give him the keys to the place in La Caja?"

"He got 'em and gone."

Cravitz breathed a sigh of relief.

"He didn't leave that pretty gun, though. That Mexican ain't dumb as he looks. Th' chump oughta give it to me. Woulda been mines long time ago if I'da had my way."

"I don't know why Yip is so spooked."

"And, honey, is he. Talkin' freakish. Didn't even sound like hissef," Cash said, then added with an amused cackle, "Yip fuckin' somebody's wife?"

"Yip's a choirboy."

"Oh, he fuckin' somebody's boyfriend then. Somethin' up," Cash said, then dropped the subject. "When you comin'?"

"Now," Cravitz said.

"Well then, c'mon, boy. I done took care of y'friend. Now I needs you t' take care of some messy bi'ness, f'me."

Cravitz knew his brother, a man of fixed habits, was taking his morning grits and waffles at the Chit Chat Room, his four-star Southern-style eatery in the mezzanine of the Château Rouge. He was feeling happy, frisky, and evil, and, as usual, trying to bum a little free labor.

"How messy?" Cravitz asked.

"Middlin' messy, I figure," Cash went on with a chuckle, "You remember Bingbong Jackson? You know, that piecea pimp I used to hang wit from Vegas?"

"Umhuh."

Cravitz had a low opinion of Bingbong. He had won his distinctive moniker during childhood. Every time he tried to snatch the purse of some unsuspecting grandmother, he'd whack her in the mouth—*bing!*—but then she'd take her purse and clobber him with a haymaker—*bong!* Bingbong Jackson, whose real name was Ernest Grandvale Jackson IV, might have been the most low-rent, beat-up, wannabe hoodlum-pimp on the whole Left Coast.

"Well, he done hooked up with a pretty yella bitch name

Bennita. They got a pad up in Vegas. They be staying at the Château Rouge f'Halloween. We gots a job f'you."

"Bingbong Jackson ain't done a sane act in his whole life," Cravitz said darkly, "What's that shitheel getting you into now?"

"They in th' music bi'ness. Gots fo', five little hoodlums from the projects with 'em," Cash said thoughtfully, ignoring his brother's rebuff. "Bingbong say these little thugs goin' platinum. Some new kinda rap shit. Call theysef Fluboor, Flowbird . . . some shit like that."

The Flo Boyz were a sensational new gangsta rap quartet out of Vegas. They were riding the crest of a publicity wave because of a violent spat they'd had with Strongbeach Posse, one of L.A.'s hot rap groups.

"I think this Bennita gonna let me smell her pussy if I book these boys on the main stage at Satin Dolls. They s'pose t'be th' shit. Jes look like snotty-nose hoodlums t'me," Cash went on. "Y' wont me t' send round the car?"

"Naw, play-ah," Cravitz said wearily. "See ya at the Château."

Cravitz rolled out in his '56 T-Bird rather than the Escalade. The classic candy-apple sports car better suited his sly, nostalgic mood. Besides, the goddamn thing glittered like jewelry on the streets. He threw on his red T-Bone Walker T-shirt, his $2,000 snakeskin boots, and his favorite ragged jeans. The T-shirt slouched nicely over the big .45 Beretta he always carried, strapped on his left hip. He jetted down Stocker and when he hit Crenshaw, turned north to King.

Feeling suddenly impish, he slowed the roadster to a crawl and slouched low in his seat, kicking it old school with The Shirelles blasting on the box, like some *vato Negro.*

The Château Rouge, with Satin Dolls, its notorious adjoining bar, was situated on Martin Luther King Jr. Boulevard five blocks west of Crenshaw. It was a ten-story structure built in 1958 by renowned Los Angeles architect Paul Williams. Its façade was polished black marble, steel, and glass. It looked like a fat stack of bop records ready to be played. The white-boy architectural critic for the *Times* in 1958 tried his best to dismiss it as "a licorice battleship." But black folk loved its swank curvilinear forms.

The hotel's main driveway was already bumper to bumper with fancy automobiles when Cravitz slid up—twenty patrons were lined up for the Chit Chat Room. It opened at 5 a.m. and featured the best and cheapest break-fast in town: two eggs, Louisiana sausage, bacon, grits, two biscuits, and a cup of java for five bucks. The menu also fea-tured New Orleans seafood, chit'lins under glass, East Texas hot wings, smothered chops, ham hocks and brains, and Johnnie Walker Black.

For Halloween, all the valets and chauffeurs wore black satin masks along with their red satin togs. Darlinda Smalls, the valet captain, waved him to the front of the line.

"Us girls got something for you, Quick," Darlinda said, and all the girls started singing Stevie's version of "Happy Birthday." When they were done, Aleta Wright, one of the fine-ass Château Rouge lady chauffeurs, took Cravitz's keys. It was already eighty degrees and Aleta was dressed for the weather in the Château Rouge's trademark peek-a-boo red satin tux.

"Hey, bitch!" a voice behind him growled.

Cravitz turned. Behind him stood a quartet of young men. One of them, a tall pasty-faced yella boy with bling braces, held up his fists and showed two sparkling rings, each one spanning a hand, spelling: *FLO BOYZ*.

Another brandished a sawed-off shotgun.

"Hey, Monster," the pasty-faced boy said to the kid with the shotgun, "cover me."

"What's your name, son?" Cravitz said to the young thug with the gun.

"Monster P," the boy said.

"That what your mama named you?"

"You betta recognize, grandpa, you jumped in line ahead of us," the yella kid with bad acne replied. Monster P, huge and grinning, circled to his left. Cravitz noted that Monster wore his new $100 Lebron James sneakers untied.

"Well, bitch, you gonna move out th' way? Or do we need to move you?" the pimply faced boy said.

"You from the Floorboards?" Cravitz said.

"Hey, sucka, you mean the Flo Boyz."

Normally, a slap across the lips was his remedy for obstreperous brats. The challenge of his birthday vow, however, posed a dilemma for Cravitz.

Cravitz was pondering this when he heard, "Drop the weapon, Twinkletoes."

It was the voice of his childhood hero, Ramon Yippie Calzone. Cravitz turned to see Yippie with Esmeralda in his hand.

Monster P held his shotgun limply, then let it slide to the ground.

"I'm saving your lives," Yippie Calzone told them. He pointed to Cravitz. "That young brother there is one of the killin'est *hombres* on the whole damn planet. Just look at them cold, gray eyes . . . I'm a mutherfuckin' killer, too. Just a few months back, shot down two little boys with this pretty gun. Ain't that right, Quick?"

"Gospel," Cravitz said.

The young men gawked at Esmeralda.

"We won't kill you this time, boys," Cravitz said. "But grown folks gotta talk now." Cravitz gave Aleta a twenty and said, "Help my friends. I ain't in a hurry."

Yippie turned to Cravitz and whispered, "We gotta talk."

The men met in a quiet booth in Satin Dolls.

"I saw something when I arrived at the Château Rouge this morning—someone," Yippie Calzone said.

"Someone?"

"A woman. A bad woman."

"Well?"

"I can't tell you much. Shouldn't be telling you this. But this *hina* is bad news. She is a drug dealer. A killer too. I didn't know she had got this far west."

"And she's here to . . . ?"

"Not sure. Her operation is in Nevada. She's helping her man Paco Santiago make Vegas the new drug hub," Yippie Calzone said. "If she's here, your brother is involved. I didn't see them together; but I'm sure she's staying here. She had on a mask, but I recognized her. I don't think she saw me."

"Cash has been legit since '92."

"He ain't." Calzone opened his briefcase and pulled out a small plastic baggie filled with a few teaspoons of yellow powder. He handed it to Cravitz. "The new teen poison."

The dope had a faint lemon scent.

"It's treated opium. It's been cut with strychnine and

baking soda and some other trash. The high's killer," Yippie said grimly.

"How's it get this weird color?"

"Food coloring," Yippie said. "They call it butter."

"Shit," Cravitz said.

"*Simone*," Yippie Calzone said.

"You're giving me classified information."

"It's a final gift, birthday boy. I'm settling all my accounts." Yippie Calzone was not smiling now. "You helped me. Cash helped me. Now I'm helping you. I'm sure this chick brought some of this dope with her. Cash might not know what he's in for."

Yippie promised to give Cravitz seventy-two hours to find the dope and get it out of the Château Rouge before he dropped a dime to Vargas.

"That's it," Yippie said finally, standing. "I've bent the shit outta the law for you, my brother. Now I'm gonna disappear."

Yippie Calzone left.

"Hey, Quick!" a familiar voice said.

He turned to face Hi-C, his brother's personal bodyguard, striding toward him. Hi-C was 7'2" without an ounce of fat. He was dressed in the livery of a Château Rouge bouncer: red satin top hat, red satin bowtie, sleeveless red satin shirt, red satin slacks, red satin cummerbund, red patent leather boots. C also wore a black satin mask.

To Cravitz he looked like a masked pillar of fire.

C said, "I been lookin' fo' ya all ovah, Quick. Mista Omar say f'you t'meet him in the conf'ence room. He wont me t'fetch ya."

One did not argue with a pillar of fire.

* * *

The penthouse conference room was located on the tenth floor. Its wall-length windows looked out over King Boulevard, framing the pale blue sky and the San Gabriels thirty miles north.

Cash was seated at the head of the long table, dressed like an eighteenth-century pirate. A black satin mask covered his eyes.

Seated in chairs on the table's other end were a woman and a man, both wearing black masks. The man was dressed all in white with a visor cap, like a 1940s Good Humor man. The woman was Cleopatra—a brass serpent coiled about her paste tiara.

"You remember my road dog, Ernie Jackson?" Cash began with a grin.

"Oh yeah, Bingbong. W'sup?" Cravitz said, with a slight nod.

The woman stood up and slowly walked around the table toward him. She was statuesque, voluptuous. Behind that satin mask, Cravitz could see her eyes flashing with golden fire. Her face was framed with braids that fell below her shoulders.

⌈She held out her hand. Cravitz fought off the urge to gobble her whole.⌉

"Bennita Bangs," she said simply.

Cravitz took her hand, feeling an electric thrill surge through his bones.

He wondered whether a woman that fine could be a thug and a killer and what it would be like to nibble her honeyed skin.

"Bingbong—I mean, *Ernest*—and Bennita startin' up a new record label," Cash said. "Bennita here done already sweet-talked me into dropping a little pieca change in the boodle. Since it's yo birthday, I figure I might spread 'round some of th' good luck to my baby bro . . ."

[Cravitz was still not listening. He was trying his best to crawl into those topaz bedrooms Miss Bangs used for eyes]

"My fiancé is a fox, ain't she, Quick?" Bingbong Jackson said uneasily.

Cravitz cast a killing gaze at the hustler. "What's all this good luck gonna cost me?"

"We need to raise two million, Mr.—" Bennita began demurely. "I'm sorry, what should I call you?"

"*Baby* would be nice," Cravitz said.

"We asking our initial investors to pony up what they can—*baby*. Twenty thousand, a hundred," Bennita Bangs said.

"I'm tapped out at the moment." He turned to Cash and winked. "But thanks for lookin' out, big bro."

Cash got up and shut the blinds. Even in the dim light of the room, Bennita Bangs glowed.

"Oh, I ain't asking you for money, birthday boy," Cash said, "We need you t'provide a little sweat equity for the home team."

Cash walked over to the safe, which was hidden behind a velvet painting of James Brown onstage at the Apollo. He pulled out a money bag and laid it on the table.

"Happy birthday, partner," Cash said, choking up. Cravitz opened the sack and pulled out a bag of yellow powder. As he turned it in the light the powder took on a gold, metallic glow.

"This is just a one-time deal. Kinda like a crime-*ette*. We make this little nest egg, then *boom*, we back legit."

Cravitz turned to Bingbong Jackson and said, "Who'd you steal this from, asshole?"

Bingbong protested, "I got this shit legit."

"I'm counting on you to get the word around. Pass out a taste or two."

"That little-ass bag of shit go for two-fiddy large, once we cuts it," Bingbong said.

"I got two words for you," Cravitz said, fixing his gray eyes on his brother, "Pelican Bay."

Cash blinked. That stint at Pelican Bay had nearly killed him. When Cravitz stumbled out of there he had called in some chits. Within a decade, the monster—his big brother—had been transformed into an avatar of L.A.'s high society and culture. It was insanity to throw it away.

Cravitz jerked a thumb toward Bingbong Jackson. "I'm 'bout to kick his pindick out of here."

"You owe me," Cash said evenly. "You gonna show me love or not?"

"I need some air," Cravitz said.

Cravitz got back in the T-Bird and called Yippie on the cell phone. "Yes, the broad is there. I'll get back to you. Remember, keep Cash out of this."

"You got my word," Yippie Calzone said.

His birthday was not going well.

At Pico and Dunsmuir, Cravitz pulled into the parking lot of St. Benedict's. The church was quiet and cool. In the solitude of his meditations, Cravitz began to form an idea. He'd bust into his brother's vault and remove the dope. Tit-for-tat, his brother would have his goons break into his View Park pad and reclaim the contraband.

Cravitz didn't care. He was determined to do the right thing.

He thanked St. Benedict for the tip.

* * *

The Château Rouge was packed when Cravitz returned. There was one masked face he'd recognize even in a coma— a girl from his past, Athena Powers.

They were a heartbeat from colliding.

He shut his eyes and cheerfully awaited his fate.

Then he felt Athena's grip on his arms and the soft press of her boobs against his chest.

"Hey! Quick! I almost ran into you. What luck."

Cravitz stared at Athena Powers with undisguised delight.

"'Member me? Thena? Jordan's little sister!" she finally exclaimed.

Fuck yeah, I remember you, you gorgeous doll, he wanted to say, but he just nodded his head and grinned. He had done a year with Jordan Powers at Juvenile Hall when they were thirteen.

"Jordan told me you was a cop or something. Y'must be on a case. Not a damn murder, I hope."

Athena chattered on, the patrons at the Château Rouge fading around them.

Then Cravitz blurted out, "You sure have grown, Thena."

"Yeah," the young woman said, blushing. "I'm an old woman now. Downside of twenty-five and sinking fast." Athena pulled nervously at her hair. "Oh my god, I must be a wreck. I been runnin' all day."

"No, no," Cravitz said, "you look . . . cool." The last time Cravitz had been this close to Athena she was sweet sixteen, and he was twenty—her brother's hoodlum friend. On that day, while she was giggling among her cousins and dressed in her great-grandmother's antique silk gown, he saw her budding into womanhood before his eyes.

"You staying at the Château Rouge?"

"Just for the weekend. I write for *Ebony*. Can you believe it? We're doing a story on black Hollywood. So I figured I might as well catch the Halloween bash at the Château Rouge."

"You got a date?" Cravitz heard himself asking.

"Oh my," she said. "Are you asking me?"

"'Might give you a shot," Cravitz said evenly.

"Y'know, Jordan is still a thug. He's gonna kick your ass when he hears you're trying to get with his little sister," Athena said.

"Jordan don't want none a this," Cravitz replied, spreading out his arms above her head and standing the full measure of his 6'5" height. His dark magnificent head hovered over her.

"I'm in room 313," she said, then disappeared in the crowd.

Cravitz took his usual route, up the rear stairwell to his brother's private suites ten floors above. He'd watched his brother work the combination many times.

He cracked the safe within minutes, removed a liner from a trash can, and stuffed the dope inside. Then he drove wearily out to the safe house in La Caja.

Yippie was elated when Cravitz arrived. He put the dope in his briefcase. Esmeralda was poised on his nightstand.

"I think we can keep your dumbshit brother out of the slammer this time but you gotta get that Vegas bitch out of there," Yippie said. "If Vargas finds out Cash is dealing again . . ."

Cravitz said he would, and told his friend he'd see him in the morning.

Cravitz took the streets home. Halloween decorations were up everywhere. Hollywood was crowded with phony vampires, angels, wolfmen, and movie stars.

Back home in View Park, he changed into his costume— Priest, from *Superfly*, replete with pimp hat, Jheri curl wig, platform shoes, polyester shirt, bell-bottom trousers, and rose-colored shades. Then he picked up Athena Powers, who was dressed as a sexy Belle Starr, with bells on her six guns and spurs, and starry skies painted across her sheer silk blouse.

That night the main ballroom at Satin Dolls became Ground Zero of Afro-Hollywood. The Flo Boyz played. At midnight Dwight Trible sang, the great jazz pianist Nate Morgan performed, and everyone joined in for "Happy Birthday, Quick!"

Finding his brother, Cravitz explained he needed a few more hours to decide. Cash never suspected he was already jacked.

Athena Powers and he danced until 2. Then she invited him back to her suite and Belle Starr easily convinced Superfly to break his fast on pussy and booze.

"Where you goin'?" Athena protested when Cravitz got up at 4 and changed back into his jeans and a funky shirt and strapped on his big gun.

"Got to check on a buddy," Cravitz said.

"Can't it wait?" she asked with a sly smile.

"Can't," Cravitz said simply.

They made love one more time and he was on the road to La Caja at 6.

3.

About 6:06 that morning, back in the safe house thirty miles north, undercover detective Yippie Calzone was awakened by whispers.

Quick as a cat, Yippie snatched up Esmeralda from the nightstand and turned.

In the flash of glass and buckshot that erupted through his window at that instant, Calzone witnessed the fiery unraveling of his final moment.

He had no time to say *oh shit* or *oh fuck* or *goddamn* or *God bless* or *forgive me* or *what the hell* or anything.

He tried to move, but his legs felt aflame. His big arms twitched and flopped against the bed. He gripped Esmeralda hard, and a shot rang out.

Esmeralda recoiled and banged against the nightstand.

Yippie's hand jerked flat, and Esmeralda, blood-splattered but voluptuous even in this light, laid upon his quivering right palm, her buxom body sparkling silver, her hair-trigger demurely cocked. Yippie could dimly feel his own heartbeat; and then, faintly, the renewed whispers of his assailants.

Dogs barked. He heard a distant siren, the droning of helicopters.

He tried to move his fingers. They felt heavy and wet and hot. Just below them, he felt Esmeralda tingling, her body cool, waiting.

Lights went on up Orchid Street—on Sagebrush Road and Terra Vista, the next streets over. Neighbors came out onto their porches.

Still lurking at Yippie's window, the killer could feel his own hot sweat, each drop a burning heartbeat. As for his heart, he felt it drumming in his chest, confident and strong.

He chuckled and stood up. He was dressed, as were his fleeing cohorts, in a ninja outfit.

"Butterbrains," he muttered, watching them struggle over the back fence.

He could hear neighbors, slightly louder now, calling out in alarm.

The killer lifted the sawed-off shotgun through the jagged gaps in the wood and glass.

Three more blasts followed for good luck.

A curtain of fire lit the room.

[Rooster-tails of splatter dripped down the walls.]

Esmeralda slid from Yippie's big fingers and clattered onto the floor.

The good cop was dead.

A dozen neighbors were milling around the front gate gossiping anxiously when Cravitz drove up twenty minutes later.

He fumbled with the keys, unlocked the gate, and hurried inside.

Unholstering his Beretta, Cravitz moved through the shadowy rooms and hallways. Then he went into Yippie's bedroom. Ignoring the bed, Cravitz looked around at the shattered window, the floor covered with splinters and glass, the streams of blood and flesh drying on the walls. He walked to the window and peered into the yard. He could make out a few footprints in the dust.

Cravitz gathered himself and turned to face the bed where his old friend lay.

He walked over and stared down at the body.

His hard gray eyes began to work, running along Yippie's corpse.

Displays four shotgun wounds, three penetrating and one grazing. Hard to figure the sequence in this light.

He lightly touched his old friend's forehead.

The lacerations and abrasions from the wounds formed linear patterns. The skull was shattered. His buddy must have been rising up when the killer struck. Cravitz got down on the floor and retrieved some black threads he noticed among the splinters.

He wrapped the threads in a handkerchief and left the lion's share for the cops. On the edge of the shattered window sill, Cravitz noticed a bullet hole.

He got a shot off. So where's Esmeralda?

Cravitz turned sharply and stared at the bloody nightstand. The briefcase with the dope was gone too. There was a pool of blood gathering just below Yippie's outstretched hand.

"Esmeralda fell there," Cravitz said out loud. As he looked closer, he realized the killer had stepped in the splatter. "I know who did this."

Thirty minutes later L.A.P.D. Homicide detective Manuel Maximillian "Manny" Vargas and his partner Will Dockery arrived. Cravitz, who'd met the detectives through Yippie, walked them through the murder scene.

As Cravitz turned to leave, Vargas said, "You have anything to do with this, Cravitz?"

"I'm a suspect, Vargas? I called you, remember?"

"Just humor me—you do this?"

"Naw, but there are fibers on the window from someone who did. Enough for Dockery here to make himself a skirt."

"This Yippie's place?" Vargas asked.

"My brother's," Cravitz said simply. "Yip was thinking about buying it. Cash let him try it out for the month—"

"Bullshit," Dockery said.

"Stay where we can find you, Quick," Vargas said.

"Yeah," Cravitz replied.

Cravitz blazed past the afternoon traffic like a bolt of light.

Cash was standing at his safe, smoking a long Cuban stogie, when Cravitz barged in. The safe was open. A 9mm pistol lay on the conference table.

"Where's the smack?"

"Robbed," Cravitz said.

"You messin' with my money, lil' brother. I could kill you, if you wasn't kin. Might kill you anyway," Cash said quietly, expelling a jet of smoke. His hard brown eyes turned black.

"You kill Yippie?" Cravitz said.

"What th' fuck?"

"He's murdered. You do it?"

"Why pick me, boy. I'm straight as a stick."

"Bennita," Cravitz said. "She put you up to this?"

Cash extracted a fresh cigar from his humidor, clipped it, and handed it to his brother. Cravitz hesitated, then took the smoke and bent over the table as his big brother lit it.

"Her brats wrecked the damn room. They was mad when they heard you took the yella dope," Cash said. "Hi-C an' nem had to bust 'em up a bit. You think Bennita and them punks whacked Yippie?"

"One of the killers stepped in the blood. That print is from the new Lebron James sneaker. Monster P had on a pair this morning when Yip and me had to spank them. Whoever did this got Esmeralda and the dope too."

Cash buzzed in Hi-C and picked up his pistol. "Let's go find these mutts," he said to Cravitz.

* * *

Cash banged on Bennita and Bingbong's fifth-floor suite with the barrel of his 9mm Glock. Then he used the pass key to go inside.

Brain splatter covered the walls of the suite. Bingbong Jackson lay dead in a pool of blood. A hole resembling a teardrop perforated his brow.

"Esmeralda," Cash said.

"Bennita Bangs," Cravitz said.

Cash got on the horn to his lowlife friends. He'd pay $5,000 to the snitch who led him to the killers.

Cravitz cellphoned Vargas. "I suggest your boys shoot to kill."

Vargas said, "If you kill anyone we'll arrest you, Cravitz—like any other thug. We're bringing 'em in alive."

"Umhum," Cravitz said, and hung up.

He called his office manager, Betty Penny.

Within an hour, the Central Detection operatives had leaped into the hunt.

They hit the liquor stores and barbershops, the newsstands and pool halls—spreading the word that Yippie Calzone, the storied L.A. champion of the streets, had been ruthlessly cut down, by outsiders, busters *from Las Vegas*.

One of mothers of the boys that Yippie Calzone had killed went on TV and said it was God's will, and that the pig should burn in hell. The other mother said that no one, not even a bad cop, should be murdered in his sleep.

Folks recalled good things Yippie Calzone had done.

He had mentored kids in South L.A.—black, brown, yellow, white. He was a good man.

The dashing new mayor, Arturo Quijada "Miracle" Mendez, a man for whom Yippie Calzone had been a boyhood hero, gave a public address.

"These are dangerous days," the visibly shaken mayor told the people. "We ask for calm."

Willie Song, one of the top gun dealers in L.A., called Cash to confirm he'd sold not one, but four shotguns to the Flo Boyz and they'd tried to pay him with some shit called "butter."

Fast Al Townes, one of Central Detection's top operatives, tracked the fibers that Cravitz had retrieved from the murder scene back to the Dream Closet, a Silverlake costume shop. A sales girl recalled renting four ninja costumes—now overdue—to some rude young men on Halloween eve.

Diss 'N' Dats Records, the Vegas label that first recorded the Flo Boyz, FedExed publicity stills of the quartet, and Vargas emailed them to all the local news outlets.

A man named Francisco Hernandez called the L.A.P.D. crime hotline to report that he had sold a tan late-model Ford Falcon to *una cabeza de quevo*—a dickhead—named Monster P, from the Flo Boyz, the kids wanted on TV.

Flagg Jackson, dumpster-diving out back of the Amarillo Bar on Lankershim Boulevard, was the first to drop a dime. He called the Château Rouge and told Hi-C he'd seen the punks go inside the bar. Their jalopy was stashed behind his favorite dumpster. He was sure they were packing. Cravitz called Vargas and told him to meet at the Amarillo in an hour.

It took Cravitz fifteen minutes to drive the twenty miles to the Amarillo. Two dozen Harleys leaned against one side of the bar. At the end of the line of hogs, Flagg Jackson waved and pointed to the front of the bar.

Cravitz took a long pull from his cigar, cocked his Berretta, and headed for the door.

Behind a curtain of beads he saw four young men, each one at a corner of the bar, armed with shotguns.

About twenty customers were lined up against the walls. In the center of the room there was a pile of wallets and jewelry.

Cravitz pushed aside the curtain with his big Beretta and stepped in.

"Well, well, well. If it ain't that bitch from the Château Rouge," said Monster P, training his shotgun on Cravitz.

Cravitz could hear distant sirens, coming closer. He figured he could kill two, maybe three of the boys without any problem. That fourth would be tricky.

"Drop the guns, boys," Cravitz said.

Now all four young men aimed their weapons at Cravitz.

"Tha's a bad idea, fella," a voice growled from behind the bead curtain.

Hi-C stepped in, his red satin top hat seeming to scrape the ceilings. He held a nasty-looking, TEC-9 assault weapon in his hands. Behind Hi-C was his boss, Cash Cravitz, followed by his crew, ready for a bloodbath.

"You got shit in your ears, boy? Drop them gats," Cash growled.

All but Monster P complied. He cocked the shotgun and smiled. "I ain't afraid to die. But I'm gonna kill you first, bitch."

Cravitz smiled too. Lazily, he strolled up to Monster P and flicked the drooping ash from his Cuban stogie onto the boy's pretty new sneakers. He hurled his 6'5" frame forward and batted the shotgun aside with his Beretta. In the same lighting motion, he smacked Monster P across the face with his free right hand. Monster P saw the flash of a broad, shadowy palm, then felt the blunt imploding thud of his head crashing against the steel base of the classic country-and-western jukebox twelve feet away.

Uniformed cops took the other Boyz away in cuffs while the cops questioned Monster P and Cravitz at the scene.

Cravitz said, "Why'd you do it, you little shit?"

"That bitch was gonna cut me in," Monster P replied.

"Bennita put you up to this?"

"Bennita? Hell naw. Some other bitch—" Monster P said.

"Other bitch?" Vargas said.

"—called herself Belle. Said we was gonna be rich, and we was gonna live in a fabulous house. Anyway, she knew I was pissed 'cause that old man tried to fade me. Fade *me*, Monster P!"

"Calzone dissed you so you killed him?" Vargas said.

"He called me *Twinkletoes*," Monster P said, genuinely hurt.

Cravitz drove home in a funk.

He remembered something Yippie had said that morning: *She had on a mask, but I recognized her. I don't think she saw me.* Suddenly his blunder hit him. He couldn't believe what a fool he'd been. He got on the phone to Vargas.

Arriving at the Château, he bounded up the back steps. Three minutes later he was knocking on the door of suite 313.

Athena Powers was smiling when she opened the door.

Esmeralda sparkled in her pretty hands.

The light in the suite was dim, but Cravitz could see that Athena had her suitcases out.

"Going somewhere?"

"Afraid so, boo. Sorry I can't take you."

"So you're the bitch assassin? Don't they pay you enough at *Ebony?*" Cravitz said.

"Everything I've told you was a lie. All except the pillow talk. When you were fucking me. I told you the truth about that, sweetboy. Anyway, *bitch* is a little harsh, don't you think? I prefer . . . Belle."

"Belle Starr, the outlaw queen. Nice touch," Cravitz said, handing her his Berretta and walking into the suite.

"I try," Athena Powers replied.

Luggage and bricks of yellow opium were strewn across the bed. Bennita Bangs was tied up at a desk with duct tape over her mouth. Her pretty topaz eyes flashed terror. She'd been beaten and there were nylon cords around her wrists.

"Nice knots," Cravitz said.

"I was a Camp Fire Girl, didn't Jordan tell you?"

4.

Cravitz got comfortable on the bed and pulled out a fresh cigar. "You kill Bingbong?"

"Had to," Athena Powers said.

"So you work for that Vegas pig—Paco Santiago?"

"Yeah, Paco bought a little piece of my time. My Bloomingdale's bill is a bitch."

"So, you and Paco . . . ?"

"That's right. He's like you—a pussy freak. It didn't take long for him to realize I was irresistible. But this butter deal is big. And when Ernie stole his shit, Paco sent me down here to kill him."

"So now you stiffin' him?"

"I'm afraid this cowgirl has outgrown little Paco."

"Paco is not a forgiving guy," Cravitz said.

"Believe me, I didn't plan this. I just came down here to do my job: kill Bennita and that dickhead Ernie, grab the smack, and haul back to Vegas for my payday. I didn't figure on falling in love with you," Athena Powers said.

Those deep brown eyes that once seemed so warm, so welcoming, now seemed aflame, cruel.

"Where did the Flo Boyz come in?"

"Just stupid kids," Athena Powers said. "I laid out a couple of lines of butter, promised them a cut of the profits, and *voilà*, instant killers. Anyway, they were already pissed off with your boy Calzone. When Paco called and told me that he had word from his L.A.P.D. snitches that a broke-down cop named Calzone might be on to me, I realized he had to be stopped. I didn't have a clue how to find him. That's where you came in. The Boyz followed you right to his hideaway." She looked at her watch. "Oh where does the time go? I've got to catch my jet."

"I'm gonna let the girl go," Cravitz said, and got up. He untied Bennita Bangs and tore off the duct tape.

"Such a gentleman. I wish I didn't have to kill you both."

"Bennita too?"

"I could have used her. She's the prettiest mule on the West Coast. I tried to talk her into double-crossing Ernest, told her we could split the spoils—it was a lie, of course—but she betrayed me . . . and what did she get for her troubles? Tell him, baby."

"After she killed Ernie, she beat me with that ugly gun," Bennita Bangs said, shuddering at the memory.

"And all for this junk?" Cravitz asked, lifting one of the yellow bricks.

"Dope is power. Love will only take you so far," Athena Powers smiled. Esmeralda sparkled in her steady hand. As she stepped forward, Cravitz burst the brick of butter in his bony hands and dashed its contents into her eyes. She cried out and pulled the trigger.

Esmeralda did not fire.

Cravitz cracked her stiffly across the jaw. Athena Powers dropped like a stone, through the clouds of golden dust.

"Baby, can't you save me?" Athena said to Cravitz thirty minutes later as two uniforms led her out to the police van.

"Fresh outta love, boo," Cravitz answered.

Athena kissed him tenderly on the lips. "You'll never get me outta your mind."

"*Simone*," Cravitz said.

"How can you do this to me?"

"It's a gift," Cravitz said.

That night Cravitz's dreams were restless reenactments of the murder scene. He imagined his old friend sleeping peacefully on the bed, Esmeralda nearby, Athena working the murdering minds of the Flo Boyz like marionettes, easing them fretfully through the night. His vow of a good deed had failed.

The following morning, before Yippie's funeral, Cravitz drove to St. Benedict's. There was one penitent there, an old woman bending over her rosary before the altar in a frayed frock and shawl. A tattered handbag sat on the pew beside her. The pair prayed in silence. Cravitz ruefully promised St. Benedict that on his next birthday he'd do better with his good deed.

When he was finished, Cravitz stole quietly near where the old woman kneeled and dropped a $100 bill atop her ragged purse. On his way out, he scribbled the name *Ramon Calzone* onto a Central Detection envelope. In it he placed a tithe of five $1,000 bills and slid it into the collection box.

MIDNIGHT IN SILICON ALLEY

BY DENISE HAMILTON

San Marino

They caught up with Russell Chen as he drove home from work, running his Lexus off the frontage road by the gravel pits of Irwindale. There were four of them, wearing reflective sunglasses and trucker caps pulled low, and for one terrified moment Chen though they meant to jack the car, kill him, and throw his body on the gray mountains of slag.

When they shoved him into a Lincoln with tinted windows, his sphincter almost let go with relief. Then fear throbbed anew as he considered the endgame. The bleakness of his situation mirrored the landscape: industrial parks rising like toadstools from the desecrated earth. In the rearview mirror, Chen watched his computer chip factory shrink to a snowball panorama, then disappear.

"The captured pigeon trembles with fright," the man in the front passenger seat said in Chinese. He craned his head and laughed uproariously to see Chen squashed between two thugs wearing cheap ties and wool-blend jackets. One of the thugs held a gun to his ribs.

The laughing man was the boss. For weeks his people had shadowed Chen, watching him kiss his wife and children goodbye each morning, clocking his drive to work. Children were good, they liked that and took note. In the evening they watched it all in reverse as Chen's car left the parking slot that read, *Reserved for CEO*. The gang had their mole inside too, a low-level employee who kept to himself, ate Hunan takeout each day from the same strip-mall restaurant on Garvey, and gave his fortune cookie away because he already knew the score. The mole had sketched out the factory layout, marking the doors and the alarm system and explaining how many seconds they'd have to disable it. They had the map with them now, singed brown where ash from the mole's cigarette had fallen as he drew.

Yes, the boss had been patient. And thorough. He knew all about the garden apartment in Arcadia where Chen stashed his mistress and their newborn son. But he'd been surprised to discover the brothel that Chen visited each Friday noon, tucked inside a tract home in South San Gabriel where the scorched lawn fought a losing battle against the sun and polyester lace curtains stayed permanently drawn. He'd dispatched a man to pay the fee and climb the stairs to the rooms where a sad-eyed Mainland teen sat behind every door, brushing her hair and gargling with an industrial bottle of mouthwash she kept next to her Hong Kong magazines, baby wipes, K-Y jelly, and condoms.

An hour later, Mr. Chen would emerge, looking pensive and smoking a cigarette.

Greedy, greedy, the boss said, shaking his head.

On Friday afternoon, he handed out ties, jackets, and machine guns, and the gang, now camouflaged in business attire, set off with military precision. There were fourteen men and four cars in all—one to retrieve Chen, two for the factory, and one for the special errand.

Pulling up to the discreet sign that said only *RIC Corporation*, the men swarmed the entrances, overpowering the $9-per-hour guards and disabling the alarms, which were right where the mole had said. After taking everybody's cell phones, they herded the workers into a room.

They ignored the offers of purses and wallets. They were after the silicon chips, a negotiable tender akin to diamonds, gold bullion, heroin, C4, and enriched uranium. Lacking serial numbers, chips were untraceable and no law prohibited their flow across borders. Best of all, twenty million dollars' worth fit neatly into a slim briefcase, with room left over for a passport, airline tickets, and a paperback novel. You could stroll right through security and onto a plane. Within sixteen hours, they'd disappear into the gray market that flourished in the backstreets of Hong Kong's hi-tech district. Silicon Alley, they called it. Eighteen more hours and the chips would circle the globe, coming to rest in Zurich and Johannesburg and even boomeranging back to California's Silicon Valley.

Except in this case, the chips weren't in the locked metal cage where the mole had sworn they'd be. They relayed the news to the boss, who cursed but didn't despair. This, too, was a contingency he'd planned for. In the black town car inching through rush-hour traffic along Interstate 10, the boss applied the screws to Chen.

"In your office, there is a safe built into the wall," he said, watching Chen the way a butcher assesses a slab of meat. "We need the combination."

For emphasis, cold metal nudged further into his ribs.

Chen pressed against his other captor, who shifted and gave off a garlicky body odor. How was it that garlic could savor food so divinely, yet be such an abomination when released through human pores, Chen wondered, as he considered their demands. He was amazed he could hold both thoughts at the same time. What a supple organ the brain was. He hoped he would not lose control of his bowels.

The prodding grew more insistent. Oxygen ebbed out of the car, making his chest tighten. Was this what a heart attack felt like? If he died, they'd never get the combination. It would be a fitting trick from a god he'd stopped believing in five minutes ago. No. He wouldn't tell them. He'd be ruined, his family turned out. This was his biggest order yet, twenty million dollars' worth of chips with a bonus for early delivery, and he was days away from completion. He'd gambled everything, even borrowed money from loan sharks to hire more workers. How could success be snatched from him now? Chen would rather die. If he sacrificed himself, his wife could take over. At least his children's future would be assured—all of them. He had amended his will last month to reflect the birth of a male heir. His mistress Yashi hadn't believed it until he'd shown her the papers. Chen had even left a generous gift for Mieux Mieux at the brothel.

The butt of a gun came down against his temple so hard he felt his brains slosh inside his skull. His head throbbed and something splashed off his brow. He stuck out his tongue and tasted warm salty liquid. Red tears, he thought. I am crying red tears. He raised a hand to probe the wound, but someone grabbed his arm and pinned it to his side. Other hands tugged at his tie and he felt a ripple as it slid loose. Now his hands were shoved together and the tie, still warm from the heat of his body, was looped around his wrists and tightened.

His wife had given him that tie. It was silk. Some Italian designer whose name he couldn't pronounce. Now it bound their love together, he thought. What he would do to save his family.

"The combination," the boss repeated.

Again Chen shook his head, bracing for further blows. He hoped he'd pass out if they hit him again. He knew his life hung by a filament not much thicker than the fiber optics that wrapped his beloved and lucrative circuits.

"Open your eyes," a voice ordered.

Chen did and beheld a photo of himself, his wife, and the two girls, at a park near their home in San Marino. Chic and perfectly coiffed even on the weekend, Leila wore a quilted pink warm-up suit and clapped her hands as the children rocked on a seesaw. Chen stood off to the side in blue jeans, a white polo shirt, and tasseled loafers, talking into a cell phone. He remembered that day. An unseasonably warm Sunday in February. They'd eaten dim sum at a new place on Valley Boulevard and then, bellies full and relaxed, had given in to the girls' pleas and taken them to the park.

"We have people inside your house," the boss said, his voice the sibilant hiss of a snake that Chen had been told lurked in the arroyo, with diamonds on its back and rattles that sang as it struck.

At these words, Chen's vision constricted to a pinhole, seeing only his children, their fragile limbs, their trusting eyes. He thought of the evil that lay camouflaged, coiled in wait in this hot dry land so unlike the humidity of home. He and Leila had made a safe place for their family in this New World, though Leila had never stopped pining for the southern province of her youth. They had sheltered their children in ways their own lives had not been, growing up under the lamentable excesses of the Cultural Revolution. Chen himself had been guilty of an excess of zeal, but that was all in the past. The American gold rush was on, and so he had emigrated and found a little door when the big one was closed and built up his business and used his skills. It meant long trips to Asia to search out the best price for raw materials, and he missed his family terribly, but such was the sacrifice one made. And after all, hadn't he met Yashi there, and banished his loneliness in her arms, and brought her back and set her up in Arcadia as his mistress? He'd even bought her a townhouse on Huntington Drive. He hadn't expected her to be so hot-tempered, his Yashi, with her flashing eyes and ebony hair rippling like a curtain. Yashi with her greedy red mouth fastening upon him, fingertips fluttering like tiny moths against his skin.

The boss gave a buzz-saw laugh. He punched some numbers into a cell phone and gave an order. Then he put the phone on speaker.

"*Russell.*" His wife's quavering voice filled the car. "*They promise that if you do what they say, they won't . . .*" her voice choked. "*The children . . .*" she said hoarsely. "*They've got the children.*"

There was a scuffling as the phone changed hands.

"Say something to your father," a male voice demanded.

Then a wet whimper. "*Daddy?*" said six-year-old Pearl.

And when he heard that voice, usually so bossy, now reduced to a high whine of fear, something broke inside of Chen, and he slumped in his seat.

How could he give these people what they wanted? How could he not? Even if his family was saved, all would be lost. He knew his wife—she expected a certain standard of living. A big house. Country club membership. Fancy cars. Ivy League schools for the children. The education they had missed out on, because of the situation at home. Then he heard his daughter's gasp again, and he knew there was only one solution.

He told them.

The boss turned in his seat and his lips parted in a ghastly smile. Then he made a new call and repeated the sequence of numbers into the phone. In the chip factory, with its modest gray carpet, black lacquer furniture, and framed invoices for ever larger orders, Chen knew that someone was giddily twirling the dial.

He closed his eyes again. Soon they'd have what they wanted and they'd let him go and his family would be safe. He could always start over. What did it matter, balanced against their well-being? These were white-collar criminals. They didn't like leaving behind bodies, messes.

With a sudden jerk, the car wheeled off the freeway and sped north along Rosemead Boulevard. Up they went, past Bahooka's, the faux-Polynesian restaurant with the shellacked swordfish on the walls and the sticky red-syrup sauces. He had taken Yashi there, a place few Chinese immigrants were likely to go. Unlike San Marino, which was more than half Chinese now and a village when it came to gossip. They hit the 210 freeway and drove west.

Chen felt a spike of fear. "But you promised," he said.

"Shut up," the boss grunted.

"Where are you taking me?" he gasped some time later, as the car swung off the freeway and wound up Angeles Crest Highway into the San Gabriel Mountains. This was where criminals dumped bodies. He read the *Los Angeles Times* enough to know that. It had always given him a broody comfort to know he lived in a hushed and leafy suburb with the lowest crime rate and highest school test scores in all California. He led an orderly, honest life. He took precautions, paid for armed guards, assiduously wooed the big companies like Intel and Pentium. And each time he opened the *Wall Street Journal* and read another headline that said, *Chip Demand Continues to Outpace Supply*, his heart swelled with pride and satisfaction at how he provided for his family. At

Yashi, now the mother of his son. A prickle of unease filled him then, something he'd have struggled to put into words in a calm setting, much less now. He recalled Yashi throwing plates, demanding that he divorce his wife. Young passionate Yashi. She'd been acting strange lately, and he'd put it down to the new baby. Cooped up by herself all day in the town-house. Really, he would have to mollify her with a gift. He thought of his favorite jeweler in the San Gabriel Village Square on Valley and Del Mar, the heart of suburban Chinese immigration. The tiny proprietor, Overseas Chinese from Burma, with his wizened face and appraising eyes. A bracelet of imperial jade, perhaps to mark the birth of a son.

It was dusk when they pushed him out of the car on the mountain road, hands still lassoed together by his designer tie. They pulled his shoes off and hurled them down a ravine, startling some unseen animal that crashed through the undergrowth and was gone.

"We're sorry, uncle, we need time to get away," one of the underlings said. Chen sensed a curious undertow to the hon-orific and wondered if they regretted their mistreatment of him, now that he had given them what they wanted.

Yes, he thought, almost approvingly. They couldn't have him sounding the alarm too soon. They were smart, meticu-lous people. They thought of everything.

From the side of the road, he watched the car pull for-ward, then turn and head back down. It slowed as it drew near him, mute and penitent in the gloaming, his wrists tied before him, hands curved into a begging bowl.

"In the name of God, at least untie me!" he shouted. "I'm no threat to you anymore!"

The car stopped. "He wants us to untie his hands," came a lazy voice from inside the car.

A pause then, as though the matter was under consideration.

"Stop toying with him and do as he asks," said the boss, sounding weary. "She was very insistent."

The first bullet shot through his knotted tie, shredding it into charred fibers that soared upward, then drifted down to the pine-needled ground long after Mr. Chen himself had slumped to rest. Two more slugs tore into his chest. A fourth caught him on the temple. He was long gone by then, dreaming of Mieux Mieux from the brothel, sad forlorn bird from his home province of Fujian, and the tricks he had taught her.

"One down, two to go," the boss said. He opened his Thomas Brothers Guide and flipped the colorful grid pages until he came to one marked *Arcadia*. His finger drifted across the map and found Huntington Drive. The car sped down the mountainside and disappeared into the night.

Three hours later, Leila Chen and her two girls walked out of a large Tudor house in San Marino and climbed into their Mercedes.

"Los Angeles International Airport," she said, and directions began to scroll across the screen embedded into the dashboard.

"Won't Daddy be surprised when he learns it was all a joke?" Mrs. Chen said gaily. A slim briefcase of fine-grained leather lay across the front seat, filled with silicone chips. There was plenty of room left over for passports, one-way tickets to Shanghai, and a paperback novel. They would stroll right through security and onto a plane winging its way over the Pacific.

"Are you sure Daddy's going to meet us there?" asked Pearl.

"Daddy, Daddy," chanted four-year-old April.

Leila Chen pursed her pastel lips and allowed herself a moment of silent triumph.

"Of course he will, darlings," she said finally. "You two are the *only* children he's got, and he loves you madly. That's why he works so hard. To give you *everything* . . . But you know your Daddy," she added in a singsong voice. "His business trip could take a long time. In the meanwhile, there's a new uncle that Mommy wants you to meet. I think you're going to like him very much."

PART II

HOLLYWOODLANDIA

THE METHOD

BY JANET FITCH

Los Feliz

I t was cold in Los Angeles. Fifty-eight, sixty degrees. In Nebraska, I'd have been scraping ice off the windshield while the wind bit my face like a Rottweiler, but in L.A., when you have to put a sweater on, that's winter. The dark deodar cedars brooded over Los Feliz Boulevard, trailing their boughs over the traffic creeping toward Griffith Park and the DWP Holiday Tunnel of Light, all eighty million drive-through lightbulbs of it. Christmas. People complained about being "stuck here" for the holidays, joking about the ribbons on the palm trees, saying how it just didn't seem like Christmas without the old yule dog. But not me. You'd never catch me whining that I couldn't get back to Kearney for the holidays, sit around listening to Paul Anka and tracking Aunt Phoebe's phlebitis.

If you met me, you might think you knew me—a small-town girl, fresh from state college productions of *The Boyfriend* and *Annie Get Your Gun*. Up against Stepford armies of five-ten leggy blondes, former Miss Iowas and Texas, with kilowatt smiles. I'm just five-two, dark-haired, with a small sharp chin and big baby blues. I know, you'd think *lunchmeat*. But you don't know me.

I was working the 5-to-11 shift at Orzo, a trattoria on Hillhurst that catered to the Los Feliz/Silverlake hipsters, men in leather jackets and perfect two-day stubble, women with clean hair and long knitted scarves. That night it was busy, customers lined up out the door. Whenever the thermometer plunged below sixty, everybody wanted Italian. A man sat in my section; if I'd seen him on the street I'd have thought he was too broke to eat at a place like this. Dark and bald, in a thick turtleneck and a beat-up leather jacket, about forty-five I'd guess. But there was something about him. I can't say what it was and I can't say I liked it. The way he looked at me when I came over and took his drink order.

"What do you recommend?" Brown eyes, with a funny light in them, like he was enjoying a private joke and I was the punch line. He pissed me off. Like me or don't like me, I don't give a rat's ass, but there's nothing funny about me.

"We have a Barolo, by the glass." It was fourteen bucks. Even the cuffs of his jacket were worn.

"I think . . . I'll have the Classico." He pointed at the board with a languorous finger, a gay gesture though he didn't seem gay. He seemed like a straight guy who was being annoying. I guessed him for a writer. They've got a look about them. They come alone, watch everything from some corner, sometimes they take notes. This guy didn't have a notebook, but he had the look.

I brought him his Classico and recited the specials.

"Would you say the ahi, or the osso buco?" He stroked his lips with long fingers. They had hair on them. I imagined shoulders like a gorilla. Hair everywhere but that dome. Too bad for him.

I knew if I said the ahi he'd order the osso. I wanted to tell him to stop wasting my time, it wasn't intriguing and he was twenty years too old for me. "The osso's our specialty."

"Then bring that." He folded his menu and handed it to me. "And the heirloom tomatoes to start." He spoke better than you'd think, with a jacket like that and the edge of his turtleneck unraveling.

It got crazy busy then. People and wine and opinions, big steaming bowls of pasta, steaks, and veal between closely packed tables. I didn't have a moment—and yet, I could feel his eyes, following me, from the corner table by the exposed brick wall. I'm an actress. When I have an audience, I act. Even if I don't, the non-acting is also acting. He made me aware of each small movement, the way I carried an armload of plates, uncorked a bottle of wine, flourished the pepper mill over a bowl of penne regate. He lifted his glass, showing me he needed a refill. I brought it over.

"I'm Richard," he said as I filled his glass.

"Enjoying your meal?" I said, distant, professional. In case he couldn't see I had five tables waiting.

"You've got a spot, exactly . . . there." His long finger, pointing to my left tit.

I glanced down and saw he was right, I'd somehow got a spatter of red on the white linen right over the nip.

"It's very provocative," he said, looking at me over the rim of his wine glass.

I purposely didn't do anything about it. First of all, if I tried to clean it up, it would just make a bigger spot, right there on my boob; and two, I didn't want him to think I cared what he thought. He was trying to throw me, but I wasn't that kind of girl. Not even then. I did better with an audience.

When I brought him his check, he asked, "Do you ever go to the Firehouse?"

A trendy bar on Rowena. "Sometimes," I said.

"I'm going over there later," he said. "Why don't you join me for a drink after you're done?"

"I'm going home," I said. Forcing myself to meet his eyes. "I have to wash my shirt."

He shrugged, paid the bill. "I hear they make an elegant martini. If you change your mind, I'll see you over there . . . Holly." He put his long finger to his mouth, hooking it over the lower lip, a good gesture, maybe I'd use it someday.

I was startled he knew my name, until I remembered that I'd signed the check. Anyone could have seen it, but people were rarely that observant.

He rapped the check on the table, left it there. "See you later." He was taller than I thought he'd be, slender, his posture relaxed and surprisingly graceful. He didn't move like a writer, none that I knew.

When he left, the place went flat, like old soda pop.

After I cleaned my tables and tipped my busboy, I walked around the corner to my apartment, a two-story '40s court on Los Feliz Boulevard. Twelve units facing an identical building across a little yard where a box hedge corralled a flock of white calla lilies. Most of the residents were old ladies living on dead husbands' pensions. A genteel crowd, these broke old grannies. We all lived here for the same reason: the address. *Los Feliz Boulevard* called to mind the mansions in the hills north and south of the street, but this was Granny Los Feliz, who counted her pennies and voted Republican, who drank cream sherry out of cut glass.

Most actresses who came here went straight for Hollywood. Three roommates and cereal for dinner, green apple martinis, X-bras from Victoria's Secret. Others chose Silverlake, a bass player boyfriend in a punk band, a new tat, and an STD for every six months you lived there. But Los Feliz meant you could take care of yourself, you'd been here long enough to know your way around. Sometimes I drove up into the hills, imagining how it would feel to have money like that, old money, houses from the teens, silent-screen stuff, before Beverly Hills was even a gleam in some developer's eye.

I let myself in, turned on the lights. Nothing but the glorious emptiness of no roommate. It was a luxury I could ill afford, but the last one, a dancer named Audrey, just got a show in Vegas. I liked dancers the best, they were never home, they weren't sociable, they didn't cook. Someday I wouldn't need a roommate at all. It was just a matter of time. I sat on the flowered couch and counted my tips. You'd think people who could spend fifty on dinner could cough up ten for a tip.

I changed out of my work clothes, soaked the shirt in some bleach. I looked at myself in the mirror. There was nothing wrong with me. I was just small. Small ass, small tits, short legs, a bit bowed, but I knew how to dress, you'd never notice it. Big blues and bright skin, though nobody had seen my skin in quite a while. Okay, I had a problem with men. I was easily bored.

I reached for my pajamas and thought of the guy Richard, waiting for me at the Firehouse. The quick brown eyes, the mocking quality of the mouth, those gestures, their ironic self-consciousness. The graceful looseness of his walk. He looked like a writer but he moved like a dancer. Slouchy but light on his feet. I wondered what his story was. I kept thinking of the way he looked at me, like he had a secret he was enjoying. People I knew didn't have secrets. They told you every microscopic detail of their lives. A leaf blew across a sidewalk and you got fifteen minutes worth. The upstairs neighbor went to the bathroom twice, God, do you think he's got prostate? I wasn't like that, and I could tell this guy Richard wasn't either.

That time of night, you could park on Rowena without having to hike a mile. The Firehouse still had the high tin ceilings from when it was a working fire station, the wooden bar long and narrow. Richard sat halfway down, drinking something brown on ice. It wasn't crowded, a few older guys scattered along the bar who watched me walk down to the bald man in the beat-up jacket. Richard didn't say hello as I took the stool next to him. He didn't even look at me. "Did you get the spot out?" he asked, lifting his drink to his lips in that stylized, mannered way of his. Slower than necessary. With the elegant pause.

"Out out, damned spot." I flagged the bartender, asked for the wine list. They had an interesting-looking Dry Creek Zin. That made me feel good, a girl from Kearney who could look at a wine list and know the Zin from the Cab, prefer the New Zealand Sauvignon Blancs to the French. Waiting tables had educational advantages.

The Zin came, plummy, I could even taste figs, and pepper too. Richard put the wine on his tab. Touching those long fingers to his lips, again, that slightly gay self-consciousness, as if placing every motion in ironic quotes. Suddenly I knew. *Actor. Actor actor actor.*

"How are you liking L.A.?" he asked.

I knew it was intended to startle me, like using my name, but it was such an easy bet. Everyone here was from somewhere else. I wanted to show him I could return a serve. "I like it," I said. "I like every fucking thing about it. How about you? Where are you from?"

He shook the ice in his drink, looking down into it with

a half-smile. He raised his glass to his lips slowly and spoke before it arrived. "Right here."

"Bullshit," I said.

"Oh yes," he said. "I went to Marshall. A mere five blocks away. I'm nostalgic already." He pointed west. "King Junior. Franklin Avenue Elementary."

"Hard to picture you as a child," I said.

"I was a difficult child." He posed, lifting his drink as if it was the skull in *Hamlet*. "I never lived up to my potential."

"I did well," I said, sipping my wine. "I was valedictorian. I played flute in the marching band."

"And then you decided to act. At . . . Champaign-Urbana? Or was it Lawrence, Kansas?"

It was Lincoln, but I didn't need to confirm a run of insight that was now getting eerie.

"And now you're here to break into the big time. How's the climb to fame going?"

"It seems they tore Schwab's down awhile back, but nobody told me."

"Naturally, you take class. Boyd Stocker?"

"Chris Valente."

"Ballet at 3rd Street—"

"Tap."

That made him smile. I smiled too. I knew it was stupid but I really liked tap, it reminded me of old Busby Berkeley movies.

"You've come close," he said, "but so far, the star never broke her ankle."

Asshole. "Actually, I had a feature."

"Never released."

How could he know these things? Well, of course, if the feature had been released, I wouldn't be slinging pasta at

Orzo. Not that I'd have any money, but I wouldn't want people to see me working for a living.

"There was a problem with the funding."

He drew his finger across the condensation on his glass. "These things happen. But you'll catch on. You've got something, a certain sense of authority. People watch you. All you have to do is soften up a little. You're all barbed wire."

Chris Valente said the same thing. *Show your vulnerability, Holly.* It just made me want to slug him. I lost my vulnerability a long time ago. Along with my innocence. Or so I thought then. "Maybe I've got a corral to fence."

"There's nothing wrong with it. You just want to layer, hold it in reserve, until it's time to show it." He looked down the bar to where the bartender, a blond boy with shaggy hair in a tight black shirt, stood laughing with an older man. "Miles, I'll have another Jack Daniel's, if I may."

The bartender came down and took Richard's glass, giving him a sweep of blond eyelash.

"So why don't you act anymore?" I asked. Seeing if I could play the clairvoyant too.

He turned toward me, propped his head on his hand. He looked at me very directly, and I felt the full force of his personality in those eyes, that mocking mouth. "What is the attraction of acting? Seeing where our personalities line up with those of fictional characters? Infusing them with the stuff of life? But the day comes when one's own personality is more interesting than those one is paid to animate."

Miles handed him his new drink. Richard made me wait while he took a sip. Controlling the silences. God, he was good. What a shame he'd stopped acting.

"So what do you do now?" I said. "Unemployment?"

"Write. Coach. A number of things. Mostly I study the

human condition." He paused a beat. "I saw something in you tonight, Holly. Something I've been looking for."

I smiled inwardly. He was too old for me and bald to boot, but he fascinated me, with his slightly gay gestures that contrasted with the bright brown wolfishness of his eyes, the flat wide mouth playing with its private joke. I itched to know that joke.

"Do you like animals, Holly?"

Just when I thought I knew what he was talking about. "Animals? You're kidding."

"I have a little problem," he said, steepling his long fingers with hair on their backs. "Can I be frank for a moment?"

I had the feeling that he couldn't be frank on his own deathbed.

"I found a dog. And I need to return it," he said.

"So why don't you?"

He moved his wide mouth around, pursing the lips, pushing them from side to side. "It's not that simple. The dog belongs to Mariah McKay. Do you know who that is?"

An actress from the '70s, sexy, sort of a dark Kathleen Turner.

"I found it on Los Feliz Boulevard. One of those little greyhounds. I saw the name and address on the tags, and was about to return it, but then I wondered, what if they think I stole it?" He opened his eyes wide, to show how innocent he was. "A problem, don't you think?"

"Only if you want a reward. Otherwise just be a good neighbor." A shitty little scam. I had to laugh.

He smiled. He knew I knew he was full of it. I was liking him more and more. "But I'm not such a good neighbor, Holly. I really do want the money." A fucking petty crook. I finally meet a guy in L.A. who is actually interested me, and he's into some shitass doggie scam. "It's probably good for a couple hundred. If you found a hundred dollars lying in the street, would you give it back?"

I looked at us in the bar mirror—Richard with his dark, sharp-peaked eyebrows, and me with my pale face and pointed chin, my dark curls caught up in a ribbon band. And I knew we were the same. That's why he recognized me. I smiled. "I'll let you know when I pawn my Girl Scout patches."

The McKay place was off Commonwealth, up in the hills, a Spanish mansion that had seen happier days. In the morning light, you could see the paint peeling off the pink stucco. I parked down the hill and made like I was jogging. The little greyhound had a tag that said, *Gilbert*, with an address and phone number, but nowhere did it say he belonged to Mariah McKay. Richard's story stunk, but so what. He fucked like an angel, and I could use a hundred bucks.

Wearing my track pants and *U of Nebraska* sweatshirt, holding onto the shred of rah rah Americana I could remember, the marching band at halftime on a November Saturday, I jogged up the steep hill in the cold December damp. The little dog easily kept pace with me. It was about 11:00, nobody around but a couple of mow and blow gardeners. When we got to the house, I pocketed the leash and held the dog in my arms. I rang, then knocked. Making sure my barbed wire was tucked out of sight.

A little window in the door opened. "Yes?"

I figured the maid. "Yes, excuse me. I was running down on Wayne and I found a dog . . . ?"

The door opened. It wasn't the maid. It was a dark-haired, older woman with the odd puffy lips of an actress who'd had work done, and she held her arms out to the little dog, who jumped into them. She kissed that narrow, hard head. "Where the hell have you been, mister? You've had me worried sick." She smiled at me. "Please, come in."

Though it was high noon, the living room was dark and smelled of mold. A row of red theater chairs sat against one wall instead of a couch. A TV, squatting on a wire cart, played a soap opera. If she'd made money in the '70s, she hadn't hung onto it. She put the dog down and he skittered out of the living room, probably toward the kitchen and his bowl. I gave up on a reward. She could probably cough up a twenty, but no way was Richard seeing any three C's. Couldn't he have stolen a richer woman's dog?

"I can't thank you enough." Mariah extended her hand, large, the back grown ropy with age. Her famous voice was throaty as ever. "Damn dog got out of the yard. I can't find the hole either." She took a pack of cigarettes from a pocket in her goat-hair sweater, lit one, coughed. "What's your name, baby?"

"Holly," I said.

"Very Christmasy. I was just making some coffee, Holly, want some?"

Should I tell her I'd seen her movies? "Yeah, that'd be great."

She shuffled in her mirrored Indian slippers back the way the dog had gone, and I followed her without an invitation. There was a dining room up some steps, the long dark Spanish table covered with mail and piles of junk, and then into the kitchen painted salmon with black trim, a Deco feel. The sink was full of dishes. She put a battered blue enamel kettle on the stove and ground some coffee in a small grinder. No maid, no help. The whole thing was pathetic beyond words.

"Have you lived here a long time?" that high school flute player asked.

She opened a cat food–sized can of dog food and scraped it into a dirty dish. "Thirty years, give or take. Shoulda sold it when the market picked up, but the mortgage's paid off now, I couldn't rent a one-bedroom dump for what this costs me. Except the roof's gone." Her dark hair was rough and unbrushed, the mustard-colored shapeless sweater did nothing for her legendary figure.

She had on some ugly fake emeralds in her ears, and a cluster of pink and green glass on her bony right hand. "I've seen your movies," said Miss Teen Americana. Striking a perfect balance between girlish excitement and Midwestern abashed modesty. "You're one of my heroes."

"Acting," she snorted. "I like animals. They never act. They're entirely authentic." The little greyhound was pushing his dish around the broken tile floor.

Easy for her to say, now that the work no longer came. "I love acting. It lets you live all kinds of lives. I'm studying with Chris Valente."

"You got lucky. All kinds of creeps out there, preying on the hopeful." She gave me a pitying look. "How long have you been in town, baby?"

"About a year." I smiled a vulnerable Midwestern smile.

She didn't say any more, as the kettle whistled and she got busy making the coffee, balancing a filter cone on top of a chipped porcelain pot, pouring the boiling water in.

"It's harder than I thought," I continued, feeling my way along. "I just lost my roommate." I played it brave—grace under pressure. More sympathetic than whining. "I'm waiting tables down at Orzo. I thought I'd be further along by now."

"Chapter and verse, baby," she said, watching the water

drip through the grounds. "Orzo. That's not a bad place. I like their osso buco."

So did Richard. "They had it last night." I tried again to redirect. "I don't mind working there, but the tips aren't as good as you'd think."

"That's tough." She took two dirty cups out of the sink, rinsed them without benefit of soap or hot water, and filled them with coffee. I prayed the boiling water would be hot enough to kill whatever had been growing on the chipped lip of the mug. "You know, I have a room," she said. "Never thought of renting it out before, but you seem like a nice kid. Any interest in that?"

"So, did you get in?" Richard asked. He'd gotten dressed, was flopped on my couch like the Crown Prince.

"You had any doubts?" I said, straddling his prone body. "But she doesn't have money. You should see that place. It's falling down around her. You'd hardly recognize her, she's shlepping around like a bag lady."

"Is that what she told you? She didn't have any money?"

"No, it's just what I saw."

"Don't be misled. That woman's got oodles."

"You're tripping."

"Trust me. Just look at that jewelry. She still had it, right?"

"Dime-store crap, you can get it in a box of Cracker Jacks."

Richard laughed, shifted me so my weight did more good. "You looked but you couldn't see. Paul Rhodes gave her those rocks back in the days of wine and roses. You can see in the magazines. She'd never part with them. I mean, the senti-mental value alone." I loved the invisible ironic quotation marks around that "sentimental." He put his sensitive fingers to his lips, dancing the fingertips. "Even if it's as bad as you describe, she's hung onto a few pesos, I can assure you."

What if those emeralds were real? Ten grand? Fifty? I tried to ballpark it, but I had no idea what jewelry like that was worth; I didn't exactly have a charge card at Tiffany. "She asked me to move in. Help with expenses."

He pressed his mouth to my neck, something that drove me crazy. "A generous offer, Holly. You should consider it."

"You think I should, do you?" I said, trying to keep some illusion of independence, but I was already slipping.

"Oh, the savings alone. And the link to a bygone Hollywood. The cachet, the entrée. Not to mention what she might have been lying about, forgotten under the couch or in a spare room. I think you owe it to yourself."

I waited a few days to return to the house off Commonwealth. Her car was in the driveway, an old blue-gray Mercedes like a tank. I knocked, figuring it was late enough that she would have slept off even a heavy drunk, but early enough that she wouldn't have gone out had she a mind to. No answer. I rang again and knocked. It was such a pretty house, it didn't deserve to be as neglected like this, leaves lying moldy, cracks running through the concrete steps.

I had just given up when the little window in the door opened. She fumbled with several locks and a chain. Gilbert raced out, danced around my legs, jumping on me, he weighed about as much as a handful of chicken bones.

"I've been thinking about the room," I said, hesitantly, vulnerable as all get-out.

Her ruined face smiled. Her hair still hadn't been washed, either that or it always looked that way, long and dark and stringy. "It hasn't been used in a while," she said, leading me through the cloisterish living room with its heavy beams, and up through the dining room, around to the kitchen and a set of wooden stairs I hadn't noticed before, narrow with an iron handrail and a sharp bend under a low overhang.

"Myrna Loy lived here in the '30s," Mariah said. "Gale Storm."

We climbed the stairs into a little hall flanked with a couple of doors. She opened one. A dirty window illuminated an odd-shaped room full of boxes, obviously a former maid's quarters.

"Of course, we'll move this crap somewhere." She stood in the doorway, scratching her dirty hair. "So what do you think?"

It was cold in the room, though I couldn't tell if it was because it had been closed off or because the heat didn't work. A stained mattress leaned against the wall. What a fucking dump. But it would probably save me close to $800 a month and there might be some fringe benefits. "How much would you want?" I asked her.

She shrugged. "Oh, I don't know. What do you think? Couple hundred?"

Not bad, for in a mansion in Los Feliz. Wouldn't that look good on my portfolio. Even if I would have to wash the dishes in bleach.

And so I joined the ranks of the oddly housed. Los Angeles is full of us—house sitters, subletters, permanent house guests. It wasn't much of a move—clothes, a few books, a TV and boom box, and my laptop. But it took two days to clear the boxes out of the room. Memorabilia, just as Richard predicted. A gold mine. Letters from Belmondo and Bertolucci and Bianca Jagger, David Bowie's *Aladdin Sane* shirt, a drawing by Larry Rivers on a restaurant placemat. A lamp she'd taken from the set of *Riverside 88*, the Paul Rhodes film that put her on the map. YSL gowns in the closet, still in their designer bags. Old scripts marked with her handwriting, photographs, scrapbooks of reviews, and fashion layouts she'd been in, *Bazaar* and *W* and *Interview*. We sat on the floor and looked at a spread of her in *Vogue*, wearing Oscar de la Renta and Halston. She showed me the gown in the photograph, a Russian velvet dress with mink on the sleeves.

But the pictures made me sad. How bright she had been, blindingly alive, lit up from inside like a circus midway. And now here she was, a single lightbulb that had almost burnt out. I could smell her sadness, sitting next to me, in a pilled mustard sweater, and those lips, and her square cut emeralds dull with dirt. The way people's lives turned out when they just ran them into the ground, like a rental car.

As we moved the boxes into another room across the hall, I saw something I didn't much care for—rat droppings in the corners. Mariah said not to worry, she used these little traps that didn't hurt the poor rats, you could carry them out to the backyard and let them go. I didn't say anything, but later went out and bought some traps big enough to kill a cat. When I heard them pop in the night, all I felt was satisfaction.

So I hung out with Mariah, and took class and visited Richard in his apartment, around the corner from the bookstore on Vermont, the second floor of an old Spanish quad. It was small but dramatically decorated with handpainted red walls and gilded beams. Not at all what you'd expect, but that was Richard. His bed took up most of the floor, covered in brown-and-black–striped cotton. Made seductions simple—there was nowhere else to sit. I teased him, that he should just come to my place sometime.

"Oh, you don't want a stream of men interfering with your new friendship," he said, tracing spirals on my skin.

I tossed the Bertolucci letter onto the bed, lay back, and folded my arms under my head. "She knows you, doesn't she?" I asked.

He didn't say anything, opened the letter, read it.

I pinched him. "Tell me. Was she a good fuck? Good as me?"

"She was very beautiful."

It hurt. I was surprised how much it hurt.

He laughed and caught my hand, put it on his cock, which moved again. When I fucked him, I didn't care how beautiful Mariah McKay had been, she looked like a bag lady now, and she wasn't fucking anyone, unless it was the delivery guy from Whole Foods.

"I want you to do me a favor, Holly," he said. He sipped his wine, arm tucked behind his head, the pillows piled up there, the fan of his pit hair like a dark blossom. His smell drove me mad.

I pulled gently at that nest of hair. I knew I would be attracted to hairy men for the rest of my life. "It wouldn't be anything illegal, would it?"

"Oh, Midwest," he said, drawling with irony. "Oh, Pioneers."

I sat with Mariah on her row of theater seats, watching *Valley of the Dolls*. Mariah knew all the dialogue. "*So now you come crawling back to Broadway*," she said along with Susan Hayward. "*But Broadway doesn't go for booze and dope.*" Then

Patty Duke snatched her wig and flushed it down the can. *"Meow,"* she said as she drowned it, Hayward pounding on the stall door.

What I could do with a part like Neely O'Hara. Not fucking Laura Wingfield, whom Chris had given me. He wanted me to find my soft side. Talk about miscasting. "It's your job to find her, Holly. Allow her to live in you."

I watched Mariah in her weird crocheted sweater and tights, unconsciously splitting the ends of her ragged hair. Her and Richard. Really? I wondered whether he was just yanking my chain. And how long ago?

"Poor Sharon," Mariah said, watching the screen, Sharon Tate doing her breast exercises. "Did you know the La Bianca house is right around the corner, across from the nuns?"

The first Manson killing. Right here in Los Feliz. *Better look out for Charlie's girls . . .*

It was a cold afternoon and I shivered, thinking of that freaky guy with his flock of bizarre little girls, exactly the kind of thing people in Kearney worried about when they thought of L.A. I wrapped my fingers around the packet of white powder Richard had given me. I was supposed to put it into Mariah's drink. Some ground-up barbs to knock her out for a few hours. So far I'd taken a few things—a letter here, a signed picture there—but it was time to get into her Deco bedroom for a little scout around.

Yes, Grandma, there was lots to worry about in L.A., and they didn't always look like Charlie and his girls. There were people like Richard. People like me.

And yet, I couldn't help wondering how he knew her. If they'd really been lovers. She might have known him when he had hair, and she was a movie star. I was jealous of her, having had him, this fuzzy-headed has-been in the goat-hair sweater. I could imagine them together, how it was. I thought of it all the time, knowing what it was to have Richard; I'd never known sex could be like that. He was a drug. He hardly even came, just got you off about twenty times. I couldn't stop thinking about it.

"I met this guy at Orzo's," I said, sipping my Corona. "He said he knew you." I was taking a chance, but couldn't stop myself. I didn't know one fucking thing about Richard. Who his friends were, what he liked to do besides fuck. "His name was Richard something."

She shrugged, sipped at her Scotch, watching Sharon Tate and Lee Grant on the flickering screen.

"Kind of intense, brown eyes?" I added.

The speed at which she turned to me, I knew. And it was either big or recent. But it hadn't been good. She looked downright scared. "Was he tall, lanky? Attractive in a sort of reptilian way?"

I backpedaled fast. I didn't want to tip her off. "No, this guy was stocky. Sort of like a wrestler. He said he interviewed you in the '80s. You snorted coke together."

She relaxed, went back to watching the TV. "Oh, a journalist. Yeah, I seem to remember someone like that. Richard somebody. Stevens. Sheehan."

Onscreen, Sharon Tate was launching a porn career to care for her declining husband.

"So," I said, natural as all get-out. "Who was this other guy?"

"Someone I had a thing with," she said, not turning away from the TV. "Years ago. But what a psycho. I had to get a restraining order."

I thought of Richard. Had he threatened her, had he hurt her? Was he capable of that? I had imagined him as dark, but was he dangerous? *You've got to layer. Hold something in reserve. Easy. Casual.* "What was his name?"

"Anthony. Karras. I had him fired off a set. People don't take too kindly to that."

"That's kind of harsh, isn't it?" I searched for my inner Laura. "Makes you kind of feel sorry for him."

She patted my leg. "You're a nice kid. Don't feel too sorry for him. He was one of those guys who's exciting in a kind of bad boy way . . . and then you get involved, and they're just freaks. I got wise and told him it was over, to move the fuck out, but he wouldn't. Had to call some people to get rid of him. He said he'd kill me. Showed up at my house. Called my friends. I took him off the picture and got a restraining order. Told the casting agents to watch out for him, he was a definite freak." She got the remote, turned up the sound. "Learned my lesson, baby. No more smart men. Only nice and dumb and hung."

I thought of the white powder concealed in my hand. Gilbert shoved his nose under my arm to be petted. I could feed him this shit, but he was a nice dog. I excused myself and went back to the kitchen, found Mariah's stupid catch-and-release rat trap in the pantry. I opened the odiferous refrigerator—I'd scrubbed it out once, but it had lain rank too long, the smell was now part of the enamel—cut a little chunk of her $20-a-pound Whole Foods cheese, and blended it with a pinkie-nail's worth of white powder. "Bon appetit," I whispered as I pushed it through the door of the rat trap with a pencil. "My name's Holly and I'll be your rat-waitress tonight, we're serving Humboldt Fog with a reduction of Nembutal." Stuck the trap back into the pantry.

By dinnertime, there was a nice big guy in there. Stone cold dead. Teeth bared and claws curled to a chest solid as a pit bull's.

* * *

I thought of it all through dinner. Richard sitting in his red room above the market, pouring himself a glass of wine, thinking he'd gotten away with murder. With me to take the rap. How satisfied he was with himself. *You're such a special girl, Holly. You're going to go far.* Yeah, I was going to go far. Right to fucking prison. Was he jerking off, imagining her dying? He sure as hell wasn't thinking of me, walking away in handcuffs, trying to explain that my boyfriend put me up to it. *I didn't know, I just thought I was going to knock her out and rob her.*

To think I'd imagined he really was hot for me, wanted me. He hadn't even *seen* me. He'd been fucking me and thinking of her. How he was going to screw her. Thinking of her not as she was now, but as she had been back then, beautiful and famous and spoiled, when she'd had him thrown out and the locks changed. Just because I'd gotten the best screwing of my life, I was assuming it meant something. *Oh, Midwest. Oh, Pioneers.*

Well, I'd always known he was a wrong guy, fake as ten-dollar Prada. That every word out of his mouth was a lie. But not about us. Not how beautiful he thought I was, how exciting. *Such a special girl. You're going to make it. You just have to hide the barbed wire.*

I'd hide it all right. Now he'd see how special I was.

At about 11:00 the phone rang. I picked up. Mariah didn't like to answer her phone if there was someone else to do it. Hard not to have help when you're a former film goddess. "Hello?"

It was Richard. I imagined how shocked he must be, hearing my voice, that son of a bitch. I listened for the tell, the little gasp, the hesitation, but he was good, he was always so fucking good. He didn't waver for a second. "Holly. I thought you were going to call me. Did you do it?" He was calling to see if Mariah was dead.

Quickly, I scraped my own part together. Naïve cock-struck dupe wasn't much of a stretch. "Yeah, but it sort of didn't work out," I said. "I put it in her Scotch like you said, but the dog knocked it over."

"That's too bad," he said, carefully. "Did you use it all?"

"Yeah." I lowered my voice, conspiratorially. "I didn't want her waking up as I'm taking an earring out of her ear, right? Hey, I miss you."

"What are you doing right now?" he asked.

"Working on my scene. Laura. It's coming pretty well," I said. "You'll be surprised."

"Come over here and surprise me."

It was late, but he never went to bed before 2 a.m. He answered the door, wearing his tattered red brocade smoking jacket and a pair of jeans. The jacket would have looked ridiculous on any-one else. On him it hit just the right decadent note.

I let him kiss me. It surprised me. It felt just the same. Goddamnit if I didn't still want him like a house on fire. It was insane. I felt like I was losing my mind. He poured us some wine. I tried mine and frowned, said it tasted weird, but he drank his and said it tasted fine. We made out on his bed and I took off my shirt, concealing our glasses of wine from him. I handed him his glass. "To Laura," I said.

We toasted, then drank. He frowned and worked his mouth, his tongue, tasting, grimacing. "That *is* off."

And then we made it. We did everything: me on top, him on top, sideways, scissoring. I was getting the best lay of my life. I came up with ideas I didn't even know I had. I was sad I wasn't going to have this anymore. But nobody fucks around with me. Nobody takes me for a ride.

Finally, he lay on his back, rubbing his arms, his chest. His breathing had grown audibly labored, though his cock was still working fine.

"Are you okay?" I asked, concerned.

"What time . . ." He was having trouble breathing. He turned over and squinted at the clock, his vision must not have been working so well. It was only 12:45.

"Feeling cold?"

His back arching, jerking. I rubbed his back, his arms. I could feel the rigidity, the tremor, the poison spreading. I hadn't seen the rat die, I didn't know quite what to expect. It was very instructive.

After a while, he pushed me away. "That's . . . not . . . helping." He lay on his back, his jaws clenching, his eyes luminous and big with fear. "Holly . . ."

"Can I get you something? Water? Aspirin?"

He nodded.

I fucked around in the kitchen, killing time, running the water, filling the glass a couple of times. As I held his water with one hand, I stretched out the other before me. Perfectly steady. I raised a palm up, inspected. The hand of someone I hadn't known until tonight. We really could have had something, Richard and I. We were perfect for each other, like Bonnie and Clyde. But he didn't see it. He just threw me away like a gumball prize.

When I came back with the water, he was rigid, his hand up by his throat, he could barely breathe. I held the water for him, let him drink. He choked a little, I backed off. He croaked, "Hosp . . . 911."

"Should I call 911?" I said.

His face was pale with a greenish cast. Reptilian, yes, definitely. His eyes pleaded. Oh yeah. Now you notice me.

I called 611 and waited. Let it ring. I braced the receiver to my breast. "It's busy, they say to hold. Oh God, Richard, what should I do?"

"Christ—" he gasped.

"Wait . . ." I said, as if someone was coming onto the phone. His back arched like he was in some yoga pose. "Oh fuck, it's still busy, oh shit, Richard, what should I do?!" Crying a little. Was I overplaying it? Maybe just a bit. "Are you going to die?? Richard, don't die!"

He tried to sit up on one elbow. "Help—"

"And . . . end of scene." I announced. I hung up the phone, dropped the panicked-girlfriend routine. Now his eyes were bugging out of his head.

"You know, Anthony," I said, pulling on my underwear, "I never did use that shit on Mariah."

I was sure he would have taken a deep breath if he could, but he wasn't breathing much at all. And yet, even like that, from somewhere, he found the strength to lunge at me. But he was rigid and in pain and all that happened was that he fell off the bed with a thud onto the Cost Plus rug.

"You know, I was crazy about you. I would have done anything for you. But you didn't care what happened to me. All you cared about was getting back at her. For dumping you. You stupid fuck. She called you a psycho, you know? And I could be in jail right now, making my one call. Now, should it be to a lawyer? Or my darling boyfriend."

His eyes looking up at me from the carpet, upside down, his back was so contorted, the whites were red and the irises full of horror and surprise. White frothy shit coming out of his nose, his mouth. I didn't know how it would go down, how I would feel watching the man I adored die. It was like watching a part of myself die. The part that was good and decent. Well, good riddance.

"You know, I might have even offed her for you, if you'd sold it right. Then you could have had it all. Revenge, the swag, the whole deal. But you got sloppy. I won't make that mistake."

As he wheezed and convulsed, I busied myself cleaning up, wiping down the bottle and the water glass. I washed my wineglass but left his.

"Nobody's going to think twice about this, Richard. Only Mariah. I'll show her the headline, would you like that? *Actor Dies in Los Feliz Apartment. Despondent over stalled career, bit player Anthony Karras . . .*" I looked to see how he was liking my performance, but he had stopped breathing altogether. His eyes stared glassily at the leg of the coffee table, his right shoe. He was dead as the rat in the catch-and-release cage. I kneeled by him on the floor. "Am I good enough now, Richard?" I said softly to the body, his inert, splayed mouth open on the rug. I finished cleaning up, locked the door on the inside, wiped the knob, and then closed it with my shirttail.

MOROCCO JUNCTION 90210

BY PATT MORRISON
Beverly Hills

Drive west along the Sunset Strip, out of the twenty-dollar-boutique-martini zone they call West Hollywood, and you know it without even seeing the signs: You're in Beverly Hills.

Suddenly, the road under your wheels isn't asphalt anymore. It's butter. Beverly Hills must have a law: *Pavement shall at all times be as smooth and creamy as the faces of the makeup-counter girls at Saks.* Not so much as a dimple allowed in the roadbed to shiver the undercarriage of a Bentley.

Even in a geriatric ride like mine, with tires as bald and thin-skinned as Jesse Ventura, you can feel the difference. Besides, for me, rolling onto Butter Boulevard means I'm home. I live here.

I don't live in Beverly Hills the way the Sultan of Brunei lived here, or even the way the Beverly Hillbillies did. I sure don't drive anything like whatever His Sultanity kept in his garage—though my grungy old AMC Gremlin would give the Clampetts' jalopy a run for the ugly trophy.

But I'm still a local.

For as long as Beverly Hills has been here, the Quires have been here, which is more than I can say for a lot of the fast new crowd. During the glory days of the big studios, my father, Harold Quire, headed up security for one of the biggest. He never got anything like rich, but he made good money and he kept his mouth shut, which got him connections and friends money couldn't buy.

My father also bought a little hunk of land in a wild, scrubby canyon and built a Craftsman house on it, long before the neighbors started putting up Mediterranean villas. Anywhere else it'd be a classic, but in Beverly Hills it makes me a one-woman slum.

That's what my father left me, that and the legacy of his reputation. It has helped me carve out a nice little niche for myself tutoring actors. I choose my own clients, make my own hours, and am generally free to tool around town indulging my hobby, dabbling in what my father did best— intelligence gathering.

It turns out that the best intelligence network in town is the cleaning ladies. Most mornings, I pick them up from the bus stops on Sunset and give them a lift up the hill to the mansions where they work. That's how I found out about the jewelry heists—from the cleaning ladies. Lots of small-m mafias operate in Beverly Hills (and a couple of big-M ones), and my favorite is the Cleaning Lady Mafia. It is very tight and usually right about everything.

On their long bus rides from Boyle Heights or Van Nuys, they have plenty of time to compare notes on their employers. What arcane plastic surgery Señora Tiffany treated herself to as a reward for hosting that godawful celebrity charity golf tournament. What little tattletale item Señor Roberto forgot to take out of the pocket of his Sea Island cotton shirt before dumping it in the hamper.

Why they haven't written their own nanny diaries, I don't know, except that their idea of celebrity runs to the blondined spitfires on the Mexican *telenovela* soap operas, not some knotty-calved, tennis-playing billionaire studio mogul whose face they've never even seen on Telemundo.

Their *patrones* live in the hills and canyons above Sunset. The roads there are too twisting to accommodate buses, and the chatelaines too busy to go get the help from the bottom of the hill. So the cleaning ladies have to make like mountain goats. That's why, before I head to my office, I give them rides to work. They accept, even though they're embarrassed to be seen in my car. In Beverly, snobbery goes all the way up and down the social ladder.

I don't mind. Beverly Hills has two kinds of rich: bank-account rich and information rich. I'm the latter. My father got buried with more ugly secrets than a prison priest. The word "karma" wasn't in his vocabulary, but if someone got what they deserved—good or bad—my father was the first to know . . . and the last to tell.

Take the murder of a certain Golden Age producer that regularly shows up on late-night TV shows about unsolved Hollywood mysteries. What only a handful of people ever knew is that he was bludgeoned to death by a dildo from his own collection of ornate sex toys fashioned from semi-precious stones—agate, topaz, tiger's eye. It couldn't have happened to a more deserving guy: He used his toys to sodomize starlets he'd slipped a Mickey, and one of them finally fought back. That young actress went on to luminous stardom. My dad knew all about it; he just got out of karma's way.

Our family rule was, if it's in the papers—or nowadays, the blogs—it's just gossip. Before it gets there—or if it never gets there at all—it's information. And information, good information, isn't easy to come by. This isn't a chat-over-the-back-fence place. Not when the fence is ten feet high and topped by Slinky loops of razor-wire. Parts of BH don't even have sidewalks. You want exercise? That's what home gyms are for. There are more unlisted phone numbers in L.A. than anyplace but Vegas, and the Beverly Hills residential phone book is thinner than Nicole Kidman's ankles. Restaurants have unlisted numbers, on the principle that if you don't know, you shouldn't go.

Anyway, the Cleaning Lady Mafia topped my "reliable sources." And on a hot July morning, I found out that my home town was getting whacked by high-end thieves. It started when Sonia announced that her *patrona's* best friend, the heiress to a cosmetics fortune, had been cleaned out by robbers. "There was nothing left," Sonia said. Except the foundation, I joked. Yessica, the youngest and hippest and best English speaker, rolled her eyes to remind me what a dumb *huera* I could be.

Then Yessica remembered that her friend's *patrones* in Bel-Air, not far from the Reagans' house, were cleaned out while they were at dinner at Ortolan. And Sonia shot back, wasn't there also *un robo* up off Hillcrest two days ago? Between them, the cleaning ladies assembled a regular police log of rich people getting cleaned out. These slick operators made the smash-and-grab looters at the museum in Baghdad look like morons who shoplift Corn Nuts at 7-Eleven.

Anywhere else, this would be big news. Not here. Here, the cops don't talk, the victims don't talk. It's like Disneyland—no crime, no litter, no frowns. The Happiest Zip Code on Earth. I've sometimes wondered whether the murder rate isn't really ten times higher than the BHPD admits, but the city long ago cut a deal with one of the big-M Mafias to smuggle its stiffs over the municipal line and dump them in Century City.

I dropped the ladies off and drove to my office—the coffee shop at the Beverly Hills Hotel. I do my best thinking on the second-to-last pink stool at the counter, cocooned in banana-leaf wallpaper.

Most days, that thinking is about how to help rich and famous clients whose thread count in their linens is higher than their SAT scores. After spending more years in grad school than Nixon spent in the White House, I'm a natural for the job.

Remember the actress starring in a World War II picture who marveled to reporters that, gee, she'd never known about all those people killed in concentration camps? Oh yeah, she said it. That's when the idea came to me. It took one call to an old friend of Dad's at the studio and I had my first assignment.

Pretty soon the word got out. Other studio execs remembered my father's reputation for discretion and then recalled mine for college knowledge. It's our local nepotism, but it's really no different from inheriting a job on a Ford assembly line. In Beverly, once you're in, you're in.

Now I discreetly tutor, shall we say, "struggling" actors. I put together an entertaining, easily digestible CliffsNotes backstory about their project of the moment: an archaeological thriller set in Greece, a movie about Madame Curie. Language, politics, science, art—I don't overstuff their brains, just pad them a little. I should have been spending this morning crafting one-syllable Civil War nuggets for an actor just cast as General Grant. But the news I'd heard was too rich to pass up.

With my fork in one hand and my cell phone in the other, I started calling: my book club, my clients, my ex-Pilates classmates. (As a lapsed Pilatesian, the choice between a German exercise regimen and the Beverly Hills Hotel's Dutch apple pancakes was no contest.)

The Cleaning Lady Mafia was right again.

All over town, the story was the same. Plasma TVs, laptops, cameras, cash in several countries' currencies—*poof*, gone. But any decent second-story man would take those. It was the rest of the hauls that made this gang special. These thieves were discerning. If they didn't actually subscribe to the glossy living-and-spending magazines, they must steal them from doctors' offices on Roxbury. *Forbes, Vogue, Wine Spectator*—they'd be regular crime primers to these guys.

They knew to take the Manolos and leave the Bandolinos. Take the real pearls, leave the fakes. Patek Philippes, but not Omegas. They carted off wine, but only top-rack stuff: Château d'Yquem, Petrus, DuMol pinots from the first Clinton Administration.

And the jewels. Drag queens don't have the nerve to wear rhinestones as big as the sparklers that were vanishing. I calculated the take just from the cleaning ladies' count: besides all the brand-X bling, the thieves had stolen baubles that little King Davey bought to adorn the scrawny Duchess of Windsor, Fabergé desk trinkets the Romanovs used as stocking stuffers, Persian turquoises brought here by genuine Persians—Beverly Hills is full of them, starting with the Shah's relatives.

Inside those fabulous houses on cliffsides and canyons, people were freaked with fear. Terrified to go out. Terrified to come home. The places they'd built to get away from it all weren't far enough away, after all.

I saved the last call for the Davises. They were old family friends, and I'd picked up a rumor that they had been hit too. My father and Mr. Davis had been a sometimes-team—a studio security chief and an attorney. Carlton Claridge Davis wasn't one of those attorneys you see on Court TV. He was good because he kept himself and his clients out of court—and out of the papers. He and my father had come to trust each other, and over the years they'd exchanged information and favors and friendship. I learned to swim in their pool. Their actor son, Winston, became one of my clients.

When the Davises heard I needed a place to stay while my house got earthquake-proofed last year, they'd offered me their daughter's old room. I had a swell time, like living in a *Father Knows Best* episode—if the Anderson family had had a private screening room and a couple of Cézannes hanging in the dining room.

The Davis house had been hit while they were away visiting their first grandchild. The usual high-end gadgets went missing, but so did some of Eloise Davis's jewelry. Her fondness for wearing her jewelry instead of stashing it in the vault was notable even in Beverly Hills. My first memory of her is on the tennis court, the *thwack* of ball on racket in counterpoint to the tinkle of bangle on bangle. Just about every piece came with a lively story about the giver, or the occasion, or both. Many were engraved with memories. Her history, in carats and karats—not bad, she'd say, for a small-town girl.

Theirs was old Beverly Hills money. Old money here meant BCTV—before color TV. Old money had more class than new money, but fewer zeroes. New money BH didn't much care whether you were Charles Lindbergh or Charles Manson, just so long as you were famous—ideally paired with rich. Old money BH, on the other hand, set great store by Bostonian virtues like discretion and civic dignity.

This was understandable. When actors first swarmed into Hollywood, they encountered signs in boardinghouse windows reading, *No Dogs or Actors*. They couldn't even get top billing in a rejection.

Once they'd prospered and swarmed into this new town and made it theirs, little wonder they began to practice their own kind of snobbery and exclusion. My father had often recounted the cautionary tale of a man who complained to the papers about getting fleeced in a Beverly Hills gambling scandal in the 1930s. In retaliation, the victim was cut from every guest list, every club, snubbed and ignored, his children passed over for good schools, his wife unable to book a good stylist at a salon. Oh, the cheater himself was briefly punished as the Old BH crowd saw fit: lousy tee times, bad tables at restaurants, little slights that mattered so much. But that was nothing compared to their fury at the man who let the world in on a Beverly Hills secret.

Old BH hated the fact that the place's original name was Morocco Junction; they thought it sounded like some cheesy hotel on the Vegas Strip, as indeed it did. In the early 1960s, a Barbary Coast stripper—one of the new silicone types whose body wasn't so much a temple as a major topographical feature—began billing herself as Beverly Hills. Old BH passed the homburg at a Chamber of Commerce smoker and presented Ms. Hills—along with a few legal documents drawn up by Mr. Davis—a nice little retirement fund, and a one-way ticket to Zurich so she could deposit it in person. New Beverly Hills would have elected her mayor.

My sympathies lay firmly with Old Beverly Hills, I decided, as Meghan finally answered the phone after ten rings. She was Eloise's assistant, a Renaissance Studies major in her first job out of college.

"Oh, Minerva, Mrs. Davis isn't here? The police called and said they found her jewelry and could she come down and ID it?" I liked Meghan well enough—but she spoke in irritating, perpetual interrogatories.

So they had been hit.

"What about the Cézannes?" I asked. Marita, their housekeeper, had once told me that she didn't see what was so special about the pair of still lifes. She called them, dismissively, "*las frutas.*"

"Oh, they didn't touch them, thankfully?"

Now I knew these thieves were pros—smart enough to recognize a Cézanne, and smarter still to know how risky it is to fence a hot post-Impressionist.

The thieves had to know that both Davises would be away. Every July, Mr. Davis went to the Bohemian Grove—that private men's club in the Redwoods where prime ministers and billionaires go to pee on trees and build bonfires. And Eloise went back to the Midwest for her annual get-together with her old college girlfriends. No women were allowed at the Grove gatherings, and no men at Eloise's "girls' weekend."

"She hurried right home when she heard about the burglars. She was in an absolutely terrible state—I'd never seen her so bad?"

Well, I'd soon hear all about it from Eloise herself—maybe after she got back from the police station. One thing I knew: Nobody would ever break into my place. My dogs regarded any creature larger than a parakeet as a potential Osama bin Laden. And my tumbledown Craftsman house screamed out, *If you find anything worth stealing, we'll both be surprised!* I was immune.

On my way to breakfast the next morning, I was surprised to find an extra passenger for my cleaning-lady shuttle: Marita, the Davises' maid, whom Meghan usually picked up. Driving along Schuyler Road is like cruising down the Loire—castles on both sides. The biggest is Greystone Mansion, where Heidi Fleiss used to screw rich men. Greystone's first owner, an oilman's son, was murdered by his own assistant. An inside job.

Hello. Switch on the klieg lights: *an inside job*. Like all these heists.

Whoa. Lights off. Yessica was right—I am a dumb *huera* sometimes. What big crimes in Beverly Hills aren't inside jobs? Back in 1929, the gang that made off with a twelve-carat diamond ring from a house in Benedict Canyon had dressed like electricians and been ushered right in the servants' entrance.

Every one of these houses is watched over by more camera angles than a James Cameron film set. Nobody just strolls in and happens upon a stash of De Beers' best. They had to know the angles, the layout, the comings and goings of everyone there.

This was bad news for the cleaning ladies. Their *patronas* would gather by their rock-bottomed pools and speculate, *Who can we trust?* Did some maitre d' tip off the thieves to when the family would be out to dinner? Or the blow-dry guy at the salon? Or maybe—and their eyes would swivel to the stolid brown women swabbing their slate floors . . . or maybe . . . *the help*.

At the Davis house, Marita hadn't set both feet out of the car when the front door opened and Meghan ran out sobbing. She yanked Marita to her feet and hugged her like she was giving her the Heimlich maneuver. They communicated in their own peculiar Italo-Spanglish hybrid, and with Meghan crying like the fountain at Spago's, it was hard to get it straight.

Eloise Davis was dead.

"*Como?*" Marita had asked several times, incredulously. "*Muerto?*"

"Yes," said Meghan. "*Sí. Morto. Morta?*" (Meghan wasn't long out of Barnard.)

Oh no—Eloise. Had the thieves come back for the Cézannes, found Mrs. Davis at home, and upped the ante to murder?

Meghan said the paramedics were on their way. She didn't know any more. If she did, I couldn't understand through the sobbing.

Meghan put an arm around Marita and they walked inside, heads dipped together in misery, one dark and one Sheer Blond Spun Gold. The immense Spanish door swung shut. I was half-tempted to knock—to do what, I don't know. Make coffee. Pass Kleenex. Just be there. Instead, I got back in the car.

The cleaning ladies, who had observed everything, crossed themselves and fell silent. They barely muttered "*adiós*" when I dropped them off.

My father's Rule Number One was: *Find out what everyone else knows.* Rule Number Two: *Don't let on that you know anything.* I'd already planned on going to the BHPD to suss out my pals about the burglaries; now I had another reason—Eloise's murder.

They all knew me at the PD. A lot of the brass had learned the trade under my dad. And my grandmother had been BH's first air cop. She had a pilot's license and a badge and patrolled on wings back when a lot of towns still sent out cops on horseback. That made me practically a blue brat.

On the way, I speed-dialed Joel, my secret source in the coroner's office. Joel loves Hollywood. He came here from one of those fly-over states the way pilgrims go to Canterbury—with reverence and awe.

I know it makes me sound like a cartoon private eye, "my mole at the morgue." Truth is, Joel's chief job is running the coroner's gift shop, selling souvenir beach towels with chalked body outlines and personalized toe-tag key chains. When the shop isn't open, he edits and files autopsy reports.

But his passion is Hollywood. To Joel, anyone who ever possessed a lot pass is touched by stardust. He knows more about the movies than folks who actually make them, every fragment of minutia from Edison's Kinetoscope *The Kiss* to next year's releases. We met because Joel sent me a very sweet sympathy note after my father died, and we became buddies.

"Skeletons in the closet, death becomes you," sang out Joel, who changed his telephone answering voice almost every day. Today it was Bogie, or maybe Mae West with a head cold.

"Not me, Joel," I said dryly. "Mrs. Eloise Davis, Beverly Hills. And it's the other way around—Mrs. Davis has become death."

He was already writing it down; I could hear the scribbly sound of the gift shop's best-selling ballpoint pen shaped like a human femur. "Eloise Davis," I repeated. "Be nice. She was. When, where, how? Call me when you know. Later, Marlowe."

I waved my way into the BHPD, chirping to the desk sergeant that I wanted to see whether my stolen emerald tiara had been recovered. "Oh sure, Minerva," he said cheerily. "In the property room, right next to the Hope Diamond."

As soon as he turned away, I zigged down the opposite hall from the property room and poked my head in at the office of the lieutenant, another Quire protégé, who'd be handling the Davis investigation. Not there. Probably at the coroner's this very minute. I'd pick his brain when he brought it back to his desk.

As long as I was there, I might as well check out what Eloise had seen yesterday—her recovered jewels. I zagged back to the property room. Somehow I'd thought the process of finding one's burgled loot would be as discreet and private as identifying a loved one at the morgue.

The line down the hallway was like the Crown Jewels queue at the Tower of London. These people couldn't all be victims. The cops had spread the table with midnight-blue cloth. It looked like Christmas at Cartier's, though Cartier has scarier security.

From the way the looky-loos were handling the goods, they might have thought this was Cartier's too. I was surprised to recognize some of Eloise's jewelry scattered here and there—from what Meghan said, I thought she'd claimed it yesterday. There were the bracelets, a couple of necklaces, and her clip-on earrings, from the era when Tiffany's believed real ladies didn't pierce their ears.

Some woman picked up Eloise's calibre-set sapphire ring. She slipped it onto her finger and was admiring it when she saw me watching and put it back down. Slags. Vulgar enough, pawing over other people's jewels. With Eloise murdered, it was downright ghoulish. Once they heard she was dead, they'd be chewing this cud for a week.

With an insouciance I didn't feel, I gave the desk sergeant my best Queen Mother wave, and walked down Little Santa Monica to Jamba Juice. I was ordering a Strawberry Nirvana Enlightened Smoothie (hey, I don't make up the names) when my phone twittered at me.

It was Winston Davis, my client and Eloise's son. He had landed his first small acting role a year or so before, as Porfirio Rubirosa in a TV bio-pic about Doris Duke, the tobacco heiress. While the Dominican playboy's chief assets were unquestionably in his polo jodhpurs, I persuaded Winston that he should know more about the Latin lover—his times, his class, his culture—to portray him convincingly and sell the film to a wider Hispanic audience.

He got just one review, but it was good: *"Winston Davis agreeably reminds us that there was something to Rubirosa from the waist up too."* Winston and his parents had thanked me as profusely as if I'd written it myself.

"Oh, Minerva," Winston began. "Meghan said you came by. I wish you'd come inside. Mom . . . you make her laugh." His tenses were as wobbly as his voice. "Made her laugh."

I made the usual condoling noises about not wanting to intrude.

"No, please come over," he said. "Katharine's here." I knew Winston's sister from Beverly Hills High, our alma mater with a fifteen-story oil well on the football field. That the well is still pumping away tells you about our local priorities; that it's been camouflaged in a trapezoidal floral condom tells you about our local pretenses. I'd earned advance placement credits in Political Science for my failed campaign to change our school team name to the Fighting Derricks.

"Please. Dad'll be glad to see you too."

For the second time that day, I drove up to the Davises' house and took the parking spot an unmarked police car was just pulling away from.

The huge Spanish door was opened again, by Winston—tall, dark, and a little less than handsome for the fatigue circling his eyes like the rings of Saturn. I shuffled down a huggy receiving line of grief: Winston, Katharine and her husband, and my father's old compatriot, the brand new widower Carlton Claridge Davis.

As I hugged Carlton back, I saw over his shoulder that the Cézannes were still in place. So there hadn't been a second burglary, or at least not a successful one.

Winston steered me up the stairs. Heading toward Eloise's suite, he must have felt me stiffen. "It's okay—she's . . . not here," Winston said delicately. "Dad found her this morning. He thought she'd had some kind of stroke. He called 911. But she was already . . ." I waited. "You know."

So maybe it wasn't murder then? At least not violent, bloody murder.

Winston started to sit down on his mother's bed, then swiveled his rear end onto the bench at the foot of it. I sat at the dressing table. He didn't want a conversation. He just wanted to think out loud. I'd done the same thing after my father died.

"She wasn't sick or anything. We asked the doctor about that right away—was she not telling something, so we wouldn't worry? Nothing. The last time the doctor saw her was yesterday, after she left the police station. He gave her something to help her sleep. She was so incredibly upset by the robbery—even though we had insurance, she hated the idea of strangers rooting through the house."

He ran his thumb along the welting on the bench cushion, a cloudlike pouf upholstered in Clarence House blue velvet. Eloise had once pointed it out to me with pride—not for the $400-a-yard fabric, but for the stiff patch where Katharine, age five, had smeared Elmer's glue pasting illustrations into her first book report.

"We thought she'd be so happy when the police found

most of her jewelry." Winston sighed and looked up again. "It was in some pawnshop in Koreatown. The cops said we were lucky it hadn't been broken up yet."

The night before, Eloise had given the family a dinner-table account of going down to the police station, groups of women wandering among the tables, just as I'd seem them doing, picking up bangles and brooches like it was a pasha's yard sale. A couple of acquaintances had spotted her and waved a bit guiltily—"Oh, Eloise, I think I saw your David Webb pin over there . . . Eloise, isn't this your Cartier panther bracelet?"

But the cops hadn't let her take her jewelry home. There were two more days of showings, in case there was some dispute, and anyway, it was evidence.

Mr. Davis's voice rolled up the stairs, the words indistinct but the tone unmistakably summoning. Winston excused himself and hustled downstairs as my phone rang. It was Joel, my coroner mole.

"Two options, Minerva," he said, cutting to the chase, this time in William Powell's Nick Charles voice. "Neither of them murder. Toxicology results will take a few weeks, but the white coats favor accidental overdose or suicide. Paramedics found empty sleeping pill bottles. And your Homicide guys just left. Keep it mum, okay? Over and out."

I felt myself go flushed and teary, and a shameful thought crossed my mind. Murder would almost have been preferable—horrible, but cleaner in its way.

Winston labored back up the stairs. If he noticed any difference in me, he didn't say so.

"Dad wondered if you'd be willing to go get Mom's jewelry from the station. The cops called and said that under the circumstances, it's okay, they have plenty to make their case.

Those guys know you, and Dad's written a note authorizing it. Here. He's in no shape to do it. And the, ah, funeral's the day after tomorrow."

I said sure.

Winston braced a hand against my shoulder. "Minerva, before you go, we all agreed that we want you to have something to remember her by." From his pocket, he fished something out and dangled it from his fingertips. A delicate rose-gold bangle as finely braided as hair. Like a Victorian mourning bracelet, fashioned from the locks of the dear departed. I had never seen it off Eloise's arm, until Winston slid it onto mine.

"You know, she always insisted she be buried with all her jewelry. She made such a big deal out of it. We always kidded her about trying to take it with her. But the lawyer told Dad it was in the will. So we wanted to make sure you got this now . . ." Winston's voice trailed away. "See you later? Marita's fixing some food, if you're hungry."

I couldn't remember ever being less hungry. For the second time that day, I headed toward the BHPD, wondering why a rich woman, a healthy woman, a happy wife, a woman who'd just had the one-in-a-million luck of getting her stolen treasures back—why would she kill herself? It had to be an accident.

The same desk sergeant who'd joked about the Hope Diamond was as solemn as a pallbearer when I handed over the note and signed for Eloise's jewelry. The white plastic property bag was unmarked, probably the only bag in Beverly Hills that didn't brag about where it came from.

Small but heavy, containing the best moments of her entire life. A woman who was well over twenty-five when she moved to Beverly Hills from some nonentity Midwestern town, and nearly thirty-five when she married the handsome kind attorney in the law office where she worked. A life like that was, as Tolstoy observed in *Anna Karenina*, too happy to make much of a story.

Except, now, for the way it had ended.

By the time I got back to the Davises', people were beginning to gather.

I slipped into the hall, past the family, and went on into the kitchen. I thought I'd get out of the earshot of the sobbing, lest I start in myself.

But Marita and Meghan were doing their own bawling, a subdued duet over a tray of de-crusted sandwiches. They mopped their eyes on Sferra Bros. linen napkins, twenty bucks each, a fact I knew because I'd priced them in a friend's bridal registry. (I ended up giving her a gift certificate to PETCO.)

"Thanks, Minerva, thanks so much?" Meghan said. "Would you mind putting it on Mrs. D.'s dressing table? I've got to lay out her clothes for the . . . service?"

Some chatelaines change their décor with every *Architectural Digest* annual "Designers' Own Homes" issue. For her rooms, Eloise had stuck to the blue, lilac, and silver palette she favored. When she began going gray, she had laughed that finally her hair went with the color scheme.

Leaving the jewels on the dressing table sounded like a lousy idea, considering the burglaries. I carried the bag into the bathroom. I'd tell Katharine I'd stuffed it in the back of a drawer full of makeup and skin goop until the funeral. My grandmother used to hide her dough in a box of Kotex. She figured even burglars and junkies would be too squeamish to look there.

I yanked too hard. The drawer came out completely and tipped in my hands, spilling mascara and lipstick and cotton balls all over the floor. I kneeled down to gather it up. Its owner would never touch any of it again, but it wasn't my place to throw it away—though I did ditch the cotton balls, scooping them up as they scuttled like Nerf balls along the floor.

When I opened my fist above the wastebasket to let them cascade, I saw something at the bottom that hadn't shaken loose when Marita emptied it. A newspaper clipping, torn raggedly into several pieces, each crumped smaller than a cotton ball itself.

I smoothed them out and assembled them on the marble floor. It was the kind of story big-city newspapers don't bother to write anymore. A young man, a doctor, a figure of some standing in whatever town it was, had been killed by a drunk driver two weeks before.

The victim's name meant nothing. But the face—it had the Davis family stamp to it: a little bit of Winston, a lot of Eloise.

And the town. I'd heard of the place. It wasn't far from where Eloise had gone to college, where she and her friends met every year for their girls-only reunion.

I read on. Friends mourned the man who had been adopted into a poor but loving family, then become a high-school standout and a fine medical school student. His parents evidently scrimping to send him there. After his internship, he hadn't run off to a fancy city practice, but returned to his hometown. He was on his way to the hospital, to take a friend's shift, when he was killed.

As I stared at the dead face on the mangled scraps of newsprint, things began to make a sad kind of sense.

Eloise hadn't been going to a girlfriends' get-together every year—but she had needed everyone to think that. She had been checking on her illegitimate son. It's not a word that Madonna's generation uses, but it was a common one, and an unkind one, to Eloise's generation. She'd given this boy up for adoption, as unwed mothers did then, and had gone to college nearby to be close to him.

Now her boy was dead, yes, but would she have killed herself over that? She still had two children and a loving husband, and her secret was safe in her poor son's grave.

As I assembled the bits of newspaper, Eloise's bracelet gleamed on my arm. The one she never took off. So much of Eloise's jewelry were mementos or gifts, so many of them inscribed—I wondered, had she engraved this one with some secret reminder of her son, like his birthdate, meaningful only to her?

I slipped it off and tipped it into the light, turned it. Nothing.

Not even a hallmark? A karat marking? I switched on the lighted makeup mirror, that lab-quality magnifier found in the bathroom of every woman in Beverly Hills, the forensic facial tool in the ruthless hunt for any hint of imperfection.

In the merciless light I could see that the bracelet was missing something else. Something less definable than a hallmark, more elusive. Something a Beverly Hills brat would know from the time she was old enough to try shoplifting at Fred Segal: the unmistakable inner glow of deep, true gold. I looked closer. Here and there, under unforgiving magnification, the tiniest pinpoints of cool metal gleamed through.

Silver. Not gold.

A fake. No, a copy.

I spread a thick towel on the marble countertop and laid

out what I'd brought back from the BHPD. One after another, in the unrelenting light, I began to notice almost microscopic clues—a jewel cut slightly too deeply, a patina a little too dull, another a little too bright. Line for line, the copies were exceptionally accomplished, but copies nonetheless.

Why? Why on earth would a rich woman have fake jewelry?

I tried to use my father's practical brain instead of my academic one. Eloise Davis *had* killed herself. She had gone back to her "annual reunion" and learned that her boy was dead. He probably didn't know about her, didn't know that his upbringing, his education, med school—all had been paid for covertly by Eloise.

Eloise, who could have asked her husband for anything but this, had sold her jewelry piece by piece, and concealed her losses by commissioning superb copies that could pass muster almost anywhere. Except, maybe, in BH.

My mind hurried down the stairs to the Cézannes that still hung in the dining room—not because thieves didn't want Cézannes, but because perhaps they too were copies and the thieves knew it.

For thirty years, the Davises, their friends, their guests, their help, had all been so used to seeing the paintings that they never noticed the switch. But the savvy thieves recognized them for what they were.

Once they'd had the leisure to scrutinize Eloise's stolen jewelry, they would have twigged to the fact that it was all fake too, and dumped it fast on that Koreatown pawnbroker, where it turned up along with some of their lesser jewelry haul.

I imagined those looky-loos at the police department coming back, looking once, twice. Somebody would eventually figure it out. In this town? You bet they would. Two girls in my sixth-grade class did their science fair project on how to test for genuine gold.

Soon it'd be whispered from salon chair to salon chair, from restaurant booth to restaurant booth. Eloise Davis's fabulous jewelry is fake.

Her suicide made a sad kind of sense: She'd rather be dead than humiliated—or humiliate her family. New BH would laugh at her pretensions; Old BH would expel the Davises for having embarrassed them in front of New BH.

Once, Eloise had owned the real things, the satin and velvet jewelers' boxes from Harry Winston and Van Cleef's, and the insurance appraisals to prove it. But once *le tout* BH knew the jewelry wasn't real, Mr. Davis, good lawyer that he is, would set out to turn up the truth about why his wife wore fake jewels. And then he'd find out about the illegitimate son and the gold and diamonds gone to pay for his upbringing, his education, maybe even the very car he was driving the day he was killed.

And good lawyer's wife that she was, Eloise had planned—so she thought—for every contingency. Her will specified that her jewelry be buried with her. Sentiment, everyone would agree. The jewels had disappeared, and the insurance company would have paid up. But instead they resurfaced, very publicly. That, on top of her boy's death, knocked her plan awry, and she must have seen only one solution—in the pill bottles beside her bed.

Oh, Eloise, you desperate, foolish, loving woman. By the time the tox results came back from the lab, she and her jewelry would be long buried.

No one would connect a Beverly Hills matron's death with a GP killed in a car crash in the rural Midwest.

I switched off the glaring makeup light and the room subsided into shadows. I pocketed the bit of newspaper and carried the jewelry out to the dressing table. Now it hardly mattered whether anyone stole it before the funeral. Maybe one of these days, another pack of thieves, less discriminating, would steal the fake Cézannes and tie up that loose end.

The family didn't know. And they never would, not from me. As I said, in Beverly Hills, the police don't talk. The victims don't talk. And I am my father's daughter. Why should I?

OVER THIRTY

BY CHRISTOPHER RICE

West Hollywood

The bus bench at the intersection of Santa Monica and La Cienega was empty, which meant that Jawbone was probably holed up in a shelter somewhere, possibly drying out from the combo of malt liquor and meth that kept him shouting at passing traffic for days on end. It was Ben's lover Ron who had given Jawbone his nickname, a nod to the fact that the guy's face was so wasted from drug use that the only solid thing left in it was his mandible. The intersection had been Jawbone's turf for years now, and the fact that he had chosen this night to go on hiatus made Ben feel all the more shameful as he walked home from a sleazy gay bar at a little after 2 in the morning.

For most of the night he had guzzled weak vodka tonics. Then he had made the mistake of buying a tab of ecstasy off a nineteen-year-old tranny that had turned out to be spit and aspirin. Because he was slightly numb and seriously nauseous, it took Ben a few seconds to realize that he recognized the giant face staring down at him from the billboard for some new cop show that had just gone up over the intersection that afternoon. Ben had slept with the handsome actor right after moving to L.A. They had shared the same agent and the same cosmetic dentist and, to Ben's disappointment, the same taste for throwing their ankles skyward in the bedroom. Now that he was being prepped for prime-time glory, it was a safe bet that the star-to-be, who had apparently changed his name from Peter Lefkin to Peter Lowe, no longer sped around West Hollywood in his Porsche convertible with Leontyne Pryce blasting from the stereo and a vial of coke tucked inside the pocket of his white jeans.

For a while, Ben just stood there, staring up at his former lover. Peter Lefkin Lowe had been given all of the same opportunities as Ben, and had adopted a few vices that Ben had never been forced to reckon with, and there he was, towering over the intersection of Santa Monica and La Cienega, while Ben, thirty-five and a year from his last acting job, stumbled home from a night spent watching adolescent go-go boys dance on top of a dirty bar.

He was supposed to be in Palm Springs getting wined and dined by his agent. But earlier that evening, an hour before he was supposed to brave rush hour traffic, Ben had taken a good hard look at the evidence and realized that his agent's idea for a weekend getaway was probably a separation hearing. He hadn't worked in over a year, not since being booted from the cast of A Passing Wind. Never mind that his four-year stint as alcoholic, sexually compulsive corporate attorney Arthur Bowden had earned him four Daytime Emmy nominations. Never mind that he had spent years training to be the kind of actor who didn't have to hit the gym three times in a single day to make up for his lack of talent. The minute Ben Campbell started to grow a belly, Arthur Bowden's life ended in a fiery helicopter crash, and now Ben Campbell was considering commercial work for the first time in ten years.

The bungalow he shared with his lover was the kind of tiny, absurdly expensive property that real estate agents referred to as charming and upwardly mobile gay couples referred to as transitional. Still, Ben felt a surge of pride as he approached it; this was the only real accomplishment he had left. Six years ago, he had convinced his lover Ron to take on the mortgage at almost ten percent interest, a testament to the fact that Ben's powers of persuasion were dependent upon the firmness of his ass.

Ron would be furious when he found out Ben had cancelled on his agent, so Ben decided to delay the inevitable as long as possible by entering through the side gate instead of the front door. Ben had spent the last 365 potential working days turning the backyard into a Zen meditation retreat, but he hadn't done much of anything in it besides sneak the occasional cigarette. Squares of white gravel held rows of faux-bonsai trees and a stone Buddha sat cross-legged in the middle of the yard, a thin stream of water gurgling from a hole in the center of its bald head. Ron's only contribution to the landscaping had been to repeatedly batter it with his gas-powered leaf blower, before one of the neighbors called to angrily remind him that gas-powered leaf blowers were illegal in the city of West Hollywood. That was Ron—ever successful in all of his business endeavors, he was convinced that this gave him license to remain ever defiant in the face of small rules designed to make other people comfortable.

Maybe I'll sleep on the sofa, Ben thought. What on earth would he tell Ron if he woke up? *Sorry, honey. I jeopardized my relationship with my agent so I could spend the night at Rudy's. You remember Rudy's, don't you, honey? That trashy dance club you and I went to last Friday when we ran out of the things to say to each other at dinner? The one where you got a hard-on for that twinky little porn star they had dancing on the bar? I even pretended to be the progressive gay wife while you slid a five-dollar bill into his sweaty jock strap, remember?*

When he closed his hand around the knob, Ben realized that the back door was slightly open. Like most of their friends, they had come to a specific agreement about sex outside of the relationship. Unlike most of their friends, however, they had both agreed not to have any. Suddenly, Ben realized that he had executed the kind of detective work a suspicious wife usually took weeks to plan—he had convinced his lover he would be out of town and had not given any indication that he was returning home early.

A fluid-filled groan came from the direction of the master bedroom, too low to be heard by anyone besides a startled lover hovering on the back steps. Ben was confident that Ron had made the sound, and in his mind's eye, he saw the nubile young porn star from Rudy's straddling Ron's hairy chest, the kid's hands gripping the headboard in front of him as he jammed his erection down Ron's throat. Force-feeding was Ron's favorite position and Ben had assumed it countless times, fearing the day when he would be too heavy for Ron to accommodate him without cursing. From what Ben could remember, the kid had almond-shaped blue eyes, enormous bleached teeth, and a compact body that was still one-quarter teenager. The night Ron tipped the kid so handsomely, Ben had gone online and found out that the kid's professional name was Mike Ellis and his most recent credits included *The Boners* and *Farewell My Daddy*. In terms of output, the kid's career was outpacing Ben's two to nothing.

The bedroom door was open. His fingers going numb as he gripped the edge of the doorframe, Ben peered in and saw the lower half of his lover's body, his back resting against the bed's footboard, his legs splayed on the carpet in front of him. The white soles of his sneakers stared back at Ben like eyes without irises. Ron's head and torso were blocked by the towering figure standing in front of him. The exertion of the guy's thrusts drove his baseball cap back over his mop of shoulder-length hair. Ben couldn't see the stranger's hands but he figured they were gripping the back of Ron's head.

Ben had left the back door open behind him. He stepped out of it, just as silently as he had entered, when Ron let out a sharper, more high-pitched sound that suggested the activities being carried out in the bedroom had grown more penetrating. Ben made it to the box hedges that concealed the back fence, then he fell to his knees and threw up. After he caught his breath, he realized what a tragic irony it was that he had rid himself of all the chemicals that could have kept him numb during this.

TV movies had taught him that there would be certain pivotal moments in his life, so like a good little actor, he had rehearsed for them. The emotional press conference he would have to give after his adopted daughter was abducted off their front lawn. The moment when Ron finally sank down on one knee and officially proposed. And, of course, the black day when he would walk in on Ron in bed with someone else.

Where was the tearful rage he had practiced? What had become of the venomous one-liners he had meant to hurl at the offending home-wrecker as he made a mad dash from the bedroom? Indeed, it was Ben who had headed straight for the back door, not the tall baseball cap–wearing stranger. Now, down on his knees in a dark corner of his own backyard, he tried to read some meaning into his own strange instincts.

Why had he run? Why was he still hiding? Because it wasn't a confrontation he wanted. He had to get a good look at the man who had led Ron to stray. He had to observe him. Pinpoint just what qualities the man had that Ben had squandered. Maybe Ben could get some of those things back, even if he had already lost Ron.

He drew his knees to his chest and wedged himself between the back fence and the box hedge, readjusting until he was in a position that allowed him to see the back door. After only a few minutes of this, his back started to tense up, and his stomach clenched at the thought that Ron might ask this stranger to spend the night with him in their bed. Their friends Phil and Tom had been in an open relationship together for years, but both of them were always eager to recite their number one ground rule: *Never in our bed.* If the wait became unbearable, Ben would use his cell phone to call the house, claim that he and his agent had had it out and he had pulled over to collect himself on the drive home. Would be there within minutes. Surely that would send the tall dark stranger racing out the back door.

The stranger had been too tall to be Mike Ellis, prince of the sweaty jock strap. That left the blond Yale Law graduate he and Ron had met at a fundraiser cocktail party for the Equal Liberties Defense Fund two weeks earlier. Yalie had made a beeline for Ron after spotting him across the buffet table. The arrogant little prick didn't even bother to extend his hand to Ben when Ron finally introduced them after several agonizing minutes of small talk. Like every other twenty-something queen fresh off an American Airlines flight from JFK, Yalie heaped generous amounts of disdain on a city that had already granted him a flawless tan and the most spacious apartment he had ever lived in, all while undressing Ron with sparkling chestnut eyes.

Overboard. That was the expression Ron had used when Ben had vented his annoyance about the little son of a bitch on the ride home. When he saw the look on Ben's face, Ron had tried a sheepish grin and said, "Relax. I said over*board*. Not over thirty."

The touch of cold steel brought Ben back into his body, and he realized he was standing in front of the garden shed, fingering the padlock on its doors. The lock had been left open and the gas-powered leaf blower abandoned on the dirt floor inside. Another image struck him. Ron hearing the phone ring over the leaf blower's dull roar, tossing it inside the shed before he ran back inside the house, steps quickened by arousal and anticipation. A set of manual hedge clippers hung from a nail inside the shed. Ben could just make out their silhouette, knew that if he opened the doors a few more inches the security light over the back gate would throw them into sharp relief, transform them into an invitation he might not be able to turn down. *When Lorena Bobbit cut off her husband's dick, it didn't actually kill him,* Ben thought. *Ergo, while cutting a man's dick off is a very dangerous thing, it doesn't always end in death. Castration and attempted murder are two different things.*

He was growing impressed with this quick logic when the back door to the house slammed shut. Ben spun around just in time to see a shadow streak through the security light's halo and out the side gate. The hedge clippers forgotten, Ben took off after the guy.

By the time Ben reached the sidewalk, the stranger was a block away, moving at a steady clip with his shoulders hunched forward and a backpack jostling against a puffy waffle-print coat that was too heavy for the spring evening.

The stranger somehow sensed that he was being pursued and whirled around. Ben threw himself behind a sycamore tree before he could be seen. He listened to the man's frenzied whispers, tried to make out his words but couldn't. After surveying the lay of shadows all around him, he decided to venture a peek. Half a block away, the stranger rocked back and forth, his head pivoting as if he had been scanning the sidewalk behind him and some internal gearshift had gotten stuck. A nearby porch light illuminated his matted shoulder-length hair but not his face.

The stranger backed up until he was at the mouth of an alleyway that ran behind the businesses on Santa Monica Boulevard, a once-important West Hollywood thoroughfare that had born the nickname Vaseline Alley before the sheriff's department had planted traffic barriers at either end to keep the predators from cruising it after dark. When the stranger saw this new path of escape, he turned on his heel and entered it.

As soon as he reached the mouth of the alleyway, Ben called out to the stranger, who backed away from a dumpster he was trying to open with one hand.

"Jawbone," Ben whispered.

The resident lunatic stared back at Ben with cue-ball eyes, chapped lips parted over yellowing teeth. Not a porn star. Not an Ivy League graduate. A deranged drug addict. He held a bulging black backpack in his right fist. The front flaps of his waffle-print coat were smeared with blood and it looked as if the bag was as well, even though the color partially masked the stains. Jawbone's lips were moving rapidly, forming words Ben could barely hear.

"'Cause he wasn't listening none, that's why. 'Cause that thing was a-blowin' and he wasn't listenin' none to what I say, so I had to . . . had to . . . had to . . ."

Displaying both of his palms at waist level, Ben started moving toward the man, trying to put nothing but supplication on his face even as he strained to hear the content of

Jawbone's frenzied speech, made even less intelligible by his heavy Southern accent.

"See I was tryin' to get him to come out and see that there wasn't somethin' in his trash. Somethin' movin', alright? But he couldn't hear me none over that blower . . ."

The leaf blower. Ron had been using that damn leaf blower and for some reason Jawbone, blitzed out of his head, had come into the yard, wanting his attention.

A few steps away from Jawbone, Ben lifted a hand and opened his mouth to speak. But before Ben made a sound, Jawbone spun, pulled the dumpster's lid open with one hand, and tossed the black backpack inside. Then he took off running.

Everything inside of Ben seemed to rear up, trying to force him to chase Jawbone down the alley. But by the time this physical intention resolved itself into a coherent thought, Jawbone was gone. *Go back to the house,* Ben told himself, even as he pried open the dumpster's lid with both hands. *They weren't fucking. Go back to the house now.* But a more reasonable-sounding voice in his head told him that Jawbone had simply robbed them, that the blood stains all over him had been old, probably the result of some accident, and who knew what stereo equipment or old watches were stuffed inside the bag he had been so eager to get rid of.

Ben pulled a trash can over to the side of the dumpster, lifted the lid with one arm, and reached down for the bag with the other. When his fingers finally grazed a strap, his center of gravity shifted and suddenly he was eating plastic, having landed face-first on the mess of trash bags inside. The lid slammed shut and he jumped to his feet, pushing it back open, and set the bag down on the trash can's lid.

Once his feet were on the pavement again, he heard a

rustling sound behind him. He turned. The bag was rolling toward the middle of the alley, each revolution slightly lopsided, leaving a trail of blood smears across the pavement.

As soon as it came to a stop, Ben crouched down over it and tugged the zipper open.

He was still kneading the matted hair inside, wondering if all hair felt the same once a person's head had been removed from his body, when a harsh spotlight pierced the alleyway and fixed on him. For a few dazed seconds, he thought the sheriff's cruiser would continue on, leaving him alone with his lover's severed head. Then he heard the clipped, hollow-sounding voice of the deputy speaking into his radio, followed by the squeak of rubber boots heading toward him.

When the deputy was a few feet away, Ben peered up at the squat shadow standing in the spotlight's unrelenting glare, his right hand resting gently against the holster he had just unsnapped. Ben heard himself say, "I need to go home now."

ONCE MORE, LAZARUS

BY HÉCTOR TOBAR

East Hollywood

Before they found the gun, they were running through the trenches at a construction site, throwing dirt clods at each other. But for their overgrown adolescent bodies, an adult standing nearby might have mistaken them for grade-school boys playing cowboys and Indians. They'd stand up in a trench, "fire" at the boy in the next trench over, and laugh and duck when the clod exploded on the other's shirt, leaving a faint brown circle of clinging dirt crumbs. Throwing dirt clods was more fun than vandalizing the tractor and the backhoe, both of which were immune to much vandalism anyway, sitting there stoic and yellow-metalled at one corner of the construction site, impervious to dirt clods and rocks and globs of tar and even a splash of urine. It was Elliot who peed on the tractor treads, to little or no effect other than the stinking mist he sent into the air, and it was Elliot who found the gun a few minutes later, lying on the bottom of the trench.

Actually, Elliot stepped on the gun. Or, to be more accurate, he tripped over it. This is what he told Detective Sanabria. Elliot was an especially bright fourteen-year-old, and he sensed that telling the story to Detective Sanabria with all its details was going a long way toward exculpating him of any guilt, and that each little twist and turn he could remember was keeping him out of the squad car now parked at the edge of the construction site. The gun itself needed no describing, having been photographed by Detective Sanabria, and then catalogued and tagged and carried away in a plastic bag. Elliot said he thought it was a toy at first, and this was true, until he picked it up, at which point its mass gave away its identity instantly, as did its intricate assemblage—the tiny screws above the trigger, the patterned indentations in the handle, the mysterious metal latches and slides, and the letters stamped into the black metal: CAUTION: *capable of firing with magazine removed.*

Detective Sanabria had grown up in this very East Hollywood neighborhood, gone to the very school across from the construction site, and could imagine the scene as if he had lived it himself. Danny, the victim, was the first bystander to run over, drawn by Elliot's sudden stillness and silence before the object he was holding. Soon that same wordlessness had overtaken all the other boys, their shouts and laughter replaced by the identical frozen Os of their stunned adolescent mouths. Across the street, sinewy third- and fourth-grade girls were running and playing tag and kickball on the school playground, without a clue about what these older kids were up to. Elliot slipped out of the momentary trance, smiled wickedly at the other boys, and raised the weapon and pointed it at the ponytailed girls. The girls didn't notice, they just bounced a red ball rhythmically against a narrow wall that jutted like a sail from the playground's asphalt blacktop, singing a song, while Elliot closed one eye and pretended to aim, looking down the stubby barrel.

Elliot laughed, and then passed the gun on to the victim, this boy they called Danny but who Detective Sanabria would soon identify as Daniel José Cruz Jr., age fourteen and a half, born in San Vicente, El Salvador, a resident of 5252

Harold Way, Hollywood, California, and just as American as fried chicken and potato salad. The victim had taken the gun, and like the little boy and the knucklehead he really was, he had turned the barrel toward himself to look inside.

Knucklehead: It was not a word Detective Sanabria used growing up in this neighborhood, where Spanish and Armenian were starting to crowd out English, causing it to retreat from whole chunks of the day. Knucklehead was an appellation used at the station for bank robbers who got caught in the parking lot fiddling with the ignition in their getaway cars, shoplifters wearing pilfered sweaters with the price tags still attached, murderers who shot off their own fingers and their girlfriends with the same bullet.

If Danny had not been shipped away to intensive care at the Children's Hospital (Detective Sanabria's least favorite place to visit on earth), Detective Sanabria would have given him a good knucklehead slap at precisely the spot where the bullet entered his brain.

"*¿Tienes miedo? No te agüites.*"

Danny turned his wrist to look at the inside of the barrel, which was his way of answering Elliot's taunt: No, he wasn't afraid; he could stare into the most dangerous part of the gun, the part that could kill you. He wanted to show all the other boys his lack of fear. The circular cavity was coming into view when a light flashed and he heard a roar that somehow penetrated into the darkness that followed, the sustained thunder of a river tumbling over a cliff or a zoo of animals letting out a simultaneous roar, followed by the absolute silence of a dreamless sleep.

He opened his eyes to the soft glow of fluorescent lamps, and caught the sharp glint of light reflecting off stainless steel. He was on his back, suddenly, in a bed. His first fully formed thought was that it was not right that he could close his eyes and be transported from one place to the next, from the ditches and the dirt of the construction site to this strange room of glowing light with—what was this?—tubes taped to his arms. He fell asleep again, drifting in and out of wakefulness many times, and had the sensation that he was floating above the bed in a slow tumble. Finally, his eyes became fixed and steady and he could tell exactly where he was: a hospital. In a corner of the room, he saw a stocky and familiar figure, a woman in a blouse that fit too tight against her round belly, asleep in her chair, her open mouth facing the ceiling like the top of a snoring chimney.

"*Mamá*," he said.

His mother startled awake. She looked at him with a perplexed, confused gaze, and he quickly understood that being awake was not something expected of him, that sleeping was now his natural condition.

"*¡Hijo!*" she shouted, so loud that the sound waves reverberated in his skull, which, he now realized, was covered with a helmet of gauze bandages. His mother brought her hands together and fell into prayer, closing her eyes, looking much as she had just a moment ago when she was snoring, words he could not hear drifting skyward from her lips like steam.

Danny soon forgot about her, raising his arms to inspect the tubes that fed a silky liquid into his wrists, lifting his fingers to touch the bandages, probing very gingerly for the place the bullet had entered. Inside his skull there was now an opening, a round path through his head, a cylinder as long and wide as the barrel of a gun.

* * *

"So you shot yourself," Detective Sanabria said. "Good job, knucklehead. Do me a favor. Make that the last shot you ever fire from a gun."

Children and guns were Detective Sanabria's obsession, his off-hours hobby. The other detectives in Hollywood Division left copies of their reports on Sanabria's desk whenever they handled cases in which children were shot, or in which children shot at other children. A ten-year-old shooting his sister in the shoulder with a .22; a two-year-old shot through the heart while in his playpen, the bullet crossing through three walls thanks to the penetrating power of an AK-47. Detective Sanabria could not explain why or when this obsession began, though his old partner Detective Nazarian knew perfectly well: He had been Sanabria's friend since way back in the academy, and had been at the scene of Sanabria's first homicide (it was also Nazarian's first), which just happened to be four blocks from the elementary school they had both attended, an old brick edifice built in the early glory days of Hollywood, with the dusty pictures of silent film star alumni growing moldy behind a glass case in the office. Nazarian had seen the stunned look on then-probationary Officer Sanabria's face when he looked down at that bleeding, dying eight-year-old whose walnut-shaped eyes and copper skin bore a striking resemblance to Detective Sanabria's own.

In the case of Daniel "Danny" Cruz, Detective Sanabria's investigation and the trace of the nine-millimeter gun that had placed Danny in this bed had been as fruitless as it usually was. Manufactured by the American Patriot Gun Co. of Waukegan, Illinois, the weapon had been sold to the Guns R Us Mart of Phoenix, Arizona, and then to a certain Andrew Palazzo, who, when contacted by Detective Sanabria by phone, said that he had sold the gun at a swap meet in Mesa, Arizona some six years ago.

"Untraceable," Detective Nazarian had remarked when Sanabria told him the results of his two-hour investigation. "Unknowable."

Detective Nazarian had seen enough cases of children and guns that he wanted to get out of police work, which was why he was going to graduate school and starting to toss around words like "unknowable," which everyone in the Hollywood LAPD station found annoying, especially Detective Sanabria. But it was probably true: How and why some idiot had left a loaded gun in the construction site across the street from an elementary school was probably unknowable. So that left the victim Danny to talk to.

Detective Sanabria could not pretend he was here for any investigation. He was here for something else—to do something he did not know how to do, that he felt queasily uncomfortable doing, which was to make the speech and twist his face into the angry I'm-gonna-kick-your-ass-young-man stare that would keep Daniel "Danny" Cruz away from guns the rest of his life.

He stood staring at Danny with a lingering, pathetic, hopeless absence of words. "Now you know what a bullet can do to you," was the best he could do. "Or maybe you don't really know yet. Because you're still alive, aren't you? And you shouldn't be."

Only much later, days after Danny had taken his first, light-headed steps away from the hospital bed, after the nurses had helped him walk through the ward, after listening to the doctor give his mother a much-too-long list of instructions for his care, when he was back in the familiar and messy nest of his room, did he realize exactly what had happened to him.

He had shot himself in the skull and survived.

He had been in a coma for two weeks, at one point nearly left for dead.

"You cheated death," his mother said. "We even had a priest here."

Danny remembered the first time he had understood what death was, in bed under his covers when he was still in elementary school. In the darkness of his room, hours after watching a movie filled with medieval battle scenes in which one of the protagonists had exited the world of the living with an especially poignant soliloquy, the abstraction of death had become real for the first time. It was perfect blackness, a sleep from which he would never awaken, forever tucked under the football helmets on his comforter, the bedroom lights permanently off.

Danny the hospital patient had a new appreciation for what death meant and, at the same time, could now see the possibility that he might "cheat" it. He could run away from death like those quick-footed boys in that game they used to play in gym, "War," where you stood with your friends in a cluster of bodies and dodged the rubber balls your classmates threw at you, until only one boy was left—the winner. Danny had done something like that: A brass bullet spinning through the air, on fire, had taken aim at his brain and he had twisted away just enough to avoid being killed.

The more he thought about it, the more he saw his survival was an act of will, rather than a stroke of luck. Danny was not yet fifteen and unprepared to accept the idea that his life could end so stupidly. He noticed adults shook their heads when they looked at the scar under his eye socket, a pushed-in nub of darker, stringy flesh. He saw in this a gesture of admiration for his strength and courage. Elliot looked a little afraid of him, which made Danny feel happy and triumphant. "Jesus, man, you lived," Elliot said. "I don't know anybody who's taken a bullet in the head and lived."

Before he had been shot, the most daring thing Danny had ever done was back in his days at LeConte Junior High School when he broke into the campus after hours—with Elliot—walking through the empty hallways trying to crack open the odd locker or two. He had never been a good vandal because he always heard his mother's voice when he tried to do those things. In the years since his father had left for El Salvador, never to return, Danny's numerous Los Angeles relatives had reminded him that a boy should respect his mother, that he shouldn't dishonor her: They were all alone, a working woman and her young son, and any bad thing he did would be a reflection on her. His mother, in turn, doted on him. She bought the blankets and curtains printed with the logos of football teams that decorated his bedroom, with their one-eyed pirates and stylized birds of prey. She had bought him the dragon poster that loomed over the bed on which he was now sitting. These things belonged to a boy, and he wasn't a boy, not anymore. He was suddenly angry at his mother, for no other reason than he felt her protective presence everywhere in his room.

Danny stood up and walked out of his room, then through the living room and the smell of soup and cooked meat that always lived there, and out the front door. Reaching the sidewalk, he stopped for a long time to examine the other stucco bungalows on the block, the palm trees that all leaned toward the south, the cars and vans parked in the driveways, their dented bodies covered with white patches. It all looked familiar, and at the same time, completely different. The pinks and yellows and blues of the houses were faded and sun-bleached, the palm trees were sad and weary. For his entire life he had lived on this block, he had pushed toy trucks and ridden tricycles and bicycles up and down the sidewalks. Everyone on the block knew his name.

Beyond this quiet little neighborhood was the real Hollywood, the thoroughfares of liquor stores and hotels, motels and sex shops, which had always existed on the fringes of his boy consciousness as a forbidden, dangerous hinterland of gaudy marquees. Danny the boy used to ride the bus home from school and stay away from the freaks on Vermont and Western. Danny the wounded warrior decided it was time to take a walk, toward the thick metallic sound of traffic on the avenues and the rising cry of firetrucks and police patrols. In a few minutes he found himself facing the din and the carbon-tinged air of Hollywood Boulevard, its long parallel rows of street lamps just beginning to glow white in the twilight. He was standing near the bottom of a gentle slope several miles long, the boulevard a buckling line of asphalt rising into the distant hills toward a gleaming array of billboards and hotel towers that clung to the mountainside, far away but reachable.

Danny had walked just half a block when he stopped, frozen in place by an image glowing from the side of a bus shelter. It was an illuminated movie poster depicting a man in a charcoal suit who held a gun at his side, a thin woman in a short skirt leaning against him, holding a gun too, but with two hands instead of just one. *That's the way you're supposed to hold a weapon. Away from your body, pointed downward.* The steel glint of their guns seemed to match the sheen of their clothes, the breathlessness of their pose. They stood, magically, on a platform of letters that spelled out the movie's title: *NO TIME TO LOSE.* Behind them rose a city of shadows, the silhouettes of tall buildings standing before a black mountain, the same city that stood before Danny in real life, a warren of alleyways where adversaries lurked in ambush, a place where a man might do battle with other men, each holding his weapon smartly between his palms, ready to guide bullets on the paths bullets were meant to take.

When he drifted back home and turned on the tiny television in his room, he saw the gun-holding couple from the poster in a commercial. *"In the dark corridors of a violent city,"* the voice-over intoned, *"there is no time to lose."* Weapons, he noticed, were being drawn on about half of the channels on his cable system. There were soldiers carrying rifles, villains swinging machine guns from their hips, housewives cowering in closets with silver-plated .22s, ready to fend off intruders and rapists. Some of the scenes were filmed in squat palm-lined residential neighborhoods that looked much like his own. People fired guns while crouched behind cement walls; they fired guns in kitchens; they fired guns while falling from airplanes; they fired guns and then jumped into lakes and rivers; they fired guns in warehouses, pinging bullets deflecting off iron beams.

Danny had become a member of the fraternity of gunslingers, and, like the people on the television screen, he began to feel looked-at. When he finally returned to school at Hollywood High, he drew stares everywhere he went. One of the football players said hello and gave him a hearty, friendly punch on the shoulder. Girls touched his scar with soft fingers that brushed against his cheek. Sandra, the one with the flowing black curls, the girl he had stared at for months without saying a word, cornered him by surprise in a hallway. For the first time, he was close enough to take in the scent of her perfume, a basket of overripe peaches that had dissolved into the air around her. Like everyone else, she had heard about his accident.

"Are you okay? I mean, that must have been awful, to be in a coma," she said. "Are you totally, you know, like healed?"

No other schoolmate had asked about his health. Only Sandra had been thoughtful enough, which to Danny immediately confirmed what he had always imagined: that she was as saintly as she was beautiful. Now he was speaking to her, his nerves steady because he was a wounded warrior, not a boy. They talked about his accident, about life and death, about the school and how stupid everyone was. Sandra wanted to know what it felt like to be dead: She was convinced that he had "passed over to the other side and come back." He made up a story about seeing clouds and angels that brought tears to her eyes.

Part of it was true; the old Danny *had* gone to sleep and died and this new Danny had taken his place, a Danny who wasn't afraid to touch Sandra's hand the third time they talked, a Danny who knew when to reach over and kiss her, how to wrap his arm around the arch of her back when they necked. A few days after they first spoke, they were under the bleachers at dusk, tugging awkwardly at each other's clothes, scattered cups and hot dog wrappers at their feet. A week after that half-consummated encounter, they were in his room, fully naked on the bed with the football curtains and his baseball glove as witnesses.

When they said their goodbyes and he watched her walk away down the sidewalk from the perch of his bedroom window, he knew for certain that the old Danny had died forever. He felt possessive of her in a hard, brittle way: Her blue jeans belonged to him, her lips, and the small scar on her chin. It was an unexpected thing to feel; tenderness and vulnerability at one moment, and then a kind of anger the next. The third time they were alone in his room, he pushed her arms forcefully against the floor. He was about to pull his hands away and apologize, but when he looked at her eyes he saw that roughness was what she expected from him all along. The boy who had been shot had to have a core of steel.

Danny took to greeting everyone, all the time, with an angry gaze and found himself losing his patience for the routine and rhythms of the school day. By late morning, he was already squirming in his seat, daydreaming about fistfights, doodling pictures of fanciful weapons. On the bus home, he looked at the other passengers and wondered which one would challenge him, and how he would strike back with balled-up fists and kicks. He always won these imaginary fisticuffs, standing triumphantly over his bleeding adversaries. Finally, and without any good reason, he found his real-life self decking a tenth-grader named Pedro Carrillo in the cafeteria. The guy ran off, sobbing, and for the first time in his life Danny felt like a stupid bully.

In the days that followed, Pedro walked around the school with one eye swimming in a purple cloud of cracked veins. The word on campus was that there would be a settling of accounts with Pedro's older brothers, a portly senior and even more portly dropout who held court several hours each day in front of a tattoo parlor on Vine Street, next to the star on the Walk of Fame honoring Rin Tin Tin. It was said that one of the Carrillo brothers would jump Danny on the football field during PE, or ambush him in the cafeteria, or that the other would shoot him on Wilton Place after he stepped off the bus. Danny was one young man against three brothers.

Asking Elliot for a gun to even the odds seemed like the logical thing to do. Elliot produced one two days later, a snub revolver that bore no resemblance to the sleek weapon Danny had shot himself with. "I got it from a guy on Western, a guy my brothers told me about."

Danny was headed home one Friday, walking past the elementary school, walking almost at a trot because he was going to pick up Sandra and take her to his room, when something cut past his ear. A half second later he heard the unmistakable report of a gun. Instinctively, he fell to the ground, looking up to see the largest of the Carrillo brothers walking toward him from across the street, a gun at his side, trying his best to assume the fierce and demented look of an actor shooting his way through an R-rated thriller. Danny stood up, quickly grabbed his own weapon from his backpack, and pointed it at Pedro's brother, stopping him in his tracks. For a moment, the two gunslingers looked at each other with childlike befuddlement. Then Danny began firing, squinting his eyes against the explosions of his gun. Pedro's brother started running, across the street and into the construction site, where he jumped into a ditch lined with metal rebar. From just a few paces away, Danny fired again, not squinting so much now and sure he would hit his target, but instead he felt a burning pain in his back. He fell, as stiff and heavy as a downed tree, and plopped down into a pile of earth, face first. A woman screamed from across the street. Pedro's brother moaned from the ditch, calling out, "You shot me, you shot me," in a pleading voice that seemed to belong to a five-year-old. Danny moved his head, an act of will against the currents of pain that ran up and down his spine, and looked into a deep hole carved into the soil. He saw chunks of mud floating about a pool of black water, and wanted to cry because he knew he would be buried soon, dressed forever in wet earth.

The daylight around him dissolved quickly. He entered a self-conscious dream, lifting himself from the ground and beginning to run through a dark corridor, stumbling toward home and his room, to the bed his mother always made for him. If he could lose himself under the blankets, his mother would kiss him goodnight. The dream ended and he was vaguely aware of being on a bed that was not his own, of lights shining beyond the black universe inside his skull, of his limbs being lifted and prodded, of formless voices chattering about him. He wanted desperately to open his eyes; he tried lifting his arms and kicking his feet, but he had turned into something heavy and immovable After the longest of efforts, he succeeded in opening his eyes, seeing what had to be an apparition: a dark man standing at the center of an aura of yellow light, a glint of metal on his chest, his lips moving but the words unintelligible. Danny slipped back into his nothingness.

"Danny. Danny. Danny." It was a familiar voice, his mother speaking calmly, evenly. "Danny. Danny. *Aquí estoy.*"

He opened his eyes easily, naturally, without much effort at all. "*Mamá,*" he said.

She was standing over him, as was Sandra, the two women on opposite sides of the bed, each clutching one of his hands in theirs, rubbing his fingers and his palm with identical strokes. No one spoke. For the moment he merely looked at them—the familiar, round figure of his mother, and Sandra, who had changed in some way he could not put words to. Sandra stared at him with brown eyes swimming in a pool of tears, fixed on him with a strange and desperate intensity.

"You look older," he said. Danny sensed that many days, weeks, maybe even months had passed while he was asleep. The skin of his arms and hands had turned soggy and the sunlight outside the hospital window belonged to a different, colder season than the one he remembered. The world had aged in his absence.

"She's having your baby," his mother said.

He lowered his chin to look at Sandra's belly, which did, in fact, rise slightly with an unfamiliar roundness. She brought her hands to the roundness and cradled it.

"*Our* baby," she said.

Danny felt the blood rushing to his skull, and let his head fall back on the pillow. Being awake was too complicated, so he closed his eyes and waited, in vain, to slip back into sleep.

"*Hijo, hijo*, are you okay?"

"I knew we shouldn't have told him," Sandra said.

"What do you mean? You think he's not going to notice you with your belly?"

"We should have waited . . ."

The two women argued, the words bouncing back and forth over his prone body, until he spoke again.

"How long have I been asleep?" he asked with his eyes still closed.

"Three months," his mother said.

"Almost four," Sandra added. "The detective was here yesterday and he said he saw you open your eyes. So we came here to sit with you."

"And to pray," his mother said.

He fell asleep to the sound of the two women whispering Hail Marys in different languages, his mother's ". . . *y en la hora de nuestra muerte* . . ." tangled up with Sandra's ". . . pray for us sinners . . ."

Detective Sanabria sat at the foot of the bed, the round and vaguely Olmec features of his face molded into a tense mask of irritation and befuddlement. "Paralyzed. Both you and the other knucklehead, Beto Carrillo. Poetic justice. That's what my partner called it. You guys shot your legs out from under each other. Good work, *pendejo*. Me and the D.A. figure you've both been punished enough already so there will be no ADW charges. Your friend Elliot's in juvie—he's going to do time for you . . . Yeah, I found out he gave you the gun. Won't tell me where he got it, the little brat."

Danny thought that he, too, would like to know where the gun came from. He thought of what the grip felt like in his hands, remembered wincing when he fired it, and wondered who else had touched it, what other damage it had done, which other children had played with it. On his back in this hospital bed, with his mother standing over him, Danny was starting to think of himself as a boy again. Somewhere there was a factory that churned out toy trucks and bullets for children, passing them on to toy stores, and to gun traffickers who operated in the alleyways of East Hollywood, selling them to boys like Elliot. The bullets in the gun Danny bought had cut the wires to another young man's legs, just as the wires to his own legs had been cut, forever.

Forever is a long time when you're fourteen years old. None of the doctors who came to see him used that word, though it was clearly the word they meant to use every time they talked about his condition. The doctors were specialists in fields whose names were too complicated to remember. There were coma doctors, spinal cord doctors, doctors interested in his moods, and doctors who talked about rehabilitation. They shined lights in his eyes and wrote notes about what they saw; they poked and prodded his legs, attached sensors to his skull and watched his brain waves on a monitor. As a whole, the doctors were optimistic about his "recovery," but fatalists when it came to his chances for walking again. After a few days, a burly hospital worker lifted him off the bed and onto a wheelchair with a cheerful, "Your new wheels, dude!"

From now on, Danny would see things from four feet off the ground. Melancholia robbed him of speech, he could barely grunt a yes or a no when Sandra came to see him again, her belly rounder still. Every few days she seemed to get bigger. He was helpless before her stomach, the child growing underneath the hard shell of a belly she forced him to touch. "You're going to walk again," she said emphatically. "You are. I know it."

When he went back to school, he became, briefly, an object of curiosity. The girls took turns wheeling him around and putting their arms on his shoulders. One girl rubbed her fingers through his hair affectionately, but this only depressed him more because it reminded him of those parts of his body where he could no longer feel anything. For a week or so, the guys on the football team took turns pushing him around school, and for one game he sat in his chair next to the team bench, the helmeted players patting him on the cheek near the scar of his first bullet "for good luck." Danny sat and sulked all game long. They didn't invite him back.

People began to avoid him, ducking into side passages when he wheeled down the hallways. No one asked to see the scar left by the second bullet, the angry red welt below his ribs, and the meandering scar in his back where the doctors had removed the metal. No one asked to hear stories about what it was like to be dead—a second time—and to come to life again. He became a ghostly, solitary figure, haunting the campus, pushing himself across the quad, inching forward with a stop-and-go roll. Sandra sometimes followed alongside him, until she became too big and round to go to class. Eventually he stopped going to school too, despite the pleas of his mother, who grew frustrated and irritable with him. "*No seas mujer,*" she snapped at him. *Don't be a woman.* But even that insult couldn't shake him from his leaden mood.

Mostly, he watched television. In the movies, he noticed, people who got shot were never paralyzed. They bore their wounds with a grimace and rose to their feet, chasing after their enemies; or they died dignified deaths, giving long speeches before they closed their eyes forever. No gunslinger ever suffered the humiliation of sitting all day in a vinyl chair, trapped with the vinegar smell of his inert legs, forced to endure the protracted lamentations of his mother and his pregnant girlfriend, who both wondered how they would feed the baby, once it was born.

After a week rooted like an angry weed to the floors of the bungalow, Danny finally got fed up and decided to wander the neighborhood in his wheelchair, joining the parallel universe of mumbling bottle collectors and lunatics who made their home on the sidewalks. He inched along slowly, deliberately, pushing hard to roll the wheelchair over the concrete squares where tree roots had raised the sidewalk, and up the steep ramps that were cut into the curb at each corner. It was during one of these excursions that, one afternoon, three blocks on from his house, he coasted down a slight slope, half hoping he would gain speed, lose control, and bounce into traffic. Instead, he came to a stop at the construction site across the street from his old elementary school. The dirt trenches were gone and the ground was covered with a vast table of concrete. Twice he had been shot here and left for dead. His manhood had arrived and slipped away from one moment to the next. A sense of injustice rose through his body, a muffled crimson scream. He stared directly into the yellow, fiery light of the sun, then turned away and cried, burying his hot face in his hands, weeping until his chest felt as weak and drained as his legs. Finally, he sat up, opening his eyes to the sight of girls running up and down the playground across the street, skipping with strong, healthy legs.

Danny was headed back home, very slowly, because his arms were tired of pushing, when he found his path blocked by a pair of standing denim pants on the sidewalk. They belonged to a rather large and roundish teenage girl.

"You prick," she said.

Danny looked up and gave her a quizzical, annoyed look. "Get out of my way," he mumbled, without much conviction.

"Who's going to take care of Beto, you prick?" The girl reached into the backpack that dangled from her shoulder, a pink affair decorated with a pouting Betty Boop, and produced a small chrome gun, barely bigger than the palm of her hand. "Who's going to take care of him, you prick?"

Danny grabbed the rubber tires of his wheelchair and pushed backward, first calmly and then with panic, as the girl raised her toy-sized gun and pointed it at him. He looked at the tiny opening of the gun's barrel and pushed harder, but couldn't get any distance between him and the girl, who kept marching toward him, mascara rivers racing down her cheeks. He tried to turn around, bouncing the chair and its wheels the way a therapist at the hospital had taught him, but he succeeded only in tipping the chair over, falling to the ground with a thud and a crash, his cheek crushed against the cement sidewalk.

Without hearing the gunshots, he felt the impact of the bullets on his body, the first striking him near the waist, the second at the base of the neck, sending a starburst of blue light across his eyelids. His skull became a bell made of bone. All at once, everything turned mercifully quiet.

He slipped into a dream in which he saw himself sprawled on the sidewalk, being lifted by men in black suits, the girl with the Betty Boop backpack standing against a nearby tree, sucking her thumb. Small chunks of silver and brass dripped from his back. He saw Pedro's brother standing waist-high in a ditch, his arms raised in a plea: *Help me.* Elliot came to place a finger inside Danny's first wound, the one in his cheek, wiggling the finger about like a worm. Danny shook his head and tried to push him away, and startled awake to see he was inside an ambulance, a paramedic's latex gloves pulling back his eyelids. "Hey, Louie, we got him back!" the paramedic shouted. Danny passed out, tumbling into a warm dreamlessness, and then woke up again, alone, months later, in a room with green walls. For a few minutes he listened to the beep of a machine that echoed his own heartbeat until the steady, soft sound made him drowsy and he closed his eyes again.

When Detective Sanabria came to the Children's Hospital some time later, he spent a good two hours at the foot of Danny's bed. He felt especially useless before the sight of this boy's prone body. Sanabria was beginning to question his place in the world, the assumptions about goodness, strength, and perseverance that had informed his life up to now; the hours of study in community college, his struggles at Cal State L.A. in classes like Applied Psychology and Urban Criminology, his monklike devotion to the reading of prolix police manuals that had ended with his consecration as detective. Here on the bed before him was a boy who had managed to get himself shot not once, but three times, twice with Sanabria looking after him, as it were. The girl with the gun in her Betty Boop backpack was in juvie, learning to draw pictures of weeping girl-clowns from her fellow inmates, and as unwilling as the rest of the knuckleheads to give up the name of the person who had sold her the gun. The gun traffickers operated a machinery of violence that churned up the fertile ground in Detective Sanabria's corner of East Hollywood. He saw them as blood merchants filling a charnel house with the bones of children, stacking femurs and punctured skulls harvested from the streets, lining their foul clothing with the quarters, the nickels, and the rolled-up dollar bills of children.

The doctors' prognosis was that Danny would never again awaken, that the forever of his wheelchair had become the forever of his sleep. Detective Sanabria stood up from his chair, walked over to the bed, and stood over the boy. He kissed Daniel "Danny" Cruz Jr. on the forehead, and then painted an invisible cross there with his thumb, a gesture the detective's own Mexican mother annoyingly repeated each time they parted.

"God, I hate this fucking hospital," he said, and left.

Two weeks later, Danny was awakened by a distant, high-pitched wail, and saw a fuzzy object at the foot of his bed, a human-like figure that persisted in its unfocused, blurry state, until he blinked several times and it began to take form: First he saw Sandra, her face bloated and paler than he remembered, and then the infant she cradled in her arms, a baby girl with an even chunkier face and a broad, flat nose. "What's going on?" he said abruptly, causing Sandra to startle and look up at him, and the baby to stop crying and look at him too.

"You're awake!" Sandra called out, as the baby began to gnaw at her own wrist with toothless gums, sucking with a cracking sound that was like bubble gum popping. For a moment, Danny was hypnotized by the sight of the baby, by the two pink barrettes attached to her thin black hair, the way her jaws moved as she chewed, and by the flower-bud mouth that was revealed when her wrist fell away.

Suddenly, he felt the urge to sit up, to lift his back off the bed. He grabbed hold of the aluminum bars at his side, rose up, and felt the blood rush to his head, his eyes beginning a slow roll backwards, until he shook out the dizziness. Without saying a word, Sandra passed the child to him and he held her, feeling her tiny chest rise and fall against his shoulder. He listened to the fast, desperate pant of her breathing, and felt the warm flow of baby drool as it soaked through his hospital smock and dripped down his chest, past the wounds near his ribs.

Danny raised a finger and gently tapped her nose. For a moment, he worried he might hurt her, that the needles in his wrists might stick her, but the fear passed. Time ticked forward with no other sound than the occasional trumpet-blaring of Sandra blowing her nose, and he noticed that the frame of the hospital room window was being filled, quickly, with the tangerine hue of a disappearing California afternoon. Danny saw his daughter's future unfolding, the yellow march of many suns across the heavens, and the slow, slow progress of the months and years they would live together in the waking world, an epoch of quiet never broken by the sound of gunfire.

Sandra wiped her nose and got up from the chair, then looked at the baby and broke into a bright, childlike smile of wonder. "She fell asleep in your arms!"

Danny listened to his daughter's breathing grow steady, and felt rhythmic puffs of wind beating softly against his chest. He kept very still.

PART III

EAST OF LA CIENEGA

THE GOLDEN GOPHER

BY SUSAN STRAIGHT

Downtown

Nobody walked from Echo Park to Downtown. Only a walkin fool.

But in the fifteen years I'd lived in L.A., I'd only met a few walkin fools. L.A. people weren't cut out for ambulation, as my friend Sidney would have said if he were here. But the people of my childhood weren't here. They were all back in Rio Seco.

The only walkin fools here were homeless people, and they walked to pass the time or collect the cans or find the church people serving food, or to erase the demons momentarily. They needed air passing their ears like sharks needed water passing their gills to survive.

But me—I'd been a walkin fool since I was sixteen and walked twenty-two miles one night with Grady Jackson, who was in love with my best friend Glorette. I'd been thinking about that night, because someone had left a garbled message on my home phone around midnight—something about Glorette. It sounded like my brother Lafayette, but when I'd listened this morning, all I heard was her name.

Grady Jackson and his sister were the only other people I knew from Rio Seco who lived in L.A. now, and I always heard he was homeless and she worked in some bar. I had never seen them here. Never tried to. That night years ago, when he stole a car, I'd wanted to come to L.A., where I thought my life would begin.

But I had thought of Grady Jackson every single day of my life, sometimes for a minute and sometimes for much of the evening, since that night when I realized that we were both walkin fools, and that no one would ever love me like he loved Glorette.

I came out my front door and stepped onto Delta, then turned onto Echo Park Avenue. My lunch meeting with the editor of the new travel magazine *Immerse* was at 1:00. I had drunk one cup of coffee made from my mother's beans, roasted darker than the black in her cast-iron pan. When I went home to Rio Seco, she always gave me a bag. And I had eaten a bowl of cush-cush like she made me when I was small—boiled cornmeal with milk and sugar.

All the things I'd hated when I was young I wanted now. I could smell the still-thin exhaust along the street. It smelled silver and sharp this early. Like wire in the morning, when my father and brothers unrolled it along the fenceline of our orange groves.

All day I would be someone else, and so I'd eaten my childhood.

When I got close to Sunset, I saw the homeless woman who always wore a purple coat. Her shopping cart was full with her belongings, and her small dog, a rat terrier, rode where a purse would have been. She pushed past me with her head down. Her scalp was pink as tinted pearls.

At Sunset, I headed toward Downtown.

Downtown, receptionists and editors always said, "Parking is a bitch, huh?" I always nodded in agreement—I bet it was a bitch for them. If someone said, "Oh my God, did you get caught up in that accident on the 10?" I'd shake my head no. I hadn't.

And I never took the bus. Never. Walking meant you were eccentric or pious or a loser—riding the bus meant you were insane or masochistic and worse than a loser.

I had a car. Make no mistake—I had the car my father and brothers had bought me when I was twenty-two and graduating from USC. They wanted to make sure I came home to Rio Seco, which was fifty-five miles away. My father was an orange grove farmer and my brothers were plasterers. They drove trucks. They bought me a Chevy Corsica, and I always smiled to think of myself as a pirate.

I was like a shark too—or like the homeless people. I needed to walk every day, wherever I was, traveling for a piece or just home. I needed constant movement. And every time I walked somewhere, I thought of Grady Jackson. Now that I was thirty-five, it seemed like my mind placed those rememories, as my mother called them, into the days just to assure me of my own existence.

I'd have time in the Garment District before lunch. One thing about walkin fools—they had to have shoes.

I had on black low-heeled half-boots today, and flared jeans, and a pure white cotton shirt with pleats that I'd gotten in Oaxaca. It was my uniform, for when I had to move a long way through a city. Boots, jeans, and plain shirt, and my hair slicked back and held in a bun. Nothing flashy, nothing too money or too poor. A woman walking—you wanted to look like you had somewhere to go, not like you were rich and ready to be robbed, and not like a manless searching female with too much jewelry and cleavage.

Down Sunset, the movement in my feet and hips and the way my arms swung gently and my little leather bag bumped my side calmed me. My brain wasn't thinking about bills or my brother Lafayette, who'd just left his wife and boys, or that Al Green song I'd heard last night that made me cry because no one would ever sing that to me now and slide his hands across my back, like the boys did when we were at house parties back in Rio Seco. When we were young. *"I'm so glad you're mine,"* Al sang, and his voice went through me like the homemade mescal I'd tried in Oaxaca, in an old lady's yard where only a turkey watched us.

No one I knew now, in this life, at all the parties and receptions and gallery openings, felt like that—like the boys with us back home, in someone's yard after midnight. [Throats vibrating close to our foreheads, hands sliding across our shoulder blades.] Girl, just— Just lemme get a taste now. Come on.

When I was home lately, I had trouble working. I looked at old things like my mother's clothespins and a canvas bag I used to wear across my shoulder when we picked oranges in my father's grove.

But walking, I was who I had become—a travel writer everyone wanted to hire.

I'd written about the Bernese Oberland for *Conde Nast*, about Belize for *Vogue*, about Brooklyn for *Traveler*.

I passed vacant lots tangled with morning glories like banks of silver-blue coins, and the sheared-off cliffs below an old apartment complex, where shopping carts huddled like ponies under the Grand Canyon.

I looked at my watch. 8:45. I smelled all the different coffees [wending] through the air from doughnut shops and convenience stores. Black bars were slid aside like stiffened spiderwebs. Every morning in late summer, my mother and I would brush aside the webs from the trees in our yard, the ones made each night by desperate garden spiders. Here, everyone was desperate to get the day started and make that money.

My cell rang while I was waiting for the light at Beaudry.

"FX?" It was Rick Schwarz, the editor.

"Yup," I said.

"So what does that stand for?" He laughed. He was in his car.

"It stands for my name, Rick."

He laughed again. "We still on for 1:00? Clifton's Cafeteria?"

"Sounds fine," I said.

"So—I don't know what you look like. You never have a contributor's photo."

"I look absolutely ordinary," I said, my body lined up with a statue in the window of a botanica. "See you at 1."

I stood there for a minute, the sun behind me, tracing the outline of the Virgen de Soledad. These people must be from Oaxaca, because this virgin, with her black robe in a wide triangle covered with gold, her face severe and impassive, was their patron saint. I had prayed before her in a cathedral there, because my mother asked me to do so each place I went. My mother's house was full of saints.

Across Beaudry, I could see the mirrored buildings glinting like sequined disco dresses in the hot sun. My phone rang again.

"Fantine?"

"Yes, Papa," I said. I tried to keep walking, but then he was silent, and I had to lean against a brick building in the shade.

"That your tite phone?" he said. My little phone—my cell.

"Yes, Papa."

"You walk now?"

"I'm going downtown," I said. "Does Mama want something? Some toys?" I could stop by the toy district today, if my nephews wanted something special.

My father said, "Fantine. Somebody kill Glorette. You better come home, *oui*. Tomorrow. Pay your respect, Fantine."

Then he hung up.

No one ever called me by my name. I had been FX Antoine for ten years, since I decided to become a writer. Only my family and my Rio Seco friends knew my name at all.

That was why I'd always loved L.A., especially Downtown. No one knew who I was. No one knew what I was. People spoke to me in Spanish, in Farsi, in French. My skin was the color of walnut shells. My hair was black and straight and held tightly in a coil. My eyes were slanted and opaque. I just smiled and listened.

But Glorette—even if she'd worn a sack, when she walked men would stare at her. They wanted to touch her. And women hated her.

Glorette had skin like polished gold, and purple-black eyes, and brows like delicate crow feathers, and her lips were full and defined and pink without lipstick. She was nearly iridescent—did that fade when blood stopped moving? Now she was dead.

I bit my lip and walked, along Temple and down to Spring Street, where crowds of people moved quickly, all of them with phone to ear, or they spoke into those mouthpieces like schizophrenics. And the homeless people were talking quietly to themselves or already shouting. Everyone was speaking to invisible people.

My father's voice had lasted only a few minutes. *I don't talk into no plastic and holes*, he always said. *Like breathin on a pincushion.*

He'd said Glorette was dead.

I stopped at the El Rey, one of the tiny shacks with a drop-down window that sold burritos and coffee. My father, when he came from Louisiana to California and began working groves, learned to eat burritos instead of biscuits and syrup. I wanted horrible coffee, not good coffee like my mother's, like Glorette's mother's, like all the women I'd grown up with on my small street. All of them from Louisiana, like my parents. The smell of their coffee beans roasting every morning, and the sound of the tiny cups they drank from even after dark, on the wood porches of our houses, when the air had cooled and the orange blossoms glowed white against the black leaves.

But the man who handed me the coffee smiled, and his Mayan face—eyes sharp and dark as oleander leaves, teeth square as Chiclets—looked down into mine. I put the coins in his palm. Pillows of callus there. I sipped the coffee and he said, "*Bueno, no?*"

So good—cinnamon and nighttime and oil. "*Que bueno*," I said. "*Gracias.*" He thought I was Mexican.

Then tears were rolling down my face, and I ducked into an alley. Urine and beer and wet newspaper. Glorette was dead. I closed my eyes.

Glorette—when we were fourteen, we walked two miles to high school, and her long stride was slow and measured as a giraffe's. Her legs long and thin, her body small, and the crescent of white underneath the purple-black iris that somehow made her seem as if she were sleepily studying everyone. Her hair to her waist, but every day I coiled it for her into a bun high on her skull. All day, men imagined her hair down along her back, tangled in their hands. I wore mine in a bun because I didn't want it in my way while I did my homework and wrote my travel stories about places I'd made up. Always islands, with hummingbirds and star fruit because I liked the name.

Every boy in Rio Seco loved her. But I talked too much smack. I couldn't wait to leave. If someone said, "Fantine, you think you butter, but your ass is Nucoa like everybody else," I'd say, "Yet all you deserve is Crisco."

Grady Jackson had fallen for Glorette so hard that he stole a car for her, and nearly died, but she felt nothing for him, and he'd never forgiven her.

Grady Jackson and his sister Hattie were from Cleveland by way of Mississippi. Grady. He hated his name. He was in my math class, though I was two years younger, and he wrote *Breeze* on top of his papers. Mr. Klein gave them back and said, "Write your proper name."

Grady said to me, "I want somebody call me Breeze. Say, I'm fittin to hat up, Breeze, you comin? Cause my mama name me for some sorry-ass uncle down in Jackson. Jackson, Missippi, and my name Jackson. Fucked up. And she in love with some fool name Detroit."

Glorette. We were freshmen, and a senior basketball player who had just moved here was talking to her every day. "Call me Detroit, baby. Where I'm from. Call me anything you want, cause you fine as wine and just my kind."

But Detroit had no car. Glorette smiled, her lips lifting only a little at the corners, and turned her head with the heavy pile of hair on top, her neck curved, and Detroit, who had reddish skin and five freckles on top of each cheek, said, "Damn, they grow some hella fine women out here in California."

He didn't even look at me.

That weekend, I was on my front porch when Grady Jackson pulled up in a car. My brothers Lafayette and Reynaldo had an old truck, and they jumped down from the cab. "Man, you got a Dodge Dart? Where the hell you get the money? You ain't had new kicks for a year. Still wearin them same Converse."

Grady looked up at me. "Glorette in your house? Her mama said she ain't home."

I saw his heavy brown cheeks, the fro that wouldn't grow no matter how he combed it out, and his T-shirt with the golden sweat stains under his arms. Should have just called himself *Missippi* and made fun of it, learned to rap like old blues songs and figured himself out. But Cleveland had already messed him up. I said, "She's home. She's waiting for Detroit to call her after his game."

He spun around and looked at Glorette's house, across the dirt street from mine, and said, "She think that fool gonna take her to L.A.? She keep sayin she want to go to L.A. I got this ride, and I'm goin. You know what, Fantine? Tell her I come by here and I went to L.A. without her. Shit."

Then Lafayette said to him, "Grady, man, come in the barn and get a taste."

My brothers had hidden a few beers in the barn. When Grady went with them, I didn't even hesitate. I'd wanted to go to Los Angeles my whole life. I got into the Dart and lay down in the backseat.

When Grady started the car, he turned the radio up real loud, so Glorette could hear it, I figured, and then he spun the wheels and called out to my brothers, "Man, I'ma check out some foxy ladies in L.A.!" I could smell the pale beer when his breath drifted into the back. He played KDAY, some old Commodores, and then he talked to himself for a long time. I knew the car must be on the freeway, by the steady uninterrupted humming. I had never been on a freeway.

"She always talkin bout L.A. Broadway. Detroit don't hear nothin. He don't know how to get to L.A. He know Detroit. She coulda been checkin out a club. Checkin L.A."

I fell asleep on the warm seat, and when the car jerked to a stop, I woke up. Grady was crying. His breath was ragged in his throat, I could smell the salt on his face, and his fists pounded the steering wheel. "There. I seen it, okay? And you didn't. You didn't see shit cause you waitin on some fool-ass brotha who just want to play you."

I sat up and saw Los Angeles. The city of angels. But it was just a freeway exit and some narrow streets with hulking black buildings. I remembered one said *Hotel Granada*, windows with smoke stains like black scarves flying from the empty sills.

Grady looked back and said, "Fantine? What the hell you doin in here?"

I walked down Broadway, where the butt models showed off curvier jeans than you'd see on Melrose or Rodeo. No mannequins in the doorways of some stores—just the bottom half, turned cheeks to shoppers. All the stereos blasting *ranchero* and *cumbia* and salesmen calling out and jewelry flashing fake gold.

L.A. I had come here for college, and that was it. I wanted to live in an apartment with a fire escape so that I could see it all. See more than orange groves and my father's truck and the ten grove houses set along our street. I wanted to live above a restaurant, to watch people all day long, people who weren't related to me. I knew everyone's story at home, or I thought I did.

Now I lived in a lovely Mediterranean castle building, and I had a lunch meeting, and I wanted shoes. I wasn't going to think about Grady and Glorette. I walked along Broadway, turned on 8th, and then headed down Los Angeles toward the Garment District.

"No one shops downtown," people always said to me at receptions or parties in Hollywood or Westwood. When I was at a tapas party in Brentwood the week before, someone said, "Oh my God, I had to go downtown with my mother-in-law because her Israeli cousin works in the Jewelry District. I thought I would die. Then she wanted to see another cousin who sells jeans wholesale in some alley. Nobody speaks English, people can't drive, and we took a wrong turn and ended up in Nairobi. I swear. It was like Africa. All these homeless people on the street and they were all black."

"African American," someone else said smugly, holding up his martini glass.

"They were tribal. Living in cardboard boxes."

"But is that better than dung huts in Africa?" the same guy said. "Did you know that people are so resourceful they make houses out of crap?"

I drank my apple martini. The color of caterpillar blood. Had they ever cut a caterpillar in half after they pulled it off a tomato plant?

I said, "People made houses out of shit everywhere. Sod houses in the Great Plains—back then, there must have been old poop in that grass and earth. Adobe bricks—must have been some old mastodon shit in that. Dung houses just seem more unadulterated."

They looked at me. I thought, *Where did that word come from? No adult added?*

"Sorry. I'm—I'm Tom Jenkins," the guy said.

"FX Antoine," I said. Then the woman's face changed.

"You're FX Antoine? I love your stuff! I do ads for Lucky."

I smiled. I drank my caterpillar blood and turned gracefully away while she studied me, reaching for a crusty bread round spread with tapenade.

The sidewalks were wet here, as I passed the Flower District with gladiol spears in buckets, and carnations that didn't smell sweet. I still loved these streets, the doors sliding up to reveal roses and jeans and blankets. I slowed down in the Garment District, with rows of jeweled pointy-toed pumps everyone wanted now, and the glittery designer knockoff gowns. Usually everything looked like pirate treasure to me.

But today the voices were harsh. The men from Israel and Iran and China and Mexico hollering at the sales clerks and delivery guys, looking at me and dismissing me. I wore no veil, and I wasn't a buyer. They wanted wholesalers, not women who were headed to work, trying to get a bargain.

I ain't no blue-light special. Hattie had said that. I shop in Downtown L.A., she bragged to us when she came home to Rio Seco once after she'd moved here to become an actress. That was Grady's sister's name. Hattie Jackson. She said she'd never go to Kmart again in her life. But I still hadn't seen her on television or in a movie.

I sat in one of the tiny burger places and called my brother. "Lafayette?"

"You heard?" he said. His radio was going, and my brother Reynaldo was singing. They must be on a job.

"Yeah."

"Man, Glorette was in this alley behind the taqueria, you remember that one close to here? She was in a shoppin cart. Her hair was all down. Somebody had been messin with her."

He paused, but I didn't ask, and so he told me. "Look like she had a belt around her neck. But we don't know what got her. Or who."

Got gotted. I hadn't heard that for a while. She done got gotted. Damn. I said, "What about Grady Jackson?"

My brother said, "Who?"

"Grady. The one she was supposed to marry, after she got pregnant and that musician left her."

"What about Grady? That country-ass brotha been gone."

"I know, Lafayette," I said. Hamburgers hissed behind me. "He lives somewhere in L.A. I should tell him."

"Sprung fool. Only one might know is his sister. Remember? She was gon be on TV. She worked in some place called Rat or Squirrel. Some bar. I remember she said it was just part-time while she was waitin for this movie about some jazz singer. I gotta go. Naldo callin me."

I walked back up Los Angeles Street toward Spring again. I didn't want shoes.

All these years, I had never wanted to look up Hattie Jackson in the phone book. I didn't really know if Grady was homeless or not—I'd just heard it when I was home in Rio Seco. Someone would say his cousin had heard Grady lived on the streets in a cardboard box, and all I could think of was being a child, in a box from my mother's new refrigerator, drawing windows with magic marker, Glorette sitting beside me.

I had left all that behind, and I didn't want to remember it—every memory made me feel good, for the smell of the oranges we kept in a bowl inside our box house, and then bad, for not being there to help my father during the harvest. I didn't want to see Hattie, or Grady.

Sprung fool. Growing up, I always heard my brothers and their friends talk about fools. *Man, that is one ballplayin fool. Don't do nothin but dribble. Damn, Cornelius is a drinkin fool.*

When I went to college, I heard Shakespeare. *The fool. Fool, make us laugh. Go tell the fool he is needed.* When I went to England, I saw the dessert Raspberry Fool. I closed my eyes, back then, tasting the cream and cake, thinking of Grady Jackson.

How you gon get sprung like that over one woman? That's what my brothers always said to him.

He came to the barn another night, and my brothers were working on a car. I stood in the doorway, watching him hold his right hand in a rag. Grady said to Lafayette, "She over there at her mama's? Glorette?"

Lafayette said, "Man, she told me she was movin in with Dakar soon as he got a record deal. Said they was gettin a place together. I don't keep track of that girl."

Grady said, "I heard him say it. Dakar. He was playin bass in a club, and I heard him tell somebody, 'I gotta book, man, I gotta get to L.A. or New York so I can get me a deal. Tired of this country-ass place.' So I hatted him up."

My brother said, "Damn, fool, your finger bleedin! He done bit off your finger?"

The red stain was big as a hibiscus flower on the dirty rag. Grady said, "He pulled a knife on me. Man, I kicked his ass and told him to go. He was gon come back and then book again, leave Glorette all the time. I just—I told him to stay away." He was panting now, his upper lip silver with sweat. "Forever."

He pushed past me and said nothing. I had already been accepted to college, and Glorette had told me she was pregnant with Dakar's child—I'd seen a swell high up under her breasts, awkward on her body like when we used to put pillows inside our shirts in that refrigerator house.

I left for college, and when I came back in the summer, my brothers told me what had happened. Grady had been driving a Rio Seco city trash truck for a year, made good money, and he rented a little house. When Dakar didn't come back, and Glorette had the baby—a boy—Grady took her in and said he'd marry her. But after a year of not loving him, of still loving a man who got ghost, she left him to get sprung herself— on rock cocaine—and she refused to ever love anyone again.

I walked through the Toy District again, the dolls and bright boxes and stuffed animals from China and Mexico. Glorette's son would be a teenager now.

Often my mother would call and say, "Marie-Therese and them wonder can you get a scooter. For her grandson. Out there in L.A."

To everyone from back home, L.A. was one big city. They didn't know L.A. was a thousand little towns, entire worlds recreated in arroyos and strawberry fields and hillsides. And Downtown had canyons of black and silver glass, the Grand Central Market, Broadway, and its own *favela*.

That's where I was headed now. I was close to 3rd and Main. If you hadn't been to Brazil, and you hadn't seen a *favela*—that's what Skid Row looked like. The houses made of cardboard, the caves dug out under the freeway overpasses, the men sprawled out sleeping on the sidewalk right now, cheeks against the chain-link.

Were they all fools for something? Someone?

Would Grady Jackson still be on the street? Would he be alive?

All the men—sleeping with outstretched fingers near my heels, pushing carts, doing ballet moves between cars—black men with gray hair, heavy beards, bruise-dark cheeks, a Mexican man with a handlebar moustache and no teeth who grinned at me and said, "Hey, *payasa*." A man my age, skin like mine, his hair dreaded up in a non-hip way. Like bad coral. He sat on the curb, staring at tires.

I kept moving. How would I find Grady among these thousands of people? And why would he still care about Glorette?

Sprung fool.

I glanced down an alley and saw a woman standing in the doorway of a port-a-potty. She lifted her chin at me. Her cheeks were pitted and scarred, her black hair like dead seaweed, and her knees gray as rain puddles. Then a man whispered in her ear and she pulled him inside by his elbow, and closed the door.

Glorette. She wanted to go wherever Sere Dakar went. He played the bass and the flute. He played songs for her. He left when she was seven months pregnant. Nothing mattered to her but living inside a cloud, and yet she was still beautiful. The bones in her face lovelier. She smoked rock all night, walked up and down the avenues like the guys who passed me now, their faces crack-gaunt.

A man waved and hollered high above me. Construction workers were gutting one of the old banks and an old SRO hotel. I saw the signs for luxury lofts on the building's roof. I turned on Spring Street.

Rat or Squirrel. What was Lafayette talking about? Hattie Jackson had a TV gig? I needed more coffee, and I needed to get myself together before meeting Rick, so I headed to Clifton's Cafeteria.

As I left Skid Row, the haunted men became fewer, like

emissaries sent out among the rest of us. The other thousands and thousands of homeless people had packed their tents and boxes and sleeping bags and coats and melted into invisibility because now the day was truly the day.

I tried, but had no heart for it. Rick was short, and thin, and handsome, and funny. He held his tray like a shield, and then put soup and salad on it and laughed at the greenery in Clifton's. I put away the notebook where I'd tried to write about Oaxaca, and mole, and mescal.

Rick sat down and said, "So, since you're a world traveler, it's good to know where you're from."

"Here. Southern California."

"L.A.?"

"No." I picked up one fry. "Rio Seco."

"Really?" He studied me. "Where's that?"

"Have you been to Palm Springs?"

"Of course! I love mid-century."

"Well, it's on the way." I smiled slightly. I didn't know him well enough to explain. "Where are you from?"

Rick said, "Brooklyn."

"What part?"

He raised his eyebrows, like black commas. "Ah-hah. Fort Greene."

"Cool," I said. "Nice coffeehouse there. Tillie's."

He grinned, all the way this time. "But I live on Spring Street now. New loft. It's echoing, I've got so much space to fill."

I looked out the window at the shoulders bumping past. "Don't you worry about all the homeless people?"

"Worry?" He slanted his head.

"Do they bother you?"

"They keep to themselves," Rick said. "Everyone has para-meters, and most people seem to respect those parameters."

I nodded and ate another fry. Like powder inside. Parameters and boundaries and demarcation. I could never explain that to my mother, or to Glorette.

Rick looked up under my lowered eyes. "But you know what? It's scary when you're walking past a guy and he looks dead. I mean really dead. Laid out on the sidewalk in a cer-tain way."

Without any parameters, I thought. Not even curled up properly.

"And then you see him shiver or snore." He moved a piece of mandarin orange around on his plate. "Anyway."

Time for work. The way Rick put down his fork meant business. He said, "Let me tell you about *Immerse*. People don't want to just take a trip. They want immersion, jour-neys, a week or two that can change their lives. Change the way they feel about themselves and the world."

No, they didn't, I thought. I looked at the haze in the window. They wanted to read about me walking down an alley in Belize, me going to the Tuba City swap meet and eat-ing frybread tacos and meeting an old woman who made turquoise jewelry. But they really just wanted a week-long cruise to Mazatlán where they never even got off the boat but once to buy souvenirs. A week in Maui where they swam on a black sand beach and then went to Chili's for dinner at the mall near the condo complex.

A woman paused to adjust her shopping bags, and she looked straight at me in the window and smiled.

I looked like anyone. A sista, a homegirl, a *payasa*. Belizean. Honduran. Creole.

"How about Brazil?" Rick said. "You look like you could

be Brazilian. FX."

"Where in Brazil?"

"Not the usual. Find somewhere different."

He was challenging me. "Have you ever been in love?" I asked him, partly just to see what his face would do, but partly because editors realized I never mentioned any Handsome Gentleman or Nameless Boyfriend who accompanied me. I was clearly alone, and because of my adventurousness and initials, mysterious.

"Twice," Rick said, looking right at me. "In high school, and she dumped me for a football player. In college, and she dumped me for a professor. Now I'm in love with my apartment and my job."

None of us, at the parties or lunches, were ever in love. That was why we made good money and ate good food and lived where we wanted to. And yet Grady, and Glorette, had always been in love, and they'd never had anything but that love.

"My name is Fantine Xavierine," I said. I looked into his eyes—brown as coffee. Mine were lemon-gold. "I was named for a slave woman who helped my great-great-grandmother survive in Louisiana."

"Okay," he said. He glanced down, at his fork. "I like that. So you'll be fine in Brazil."

I walked with him for a block toward Spring Street. It was after 2:00. I could head home now. Rick said, "You know, this place was worse than a ghost town a few years back, because the ghosts were real. But now all these hip places have shown up. There's a bar people in the office are going to lately—the Golden Gopher. I guess it was a dive before."

Rat. Gopher.

"Thanks, Rick," I said, and I touched his arm. Gym strong. He was shoulder to shoulder with me. "I'll call you."

I remembered it now. 8th and Olive. Grady had driven down dark streets for a long time, looking for it, and from the backseat, I was dizzy seeing the flashes of neon and stoplights. Then I saw through the back window a neon stack of letters. *Golden Gopher*.

I walked toward 8th. Grady had parked and then he'd seen me. He'd said, "I can't leave you here. Somebody get you, and your brothers kill me. Come on."

At Olive, I rounded the corner, and a film crew with three huge trucks and a parade of black-shirted young guys with goatees was swarming 8th Street. They didn't notice me. They were filming the tops of apartment buildings, where a young man was looking out the window of a place he would probably never live. A place probably meant to be New York or Chicago or Detroit.

There was no neon in this light. There was only a façade of black tile, and a door, and a sign that read, *Golden Gopher*. It didn't open until 5 p.m.

The security guy noticed me now. A brother with cheeks pitted as a cast-iron pot. His badge glinted in the light from a camera. "Excuse me," he said.

"You're in the movies," I said, and I moved away.

Even I couldn't walk for another two hours. I looked for a Dunkin' Donuts or somewhere I could sit, and suddenly realized how much my feet hurt, how much my head hurt. I never felt like this in Belize or Oaxaca, because I'd be back in my hotel or in the bar, listening and watching. Now I was like a homeless person, just waiting, wanting to rest for a couple of hours.

I sat at a plastic-topped table and closed my eyes.

Hattie was twenty-two then, and Grady was eighteen, and I was only a freshman. He'd pulled me by the arm into the doorway of the club, past a knot of drunken men. One of them put his palm on my ass, fit his fingers around my jeans pocket as if testing bread, and said, "How much?"

Grady jerked me away and up to the bar, and a man said, "You can't bring that in here. Underage shit."

A line of men sat at the bar, and someone knocked over a beer when he stood up. Then his sister spoke from behind the counter. She said, "Grady. What the hell."

Hattie was beautiful. Not like Glorette. Hattie's face was round and brown-gold and her hair straightened into a shining curve that touched her cheeks. Her lips were full and red. Chinese, I thought back then. Black Chinese. Her dress with the Mandarin collar.

She pushed three glasses of beer across the counter and someone reached past my neck and took them. Smoke and hair touched my cheek. I remembered. The bar was dark and smelled of spilled beer and a man was shouting in the doorway, "I'll fire you up!" and through an open back door I could hear someone vomiting in the alley.

"I wanted to come see you," Grady said. Sweat like burned biscuits at his armpits, staining his T-shirt. "See L.A. The big city."

"Go home," Hattie said. "Right now, before somebody kicks your country ass. Take that Louisiana girl wit you."

I looked at Hattie, her contempt. She thought I was Glorette. I said, "I was born in California. I'm gonna live in L.A. myself. But I'm not gonna work in a bar."

I thought she'd be mad, but she said, "You probably not gonna work at all, babyface."

Grady pulled me back out the door, and this time the hand fit itself around my breast, just for a moment, and someone said, "Why buy the cow?"

Then we were driving again in the Dart, and Grady was murmuring to himself, "They got a bridge. She said."

He drove up and down the streets, and I said, "The full moon rises in the east. Papa said. Look."

He drove east, and the moon was like a dirty dime in front of us, and we took a beautiful bridge over the Los Angeles River, which raced along the concrete, not like our river. Grady said, "We can't get on the freeway again."

"Why not?"

"Shit, Fantine, cause I stole this car, and you ain't but fourteen. John Law see me, I'm goin to jail."

He drove down side roads along the freeway, past factories and small houses and winding around hills. The Dart ran out of gas in Pomona.

We were on Mission Boulevard, and Grady said, "You wanted to come. Now walk."

I walked slowly back toward 8th. It was nearly 5:00 and the sun was behind the buildings, but the sidewalks were still warm. I was carried along in a wave of people leaving work. Homeless men were already staking out sidewalk beds in alleys. Back at the bar, the blackness was like a cave, tile and door so dark it was as if someone had carved out the heart of the building. The film crew was gone. A pink curtain waved in an open window where they'd trained the camera.

A bucket slammed down on the sidewalk, and someone began to wash off the tile. A homeless guy. Green army coat, black sneakers glistening with fallen foam from his brush and rag, and black jeans shiny with wear and dirt. His hair was thin and nappy, and a brown spot showed on the side of his head, like the entrance to an anthill.

Grady. No. Uh-uh. Grady?

He'd had ringworm in Mississippi, when he was a kid, and he'd always combed his natural over that place. Grady. His hand moved back and forth over the tile, washing off fingerprints and smudges. He was missing the end of his right ring finger.

I couldn't do it. I pressed myself against the building across the street. *Hey, Grady, remember me? I wish I could get to know you again, have lunch, tapas or sushi, and then take a couple weeks before I tell you Glorette got killed by somebody in an alley, and she still only loved a guy who left her.*

I watched him for ten minutes. He washed the tile, wiped down the door, and polished the gold handle with a different rag. Then he stepped back and turned to look at something above my head.

I didn't move. His eyes crossed over me but didn't pause. He went inside, and he never came back out.

Other people stepped in now that the door was open. Two actors from *The OC.* Three young women wearing heels and carrying briefcases. A guy in a suit.

I crossed the street and went inside. This was not a dive. It looked like Liberace had decorated, with chandeliers and black pillars and even little lamps with gopher shades in gold. I squinted. The jukebox played Al Green. My eyes hurt from saltwater and darkness, and I didn't see Grady Jackson.

The bartender leaned forward and said, "You okay?" He had a two-tone bowling shirt on, and a porkpie and sideburns.

"Does Hattie Jackson work here?" I said. The bar was cool under my fingers.

"Who?"

"She's about forty. She was a bartender here."

A young woman—Paris Hilton–blond but with cool black roots, and a satin camisole—came up behind the bar and squinted. "She means Gloria, I'll bet."

Gloria was in an alcove to the side. It was like a little liquor store, and she was arranging bottles of Grey Goose and Ketel One. Her nails were red. But her lips were thin and brown. She looked old.

"Hattie?"

"Gloria Jones," she said to me. I leaned against the wall. My hips hurt, somehow. She knew me. She said, "When I came here, you had Pam Grier and Coffy and all them. My mama named me Hattie after the one in *Gone with the Wind*. Who the hell want to be a maid? I changed my name long time ago. After you was here with my fool-ass brother."

"Was that him? Outside?"

She nodded. "Comes to clean, and then he walks again. He got five, six routes a day. You know. He goes all the way along the river till Frogtown. Comes back later." She pushed the bottles around. "I don't get much tips over here. People don't buy this shit till they ready to go to a private party."

"You've been here all this time."

She shrugged. "Seem like not much longer." She wore a wig. The hairs were perfect. "After my senior year. I was fine as wine, but even the hookers in L.A. was something else. Hollywood was crazy. I came downtown to get me an apartment and wait for the right movie. Did the dancing place for a month."

"The dancing place?"

"Over on Olympic. The men dance with you for ten dollars and they gotta buy you them expensive drinks. But they smelled. Lord, they all smelled different, and some of them, the heat comin off their underarms and neck and you could smell it comin up from their pants. Even if they had cologne, just made it worse. I couldn't do it. I came here, and I was behind the counter forever serving drinks. The guys would tip me good, all the old drunks, and I went to the movies every night after work. Now the theaters are all Spanish. I just get me a video after work. And I sleep till I come in. I live next door."

I didn't know what to say. Her eyes were brown and muddy, as if washed in tea. "They were filming your building today."

She shrugged. "Always doin somethin. Now that Downtown is cool again. Grady can't even get his food in the alley now. Miss Thang at the bar like a hawk."

"He comes back for dinner?"

Gloria looked around and nodded. "I used to take my plate out there early, before we got started. Take me two enchiladas and rice. Hold a extra plate under there and gave him half. Used to have Mexican food in here. Not now." She glanced out over her counter. "Now the little old actors be out in the alley. Think they big time."

I walked away from her alcove, past the bar, the bowling-shirt watching me with a puzzled look—*What is she? Brazilian?*—and out to the alley. It must have been just a place to dump trash before—but now huge couches covered with velvet and pillows lay at each end, and the OC boys were already collapsed on one, with two girls. It was cool to be in a dive, in an alley, drinking Grey Goose martinis.

"Where does he eat now?" I whispered to Hattie, to Gloria, as she marked off bottles on a list.

"In the other alley. Next door," she said softly. "At 6:00. Every night, I take me a smoke break out there. And I take my purse."

I waited for Grady there. I ignored the other homeless men, the drunks from down the street who stumbled past the Golden Gopher, the snide comments of one girl wearing a slinky dress who said, "Uh, the library is on 5th, okay?"

I saw him turn the corner and lope slowly toward me, steady, knees bending, arms moving easily at his sides. He stopped about ten feet from me and said, "Fantine?"

I nodded.

He said, "I been waiting for you. All this time."

His hands were rimmed with black, like my father's when he'd been picking oranges all night. His eyes were tiny, some-how, like sunflower seeds in the deep wrinkles around them. All that sun. All those miles.

"You told me you was gon come to L.A. And you left for college. I married Glorette. I married her." His four top teeth were gone, like an open gate to his mouth. "Didn't nobody know. We went to the courthouse. Me and her."

I said, "Grady, I came to tell you—"

"I knew you was somewhere in L.A. Me and Glorette went to the courthouse after Sere Dakar was gone. He played the flute. But he wasn't African. I seen his driver license one time. Name Marquis Parker. He was from Chicago. Call his-self *Chi-town* sometimes. Told me he was goin to L.A. and play in a band. Glorette was havin a baby."

"He'd be seventeen now," I said. "Her son."

But Grady stepped closer, the ripe sweet smell of urine and liquor and onions rising from his coat. "No. My son. I was gon raise him. Dakar was gon leave every time. So I got him in my truck."

I tried to remember. Grady had an old Pinto back then. "You didn't have a truck."

He trembled, and breathed hard through his mouth.

"Fantine. All this time I waited to tell you. Cause I know you won't tell nobody. You never told nobody about the car. About Pomona."

I shook my head. My brothers would have beat his ass.

"I waited till Dakar came out that one bar where he played. I told him I had some clothes to sell. Then I busted him in the head and put him in the trash truck. It was almost morning. I took the truck up the hill. To the dump."

"Grady," Hattie said from behind me, "shut up." She dipped a hand in her purse and brought out a foil-wrapped package. "Eat your dinner and shut up. You ain't done nothin like that."

"I did."

"You a lie. You never said nothin to me."

"Fantine—you was at the barn that night." He held up his hand, as if to stop me, but he was showing me his finger. "Chicago had a knife. When I got to the dump and went to the back of the truck, he raised up and took a piece of me with him. But I had me a tire iron."

I looked up at the slice of sky between buildings. Missippi and Cleveland and Louisiana and Chicago—all in California. Men and fathers and fools.

Grady tucked the package against him then, like it was a football. "I was waitin on Fantine. She can tell Glorette he didn't leave. I disappeared his ass, and then I married her. But she left anyway. She still loved him. I don't love her now. I'm done." He brought the package to his lips and breathed in.

"You left him there?" I said. Sere Dakar—his real name something else. A laughing, thin musician with a big natural and green eyes. "At the dump?"

Grady threw his head up to the black sky and dim street-lamps. His throat was scaly with dirt. "The truck was full. I drove it up there and hit the button. Raised it up and dumped it in the landfill. Every morning, the bulldozer covered the layers. Every morning. It was Tuesday." He stepped toward me. "He had my finger in there with him. I felt it for a long time. Like when I was layin in the bed at night, with Glorette, my finger was still bleedin in Dakar's hand." His eyes were hard to see. "Tell her."

"She's dead, Grady. I came to tell you. Somebody killed her back in Rio Seco. In an alley. They don't know who. I'm going to see her tomorrow morning. Pay my respects." I pictured Glorette lying on a table, the men who would have to comb and coil her hair. Higher on her head than normal, because she couldn't lie on her back with all that hair gathered in a bun.

We'd always slept with our hair in braids. My eyes filled with tears, until the streetlamps faded to smears and I let down my eyelids hard. The tears fell on the sidewalk. When I looked down, I saw the wet.

Hattie went back inside without speaking to me, and she closed the black door hard. And Grady started to walk away, that familiar dipping lope that I'd watched for hours and hours while just behind him, that night.

I had to call a cab to get home. I went to Rio Seco the next morning in my Corsica. I thought I would see Grady Jackson there, or at the funeral, but I didn't.

My father said to me, "You goin to Brazil? That far?" He shook his head. "You never fall in love with none of them place. Not one, no."

I smiled and kissed him on the cheek. I sat all that night in my apartment, listening to Al Green, hearing the traffic on Echo Park Avenue, watching out my window as the palm fronds moved in the wind.

No one ever saw Grady Jackson again. I asked Hattie the following week, and the week after that, and then a month later. She was angry with me, and told me not to come back to the Golden Gopher. "You didn't have to tell him," she hissed.

"But he would have known someday," I said.

"You know what?" she said, her fingers hard as a man's on my wrist. "I loved my brother. I never loved nobody else in the world, but every day I saw my brother. I can't never go back home, but he came to me. And you done took that away. You don't know a damn thing about me or him."

The next time I went to the bar, she was gone too.

I knew him. I figured he just started walking one day and never went back to Skid Row. Maybe he walked to Venice and disappeared under the waves. Maybe he walked all the way to San Francisco, or maybe he had a heart attack or died of dehydration, still moving.

That night, when we were young, when Grady left the car in Pomona, we walked down Mission Boulevard, leaving behind the auto shops and tire places, moving past vacant lots and tiny motor courts where one narrow walk led past doors behind which we could hear muffled televisions. Junkyard dogs snarled and threw themselves against chain-link. And we moved easy and fast, me just behind Grady. Walking for miles, past strawberry fields where water ran like mercury in the furrows. Walking past a huge pepper tree with a hollow where an owl glided out, pumping wings once and then gone.

That night, we walked like we lived in the Serengeti, I realized all those years later when I watched Grady disappear down 8th into the darkness. Like pilgrims on the Roman roads of France. Like old men in England. Like Indians through rain forests, steady down the trail. Fools craving movement and no words and just the land, all the land, where we left our footprints, if nothing else.

THE KIDNAPPER BELL

BY JIM PASCOE

Los Angeles River

Change flows swiftly through L.A. like the shallow river that cuts into downtown on its way to the ocean. But in Los Angeles there are pockets, tiny whirlpools eddying in the stream, where change cannot reach. In those places, things even worse than change can find you.

Five till 7. With the taste of second-hand smoke in his mouth, he settles into a dark corner of his favorite bar in Chinatown, early for his date, ready to dope his new girlfriend. He has two beer bottles from the bar. He sets them on the wobbly square table. He looks around the place: The loud bleached-blonde harassing the bartender, the old men drinking Crown near the door, the smoking Chinese couple, all unconcerned with the packet of crushed powder he's sifting down into the brown longneck. His eyes dart between them and his work, all the while he's doing the male math in his head: *Four dates and still no sex. Tonight makes five.*

He was proud to have walked away from the first date without so much as a kiss goodnight. If you can't get a second date, she's not worth sleeping with in the first place. It was date three that made him nervous, caused him to question his game. He knew then she wouldn't be easy. He even wondered if she really liked him.

Now, it's been ten days since they last saw each other. He

was kicking himself for letting an opportunity with someone so beautiful slip by. He had thought it was all over, until she called earlier today.

Why the call? Why the rush to meet? Perhaps in her mind they were just friends, and this is what friends do, how friends behave. Even if so, what does she want from him?

When she arrives, she looks pale. Sweat darkens the hair around her temples. Her hands look dirty.

"Is this for me?" Slumping into the seat next to him, she grabs the full bottle and lets it drain into her mouth. "Have you been waiting long?"

He stares at her. "No, I haven't been here long. Are you all right?"

"There was a problem." She finishes her beer. "I think I need your help."

"Of course. Anything. But you're scaring me."

"We've grown close in the last month, haven't we?"

"Sure."

She reaches her hand out to touch his arm. Her laughter sounds forced as it cracks, turning into something like crying. Hysteria.

He waits for her to compose herself. She looks around the dark room and says, "Not here. I can't tell you here."

He leans back, keeping quiet. He's being baited and wants no part of it. He is familiar with the dynamics of power, the rules of hunting. Give too much and you can't take. Push forward and your target retreats. Remain silent and she will open up.

He knows all this. He should have slept with her weeks ago.

She gives in, speaks: "It happened in the river."

"What river?"

"The river, the L.A. River."

"What happened?"

"I think . . . I think I just killed somebody."

He waits for the punch line, which does not come. There's no reason for her to lie to him. He fingers the empty powder packet in his suit jacket. Slowly, like powder, his plan dissolves.

He straightens up in his chair, reaches for a new plan. "Maybe we should go back to your place. You can tell me everything there."

"No. There's no time." She lowers her voice. "I'll take you to the body. You'll know what to do. I'm in over my head. I trust you."

He stammers out the beginning of an argument. She is already up, heading toward the door.

Trust. If he thinks about it too much, his muscles tense.

He offers to drive, insists upon it, concerned about her staying alert enough with the substance in her system. She won't have it. They argue. Unable to reveal why he opposes her getting behind the wheel, he concedes.

She drives east out of Chinatown. They cross the river. A dark left takes them down an industrial service road until they hit Riverside Drive. They exchange no words. She speeds and swerves. He clutches the handle above the window.

Elysian Valley. She gets out of the car, locks the door, and heads toward the entrance of a bike path that runs along the crest of cement lining the deep, empty river basin.

"Hey!" he calls after her. "I think we need a plan. You haven't told me anything. I want to help you, but I need a little more."

"It was an accident." Her words slur.

"Accidents happen."

"We should walk and talk." She takes his hand. "He knew so much about the river, more than most Angelenos."

"So do you."

"Yeah, well, that's it. I think he was stalking me. I think . . . I was next."

"An old flame?" He looks over the edge of the bike path. A knee-high barrier of loose chain-link tops an almost perpendicular sheer.

"No, I didn't know him. I mean, I hadn't ever met him. He started posting anonymous comments on my blog. Every time I wrote an article on the river, he would add his two cents. Sometimes he'd make corrections, sometimes he'd start an argument by taking a contrary point of view. At first I assumed he was with FoLAR—"

"Friends of the L.A. River?" He remembers this detail from her site.

"Yeah. But it didn't fit. I know most of the gang over there, and he wasn't anyone I recognized." Her breathing has become labored. "Later, we e-mailed back and forth. His username was Pavlov."

"A strange handle." His eyes adjust, searching for the body. The only light comes from across the river. She tells him the MTA uses this defunct Southern Pacific structure as a place to store their spare light rail train cars. To him it looks like an abandoned factory.

"Wait, wait a second, please. I gotta stop." She rubs her eyes. "I didn't realize I was so out of shape."

He touches her between her shoulder blades. "He wanted to meet you alone at night in the river? How did it get to that point?"

She walks away from his fingers. "Didn't you ever want something so bad that, well, it's not that you'd be willing to do *anything*, it's that each step adds up and soon you find that you're over the line, somewhere you shouldn't be? You've got to help me, Jim."

He does not say anything. His mind is already made up.

She points to where the body is, although he has a hard time seeing it at first. He must walk several yards farther north to where the embankment is gentle enough to descend. He makes his way down, his feet sideways so he doesn't slip.

The body lies crumpled on the bone-dry, flat edge of the riverbed, several feet away from the small swash of water tracing the center of the channel. The man is dressed in a gray sports coat and jeans. His neck is twisted. His face is down.

"Hey," he whispers, nudging the guy in the rump with his shoe. "Hey." He leans down to find a pulse. The guy's neck is cold.

She whispers down the embankment. "Is he definitely dead?"

"I wouldn't think a fall down here would kill a guy."

"He must have snapped his neck. It was a bad fall. From here it's almost a straight drop."

He looks up at her.

She says, "What? What are you thinking?"

"What aren't you telling me?"

He hears her breathing heavily through the sobbing. "He . . . he took her."

"Who?"

"Before I pushed him, he, he said I could find her . . . through . . . through the six cats. Should've went right away, but . . . got scared. Thought you could help."

"You're crazy—you're not making any fucking sense." He

continues to examine the body, looks in the guy's pockets. No wallet, no ID, a few dollars in cash. "I'll help, but you need to start filling me in."

"What . . . what are you doing?" Her voice rises like helium.

He pulls something from the body's right suit pocket. A small metal object. A bell. Caked in dried mud.

He walks to the center of the river, to the water.

"Where are you going? What are you doing?" she asks.

He tries to wash the bell. He shakes it under the water, as if ringing it. No sound comes up past the surface. The cold water is surprisingly swift, like a full-force faucet running over his hand.

"I know you want me, Jim. And I know why you think you can't have me. Doesn't matter to me anymore. Find her and . . . I'll do anything . . . I'll let you do anything."

Something in the water touches him, something that floats around his hand, something that feels like fingers. He flinches. The bell slips from his grasp.

"Shit," he says.

"What! What's going on down there?"

He splashes his hand in and out of the shallow water, but he can't locate the bell.

"Shit. That guy had something in his pocket and when I tried to clean it off in the river, I dropped it. Now I can't find it."

"Was it the bell? Was it?"

He turns around to look up at her. She screams, using all her energy. The effort actually deflates her. Her body withers, goes limp. Her knees strain against the short chain-link fence. It buckles. She topples.

The drug. His drug. Now is its time. Its damage, far from

expected, doesn't seem real. Had she stayed a couple feet back, he would be crawling out of the river, gathering her unconscious body, and returning her home.

But she is too close to the edge. The fence cannot hold her body when she loses consciousness. Her upper body folds over the edge, the momentum carrying her head down fast in a dive. Her feet flip over the fence, and she's falling. He watches her as she goes down with impressive velocity. Her limp condition might have saved a more substantial body, but her delicate frame snaps when her curved neck crashes into the dry gravel at the bottom. He runs to her, stops in front of her twisted, broken form.

He can hear the river churning, flowing fast behind him; its thimble-full of water, a flood.

He hyperventilates, looks for something to hold, to steady himself. His tongue pumps piston-like into the back of his throat.

What is happening?

He doesn't bother with a pulse this time. He is afraid to know; although he knows he knows.

He speaks out loud, hoping his voice will give truth to the lies: "This is not my fault. This is not my fault. This is not my fault."

This is a trap, he thinks, his heart still racing. *I see it clearly, this quicksand of culpability. If I do nothing, I sink. If I struggle, I go down faster. I must remain calm, go backward up along the path that brought me here, until another path presents itself. A tiny pocket. A window. An escape. If not from responsibility, from guilt.*

Her dress has come up above her knees. He glances over to the man's body. The head is cocked on its broken axis. Jim imagines the body looking back at him, even though only one eye is open. The man would say, *You can look. Take a peek. It's okay. You haven't gone any farther than the rest of us. Don't worry about crossing the line. I am the eraser. The line is gone.*

He walks away from the bodies, climbs out of the river. He takes her purse, checking for her keys and wallet. He leaves.

It takes him almost an hour to walk back to Chinatown. All the while he repeats to himself: *You can find her through the six cats.*

Who is she? How can he find her? How can he help her?

He gets to his car, drives to the dead girl's place, a one-bedroom cottage in Echo Park. With her key, he enters. He goes straight for the bedroom.

The scent of the place is familiar. It smells like her. He has been here a couple times, but never has he come into this room. He allows himself a moment to take it all in.

He opens the closet's double doors. She has pushed a four-drawer dresser into the closet, clothes hanging on either side. On top of her dresser are two photos in stand-up frames. One is a picture of her with another girl, much younger. They are laughing, standing arm in arm. Sisters. The other is a picture of a young lady, taken at the beach. The sunglasses the woman is wearing, as well as the color and quality of the print, date it. Most likely, her mother.

Starting with the top drawer, he goes through the contents of her dresser. Bras, panties, socks, scarves, sweaters. What would have been a puerile thrill has become numerous slugs to the stomach. Still, he finishes, digging under the piles of folded fabric, knocking the four corners of each drawer, hoping to uncover a hidden relic of some sort.

Secret photos, perhaps. A bundle of old love letters. A diary.

He moves onto the shelves, finds a leather-bound volume of lined paper with less than half of its pages filled. He reads the first entry. As he reads, her voice rings in his ear.

He closes the book, looks around the room. He shakes his head and feels his forehead with the back of his hand. He's hot.

He must not get distracted by emotions. There is a task at hand, he reminds himself. Whatever she was doing in the river remains unfinished. He owes it to her to see it through, all the way to the end. He remembers the list of clues he's assembled: a missing girl, Pavlov, six cats, a bell.

He opens the book again. He tries speed-reading the diary to see if any of these things are mentioned. Nothing. The information is either not there or he's too impatient to find it.

Frustrated, he turns to the last entry. Ten days ago. It's an inconsequential write-up, but it gets him thinking: Wasn't that the night of their last get-together?

Flipping through the pages, he searches for his name. He tries to remember the exact day of their first date. He finds it, an entry about that night. He reads her words. Her voice rings louder.

He rips the page from the book, stuffs the paper in his pocket, slams the book shut.

The ticking of a clock fills the quiet that remains. He's concerned that he's been in here too long. He expects a knock at the door any moment, but can't imagine who would come calling at this hour.

He sits at her desk, digs through papers there. A good number of them are printouts of online reports: girls gone missing, kidnap suspects arrested, and alleged abductors still at large.

A picture is developing in his mind.

Her computer is already on. He moves his finger across the trackpad to wake it from sleep. He starts by pulling up her blog. Though it looks like she posted daily entries, the site has not been updated in ten days. Her previous posts were all things he had seen before: conservation issues, environmental impact discussions, and public policy debates concerning the L.A. River.

He clicks off the browser and begins reading through folders and file names on her hard drive.

An electronic ding sounds off. A flashing window appears in the upper right-hand corner of the screen.

Someone is sending an instant message.

Shepherd_79: god i'm so sick of guys
Shepherd_79: he didn't call again tonight

He is tempted to shut the program down, make it seem like a glitch. Her friend would never think twice about it. But he doesn't do anything, thinking it is far less suspicious to do so.

His heart is racing, and he can feel his neck and chest flushing with color. Finding it hard to concentrate on reading her folder structure, he opts to open an image viewer and browse through her digital photos.

Shepherd_79: i should just get over him, right?

The photos are grouped into categories, mostly events: parties and a couple weddings. The largest group of pictures contains shots of the river. He opens them in thumbnail view and scrubs through them, trying to differentiate one from another. They all look the same. Graffiti-covered cement. A hint of water. Chain link, barbed wire, corrugated steel.

He clicks on a couple of images, enlarging them, hoping

to read the graffiti. But it's all senseless tagging in an indecipherable alphabet.

Next are a bunch of shots of storm-drain covers spray-painted in bright, bold metallic colors. The paint looks layered on, the iterations of multiple artists on many different occasions.

There's something familiar about the shape of these drain covers, the way the upper hinges taper off to points on either side of the large circle.

Shepherd_79: hello?
Shepherd_79: are you ignoring me too bitch!

The messages are getting to him. Someone is closing in on him, has him under a microscope.

He clicks the IM window and types, hitting the keys hard.

CAN'T TALK NOW.

A mistake? Just by typing a few words he has brought her back. A ghost in the machine. Although this ghost is thinner than smoke.

The next image of the drain covers reveals it all. The spray-painted eyes, nose, whiskers. Cats. They are graffitied to look like cats.

Another message comes through IM.

Shepherd_79: sorry . . . you okay? is there news about your sister?

He jumps up to her bookshelf and starts tearing through books.

Captions under key images begin to point him to a general location. Hopping back onto her computer, he starts opening documents and searching for keywords. *Frogtown. Atwater Village. County Flood Control. Mural Registry.* He starts sketching on the back of a piece of paper.

After much work, he has a map, a goal. He is about to leave when he notices the IM window is blinking again. He knows he will have to close the program before he leaves. Keeping it open will make for a suspicious scene, even though the books and papers he has pulled out make the ransacked place suspicious enough.

He reads the last communication.

Shepherd_79: what's the matter?
Shepherd_79: hey! HELLO!
Shepherd_79: Who are you?
(Shepherd_79 has signed off.)

He exits the program. He imagines that Shepherd is heading here, to this house, to investigate. It hardly matters now. He won't be here. He is heading back to the river.

He knows who she is. He knows how to find her. The rest is fate.

In the dim light of the riverbed, he has trouble seeing the graffiti on the drain covers, but he knows he's at the right place. Six cats, six drains. The large painted faces hang perpendicular to the ground. During heavy rains they will swing up, releasing torrents of run-off into the violent river come to life. Now they are silent, each recessed into an individual hollow in the channel's cement wall. He takes a moment for a deep, shaky breath. He twists his wrist to look at his watch, but the time doesn't even register. His mind is on what happens next.

Really, what is he doing here?

Thoughts crowd his head. He should go to the police, he should go get help, he should just walk away and pray for this day to end. He shakes his head, pulls the paper he ripped from her diary out of his pocket. With a faint click he turns his flashlight on and reads:

In real life, stories never actually end; they simply change. If you are in a loveless marriage, you can't just type "THE END" and move on to the next story. No, you make choices and you change, your story changes. A main character is swept to the side. A supporting character rises to take on more importance. New characters are introduced.

Nothing ever stops, not for a single moment.

Six cats in front of him. He chooses one. Kicks at the cover. Solid. He touches it hesitantly, thinking that it's probably dirty. The slightly moist surface is cold from the night air. It says to him, *Choose again.*

The next cat he selects reacts differently. It gives when he touches it, making a squeaking sound not unlike a low meow. One of the top hinges is broken. The cover opens easily. Beyond is a cement tunnel, almost six feet in diameter.

He steps up. Inside. The beam of his flashlight melts into black. The entire inner surface is covered in graffiti tags of multiple colors. Catching the writing out of his peripheral vision gives the illusion that the tube is slowly rotating. He tries to concentrate on the sloppy seams of the poured concrete, concentric rings that disappear into darkness. He walks slowly at first, then with determination.

The path in front of him does not appear to end. He stops and looks back. He can't see the entrance anymore. If he spun around he wouldn't be able to tell which way was out, which way was in.

He keeps walking until he reaches a hole in the curved bottom of the tube. The hole is slightly smaller, maybe four feet wide. Attached to the side is a ladder. He aims the flashlight below. He cannot see bottom.

He climbs down the ladder.

The length of the descent surprises him. When he reaches the bottom rung, he extends his leg down, swinging it to feel for some ground. His shoe scrapes against something and he decides to let go of the ladder.

He lands awkwardly, almost twisting his ankle. He shines the flashlight around. Another tube, this one perpendicular to the one he came in. His choice is left or right.

There is a scratching, scurrying sound. He thinks it's most likely a rat.

Then it sounds different. A whimper. A cry.

He looks in the direction he thinks the sound is coming from. His flashlight only goes a small distance before the beam diffuses into an off-white haze. He thinks he sees movement, but it's up high, eye-level, not crawling across the floor.

He flinches and throws some light above him. Nothing but gray cement.

His light still pointed above him, he looks forward and sees something more clearly. He turns out his flashlight and lets his eyes adjust. Again he sees it. A flickering.

A light ahead.

He runs toward it. As he gets closer, he can't quite grasp what it is. The first thing he sees is the reflection of his own flashlight.

Then he sees her.

He holds up his free hand, trying to wave the image away as he fights back the nausea. Looking around, he sees he's in what appears to be a large circular room. Off to one side hangs a camp lantern that barely illuminates the scene.

In the center of the room are two large pieces of sheet glass, hung vertically. They are sealed together at the four corners with over-sized metal bolts. Between the glass is pinned a young girl, wearing only a white T-shirt, a white pair of underwear.

The glass holds her up off the ground. She is pressed together so tightly that her face is distorted, her cheek blotchy and spread wide, her lips puckered like a fish. Her eyes are closed.

"No more." Her voice, a dry whisper. "Please, no more."

He catches himself staring with incomprehension before he snaps out of it and rushes to her, examining the glass for some type of latch or opening. Finding none, he fights with the bolts. His hands burn at the friction of the unmovable metal.

"Please . . . I'll do anything . . . I'll let you do anything," she says.

The bolts appear to have been tightened by some massive wrench. He looks around the room for it, but finds only a metal pipe.

"Just whatever you do . . . Don't ring the bell anymore."

He stops, looks at her, really looks at her. "What?"

She opens her eyelids, and her eyes searchlight the room. "Who . . . who are you? Where is he?" Her voice gets more and more excited, and her eyes go crazy. Except for this flurry, she is unable to move. "Get me out, get me out, get me out!"

"I'm trying. Just calm down. Everything is going to be all right."

He tries to pry the two panes apart, first with his hands, then with his shoe. Her cries are getting louder; his blood pressure, rising.

The glass does not budge. Now a scream: "Get me out! He's coming! He's coming back with the bell! No no no no . . ."

He tries to quiet her, tell her that he's here to help. He does not tell her that her kidnapper is dead, in the river, unable to hurt her anymore. The idea of what he did to her burns him, keeps him quiet.

Her screaming shows no sign of stopping. She screams dry, hollow, hyperventilated screams—she can't get enough air to properly bellow out. It would be better, he thinks, if she could really let it all out. But she is so constricted. Her wheeze crawls up his spine and pools into tension.

He grabs the metal pipe.

"Look. The only way I'm getting you out is to break the glass." He weighs the pipe in his hand. "But I think it's too dangerous. You could really get hurt. I'm . . . I'm going to go for help."

"No! He'll come back! You have to do something!"

"He's not coming back!"

The noise she's making reminds him of her sister's last sound, that final emptying scream. Could he have done more to help her? Should he have done less?

He can't concentrate with her crying. The opportunity is slipping by. What would he be willing to do to free her? Anything? A moral lapse? No. To lapse is to fall. This is a leap. This is worth the price.

He swings at the glass with the pipe, aiming near her upper leg. The impact makes a loud reverberating bounce that echoes through the underground tunnels. The glass does not break.

"No! Stop! That hurts! Get me out of here!"

"I'm trying—"

"Get me out!"

"I'm trying!" He swings. "I'm trying!"

Again and again, until the glass shatters. She falls forward onto the shards.

He throws the pipe away and goes to lift her up. Blood has already soaked her thin shirt. She presses herself onto him, holding him, crying deeply, allowing big gulps of air to enter her lungs.

"I'll take you somewhere safe," he tells her, but all she can do is moan.

In his car. He drives her to the nearest hospital. She hasn't said anything since he carried her up through the tunnels and out of the river. He continues to glance over at her, hoping she will say something, anything. When she doesn't, he speaks just to break the still air.

"He can't hurt you anymore."

She looks out the window. "When I woke up in that thing, he began telling me stories. He would tell me about the horrible things he was going to do to my sister. Only, every time he would describe something really bad, he would ring a bell. At some point the stories stopped. He would just come and sit next to me and ring the bell."

He grips the steering wheel tightly. "You know, I had it in my hands. I had the bell, and it slipped away from me." He looks at her, her confused expression. "It's gone now. It's all gone."

She puts her hand on the door handle, turns to him. "Who are you?"

"I'm a friend of your sister." He sees a tear roll down her cheek, a tear she does not wipe away.

She says, "I think you should just let me out here."

He turns onto San Fernando Road. "The emergency room is right there. Just let me—"

She throws the door open; he slams on the brakes. She uses the recoil of being thrown back to push herself out of the car. She gets to her feet and runs toward the hospital, flailing her arms as she goes.

There is nothing more he can do. He reengages his stalled engine. He leaves.

He puts his window down, even though the late-night air is cool. He wants to drive forever, wants the car never to run out of gas, never to stop. No acceleration, no deceleration. A constant, smooth, uninterrupted drive.

This fantasy cannot hold. He knows he needs to go home. He looks down and remembers her blood all over his clothes. He can't go home like this. He's too tired to want to figure things out, though he knows he needs to. But then, as ideas do, something comes to him.

For the last time tonight he heads to the river.

He finds their bodies, largely unchanged since he left them hours ago. He examines the man, stiff and cold, roughly his same build. First he takes off the man's jacket. Then his shirt, his pants.

They fit him well enough. At least they are clean.

He dresses the man in his clothing. Now the kidnapper is wearing the blood of the sister of the dead woman next to him. For him and for now, this is enough.

As he reclaims his personal belongings from his exchanged clothing, he finds the empty powder packet in the suit jacket. He leaves it in the possession of the corpse.

"You," he says to the dead man. "This is your fault."

Home. He tries to be quiet as he opens the door. He closes it softly. He crosses the front room, slinks into his office and into his chair. He breathes in and out, trying to calm down. His skin is clammy from the lack of sleep.

He goes into the bedroom. His wife is sleeping. He sits down on his side of the bed, trying not to wake her. He doesn't bother to undress.

She turns to him, still asleep. She manages to mutter, "Poor baby, always working late. You get a lot done?"

"Yeah."

"That's great. Mmm, I got to get up soon. Wake me up at 7, 'kay?"

"Sure."

He pulls his wallet out of his back pocket, sets it on the nightstand next to his pillow. Does the same with his keys, his change. He reaches into the suit jacket. The right pocket. He finds it there.

The bell, washed clean by the river, traveled on its journey, has arrived here.

Maybe it's the fatigue, but he's not so concerned with *how* as he is with *why*. The bell demands a story, a confession.

He holds it in his hand, examines the detail.

He does not move. He stays this way for a long time, as long as he can.

His concentration broken, he looks at the clock.

Five till 7.

Everything seems to change.

He rings the bell.

CITY OF COMMERCE

BY NEAL POLLACK

Commerce

T he call came at 4 p.m., just when I was starting my prep for the day's first bong hit. It had been weeks since I'd heard from my agent. I put down my gear and listened.

"Some cherry producer at New Line likes your treatment for *Cedar Fever*," he said.

This was a crappy horror comedy that I'd written two years before, about people whose allergies get so bad they start turning into plants. Not exactly what I'd dreamed about when I moved here. But after a while, you've sleepwalked long enough so you're not really dreaming anymore.

"No shit?" I said.

"Yeah," he said. "Stupid fuck read your book, and he thinks you can still write."

Silence, as I decided whether or not to defend myself.

"You got a clean shirt, one with buttons?" he asked.

"I *am* still married," I replied. "So probably."

"Good. Because I scored you a sit-down at 3:30. Do *not* be late to this one . . ."

He bitched at me for a few minutes, then turned nice when he asked if I knew where he could get some weed. By the time I got his ass off the phone, Karen was coming in the door, looking fine as ever. Admissions of love came less and less frequently from her these days, not that I blamed her.

One minute she was at a Santa Monica beach party getting felt up in a hammock by a promising novelist, and before she could hiccup, she found herself paying the mortgage on a two-bedroom condo in Glassell Park and coming home every day to an unshaven, unemployed stoner. She was as bitter as an unripe plum, so I was glad to have some good news for her. I just about fell on my ass when she threw her arms around my neck and put her tongue in my ear.

"You get this gig," she said, "and I'll cruise you up to Ojai for a weekend of blowjobs you'll never forget."

I hadn't received an offer like that in nearly a decade. She still loved, me, maybe. But I was feeling a little jittery at that moment, and I told her so.

"Maybe I should . . ."

She blanched whiter than a snow leopard in February.

"No, Nick," she said. "You're *not* fucking going to the casino. Not tonight. Not before the biggest meeting of your life."

"I'll play a few low-stakes hands and be home by midnight," I said, reassuring myself as much as her.

"Jesus Christ."

"Come on, babe," I said. "You know it relaxes me."

"It does anything but."

I picked my keys off the kitchen counter and headed for the door.

"You're going *now*? You're not even going to have *dinner* with me?"

"The 5 can be a real bastard this time of night," I said.

I was out the door so quickly she couldn't possibly have jinxed my opening flop.

Before I moved to California, I played poker occasionally at basement tables with ten-cent antes, where the real object was to drink as much Old Style as possible without vomiting. Winning meant zero, and losing even less. I had no idea that I was coming to a place where poker transcended hobby, leaped above pastime, and approached something near civic religion. The first couple of home games almost turned me back toward the path of righteousness; one was full of twenty-five-year-old schmucks hatching plans to date-rape a stripper in Malibu, and the other featured new dads who were busy discussing home renovations and the difficulties of finding a reliable nanny who'd work for less than seventeen dollars an hour. Neither scene appealed much. In fact, I couldn't think of *any* home game I'd enjoy, unless I were sitting around a table with nine clones of myself. Other men can be a real pain in the ass.

Then one night, a guy mentioned that he was heading out to Commerce that weekend to play in some tournament that might get him into some other tournament that might get him into the World Series of Poker. I guess it had never occurred to me that the three thousand gambling billboards I saw a week could be advertising poker rooms. And when he said that the games ran twenty-four hours a day, all year, the amateur anthropologist in me began to quiver. This, I thought, could be the ideal canvas for my art, so I went along.

City of Commerce may be the most ironically named place in America, which is saying a lot. I suppose it was once full of factories that made things. But that's not what commerce is about in this world anymore. The only commerce now is a five-cent rake on the pot. One person in fifty goes home with a profit and one in five thousand actually makes a living. If those had been the commercial odds during the Industrial Revolution, Californians would still be riding donkeys down to the San Diego Mission. Maybe we'll get there still.

From the moment I first walked in under the faux-gold-mirrored awning, lit with a circumferential rectangle of two-inch-wide bulbs, I knew I was sunk. This hardly represented the seamiest gambling scene I'd encountered—that honor goes to the Friday midnight riverboat blackjack cruise in Joliet, Illinois—but it was probably the most baroque. The place obviously prospered beyond measure. However, unlike Vegas patrons, these players required little frippery. The most lavish theme in the world couldn't draw the casual gambling tourist to City of Commerce night after night. They were here to play cards.

I've never seen garbage on the floor. Someone's always vacuuming the rugs or polishing the faux-marble, and there's no sign of chipping paint. The casino has a sushi bar and a sports bar full of flat-screen TVs. Yet the place always seems suffused with a kind of jaundice; the lighting scheme encourages the shakes, and nausea. It's ugly, almost as though the casino were deliberately trying to throw us off our game.

I prepared for my meeting, in my mind, as I whipped the Acura down the 110, and then onto I-5 as I moved through Downtown, crawling past merges like a sheep on wheels being herded off to slaughter. But by the time I was halfway to Commerce, thoughts of pitching grew cloudy, replaced by visions of flush draws dancing in my head. The landscape grew generic, sooty, industrial, less definitively L.A. to the casual observer. This town, to me, isn't most notable for its candlelit, leather-bound nightclubs or fancy Valley gallerias. Like anywhere else, it's the outlet malls and truck-stop Arby's, pathetic little trees dwarfed by ten-foot freeway sound walls. I could be leaving San Antonio, or Atlanta. By the time I get to Commerce, the empty concrete lots, smoke-stacks, and shoddy public parks call Gary, Indiana to mind. What else can I think about in such an environment but poker?

The parking lot was as full as visiting day at maximum secu-rity. I pulled the car into a spot in the back row, between a gleaming Cadillac SUV and an Oldsmobile that looked like it hadn't been washed since 1973. There was someone inside the Cadillac. I could see the glint of a cigarette through the tinted windows. I should probably have been looking in front of me instead. In my hurry to make it to the tables, I slammed my right big toe into the curb, sending a hot shard of pain up through my leg. It felt like I might lose the nail. Why the fuck did I wear sandals to the casino anyway? I limped to the awning, past the lifetime smokers getting their hourly fix, and into the California Games Room with its ridiculous Wheels of Fortune and lucky-hand jackpot tables. Then past the two twelve-foot-high gold plaster sphinxes, the casino's one con-cession to Vegas-style garishness, and on into the main gam-ing hall.

Though I recognized the woman working the board, one of an interchangeable rotation of semi-attractive Filipinas who worked there, she didn't know me from the other 1,200 low-rent fliers who'd approached her since the start of her shift, asking if there were any open spots at the 3-6 or 4-8 tables. As it turned out, the waiting list was nearly as long as that for Lakers season tickets. She did have some seats, how-ever, at the 2-4 tables upstairs.

Why not, I thought. *I'm only gonna be here a couple of hours.*

On a busy night, sometimes you'll get stuck in the overflow, a partitioned conference room on loan from the adjacent Crowne Plaza Hotel. It could have been used earlier that week for a home-equity loan officer convention, or maybe a really sad low-budget wedding. But now it was twenty tables of cheap poker, with decent coffee and tea service and complimentary plates of Chinese food on the hour. I had a five-minute wait, and then they sat me down, throbbing toe and all.

I had a pretty good night too, until the Russian showed up.

At 11 p.m., I found myself up a hundred, maybe 140 bucks. That represented a good night for me, even though I would have had to work a seventy-hour week before it started to resemble anything close to the equivalent of a decent living. Still, I'd drawn the perfect table mix of sour middle-aged Korean ladies, old dudes who bore the perfume and hairstyle of late-era William S. Burroughs, a couple of Persian frat boys from UCLA, and a pockmarked *cholo* who leaned so far onto a cane when he stood that he fell to a sixty-five-degree angle. Like so many doomed poker players before me, I told myself just one more hand before I leave.

The Russian sat down three players to my left. I call him Russian, though he easily could have been Ukrainian, or maybe from Georgia, something post–Soviet breakup, vaguely Caucasian. I never got a chance to ask. Regardless, he wore a red two-piece tracksuit and silver-tinted sunglasses, and a big gold chain with a Mercedes medallion around his neck. His tight-trimmed beard made him look particularly ridiculous, since he obviously got his fashion tips from a mid-'90s hip-hop magazine. He slapped down double what he needed to buy into the first hand. This, I knew, was a sure sign of a fast player; you should never, ever gamble until you understand your odds.

The dealer sent me a jack-ten, suited, worth playing if you're near the button, which I was. The Russian, who was way out of position, raised when it came to him, probably not surprising given his brazen opening bet. I called. The flop showed a king and queen, off-suit. This was a great straight draw for me. Before I could raise, though, the Russian beat me to it, immediately folding the other two players who remained. I re-raised. He saw me, and raised me again. I called.

A nine came on the turn. My odds at winning stood at about ninety-seven percent. Yet still he raised me. And again. And then twice again on the river. He turned over his cards to reveal pocket threes. I sucked up his chips like a coin reclamation machine at the supermarket.

"Lucky man, Dodger," he said to me, apparently referring to the Dodgers cap I always wear to Commerce, to augment my chosen posture of regular guy.

"Not so lucky," I said. "Unlike some people, I just know what I'm doing."

The other players at the table moaned and shifted a little. This wasn't what they wanted to hear. But it was undeniable.

"We'll see," the Russian said.

I smelled profit in that conference room. My watch showed 11:15. One more hour, I told myself. I'll milk this cow, and then it's off to bed.

By 1 a.m., I was up several hundred bucks, no mean feat at a low-stakes table. But the Russian knew no play other than the check-raise. He may have folded one in ten openers. Other players tried to take advantage, but I had them read as well. Finally, the old dude to my right got up, cracked his bones, and mumbled off into the sooty night. The Russian immediately stood up and plunked himself in the chair.

"Now I will show you, Dodger," he said. "Now we will play poker."

And poker I did. His aggressive play dug him deeper and deeper holes. He did win a few hands, getting me to fold when I had bupkus. But he folded nothing himself, and I just kept adding plastic trays. By 2:30, I had nearly a thousand bucks in front of me. Karen had been buzzing my cell phone since midnight, and at one point left me a text message saying, *Don't fuck this meeting up, Nick* . . . Even she couldn't argue with a thousand-dollar haul.

I stood up, taking my trays with me, sliding the dealer, another anonymous, semi-attractive Filipina, a ten-dollar chip.

"Where you going, Dodger?" said the Russian.

"I've got a big meeting tomorrow."

"So when do I get my money back?"

"Ain't your money anymore," I said, and the table exploded with laughter.

As I turned away, I didn't see the Russian seethe, and I was too busy making a joke to the cashier about unmarked bills to notice him picking up the phone. Maybe if I'd skipped going to the can, I would have made it home that night.

I was making my way past the plaster sphinxes when a 310-pound side of Slavic beef slid into my purview.

"You took boss's money tonight," he said. "And boss doesn't like to lose at poker."

Somehow I guessed the identity of his boss, and tried to pull together an instant plan of escape in my mind. I mumbled, "Sorry," and turned on my heels, angling toward where

I thought a security guard might be seated. Instead, I whirled into another side of beef. Briefly, I felt my arms getting pinned behind me, and then something heavy on my head. A vague sensation of green digital numbers, blinking in random succession, passed before my eyes, and then I said goodbye to consciousness.

I woke with John Henry pounding rocks inside my head and the impression of dusty sunlight on my eyelids. A tentative opening revealed that I was in a hotel room, and a whiff indicated that smoking was allowed. Instinctively, I felt for my wallet. It was there, but pretty thin. My cell phone was also still with me, in my front jeans pocket. I removed it to find it out of juice. I turned my head. The clock beside the bed read 10:45 a.m. Less than five hours away from my meeting.

I sat up, and then stood, and found that the pounding wasn't bad enough to prevent me from walking, or from taking a piss. In fact, the mirror showed me not looking any worse than usual, even a little better. Eight hours of sleep was eight hours, even if it was artificially induced. The sound of bad hotel porn was coming from beyond the attaching door. I opened it.

The Russian sat with six other guys, placidly watching some girl-on-girl action. Cigar smoke suffused the room like toxic waste. A poker table sat by the window, silently waiting to play its part. He turned to regard me.

"Our princess has awoken," he said.

"Can I leave now?" I asked. "My wife is worried about me. You've proven your point, whatever that is."

"We've got some poker to play," he said.

"Haven't we played enough?" I asked.

"Let me explain something to you," he said. "I don't lose. Ever. And especially not to guys like you."

"But you did lose."

One of his cronies stood, walked over to me, and smacked me across the mouth, drawing a little bit of blood from my lower lip. *Goddamnit*, I thought, *I could actually fucking miss my meeting here.*

"The game isn't over yet," said the Russian. "You took $1,000 from me, and I intend to win it back."

He explained the rules to me. We'd each get $500 worth of chips, though my chips were, essentially, air. He got to keep the money, which was rightfully his. If I won his chips, I got to go home. If he won mine, he got to shoot me in the face. Those were higher stakes than usual, and I started to sweat.

A knock came at the door. It was a Filipina, not surprisingly, pushing a cart stacked with orange juice, eggs, and smoked salmon. If these guys were thugs, at least they were generous with the buffet. The Filipina would also, the Russian informed me, serve as our dealer for the day.

"But first," he said, "we eat."

I figured it wouldn't help me to say that I was in a hurry, so I dug in. By the time we were done eating, it was nearly noon. As the first hand was dealt, I felt more jittery at the table than ever before. His cronies were playing with us, but it was obvious from the beginning that they were decoys, there to win small pots that neither the Russian nor I had a shot at; it was a two-player game, with props.

I had to make that meeting. Missing it would mean the end of my career, and maybe my marriage. So I played aggressively. This was exactly what the Russian wanted. It perfectly matched his style of play. If you re-raise a raiser when the odds are bad, or even mediocre, he will bury you. For an hour, he whittled away at my chips, and then took a huge pot when he drew an inside flush to beat my pocket kings. I looked down at my pile and realized that I was $150 away from death. That was the last thing I wanted. I took a breath and prayed patience.

By 1:45, I was back up to $500. The Russian saw what was happening, and he cursed my ability to fold a bad hand, something that he'd apparently never learned. I stayed quiet, occasionally stealing little glances at the digital clock by the bed. At this point, I knew that I was going to escape with my life, or at least assumed that I would. But if I didn't do it soon, I wouldn't have much of a life left. Still, I had to play carefully. It took me another forty-five minutes to get up to $800. There would be no time to go home and shower, but I could at least buy some deodorant at Walgreens before the meeting. It was time to roll 'em.

I drew a queen-nine, not the best opener, but winnable. It didn't matter what the Russian drew, of course. He raised me regardless. I saw him, and re-raised. He did the same back, and onward until the betting was capped.

The flop revealed a second queen and some junk cards. His chance at a flush draw was nil, and a straight seemed unlikely. I'd probably flopped top pair, so I laid down a big bet. He followed, of course, and kept laying down chips. By the river, it was pretty certain that he'd bust out. The dealer called for us to show our hands. I had my queens. He had a pair of sevens, ace high.

"Well," I said, standing up, and then backing away toward the door, "it was certainly tense, and you really proved something today—"

"Don't fuck with me, Dodger," the Russian said.

"Just let him win, dumbshit," I heard a crony say, and

then I felt everything go black again. Consciousness and I had a tenuous relationship that day. My world disintegrated around me, and it was night again.

I woke to the sensation of my head being dumped in a bucket of ice water, never pleasant under any circumstance. When I emerged, gasping for breath, one of the Russian's lummoxes was holding my shirt collar. He had a huge wad of bills, which he thrust into my hand.

"Take this and go," he said.

"What?" I said.

"Boss is asshole," he said. "I'm tired of him doing this all the time."

"I'm not the first?"

"You're not the first *this week*," he said.

"But why save me?"

"You're good at cards," he said. "I'm tired of being around people who are bad at cards."

"At least I'm good at something," I said. "Thank you."

I peeled a hundred-dollar bill off the stack and slapped it into his palm.

"Buy yourself a lap dance tonight," I said.

"Or maybe I pay rent this month," he said.

"That too," I said.

"They're eating lunch downstairs," he said. "Go now."

I took a step forward, but that wasn't happening until I vomited into the toilet. With that business completed, I saw that it was ten till 3:00. I wouldn't look good doing it, but I could still make the meeting. I thanked the lummox again, and walked into the hall.

The Russian and his cronies were stepping off the elevator. I looked around. There were stairs at the end of the hall.

I tore off toward them, with the Russians in hot pursuit. They might have caught me, too, if the room hadn't been on the third floor.

A quick orientation in the parking lot showed that I was near my car, which I found easily, even though the lot was no less full than it had been when I'd pulled in sixteen hours before. The Russians kept coming. I heard the Cadillac SUV next to me beep, and I realized that it was their car. I peeled out of my spot, flipped into reverse, and then accelerated forward at an angle, aiming for the SUV's rear taillight. It might not have done much damage, but it felt symbolic. They were far enough behind me that I was on the 5, going north, before they could figure out my direction.

Then I realized. They'd filched my wallet, so they probably knew where I lived. I needed to call Karen, to warn her. But I didn't have a working phone. The clock showed ten after 3:00. The traffic report said that there was an accident at the 101 interchange. I wasn't moving.

Even on an ordinary day, an overturned tractor-trailer can destroy your plans in L.A. I don't know why I expected anything different; my meeting was never going to happen. So I formulated a plan: I'd drive to my agent's office, so he could fire me. But I'd at least tell him the story so he could call Karen and warn her not to come home, or hire a bodyguard, or something.

Oh, man.

Was I fucked or what?

Still, I did have $1,000 in my pocket, and that was enough. I couldn't go back to Commerce for a while, and maybe never. Who knew how often the Russian haunted those well-trod carpets? My frequent-player's card, however, was good to go in Gardena. I'd check in there, get a room for sixty-nine dollars a night, and easily win that back at the tables, no problem. Even if I hit a bad streak, I could probably survive for a month with what I had left in my checking account. And if I ran into a really good table one night, I might even be able to win Karen back with a wad of bills and a tale of pure success. Greater women, I figured, have been seduced by less. It wasn't the best situation in the world. But at least I had the skills to win big.

So I turned my car around at the next exit. I drove off in anticipation of a big night, and of hundreds of nights to come. Because there was nothing like a night spent playing poker: It was the great equalizer, the great humanizer, and the great eraser of differences. Except when it wasn't. But the hope remained for every numbers nerd, every bored housewife, every laid-off trucker, every hack screenwriter, and all the other poor saps out there who woke up one morning only thinking about cards and subsequently went about overturning their lives. Like everyone else in the world, it seemed, I floated along on a current of odds. Still, I figured that a little self-understanding would make me a dangerous man at the tables. And so I drove on, along the endless highways, thinking only of flopping trips, ace high on the river.

FISH

BY LIENNA SILVER

Fairfax District

Ivan Denisovich hated fish, but was obliged to buy several kilos of the rock-frozen cod. The loud and obnoxious saleswoman wrapped it in a piece of hard brown paper, her swollen red fingers with chipped nail polish barely bending from the moisture and cold. He obediently stuffed the package into the green net shopping bag, and struggled through the shoulder-to-shoulder crowd, almost losing his scarf to the pressing comrades.

Outside, he meticulously rebuttoned his coat and patted the treasured fish in the bag with his lined leather gloves. He knew Sofia Arkadievna would be happy with his purchase. A fat *dvornik*, an old woman in a padded cotton coat and white apron, was cleaning the sidewalk, her giant spade rhythmically scraping against the compressed snow. His breath fogged around him as he walked home through the narrow Arbat streets, listening to the crisp crunch under his feet. This sound was like balm to his wounds, mitigating the repulsive inevitability of having to eat and, even worse, smell the fish for a week.

"Ivan . . . Ivan . . . wake up!" He felt his wife's elbow poke his ribs. "Come on. Turn that damn box off. Let's go to bed."

Ivan Denisovich opened his eyes and stared at the fan that was slowly spinning above his head. Where was he? *Boje moy!* Good God! The Russian snow and the fish melted away, and instead he was sitting in Los Angeles on his brown velour couch next to his wife, Sofia Arkadievna. The television murmured something in English that he couldn't understand. The Asian commentator smiled and glanced at him as if she was a guest in their living room.

The apartment was dark except for the flicker of the screen. He knew he was home, but it wasn't quite right. He put on his slippers and silently shuffled behind Sofia Arkadievna to the bedroom. He didn't want to break the spell, still hoping to return to the frosted winter day in his dream and the hated frozen cod. He yearned to follow the icy street past the familiar tram stop, across the rails and through the arch into the dirty Moscow yard, past the elderly ladies gossiping on the bench, and up the broken stairs that reeked of fried fish.

He resented that Sofia Arkadievna had interrupted his dream. Lying on his back, listening to her scratchy snoring, he stared at the trees outside through the tulle curtains. The constant summer of Southern California was gentle on his bones, but turned his heart inside out. This country gave him everything that he could dream of, except he never dreamed of it. His eyes skipped across the white-and-gold lacquer bedroom that Sofia Arkadievna bought on a layaway plan from a neighborhood store. They didn't have to wait or get permission to buy the furniture. Just went and bought it, and it was delivered a few weeks later. Same thing with the furniture in the living room. Their daughter Sveta and her husband Alex, that red-haired *putz* with an idiotic smile, bought it for them when they finally moved to their government-subsidized apartment. Nothing had any history of his life imprinted on it; nothing held memory for him. It was all new and alien, and still smelled of fresh composition board. What was there to say?

He had grown into a pattern of sleeping during the day and staying awake at night, lying in bed and remembering things. It was as if he was trying to live on Moscow time. Sofia Arkadievna was mad, and Ivan wanted to go back to normal, but somehow couldn't. Sveta said he was depressed and should see a doctor, get one of those depression pills. To hell with that. He was not taking any brain pills. What if he wouldn't be able to remember anything? Oh no. No pills would help him with his condition. And then, who said people had to be happy all the time? How would they even know they were happy if there was no difference from one day to another? Come to think of it, being happy all the time would be just as tiring as being unhappy.

Sofia Arkadievna turned on her side and made him conform. Her soft breasts and belly cushioned and heated his aching back, the only things that were comforting and familiar in his life. He put his hands under his cheek and drifted into a restless sleep.

In the morning, Ivan Denisovich took a shower, flexing his biceps as he rinsed off the soap. His skin was sagging in a rippling sack under the arm, but his muscles beneath were still firm. Satisfied, he turned off the hot water and stood under the ice-cold jet, as he had done for fifty years, until his whole body burned in a tingle.

The sweet yeasty smell of *blinis* and smoldering butter wafted from the kitchen. He could hear Sofia Arkadievna bang pots, pans, and dishes in her usual morning whirlwind of activity. She was plump but not fat, and although she had changed through the years—her cheeks drooped, and her skin and eyes had lost their luster—she had not slowed down, and she kept her commanding attitude and agile walk.

"Stop admiring yourself. Breakfast is getting cold!" yelled Sofia Arkadievna through the door.

"Coming." Ivan Denisovich looked at his stupefied face in the foggy mirror. His nose had become longer and fleshier, even bulbous. His jaw had lost definition, and jowls flapped under his mouth on both sides, reminding him of catfish whiskers. A sorry sight. He shrugged, splashed Grey Flannel over his flushed cheeks, and pulled on the blue Adidas jogging suit.

The TV was already on, Russian programming delivered via satellite right to their Southern California home.

"A nightmare!" said Sofia Arkadievna, rolling *blinis* onto her plate. "Look what those blood-thirsty Chechens are doing again! There's no end to it . . . Sour cream or jam?"

"I'll take the Nutella," replied Ivan Denisovich, sitting down.

The screen flashed scenes from Grozny, where another car had been blown up and charred corpses were strewn across the pavement. Women in flowery babushkas wept, wiping away tears with dirty rags.

"Beasts. They are not human!" exclaimed Sofia Arkadievna, and sauntered over to the refrigerator. "How can they live like that?"

"It's their home."

"You want some juice?" She ignored his remark.

"*Neh*, my stomach is gurgly." Ivan Denisovich glazed the inside of a *blini* with a generous layer of Nutella and slowly rolled it around the fork into a tube.

Home. What a strange word. Its meaning confused Ivan

Denisovich. His mother died long ago, just before the war. And his father, after being liberated from Dachau, was sent directly to the Gulag, where he died after three months of hard labor. Funny how memory worked. The thought of home triggered the image of his exhausted father. Did he know that Ivan, then age fourteen, was also shipped to Siberia, as the son of a *traitor of the people?* It all seemed to have happened only yesterday, and at the same time in another life.

Ivan Denisovich remembered how after his release from the camps, he stood at a railroad station with a small backpack. The newspaper he had wrapped around his feet instead of puttees ripped inside his boots, but he was accustomed to the feeling. He had lived like that for two years, never fully warm. The sound of the approaching train pierced the Arctic silence. He bought a ticket to Kazakhstan, because it was hot, and *ex-politicals* were allowed to live there. He didn't have any aspirations; he was sixteen but didn't feel young, or excited at the long life ahead. He just wanted to be warm and have a place to sleep, any place, as long as it was only his, without cellmates.

Ivan Denisovich looked around the room, and it seemed eerie that he was sitting in Los Angeles, half the globe away from where he started.

"Ivan, where are you? I've been talking to you, and you're like a zombie." Sofia Arkadievna shook his shoulder. "What is it? Get out of your head, all I have to say. I have an assignment for you, dearie." She pushed a piece of paper across the table. A little furry kitten with a pink bow stared at Ivan Denisovich from the top of the to-do list. Sofia Arkadievna would not allow him to sit in front of the television all day. He had what she called *responsibilities.* Canned tuna and oatmeal, that's what his life had become.

"Later." He stuffed the list into his pocket and walked over to the couch to watch TV.

"Pick up the phone, my hands are wet!" yelled Sofia Arkadievna from the kitchen. Ivan Denisovich must have dozed off again, because he didn't hear the ring.

"Vanya?" Grigory Petrovich's familiar baritone flowed benevolently through the receiver. "Are you decent? *Davai*, get down. I'm waiting. We're going fishing in Santa Monica. My women are driving me crazy."

Grigory Petrovich was Ivan Denisovich's old school friend. He had a wife and a divorced daughter with two kids. They all lived together in a two-bedroom apartment in North Hollywood. Ivan Denisovich rarely visited him at night. The household was raucous, with children running and women yelling; besides, Sofia Arkadievna didn't like Grigory's wife, Valentina. She found her gaudy and low-class, not to mention ten years younger. Frankly, it was just as well, because Ivan Denisovich's eyes weren't what they used to be, and he preferred to stay home at night.

"Why fishing?" he whispered.

"Why not? Better than sitting in front of that talking box. Think: air, waves, the sun, and girls in bikinis."

"You can't eat that fish, the water's polluted," replied Ivan Denisovich, watching his wife clear the table, all the while figuring out how to escape without telling her he was going to the beach with Grigory.

"Hell you talking about? Who cares!" roared Grigory. "You hate fish anyway."

"I was just saying."

Grigory's brown Oldsmobile had no air-conditioning. They

kept the windows open, letting the breeze play with their messy wisps of gray hair. The oppressively hot day was unusual for January, but this year the whole winter was scorching, as if it were June. Sofia Arkadievna called it "earthquake weather."

"*Hooh,* my heart goes crazy in this heat," said Grigory Petrovich, patting his chest. He was wearing an old purple T-shirt with the yellow Lakers insignia, dark blue Adidas exercise pants, and sandals over striped socks. Round beads of sweat formed on his forehead and nose, and he wiped them off with a large crumpled handkerchief. "Live it up, Vanya. Eh, live it up! Vanya, Vanya, Vanya! What are we doing in Southern California anyway, my friend?"

Grigory pushed a cassette into the player and Gypsy music burst out the windows into the Fairfax midday traffic.

"Look, look at them." Grigory Petrovich pointed at the people crossing the street in front of them. "They don't know how to enjoy life, how to live. Look, not one of them feels the music."

"Turn it down a bit," replied Ivan Denisovich, worried that they were disturbing the peace. "Stop scaring people. Not everyone likes the Gypsies."

"You used to. What, now it's too Russian for you?"

"Russian? You're some Russian yourself." Ivan Denisovich was hurt. "You couldn't get a job because you were a Jew, and here you're suddenly a Russian, dancing Cossatski. *Tphew,*" he spit in anger.

"Okay, okay. Sorry. You're boiling over today. What's up?"

"Nothing. Mind your own business, that's what."

Grigory Petrovich didn't respond, and instead belted out at the top of his lungs, together with the Gypsies, "*Eh, once, and once more, and many, many, many more . . .*"

Ivan Denisovich loved the Gypsies. He didn't know what

had come over him. A rebellion to joy. He couldn't explain it. He just didn't have a taste for anything. Grigory was his best friend, now and always. Their relationship was rare and lucky for immigrants. They had lived across the street from each other back in Moscow, gone to school together, and later, when he came back from Kazakhstan, it was Grigory who helped him find a job. Even their wives' mutual animosity couldn't ruin their friendship. Recently, however, as Ivan Denisovich reflected on his past, he wondered if he would have been here in California had Grigory remained in Moscow, and secretly blamed his friend for ending up at the Pacific shores.

"Stop at Trader Joe's. Sofia asked me to buy a few things," mumbled Ivan Denisovich.

"And it'll all sit there in the sun while we're fishing? We'll stop on the way back. I have sandwiches in the cooler. Mortadella and Swiss on white. Your favorite. I made them myself, didn't want Valentina to know our plans. We're traveling incognito."

His constant playfulness irritated Ivan Denisovich. A grown man joking all the time. What's so funny? Two idiots traveled all the way around the world to escape from home, almost returning on the other side, stopping short, it seemed, only because of the ocean. Just like in the old revolutionary song, ". . . *and at the Pacific Ocean, did they finish their trek.*" Now what?

They parked at the mall as usual. Grigory Petrovich rigged his little cooler, a bucket, and two folding chairs to the luggage wheels, and handed Ivan Denisovich the two fishing rods and umbrellas.

"Don't let me forget to stamp the parking ticket at the mall on the way back."

"Give it to me. I'll do it now. Everything has to be *on the way back."* Ivan Denisovich hated the sound of his grouchy voice, but couldn't stop.

It was much cooler in Santa Monica, and the wind hadn't lost its winter prickle. Their usual spot was taken by two teenagers with Chinese tattoos and pierced lips. Ivan Denisovich and Grigory Petrovich walked further, toward the end of the pier, and, disappointed, squeezed into a small space between the enormous fat lady with wild gray hair, a permanent fixture at the pier, and two chain-smoking hobos, fishing for dinner. At least no one would complain when Grigory smoked, but fish could not be expected at this proximity to the competition.

They set up the chairs. Ivan Denisovich's umbrella kept dragging his bargain Sav-On chair with every gust of wind, no matter how he positioned it.

"Sit down, I'll fix it when I'm done," said Grigory Petrovich, untying the fishing rods.

"As if I don't know how. Look at this wind. We'll catch pneumonia here, thanks to your stupid plans," mumbled Ivan Denisovich.

His friend ignored him, adjusting his Lakers cap that was clipped to the back of his shirt.

Ivan Denisovich ripped the umbrella off his chair. Why would he need it anyway? People know too much here. Cancer? Crap. Too much information leads to panic. He was old enough to die of natural causes before skin cancer would catch up with him.

He sat down in his chair, enjoying the view. The sun heated up his face, but it was still a winter sun, caressing, not brutal. He took off his hat and let the sun tickle his bald spot. Funny, even now with nothing left to live for, it was hard to let go of all this: the expanse of the ocean, the hazy sprawl of the beach, the seagulls, the annoying rumble of the roller-coaster at the end of the pier. It was good to be alive. No, he was not ready. He got up and covered his head, protecting it from the sun.

"Here, put some on." He handed a tube of Coppertone to Grigory, who was already casting his rod on the water below, a cigarette hanging off his lower lip. "You should quit that crap, especially with your heart!"

"Hand me a beer. And stop being my wife."

"Where is it? I just put the cooler right here." Ivan Denisovich searched behind the chairs. The cooler had vanished, and so had the two hobos. He peered at the crowd and spotted the two emaciated figures in dirty clothes escaping down the pier.

"Grisha, look!"

Grigory Petrovich pulled on his glasses and immediately dashed after the hobos. *"Dergy ih! Pivo! Moyo pivo!"* he yelled in pursuit, his sandals flapping against his heels.

People stared at him and made way, probably thinking another nut had been prematurely released from a psychiatric hospital. The hobos were younger and faster. The cooler was the only thing slowing them down, because it had no handle. They opened it on the run, each grabbing a can of Coors and a foil-wrapped sandwich, and threw the cooler on the ground. The ice spilled onto the asphalt with a loud crashing sound that made everyone turn.

"Beer, my beer!" Grigory yelled in English, but too late. He slowed down and grabbed his chest.

The crowd disapproved generally, of both the hobos and this gibbering old fool. Ivan Denisovich watched, afraid to leave the rest of their stuff behind.

"Grish, come on, *nuuh*, forget the beer," he called. "Grisha, what's up? You sick?"

Grigory Petrovich coughed, holding his chest, then made a sign to his friend to wait. People stopped gawking and went back to minding their own business. A woman in a flowing florid dress picked up the cooler and the bottle of water that had rolled out, and together with her toddler carried them over to Grigory.

Nodding at them, Grigory searched in his pockets with one hand, and revealed an old melted Tootsie Roll. He handed it to the mesmerized boy, who automatically stretched out his hand, but the mother deftly snatched it and smiled at Grigory.

"The hell with you," he sighed, and walked back to Ivan Denisovich.

"Grish, you all right?"

"I'm dandy," replied Grigory, pale and still panting.

"Sit down." Ivan Denisovich pushed forward the chair, which immediately tipped over.

"A-ha-ha-ha!" exploded Grigory, and went into another coughing fit.

Ivan Denisovich handed him the recaptured bottle of water.

"The hell with it all." Grigory picked up the chair. "It's just too bad about the beer. The beer was a nice touch."

Ivan Denisovich patted him on the back. "Let's go, Vanya," he said. "Let's go to Plummer Park and play chess."

Ivan Denisovich lived near Plummer Park in West Hollywood, and he often came here to listen to the mellifluous simmer of Russian speech and the sound of dominoes slammed against the table boards. He would close his eyes and imagine he was in Russia, especially when jasmine was in bloom.

But the park was changing. Young mothers brought children here after the city had built a jungle gym. The yuppies in the area came to play tennis at the city courts, disrupting the old-country rhythms of the park with their loud laughter and dull thuds of the ball. The commanding and confusing sound of English had already subjugated the fading sounds of Russian, as adolescents, none of them Russian, mind you, gathered to watch the endless chess games that Russian retirees played on the picnic tables. They could still teach a thing or two to this underwear-flashing generation.

Grigory Petrovich and Ivan Denisovich bought lunch at the Russian market on the way back from the beach. They sat on benches across from each other at the unusually empty end of a picnic table and opened the white paper packages. The aroma of dark rye, spicy Russian mustard, and fresh Mortadella were enough to convince them that the seven dollars they had squandered was well worth it. Grigory Petrovich bit into the crunchy half-pickled cucumbers, available only at the Russian market that, for some reason, disguised itself under the enigmatic and misleading name, The European Deli. Life was good again.

"Set them up, Vanya. I'm gonna kick your butt, as they say in America." His teeth crunched against the taut flesh of the pickle, its subtle saltiness a perfect match for the robust flavor of the sandwich.

"*Black Sea and the sacred Baikal,*" Grigory blasted, following his opening gambit.

Ivan Denisovich wiped his forehead and neck with a handkerchief. The weather made it hard to concentrate. He was convinced that hot weather was responsible for the collapse of many ancient civilizations. Who could think in the heat?

Grigory unwrapped the dry salted fish from the market, and, holding it by the tail, hit it against the edge of the picnic table to soften it up.

"You're distracting me."

"*Tugodum*, lighten up, you old goat. We're not playing for money," laughed Grigory, peeling the skin off the fish.

"Don't you dare touch the chess pieces with those fishy fingers. It'll make me vomit."

"There you are again, just like Valentina. Nudge, nudge, whine, whine."

Ivan Denisovich, nauseous from the sight of the fish, and yet feeling suddenly at home, inhaled as if it were the aroma of lilacs in spring and moved his knight to the middle of the board in what he thought was a very elegant combination. Yet as soon as he let go of the piece, he realized his mistake. How could he not have noticed that he was exposing his king? How could he be so stupid? He felt embarrassed. If Grigory didn't see it, he would convert to Catholicism and start believing in miracles. Why was he playing chess instead of shopping for Sofia Arkadievna?

"*Nuuh*, Denisich, watch out! It's over, pal."

Grigory Petrovich grabbed his Queen, leaned back in a slow swoon, as if ready for a backstroke, and suddenly plunked back off the bench, flat on the ground. The children continued to run and giggle by the jungle gym, the chess and domino players were absorbed in their own games. Ivan Denisovich thought it was some kind of a joke again. He peeked under the table, but his friend remained on the ground, clutching the Queen in this stiff fist. Ivan Denisovich carefully slipped off the bench and stared at the lifeless body by his feet.

"*Pomogite!* Somebody, help! Call an ambulance!" he screamed, and dropped on his knees in front of Grigory. "Grisha, Grish! Come on! Cut it out! Look, I'm right here! Don't go! The ambulance is coming! Grisha! Somebody, help!" he yelled at the top of his lungs, shaking Grigory Petrovich, lifting his head off the dusty ground.

The children's laughter from the playground merged with the sharp siren of the approaching ambulance. Mothers clutched their babies as if death was contagious. A few men stopped their game of chess and surrounded the prostrate body.

Two exhausted paramedics, a man and a young woman, jumped out of the vehicle and checked Grigory Petrovich's pulse. They ordered the spectators to step back and pulled a box out of the van. The man efficiently exposed Grigory Petrovich's pallid chest with its flowerbed of gray hair, and attached the defibrillator pads to his skin. The girl pressed the button on the box, following her partner's signal. Grigory's body jolted on the ground, lifting his feet and head, and sprawled back, lifeless. He was like one of those rubber frogs that leaped when air was pumped into them through a tube. They did it again, this time his feet shook longer, but seemingly without any relationship to the rest of his body. They tried once more for good measure, but it was clear—he was gone.

Ivan Denisovich stood, paralyzed. His extremities stiffened and froze, despite the heat, and his head buzzed. He watched the paramedics load Grigory Petrovich into the van and close the door. Someone pointed to him, and the young woman in the paramedic uniform shook his shoulder. She held a pad in her hand and asked him something. He didn't respond. She offered him water.

He pushed away the plastic cup and whispered, "Grisha."

She handed him a pen and held her pad pointing to the empty page. He understood, and wrote, *Grigory Petrovich Shurov—May 13, 1931, Moskva, U.S.S.R.* He wished he could add *war hero*, or something important to the line, but Grigory didn't have any distinctions, and was too young to have participated in the war.

Ivan Denisovich climbed inside the ambulance and sat across from the zipped-up plastic bag that used to be his best friend. He tried to avoid looking at the slug-shaped object laid out on the gurney, but his eyes kept drifting to the head, because the zipper was right over Grigory's large nose, and Ivan worried about it leaving scratches on his face.

He had to tell Valentina, but how could he? He remembered a Jewish joke where a man was sent to gently deliver the news to the wife that her husband had passed away. He rang the doorbell and an attractive woman opened the apartment door. "Is widow Abramowitz home?" he asked, removing his hat. "Why widow? I have a husband," she replied with arrogance. "*Bubkas* is what you have instead of a husband," blurted out the man, and ran for the exit.

Ivan Denisovich smiled and immediately started to weep, because he knew that no one except Grigory would have understood him joking now.

The door opened and Valentina stared at him from the dim apartment. The smell of burning canola oil enveloped the two of them like a nostalgic blanket.

"*Nuuh*, finally. Where's my oaf? Parking? We've been going crazy looking for you. Sofia called four times." She winked at Ivan Denisovich. "Jealous."

Valentina's blue eye shadow had caked over her eyelids,

her hair was up in soft pink rollers, and she wore white fluffy rabbit slippers. *The Queen of Fucking Everything* sparkled from her apron.

Ivan Denisovich had rehearsed his lines several times on the way from the hospital, but *Hold yourself together, Valentina, your husband is deceased* just wouldn't roll off his tongue.

"Valyusha, our Grishka is gone," he gushed, and collapsed on her shoulder.

"Are you drunk? Idiot." She shook him, trying to find his face. "What the hell you're talking about?"

"He's dead, Valya!" slobbered Ivan Denisovich. "Something's burning in the kitchen."

Valentina stood there blocking the entrance, staring not so much at Ivan Denisovich as inside herself. She pushed him out of her way and dashed downstairs, her slippers flapping against her rough bare heels.

"He's not there," yelled Ivan Denisovich, and followed her down, holding onto the railing.

Valentina darted to the corner and looked up and down the street, then froze, watching Ivan Denisovich's solitary figure approach her. His shoulders sank and his face turned sullen. He opened his arms to embrace her, uncertain which one of them needed to be held more.

"No. No, no." She pushed him away. "He can't do this to me." She folded her arms and pursed her lips as if plotting revenge for Grigory Petrovich's return.

"Come," Ivan Denisovich said quietly. "Let's go in. You'll burn down the house."

They sat on the sofa holding onto each other. The TV flickered with grainy images from Russian *Candid Camera*. A pretty young woman with fake hair glued to her back asked strangers on the beach to help her apply sunblock. Some laughed, some were disgusted and walked away, and some expressed sympathy to the poor girl, suggesting electrolysis. The phone rang ten times, but Valentina and Ivan Denisovich didn't move, staring at the TV screen.

Ivan Denisovich suddenly felt what he hadn't felt for a long time. He wasn't sure if it was Valentina or the hairy woman in a bikini on the screen. He glanced at Valentina's soft round breasts, something he had avoided for the last twenty years. That one time was a mistake, they shouldn't have done it, and Valentina and he agreed to keep it a secret from their spouses. They didn't even particularly like each other, but there they were. He always thought it was her fault, all that ass swish-swooshing she liked to do, and those low-cut dresses she flaunted. He used to tell Grigory Petrovich that this kind of exhibitionism wouldn't lead to anything good, but Grisha liked it. Ivan Denisovich later wondered if his friend knew about *them*, and even stopped seeing Grigory for a few years. He also wondered if she ever did it with anyone else. Secretive little wench. She knew what she was doing.

Ivan Denisovich watched Valentina's hand go up and down her thigh. It was like a tic. She hadn't stopped for ten minutes. Just rubbing and rubbing, rubbing and rubbing. He cleared his throat. Valentina's daughter and grandchildren were not coming back for another two hours. Was she thinking the same? Did she know what he was thinking? He suddenly wanted to undo her dress and spill her soft large body onto the sofa.

"*Oy, kak pusto! Kak strashno! Oy,* Vanya, why?" She tossed from side to side over the barely rumpled sheets. "So lonely

. . . so scary. So empty . . . so alien . . ." She glanced at him, sitting on the side of the bed. "Even you," and she wrapped her face in the pillow to muffle her weeping.

Ivan knew he should hold her, try to calm her down, but he was overwhelmed by what had just happened, and couldn't bring himself to touch Valentina again. The thought of embracing her warm, flaccid body whose faint perspiration had a completely foreign flavor nauseated him. He turned away, and another smell, Grigory Petrovich's dear smell, wafted from the pillow, and he noticed a few strands of his friend's hair on it. He simultaneously wanted to throw the pillow against the wall and bury his face in it forever.

Ivan Denisovich reluctantly patted weeping Valentina on her broad undulant back and grabbed his boxers off the chair.

The sun was down and the apartment would soon fill with children's laughter, regardless of what had happened.

"Do you want me to stay?" he asked, pulling on his pants.

"No, we'll manage. We always do, we have to," Valentina sniffled, wiping her nose on the discarded T-shirt. "You ain't Grisha, don't even try."

She stood up and undid her rollers in front of the black lacquer vanity that had been purchased from the same store as Sofia's. She suddenly seemed taller, more imposing, despite her bright pink bra and underwear. Her peroxide-blond hair slipped down her round shoulders in large stiff waves.

"*Nuuh*, what are you staring at? Haven't seen a naked woman?" she smirked, shaking out her curls like a girl.

"No, I'm just . . ." and he realized he hadn't for some time.

"Sveta, pass the fish," said Sofia Arkadievna to her daughter. "*Oy*, I still can't get over it." She squeezed Ivan Denisovich's arm in sympathy.

The TV was on, a low hum in the back of the room. Sveta and her husband Alex had stopped by for dinner. Ivan Denisovich noticed they always came to eat at the end of the month, probably ran out of money. No wonder. Her husband was an idiot, spending money on stupid haircuts and designer T-shirts. He was not a husband, he was a liability.

"*Pap*," said Alex, chewing the fish and mashed potatoes with his mouth open.

Where did she find this treasure? Well worth immigrating for.

"I have a name."

"Oh, c'mon, *Pap*, we're all family here."

"Grigory was family. And you . . ." Ivan Denisovich shook his hand.

"Stop it, Papa. What did he ever do to you?" whined Sveta.

She was not his Svetka anymore. His Svetka who used to jump and laugh until her braids were undone. She had lost her sense of humor, as if being dull meant being smart.

"To Grisha's soul, may he rest in peace." Sofia Arkadievna lifted her glass filled with vodka to the brim.

Ivan Denisovich thought it strange that his wife, who didn't like vodka and rarely drank at all, was about to chug a full glass of the clear demon.

"A good man is gone." She put down the empty glass and inhaled on a slice of brown rye. "Let's go see Valentina. I don't treat her right. I should give her something."

Ivan Denisovich realized that his wife was already drunk, and acting out of character. He gazed around the room as if he had accidentally entered the wrong apartment. He searched for something familiar, something to hold onto, and was happy to see the little yellow-and-brown throw that Sofia

Arkadievna had crocheted when Svetka was born. Russian newspapers and magazines were scattered on the glass coffee table, covered with fingerprints. The blue-and-white flowery china—one of the few things they brought with them when they emigrated—held the proverbial fried cod, mashed potatoes, and beet salad. Stolichnaya vodka in Czech crystal glasses with golden trim completed the setting. The curtains were drawn, shutting out the world, and on the TV screen an old black-and-white film with *Katyusha* missiles blasting against the night sky annihilated Nazi troops in the field. Ivan Denisovich almost believed he was back in Russia, and for a moment felt warm inside, as if the shot of vodka had spread slowly through his veins into the most remote areas of his body, pushing out the pain. He suddenly loved everyone, even his son-in-law with his idiotic spiky hair.

"*Milaya.*" He hadn't called Sofia Arkadievna "my beloved" for many years. He reached for her face and noticed she was crying. "*Milaya*, don't cry. It will be all right."

"How would you know, you old goat?" She sounded just like Grigory.

"Mama?" Sveta stared at her weeping mother from across the table. "Ma, what's wrong?"

"*Ma, ma!*" Sofia Arkadievna mocked her daughter. "That's what," and she grabbed the platter and threw it across the room. It hit the wall just below the family picture gallery, and the fish mixed with broken china slid down the wall and landed on the polished top of the bookcase.

Sveta jumped from the table, covering her mouth with both hands, as if afraid to release any sound. The men didn't move.

On the screen, a hazy-eyed war heroine sang "Moscow Nights" to a room full of somber officers.

"I'm sorry," cried Sofia Arkadievna, and plunked her head over her arms on the table. "I'm so sorry, Vanya. For everything."

Sveta made a sign to her husband to help her clean up the mess. He wanted to finish his food, but she handed him a rag and a bucket to take care of the fish on the bookcase.

Ivan Denisovich remained still. Everything in his past had to be suddenly rearranged, like a Rubik's cube when you moved one square and the whole thing collapsed and you had to start over. Only he had no time left to put it all together again. He stood up, unexpectedly sorry for himself, picked up his keys, and walked out the door.

He reached the corner. The night was cool, but jasmine filled the air. The leaning palms looked like bottle brushes against the dark red glow of the evening sky. A young couple across the street laughed, drinking out of a brown bag and smoking. Ivan Denisovich approached them and demonstrated that he wanted a cigarette. They smiled, handed him a Marlboro, and offered to light it. He nodded in gratitude and limped away, his legs rubbery from the first puff.

Cars zoomed by, up and down Fountain Avenue. An older woman with a grocery bag struggled with her keys. A black teenager coasted on his bike, hands off the bar, just like Grigory used to, back in Moscow. A Latina beauty pulled her screaming son out of a beat-up Toyota; then a paraplegic rolled past him in a motorized wheelchair and disappeared inside an apartment building.

Ivan Denisovich shivered and regretted having forgotten his jacket. He glanced at the window on the third floor that framed the orange-tinted light from his apartment. The balcony was filled with old suitcases, geraniums in clay pots, and laundry hanging from the line. Two plastic chairs, his and

Sofia Arkadievna's, stood in the middle, facing the street. They often sat there in the evenings, drinking cold tea and watching neighbors down below. He noticed that the chair cushions were still there. How many times did he have to tell her not to leave them out overnight?

He threw his cigarette on the ground, crushed it against the asphalt with his slipper, and shuffled back home.

ROGER CRUMBLER CONSIDERED HIS SHAVE

BY GARY PHILLIPS

Mid-City

R oger Crumbler considered his shave. On this his fiftieth birthday, he was pleased that while his stubble became grayer each week, he still had a head of hair—and it was still dark.

The face in his bathroom mirror had held up fairly decently for half a century. Though not for the first time he considered minor cosmetic surgery to correct the bags under his eyes, a trait among the men in his family. Was it true that Preparation H reduced the puffiness? There was a kind of logic to that since hemorrhoids were what . . . ? An enlarged vein, right? But what caused those sacks under the eyes? Fluid? He'd have to Google that. It was always good to have something new to learn.

Working the shaving gel into his whiskers, Roger smiled, mentally outlining the day ahead. At the office he had to complete a final review of the Carlson Foundation financials. There had been no major blips on the radar save for some inconsistencies on a pass-through grant from a city agency. The Carlson Foundation funded reading programs for low-income youth, and the city of Los Angeles was a partner in that endeavor. Such inconsistencies were not unusual given the accounting procedures of the bureaucrats versus the private sector. This was a minor concern, and he would resolve it with a phone call or two to his City Hall contacts.

Yet it was because of those inconsistencies that he was able to do what he'd done. For him. For Nanette.

Roger turned his head this way and the other, making sure he'd covered his face evenly as he massaged the warm foam into his pores. At one of those precious west side fundraising dinner parties saving spotted owls (or maybe it was spotted actors), a dermatologist with skin flawless as plastic told him that you should allow five minutes for your night beard to soak properly. He didn't adhere to this advice each morning, but he wasn't going to be fifty every morning either. This was, after all, a big day.

After reconciling the financials, there would be the regular weekly staff meeting. He'd already written and copied his report earlier this week, so there should be no surprises there either. The company, Nathanson and Nathanson, was a boutique CPA firm that nonetheless commanded more than eight million in billing last year, with a clientele that ranged from old-line family foundations like Carlson to heavy hitters in the film and music business. Roger was senior vice-president and was up for partnership.

That in itself was something, considering the firm had been started in the '40s, when there were still a smattering of orange groves along Wilshire. Run and grown by the founder, Sig Nathanson, then turned over to one of the sons, Gabe, and nephew Martin, in the '70s. The only other partner outside of the family had been a member of the founder's temple, and Roger was not a member. Unlike the late Sammy Davis, Jr., he'd only joked over drinks about converting. And what about Whoopi Goldberg? She wasn't really a member of the tribe, was she? Something else to Google.

He dutifully stroked his double blade through the foam.

The reassuring sound of whiskers being loped off were the low notes accompanying the chirping of birds in the tree outside his second-story bathroom window. Post the staff meeting he'd have a light lunch at his desk. He wasn't actually much for diets, but when he'd had the irregular heartbeat detected at age forty-five, he finally quit smoking and resolved to loose the fat.

Roger guided his razor underneath his jaw. Initially he'd hated running. He'd tried the treadmill at the gym his wife belonged to, but found that boring. Yet jogging through his neighborhood—*Wilshire Vista*, the upscalers called it—he had sights and sounds, and this kept him occupied. In the five years of this regime, including regular sessions with weight machines, he'd lost forty pounds. He ran a palm over his handiwork. For a man his age, his wife and girlfriend both told him amorously, he looked reasonably fit and even a little buffed.

He worked the razor on his upper lip, recalling fondly the moustache he'd also shed five, no, more like four years ago. That's when he'd met Nanette. Finished, he toweled off the excess of lather and dabbed on aftershave, then stepped back into the bedroom.

His wife, Claudia, was up and moving about. He watched with lascivious interest as she bent over to search in her underwear drawer. Usually she wore sweats or pajama pants and a top, but this morning, this birthday, she wore only lacy purple panties.

Roger sat on the bed, picturing himself as David Niven in *Raffles*. "Have I mentioned how spectacular your ass is, honey?"

"You always know what to say to a woman." She pushed him back and straddled him, nuzzling and biting his neck.

"Glad you woke me up this morning," he said, pulling her

down and kissing her full on the mouth. He was going to miss her. Yes, he certainly was.

"You didn't do too bad for an old dog."

"Careful, I might have to show you my double play."

She smiled, biting her lower lip. This always got to him, even after decades of seeing it. "I'd like to, baby, but I have to hit that inventory this a.m. You know how that tight-ass Pelecanos gets." Claudia managed a heavy-equipment rental service.

"Forget your clown boss. He couldn't find balls in a bowling alley if it wasn't for you." He slipped his hand inside her panty and caressed that wondrous backside. His wife reluctantly broke free.

"Tonight we'll have all kinds of time," she said.

"Well, I don't know. At my age, Lord knows, I need my rest."

She shook a glossy purple nail at him. "You just be ready and don't drink too much."

He chuckled. "I won't." Damn, she looked good.

The phone rang. He reached for it but Claudia moved quicker and plucked the handset loose.

"Hello?" Then, "Oh, hi, sweetie." She listened some more, glancing once or twice at her husband, frowning.

Roger languidly reposed on the bed, but a spring was winding in the base of his spine. That had to be their daughter on the phone. She attended Cal Berkeley up north. Was there some emergency? If so, what would that do to his schedule? But he had to be cool. *Can't let 'em see you sweat,* he reminded himself.

"All right, honey. We'll see you tonight."

"Why's she coming home?" he asked as his wife hung up. "There some problem?"

"Not really . . ." Claudia began.

"Not really?" he said more shrilly than he wanted. "This is the middle of the school year, Claudia." Now what did he just tell himself? *Keep it on low burn, man. Low burn.* He rose, clasping his wife's shoulders. "Sorry, I didn't mean to get all tense. You know how us pensioners get mood swings."

Claudia Crumbler-Morris looked preoccupied, fooling with a towel. "Janice's coming home because she doesn't have class until Monday, and wants to talk to us about something."

Roger wondered aloud, "Dropping out?"

"Or pregnant."

"Aw, hell no." He began to stomp around the room. "We're too damn young to be grandparents."

"No, we're not."

"Jesus."

Claudia chuckled. "I don't think she's pregnant."

"She's twenty and we've both seen how them knotheads with their pants hanging down around their cracks drool at her."

Claudia was heading toward the shower. "She's not attracted to those kind of boys."

"Even boys with slide rules like a little—"

"Roger," she admonished.

"Taste," he declared.

"Heathen." She closed the bathroom door and ran her shower. He knew she wasn't that sure Janice wasn't pregnant, and neither was he.

And if she was with child, then what of his plans involving Nanette? It wasn't like he could pull this off any time he felt like doing it. He finished dressing. It would be casual today, the pressed chinos, button-down shirt, sports jacket, no tie. It was his birthday and it was expected he'd be coasting once the Carlson file was closed out.

Putting his socks on, the ones with the blue hourglasses, he reveled in the simplicity and beauty of the virus he'd planted in his firm's computers more than two years ago. At 9:24 tonight, his new life would begin.

By then he and Nanette would be heading east, toward Texas, in the used car they'd bought more than a year ago. He'd gotten the brakes fixed, the head gasket replaced and what have you, so that the vehicle was completely reliable for the getaway. And, most importantly, the final transfer of the funds he'd siphoned off, little by little, had been completed three days ago. The computer crash would cover his nefarious deeds for weeks, time enough to set up his new life with the younger woman.

Naturally, Roger would be a suspect, but he'd be gone, no forwarding. The cops and the firm would hammer at Claudia, give her a rough going over, but she was innocent. She didn't have a clue about his plans.

"What time will you be back home? I know you're going to have drinks with Wayne and the guys."

"What time is Janice supposed to be here?"

"About 7:30, she said."

"Alone?"

His wife dangled an earring from her lobe. "Good question." She blew him a kiss. "You have such a suspicious mind."

"I'll be back here no later than 8."

"All right. See you then, Rog." She gave him a peck, then gripped his lower face in her hand. Using her tongue, but keeping her fresh carmine lips off his, she probed his mouth. "Love you."

"Love you too."

As she hummed and walked down the stairs, he stood at the railing, watching her go. He remained there, hearing her car start up and fade away. After tonight, he'd never see her or his daughter again. But he was resolved, he was going to spend the second half, well, really, if he was lucky and kept exercising and watching what he ate, the next thirty years with a woman twenty years his junior, plus some two and a half million dollars in ill-gotten gains richer.

That was an amount a bling bling rapper like 50 Cent or actor Tom Cruise might sneer at, hardly enough for them to get out of bed. But it was sufficient for a humble man like Roger Crumbler.

The down payment had been made through intermediaries on a condo in Port Saint Charles in Barbados. And through budgeting and living within their means, they'd be comfortable. They wouldn't be driving Jags or Bentleys, nor vacationing on a whim, but it's not like they'd have to subsist on Top Ramen.

And should the need or notion arise, Roger had also entertained money laundering for a select list of individuals. Certainly more than once over the years, several clients of the firm had hinted at such. Millionaires, more than the middle class, were willing to step over the line to hold onto that which they felt entitled to by birth or happenstance.

Wayne Wardlow, the Carlson Foundation's executive director, was not a possibility in that department. Though it was Wayne who had inspired Roger.

"Hell yes, I'm tappin' that ass," he'd joked. Referring to a woman, a freelance writer Wardlow had met doing an article about socially involved foundations for *Los Angeles* magazine.

"Okay, P. Diddy," Roger had remarked to the man whose

face should illustrate WASP in the dictionary. They were in the locker room getting dressed after their basketball game and shower.

"I love black pussy—you don't know what you're missing, son." Wardlow knocked him playfully in the shoulder.

"And you have lost your natural cotton-pickin' mind," Roger said, slipping into his trousers.

"Rog, getting some on the side at our age is cheaper than buying a sports car, and a damn sight more fun." He then grabbed his crotch like an oversexed sophomore in high school and bucked his hips.

Okay, it wasn't really fair to lay this at Wayne Wardlow's doorstep. Roger was a grown man. He made the decision to kindle a romance with Nanette, who'd flirted with him that day at the Barnes and Noble in the Grove. A pretty woman like her browsing in the Social Science section, able to cite the specific failures of strongman Robert Mugabe's policies in Zimbabwe, and argue the cultural significance of the late Rick James's music. How could he not be hooked?

His cell phone rang, and he knew only too well the number on its screen.

"How does it feel to be a geezer who has two women panting to fuck the shit out of you?" Nanette said huskily.

"You have a way with a phrase, have I mentioned that?"

"Are you hard? Or did the old lady drain you?"

"I want you so bad."

"Me too."

"Everything ready?"

"Ready and steady."

He hesitated—should he mention his daughter coming to town?

"What? Worried? Having second thoughts? That's understandable, this is serious."

"Don't I know. Everything's fine. I can't wait to see you." Don't say anything, don't put a jinx on this opportunity.

"I'll be thinking about you all day, Roger. Wish you were here to find out how wet I am."

"I will soon, baby."

"You got that right."

He pressed the cell off and nodded his head. They'd even accounted for this. For the last few months he'd been using disposable cell phones, also carrying his regular one for his wife's calls.

Outside, Roger sat in his idling car, looking at the house he was not going to see again after today. It was far from a palace, but they'd lived in this two-story Spanish-Mediterranean since Janice had been three. The paint jobs, the patching, the lawn that needed re-seeding, staying here while Claudia took Janice to the Valley during the '92 riots— a pint of Jack Daniel's and a revolver he'd never fired, his false fortifications. There had been the hole in the roof beneath the tiles that had ruined their bedroom ceiling, those ornery possums prowling in the bushes in the backyard he'd chased off with a golf club, the time Janice learned to ride her bike up and down the block. The house was the touchstone to a vast chapter in his life.

He backed the car out of the driveway and made a slow tour along Curson, taking it all in as if for the first time—the old timers and the others, the newbies with their walls enclosing their front yards, the redone homes with the Southwest flare replete with landscapes of cacti and native plants—how his neighborhood, his part of Mid-City, had changed in the years they'd lived here.

Roger waved at Dorothy, one of his long-time neighbors, walking her Chow mix. He choked up, but pulled it together and moved on; there was no time for cheap sentimentality. After making a turn at the signal, he picked up speed heading east on Olympic, nearing L.A. High where he'd gone his junior and senior years, lettering in basketball and track. His folks— his dad had worked for the county as a bus dispatcher for the then Rapid Transit District, and his mom a legal secretary— had saved enough to move from what they called the east side in those days, South Central now, and bought a tidy one-story on Norton just south of Pico.

His father had died in '99 and his mother, still active and working part-time at a senior center, had moved back to Oakland where she was from. How would what he was about to do affect her? Would it age her? Would she hate him? Blame Claudia? Take it out on Janice? No, his mother was a rational, strong woman. She'd probably denounce him from the pulpit of her church and pray for his lost, misguided soul. There'd be a round of "amens" and shaking of heads and comforting their troubled sister by the congregation. She'd done what she could to raise him right, some people are just born to be bad, they'd commiserate.

To get his mind off his mother's pending disappointment, he turned on the radio. He was pleased to hear that the forecast was sunny and breezy, a typical day in L.A. At Highland, he went north.

At the office he reconciled the inconsistency with the Carlson financials after one phone call and a subsequent fax from his buddy at the County. In deference to his friend Wayne Wardlow, he'd also stolen money from his foundation. If he hadn't, then Wayne would have come under suspicion and scrutiny. And that might disclose his friend's continuing relationship with his paramour, and that would surely weigh on Roger's conscience.

"Happy birthday, Rog."

"Thanks, Gabe." The son had stepped into Roger's office.

"Just want you to know, it's all downhill from here." Gabriel Nathanson was twice divorced and fifty-four.

"That's what I'm afraid of."

Nathanson clapped him on her shoulder. "I'll see you over at the Bounty, I'll buy a round."

"That's great, Gabe."

"I tried to get that drip Marty to come along, but you know how he is."

Roger dredged up a camaraderie chuckle it had taken him years to perfect. "Yes, I do." Martin Nathanson's idea of cutting loose was putting ketchup on his scrambled eggs.

"And next week, let's you, me, and sourpuss sit down, okay, partner?"

"Sure, Gabe. I look forward to it."

The son left, whistling.

There it was. Roger was going to betray a firm with a reputation for spotless honesty and forthrightness of, well, of more than sixty years. Would they recover from the taint his theft would smear them with, or sink under a sea of accusations and blame? That and the avalanche of lawsuits sure to come. And though Roger was not much of a standard-bearer for the race, there was that too. A black man, albeit middle class and middle-aged, married for over twenty years to a white woman, but a black man nonetheless, who had gained the trust of his Jewish bosses and in effect stolen from them. What would be the fallout from that? Strenuous finger-pointing at the next CPA convention, for sure.

And what of the betrayal of his wife and daughter? Wasn't that the biggest crime of all? Running off with a younger black woman, fine as she may be? His stomach gurgled as he admonished himself. This was a time to keep his mind focused, not a time for butterflies and second-guessing. He wanted to call Nanette, wanted so desperately to hear her say how much she loved him, how she'd never felt this way about a man before.

He suppressed the urge and went about his tasks, forcing himself not to watch the clock, not to mentally count down the hours till he started anew. Never again the same old 9-to-5, mortgage-paying, block-club-going Roger. The hours eked by and finally he was sitting in the back room of the Bounty on Wilshire in what was becoming part of the growing Koreatown.

The HMS Bounty was a time warp steak-and-booze emporium left over from the days of pounding down a couple of Scotches over lunch, when *cholesterol* sounded like the name of a new hair color line. It was where you could find a booth named for L.A. native Jack Webb, and across the street from the ghost of the Ambassador Hotel where presidential candidate Robert Kennedy had been assassinated in 1968. The hotel was no more, and a high school and shops were being built on the grounds.

"Here's to my ace, Roger. May the next fifty be yours for the taking," Wayne Wardlow toasted after they'd sung an off-key but effusive "Happy Birthday."

The waitress brought out a chocolate cake, his favorite.

"Of course, we only used five candles for symbolism's sake, since we didn't want to torch the joint," Wardlow joked, getting a round of guffaws.

"Here's to you, Roger," Gabe Nathanson echoed.

"Thanks, gents." Roger clinked his glass against the

others' and drank. This was his second gin and tonic and it was going to be his limit. It was seventeen past 6:00 and it was getting harder for him to laugh and seem at ease. He had to go home and find out about his daughter, a last intimacy with Claudia, he owed her that, and then Nanette. *One foot right before the other, Roger.* Just like walking across the street. Though you could get run over.

"What's up, champ?" Wardlow sidled up next to him. "Looks like you got something on your mind."

"Being fifty."

Wardlow had more of his whiskey. "I hear that. But things change, yeah? Don't want to look back and have a trunk full of regrets." He upended his tumbler and signaled for another. "Getting this age, too old to be innovative but just enough juice left in the tank to try something different, it hits you, doesn't it? You can keep doing what you're doing, stay in that rut till you maybe make retirement, and hope you can still manage to wipe your own butt and have enough to buy a few beans and tortillas. Or take a chance on some-thing." He looked off, beyond the walls.

"Exactly," Roger agreed.

Later, after the goodbyes and a promise to play nine holes with Wardlow and a couple of the fellas, Claudia called him on his cell as he headed home.

"Janice isn't here."

"What? She turn around and go back?"

"No. Her cell phone is suddenly disconnected. I couldn't leave a message, and I haven't heard from her."

"You just now telling me this?"

"Don't yell at me. It's just a little past 7:30, the time I fig-ured she'd be here."

"You're right, I'm sorry. Think she's at one of her friends' houses? Could she have stopped on the way and maybe dropped her phone and broke it?"

"Then why wouldn't she use their phone to call?"

"Look, it's not dire yet or anything. We should be calm."

"I am, I'm just, you know, could it have something to do with why she came down?"

"I don't know. We have some of her friends' numbers. Girls from high school."

"I'm going to call them."

"Okay. I'll be home shortly." He hung up and rang Nanette to fill her in.

"Why didn't you tell me she was coming to town?"

"I didn't think it was going to be a big thing."

"So what are you going to do?" she asked.

"I can't take off till I know what's going on with Janice."

"I know that, I'm not the unfeeling ho," she barked.

"That's not what I meant. I can't stop the virus. Anyway, everyone's gone home, it would be my code and time stamp registered on the alarm pad if I went back to the office now."

Her tone softened. "What about the money in the accounts? We can access the funds at any time, right?"

"Theoretically, yes. But once the hard drives are probed, I can't be sure there won't be traces. When they attempt to resurrect the files, they'll dig deep. The virus was merely a way to give us the time we needed to get to the islands."

"Then find your daughter, darling, and call me back. It still won't make a difference if we leave tonight, tomorrow, or next week. Those computer files won't be recovered that fast. In fact, when they go down and you're around being all concerned, that will be even better, less attention on you."

"Okay. Talk to you soon."

"Okay, baby."

Roger arrived at his house and was surprised to see his wife's car wasn't there. She called him on his cell as he unlocked the front door. "Janice had some car trouble, I went to pick her up. Should be back in half an hour."

"Fine, I'll be here." Roger went inside, checking the time and gauging his next moves. The virus had launched, it was real now. He was elated. He was getting aroused as he fantasized about the money and his woman. Giddy, he took out his BlackBerry and punched in a code. The results on his screen sobered him. He put in more numbers, and again got the same results. *Zero.*

Reeling like he'd been hammered by a heavyweight's blow, Roger dropped to his knees, fighting for air. He dropped the BlackBerry before him, as if it were a totem he could invoke favor through. The accounts in the Swiss banks and the one in the Caymans were empty. He kneeled there, blinking and kneading his hands. There was only one other person who knew about them. He rose, a man with renewed purpose.

Not fifteen minutes later, Roger Crumbler was surprised when Nanette answered her door. She lived in a duplex near Motor he'd helped her rent under a false name.

"Hi, Rog," she said as he rushed inside.

"Well?" He held the BlackBerry in front of her face.

"Well, what?"

"The money, Nanette, the goddamn money I risked everything to steal. For us."

"I don't have it. Obviously."

"Really?" He stalked through the apartment, not sure

what he'd find or do as he looked in the bedroom and the closets. "You're full of shit, baby. You must have the money. No one else knew about the accounts but you."

"Keep your voice down, Roger."

"Fuck that." He was breathing hard, sweat glazing his brow. Fists balled, he blared, "You're playing some kind of game with me, aren't you? Think I'm stupid."

"Roger, if I had the money, why would I be here waiting for you?"

He grabbed her arm. "You tell me."

"Let go." She jerked free. "So let me get this straight, you're claiming the money is gone all of a sudden? The money from the accounts you set up, the money from the accounts you created passwords for? *That* money?" She glared at him, nostrils flaring.

"Oh, I see. Very clever. Make it seem like you're the innocent here. When it's perfectly clear you're trying to pull some shit on me."

"What about this, asshole. What if you planned this all along, come storming in here pretending you can't find the Benjamins, and be all outraged and get me sucked in. Then send me off to look for the money and you take off with it. Shit," she said, disgusted. "Without me giving you the backbone, you'd never have stolen that money. You'd keep being a glorified bookkeeper until you got your gold watch and your once-a-week handjob from your wife."

"Shut the fuck up. I need to think." He wanted to beat the truth out of her.

"*You* shut the fuck up." She shoved him. "And get out of here. Now that I see what a pussy you really are, I wouldn't go to the corner liquor store with you."

He was shaking in anger. "Now you hold on."

"Get out of her before I call the cops on your useless ass. You probably got all nervous and hit the wrong key, sending our money to some South American dictator's account." She laughed hollowly. "How the fuck could I have seen a future with you? You're pathetic, Roger."

"You're not getting rid of me. We're going to find that money together. This is my only chance, Nanette."

"You're unstable." She moved to the door and held it open. "Leave."

"I'm not going until I get my money." He stalked toward her. "My fuckin' money, understand me, bitch?"

"Oh, okay." She slapped him hard. "Now get to steppin'. I don't want to ever see you again. We're through—get it, motherfuckah?" she yelled. "We're through! Fuck you, your money, and your sorry little dreams."

He popped her on the point of her jaw and she rocked back, dazed. He grabbed her arms with both of his hands and shook her. "I want my money!" he screamed.

She lunged forward and bit his ear as he reflexively turned his face away. He yowled in pain and let her go. Nanette ran and grabbed a screwdriver out of a kitchen drawer. "Get the fuck out of here or so help me, Roger, I'll gut you." Red washed her teeth and mottled her lips. The lips that all day he'd longed to kiss.

"Look, let's—"

"Hey!" a voice called from below. "I've called the police on you two!" An approaching siren punctuated the warning.

"Get out of here," Nanette repeated.

"What are you going to tell the cops?"

Her eyes were pitiless. "Get going, Roger."

He ran from the duplex and ripped away in his car. The downstairs neighbor was out on the lawn, watching Roger go.

Blood congealed in his eardrum, and some of it had dripped on his jacket and shirt. His cell phone rang, and he recognized his daughter's number on the screen.

"Daddy?"

"Janice. Where have you been?"

"Waiting for you and Mom at the house. Aren't we supposed to go out to dinner with your friends?"

"What?"

"Mom called me last Wednesday and said it would be good if I came down this weekend because it was your fiftieth birthday and she was having a party for you at this fancy restaurant."

"She . . ." he began, but didn't finish. "You didn't have car trouble?"

"No. Mom told me to be home around 8:30. I got in town earlier and went and saw Ruthie and them, you know. I called her and told her that."

Roger looked at his watch. It was 9:01. "And your mother's not there?"

"She isn't. I called her cell and got her answering message. Are you on your way home?"

"Yes, dear. I'll see you in a few minutes." They severed the connection. Roger was heading toward his house but pulled over on Venice and parked. He called their mutual friends. Nothing. Hadn't seen or heard from Claudia. He called her friends. Again nothing. She was gone. He was sure of it. Took the money he worked so hard to steal. Roger got out of his car, dizzy and disoriented. He retched, vomiting into the gutter.

He sat on the curb, head in his hands, almost in tears. All his planning, his hope, his chance, gone. Claudia must have found out he was having an affair. She'd have searched through his BlackBerry, looking for a name or phone number.

The passwords to the accounts were in the PDA. And it wouldn't have been too hard for her to figure them out, as she'd chided him more than once that he used his mother's maiden name, his favorite movie, or his father's nickname way too often.

He sighed, and as if trudging through wet cement, he returned to his car. Driving aimlessly, he realized he wasn't going home. Roger knew Nanette wouldn't tell the cops anything since she risked trouble if he was arrested. But that nosy neighbor might have noted his license number. And for all he knew, the law was running his plate now.

He drove, alone and deliberate in his thoughts.

What if Claudia had a boyfriend? Had she run away with some young stud she met at the gym or that class she took at UCLA last year? Had she played him for the fool all along? Nanette's phone numbers were in his PDA. Claudia was smart, she'd put it together and hadn't given anything away. She'd waited until he'd amassed enough, and then took it from him like a vandal sacking a village.

He slowed near the 10 freeway and Fairfax Avenue. He hadn't allowed himself to imagine the depth of the disgust she'd feel once it was known he'd stolen money and run off with another woman. But now *he* could be the hero. At least he could have that over Claudia.

"Your mother has done us wrong, Janice," he told her after reaching her at home on one of his cell phones. He'd crawled through the hole in the cyclone fence to get down to Ballona Creek. It was an old tributary of water dating back to the days of the *ranchos* in this once small pueblo. But like everything else in this city, the creek was walled in with concrete. Ballona ran under the Fairfax Avenue overpasses from the freeway and meandered west for nine miles or so to the Pacific.

"What are you talking about?" his daughter replied. Then he heard a knock and a muffled voice. "Dad, there's a man at the door saying he's from the police. What's going on?"

"Tell him your mother's run off with another man." Hell, maybe it was true.

"Dad, what are you—"

"It's okay, sweetheart. She'll get hers. I'm going to find her. I'm going to make sure she doesn't get away with this." He hung up and smashed both of his cell phones against the concrete walls of the creek. There were ways of tracking you with those things.

Roger started jogging through the shallow water, which barely splashed above his dress shoes. In nearby Culver City, there was a bike path that paralleled Ballona. He and Claudia and Janice had ridden it many times out to Marina del Rey. Tonight it wasn't for recreation that he would travel it—this was his lifeline. He picked up his pace, arms pumping, legs churning. Ahead, in the dark at the curve of the concrete wall, something disturbed the water. Roger didn't slow down. Be it a possum or human predator, he didn't care. He was on a mission. Claudia would not escape him.

In the morning he awoke in the stale motel room with its walls bleached of color and greasy cracked windows. He took the toiletry items out of the black plastic bag from the 7-Eleven. Overhead yet another plane rattled the threadbare room. In the few pieces left of the broken mirror over the rust-stained sink, he studied his face while he lathered.

Wasn't there more gray in those whiskers today? The bags more pronounced? And wasn't that some gray edging into his temples? No matter. He had big things to do. Razor poised, having lubricated his stubble for the requisite five minutes, Roger Crumbler considered his shave.

PART IV

THE GOLD COAST

THE GIRL WHO KISSED BARNABY JONES

BY SCOTT PHILLIPS
Pacific Palisades

It's 2:30 in the morning and I'm all alone closing down Burberry's when my cell goes off. The caller ID says it's Cherie, which probably means a conflict with tomorrow's schedule, but I pick up anyway.

"Hi, Tate. I need you to help me out with something."

"Right now?"

"Are you almost done closing?"

"Fifteen minutes."

"Can you come out to Pacific Palisades when you're done?"

"I guess so." I live in Koreatown, so the Palisades is miles out of my way; like half the guys who walk into Burberry's, though, I have a great big boner with Cherie's name on it, and if she asked me to shovel shit I'd ask her how fast she needed it shoveled. "Where, exactly?"

She gives me an address in the highlands accompanied by minutely detailed instructions, including a warning to park at the base of the street. I rush through the rest of the closing process and on the way out buy a package of condoms from the machine in the men's room, dropping an extra fifty cents for the strawberry-flavored ones. When I set the alarm my hands are cold with sweat, and pressing a finger to my wrist I clock my pulse at eighty. Thirty-four years old and I feel like a teenager heading to the prom with a diabolical cross between the homecoming queen and a middle-aged hooker.

It broke a hundred in the Valley today for the fifth day in a row, but the night air is cool and quiet. I pull my old Saturn onto the westbound 101, so nearly deserted at a quarter to 3:00 that I hate to merge onto the 405 after a mere three exits. The 405 is even better, though, ten lanes of empty, untrammeled joy; I've had flying dreams that were less spiritually nourishing, and I'm not even speeding. Well before 3:00 I'm headed west on Sunset toward the Palisades, window rolled down for the breeze on my neck and bare arms.

The shops and restaurants of the village are dark as I pass through, the only moving vehicle in sight an LAPD cruiser that crosses in front of me just before my right turn onto Via de la Paz. At the crest, the cruiser turns left and I turn right, taking it slow, careful not to miss any of the indicated streets. The house is at the top of a nearly vertical, circular one, and when I park the Saturn at the bottom I make sure the hand brake is on and the wheels turned out.

Cherie is the ur–cocktail waitress, tall and leggy with hair dyed blond, hanging straight with an inward flip just below her jawline, and looking at her face and body you wouldn't take her for more than forty.

In which case you'd be wrong. She came to L.A. from East Lansing, Michigan to be an actress back in the '70s. Knowing that, you might take her for the embodiment of a cliché—prettiest girl in some provincial town comes to L.A. with dreams of stardom, never gets a part, ends up bitter and old, taking drink orders in the Valley—but here again you'd be wrong: Cherie did make it for a while. On cable you can still catch her in old episodes of *Starsky and Hutch* and *Barnaby Jones*, and at least one *Columbo* (in which she plays—unconvincingly—a cocktail waitress). Once in my presence she made the unlikely claim that she was the producers' first choice for the Linda Evans part in *Dynasty*, and Dean Berg, who tends bar in the afternoons, swears she did an episode of the original *Star Trek*. While we all cherished the thought of her in one of those short red uniforms with the leather boots, when he repeated the claim in front of her, she busted a gasket and said she didn't even come out here until years after the show went off the air. When Cherie's annoyed she clenches her teeth, and she's spent so much of her life in a state of annoyance that the muscles lining her cheeks actually bulge outward. Her jaw didn't unlock for three days after that.

We get guys all the time with crushes on her, some of them very young; they come in on a daily basis for months sometimes before they accept the fact that she's never going to respond to their devotion, and lots of them keep coming even after that, just to pine. She's worked at Burberry's since at least '91, long after the end of her acting career. What she did in the meantime is a mystery, but according to Dean she lived for a while with Lyle Hobart, one of the owners. Lyle is married these days to a former Playmate of the Month who doesn't let him set foot in Burberry's without her, so terrified is she of Cherie's lingering influence on her weak-willed husband. Her fears aren't misplaced; it's due only to Lyle's protection that she's still employed. I've been at Burberry's since my divorce, a year ago, and she's the most unreliable waitress I've worked with in ten years of on-and-off bartending: no-shows, bad arithmetic, ignored customers, the whole roster of waitressing sins. Her looks, combined with a certain flirtatious affability, have kept me—have kept the entire male portion of the staff—from turning on her, but the other waitresses loathe her, and she wouldn't last a week anywhere else.

The house is at the summit, the street curving downward in either direction away from it. The front door is locked, the windows all dark, so I double-check the address before ringing the bell. From the outside it looks modest, but in this neighborhood at this altitude facing seaward you'd be looking at a couple million dollars' worth of bungalow. When the door finally opens it's Cherie, and she greets me with a finger to her lips.

"Hey, Cherie," I say.

"Shut the fuck up," she hisses, beckoning me inside.

It's completely dark, and she takes my hand and leads me down a staircase into what turns out to be an enormous living room with a panoramic view of the Pacific. There's another staircase leading down, and outside I can see more house going down the hill, and I understand that this is one of those four-story houses that you enter through the insignificant-looking top floor. I try to revise my estimate of the house's worth and fail. This is one of those places you read about on the front page of the *Times'* real estate supplement, the part Harry Shearer reads aloud on the radio Sunday morning. For the first time I begin to feel uneasy about what Cherie might be doing here.

She's in her uniform, and she sidles up to me and slops her mouth onto mine. Up close she smells like cigarettes and perfume and wine, and her mouth doesn't taste half bad, considering.

I pull away, determined to find out while I still can exactly what I'm buying into. "So what's the favor, Cherie?"

"The favor is I'm horny, stud, and I want to make it with you." One of Cherie's more endearing traits is a tendency toward '70s slang that dates her in ways her face and body fail to.

"Just all of a sudden out of nowhere?"

"All of a sudden I got this great housesitting gig and I thought it was sad to be staying in a beautiful pad like this without a lover to share it with."

This is the first I've heard about any such job, and just as I'm thinking, *Who in God's name would be fucked up enough to hire Cherie as a housesitter?* I find myself distracted by how nice her tits feel pressing against my rib cage, and the sensation of her tongue in my mouth is having its own clouding effect on my wits.

"You've never shown any interest before."

"Oh, but I've been thinking about it, big boy. I see the way you watch me. Parts of me. You want a glass of wine?"

"No thanks."

"Meth?"

I shake my head no and she takes me by the hand down the other staircase and down a hallway to a magnificent bedroom, and for the first time since I got there she turns on a light, a bedside lamp. The bed is made, the walls covered with framed gold records and what looks like dark red velvet. In the light I give her a careful up-and-down appraisal and find that she looks very, very nice indeed, down to the one nonregulation item in her uniform: a pair of black high-heeled shoes, the kind that would kill her on an eight-hour shift.

"You want to get naked, or are you one of those guys who gets turned on by the uniform?" she asks, and by way of an answer I jump her.

* * *

In three and a half minutes it's over, which embarrasses me but seems to be fine by Cherie. Cheerfully she doffs the remainder of her uniform and heads for the bathroom, and while she's in there I wander to the wall to take a look at one of the gold records. To my surprise I know not only the record but the guy who produced it, Gary Hinshaw. Gary is the nicest famous person I've ever met; he used to hang around the bar when I worked at Chez Kiki, and he switched allegiances when they fired me and I moved over to Burberry's. This was a serious step downward in the hierarchy of Valley restaurants, so it was encouraging to have a friendly face following me to the new job, especially one who quickly endeared himself to the rest of the staff as a talented raconteur and prodigious tipper. The funny part is, I didn't even know what Gary did for a living until Dean told me one day.

"He's a record producer. You never heard of him?"

"I guess I've heard his name. I knew he did something in the music business."

"Starting in the early '60s. You ever hear of the Carlottas? The Essentials? Jesus, you kids have no sense of musical history." Then he went on to name some later groups, a few of whose records I remembered fondly from high school, and I was finally impressed. This also cleared up the question of how, even in L.A., even with money, a guy who looked like Gary had such a way with women. When a 350-pound man with hairplugs and a nose like a yam walks in with a different stunning woman every other week, the temptation is to think call girls, but they didn't strike me that way. Several of them became regulars at Chez Kiki in their own right, and from what I could see they mostly stayed friendly with Gary once he'd moved on to fresher game.

Gary hasn't ever brought any of those women into Burberry's; I had assumed that this was because it wasn't the kind of place you could bring the kind of woman you might take to Chez Kiki. Now that I think of it, though, one of the prime beneficiaries of his largesse has been Cherie, and it becomes suddenly obvious to me that he's one of the abject worshippers. The housesitting gig makes sense now, and I ever so briefly feel ever so slightly bad about fucking Cherie right in what I assume is Gary's bedroom.

After maybe five minutes she comes out all dressed back up.

"Maybe we can go again after we're done, if you feel like it."

"After we're done with what?" I ask, trying to come up with a graceful way of declining her request, whatever it's going to be. I have the uneasy presentiment that what she wants me to do is something horrible and pet-related: a faithful Irish Setter, dead of thirst, or maybe a million-dollar showcat roaming around the neighborhood in heat.

She leads me back up the staircase to that room with the view and through to the kitchen, where something smells funny. Not food-gone-bad funny, but it's an aroma not completely out of place in a kitchen. When the light comes on, I see that the source of it is a quantity of Gary's blood, which has pooled on the tile floor beneath his enormous torso.

"What the fuck," I say.

"Yeah," Cherie says.

He looks even bigger lying there on the peach-colored tile, the force of gravity pulling all that adipose tissue down from his chest toward the floor. There's a blood-soaked hole on his tentlike yellow shortsleeved shirt, quite low on the abdomen. I take a good long look at that shirt and note that it's moving, slowly and rhythmically.

"Holy shit, he's alive!" I yell.

"He won't be for long."

"When did this happen?"

"About fifteen minutes before I called you." She leans back, arms folded under her breasts, hips against the counter next to the sink, waiting for me to ask her what I'm supposed to do next. What I do is take out my cell and start to dial 911. She grabs for it, and I have to yank it out of her reach.

"What the hell are you doing?"

"Calling an ambulance."

"If I wanted a fucking ambulance I'd've called one myself. You're going to help me cover this up."

"Was it self-defense?"

"Are you kidding me? The big fucking ape. Take a look at this."

She unbuttons her sleeve and pulls it back to reveal a big pink rectangular bandage. When she peels away its corner there's a fresh red welt, round and dark.

"Cocksucker burned me with a cigarette, and when I objected he pulled a gun on me, swear to God."

For the first time it occurs to me how fast she's talking, and I remember her offering me a hit of meth when I first got here. "How fucked up were you guys when this happened?" I ask.

"He had some crank, we were messing around a little bit."

Something else strikes me. "How come you're in your uniform? You didn't work today."

"Sometimes I wear it on my off days." This, I know, is a lie, and under the pressure of my stare she cops to it. "Gary likes to fuck me while I'm wearing it, okay? Just like you do, so don't smirk. Sometimes he likes to tie me to a chair and do stuff. That's what he wanted to do tonight, but with him being so cranked up and things already getting out of hand"—she holds up the burned wrist as evidence—"I decided that was a bad idea. So he got the gun and started trying to force me into the chair, and I took it and shot him. Simple."

"That's a pretty good story, why don't you just flush the crank down the toilet and tell it to the cops?"

"I don't function well with cops. They give me the willies."

"They give everybody the willies, but we have to call 911 and get an ambulance."

"Like fuck we have to. Look, Tate, I want to be famous again someday, but not for being in this year's trial of the century, got it? That's why I called you."

"What did you think I was going to do? Finish him off?"

She shrugs. "He's not long for this world anyway. Just help me get rid of him, someplace where nobody'll find him for a long time. What do you think of the Angeles National Forest?"

"Never been."

"Doesn't it seem like they're always finding corpses out there? Angeles National *Cemetery*, more like." She laughs, a staccato, high-pitched giggle I've never heard from her before, and the batshit crazy sound of it scares me a little bit more than I already am.

"Won't people be looking for him?"

"Wouldn't be the first time he's taken off without telling anyone. He's a world-famous nutjob anyway, and by the time anybody figures out he's really gone, the evidence'll be cold."

"Where's the gun?" I ask, the brilliant idea being that I'll take it from her and call 911 like a sane person. When she produces it I lunge for her, and to my utter and complete astonishment she fires at the floor next to my feet, drilling a jagged hole into one of the tiles and scattering dusty shards in all directions. I drop the cell and she kicks it out of reach.

"Fucking hell, Cherie. Way to wake up the neighbors."

"I knew you were going to try and take the gun. Soon as you asked for it. Now, you listen." She raises the gun so it's pointing at my face rather than my belly. "You fucked me while he lay here dying, and that makes you my accomplice."

Rather than pointing out the flaws in her logic, I concentrate on placating her. In between our words I discover that I can actually hear the thin whistle of Gary's breath, and it occurs to me that I'd better get help to him sooner rather than later.

"All right, then, take his feet," I tell her.

"I'm not putting down this gun."

"I can't carry 350 pounds of Gary up those steps all by myself."

"We're going downstairs, to the garage. Gary's got a Hummer."

"Hummer's no good, it's too conspicuous."

"Fuck conspicuous, you do what I tell you. Take him by the feet and drag him."

I start pulling him toward the staircase. It's harder than I thought it would be, hauling a sixth of a ton of deadweight across the tile, harder still when I reach the carpet of the living room. Then Cherie starts down the steps ahead of me to turn the light on downstairs, and I step over Gary and kick her right in the ass. She stumbles—did I mention those heels?—and when she hits the landing with a squeal of pain and outrage, she twists around and fires at me. I'm already headed up that other set of stairs to the front door, though, and as soon as I cross the threshold I haul ass down the side-walk toward my car. There are low-hanging branches in my way, and ducking under one of them I lose my balance and hit the sidewalk, scraping the hell out of my right elbow.

"Get back here, you fucking coward!" I hear when she gets outside, and I keep sprinting, secure in my assumption that she's not crazy enough to open fire on the street.

The first shot hits the car parked in front of mine, and I dig in my pocket for my keys, then fumble with them for what feels like about a minute and a half before I manage to open the Saturn. I haven't got the door closed yet when I turn the engine over, and the next shot shatters my driver's side window. Wetting my pants, I say a silent prayer of thanks that I took a dump before I left Burberry's. Chugging into reverse I jump the curb, and then I ram it into gear and make a U-turn, swiping an SUV, the passenger-side mirror making a horrible scraping sound against it. In the rearview I can see her standing there in the middle of the street, taking aim, and I swerve to my right as she fires again. It misses me by a mile.

The cell is back on Gary's kitchen floor and there are hardly pay phones in L.A. anymore, not in this kind of neighbor-hood anyway. But there's a supermarket at Sunset and Via de la Paz, and on a hunch I pull into the lot and find a pair of them mounted next to the doors. My engine is still running when I make the call to 911, and I can hear a siren coming from the south. When the operator asks me the nature of my emergency, I'm momentarily at a loss. I tell her Gary's address and she says they've already got a prowl car on the way to the street after reports of shots.

Tongue-tied, I manage to get across that they'll need an ambulance too, and that an armed, dangerous, and crazy woman is probably on the premises, cranked to the gills. "She's an actress," I add, in case additional precautions need to be taken.

After hanging up I slump against the wall, illuminated by my headlights, the breeze soothing on my wet pants front. I wonder how long until the sun comes up, and in the distance to the east I hear another siren approach, this one of a slightly different timbre than the first. I can feel the tension start to drain from my shoulders, and I put my weight back onto my feet just as I catch sight of a vaguely familiar, battered red Corolla pulling into the lot and heading toward me, the face behind the wheel bearing down on mine, jaws clenched so tight they're bulging, and all I can think is how pretty she still looks.

KINSHIP

BY BRIAN ASCALON ROLEY

Mar Vista

As I pulled into my driveway I saw my cousin Veronica sitting on the bungalow porch steps with her face buried in her hands. She heard my shoes snapping acorns on the path and looked up, stood, and came toward me. Her tank top revealed the butterfly tattoo on her shoulder. A rolled-up mat stuck out of her satchel. I tossed her my windbreaker: cool damp ocean air was coming up the street. I thought maybe she'd come over after yoga in nearby Venice to see if I wanted to go surfing—something we used to do as teenagers, on afternoons after she tutored me in math—but her eyes were bloodshot.

What's wrong? I said. I noticed something blue on the side of her face and moved her hair aside. Did he hit you?

She flinched. No.

Your face is blue.

I told you, it wasn't him.

Who, then?

Please, Tomas. I didn't come over about this.

I crossed my arms. I asked her to explain. She glanced down as she fingered her satchel strap and told me she'd come to talk about her boy, Emerson.

She said, Manny went over and tried to confront the bully's father, and he got beat up after carpool. Only a few blocks from school.

Some kid has been bullying Emerson? I said. My hands fisted, the pulse hot in my knuckles.

Yeah.

How long has this been going on?

Two months, I think. That's when we started seeing bruises.

And you didn't tell me?

Sorry, she said.

I bit my lip, tasted warm blood, looked down my street. In the June overcast, no shadows cast on the silvery asphalt, but the glare was enough to make me squint. Gulls squawked overhead.

Where does it happen? I said.

I don't know. At school, we think.

And the teachers?

They don't do anything.

Nothing? I thought they were big on PC stuff nowadays, teaching tolerance for people who are different.

Veronica rolled her eyes. She said, They talked to the kid we think is the ringleader, Harley Douglas. They talked to his parents. But nobody actually saw anything, and Emerson won't say that Harley hit him, though he's the one who picks on him the most. The principal promised to investigate.

I felt the heat in my face; my cousin did not come over much anymore, and now I knew what had brought her today. Emerson had a metabolic disorder that impaired his balance, sensitivity, and muscle strength, and caused developmental delays.

Emerson can't really even talk, I told her.

He can, she said with slight annoyance; she shoved her clenched hands into my windbreaker pockets. Just not well. He claims he's been falling on the playground.

And you're sure he's not?

Yesterday someone sliced his leg braces. Here, look.

She pulled them out of her backpack. The braces, a contraption of plastic parts held together by joints and straps, had been cut clean.

Motherfuckers, I said.

Tomas.

What did the parents say?

They didn't believe us. Said we were making false accusations against their son. Then Manny went over to confront the guy, after he noticed Emerson's slit braces. The father's a soccer-dad from hell. Goes to all the school games. Eggs his kid on to commit fouls, yells at the other parents. The jerk beat up Manny in front of Emerson and Harley. He looks terrible. Needed twenty stitches.

Did he file an assault report?

She shook her head.

It might make them take you more seriously.

He thinks he can handle it by himself. But he can't, she said, then shrugged and turned away.

I clicked my tongue and shook my head. You shouldn't of sent Manny. Confrontation isn't his thing.

I didn't send him, he went over himself, she said. Veronica seemed irritated, crossed her arms and glanced away.

Wait here, I said.

Where are you going?

I need to get something from the house.

She yelled after me what was I doing, but I kept on thumping up the paint-flaking front steps. I slammed through the door and swept through the hall like a sudden gust. I moved into the back where my brother and girlfriend and their daughter lived, my brother who refuses to talk to me, blames me for having been a bad influence when we were teens. I rifled through his closet and drawers, looking, and I thought about Emerson, who until last year had used a walker to get around. He was growing stunted for his age, with his trunk becoming shorter in proportion to his legs. Veronica and Manny were in denial. They spoke as if his cheerful laugh wasn't a reflection of mild mental retardation, as if his slurred speech could really only be due to limp muscles in his neck and body. As if he'd someday win sports, avoid teasing, charm girls into giving him female companionship.

Tomas, what are you doing? my mother said.

She stood in Gabe's doorway; her hair was messy, she had probably been napping.

Nothing.

What are you looking for? she said. Gabe will be home from work soon.

You want to help me look?

She hesitated. For what?

Never mind, I said. I found it in the bedside table, took the icepick out, and palmed it, felt the weight of the wooden handle, the thinness of its blade. It looked like an enormous hypodermic needle.

She blocked the doorway.

Tomas, you said you wouldn't! she said. You're on probation. You said you were finished with that life. My mother grimaced; she had suffered through my days of adolescent rage, my anger at being a halfie.

I went to the rear window, slid it open sideways, popped out the flimsy screen. I started to step through, but then paused and turned to her.

It's not about my old life, I told her. I'm not going back. You said.

It's about Veronica's child.

She had begun crying but stopped now. She furrowed her forehead as she looked at me. Veronica was like a daughter to her. We spent five years living in my *tita's* house after coming here from the Philippines.

A kid beat him up at school. And Manny got beat up by the kid's father when he confronted him.

She touched the wrinkled lapel on her robe as if she knew it needed to be smoothed, but she didn't smooth it. Somebody hurt Emerson?

I nodded.

She looked at me for a long moment, and then stepped out of the doorway to let me pass.

I drove over to Veronica and Manny's apartment. As I headed north, the dilapidating bungalows of my inland Mar Vista neighborhood gave way to better-kept houses and lusher streets. They lived in what used to be the crappy part of Santa Monica, along the southern border, in the same rent-controlled apartment Manny's mother raised him in, up on the once-seedy hillside roads near Rose Street, just inside the Santa Monica line. When I was smaller, gangs from nearby Venice and Mar Vista claimed the blocks as territory, and I'd notice their cars patrol it, though most of the white people living in the small houses had no idea. But the neighborhood was changing. Many of the bungalows and apartment complexes had been torn down and replaced by trendy condos.

Veronica was two years older than me. Like me, half Filipino—our moms are sisters—but she grew up in Santa Monica north of Montana and went to a private alternative school founded by hippies in the '70s, full of rich white kids now, mostly affluent and movie industry. She tutored me in math—would come down south to wherever we lived at the time, in the triangle of south Santa Monica off Pico where all the Mexicans and blacks lived, the house Mom rented in Mar Vista, the apartment in Venice.

After we finished the schoolwork, Veronica would reward me with play. She took me and my brother Gabe everywhere—to the beach, the parks, movies, malls. She was a fun tomboy—wasn't afraid to play basketball in the driveway or on the courts across the street from our church. We played rough volleyball on the sand. I did well in school mostly to please her.

After she left California for Reed College in Oregon, I got into trouble. I'm sure Veronica thought it was because she left, but I was enmeshed in adolescence, a new school, new neighborhood, and I probably would have ended up gangbanging even if she'd stuck around. People act surprised when they find out I got involved in Chicano gangs at St. Dominic's—a white liberal Catholic parish. But it gave me the respect I needed after being dogged by both whites and Asians. I knew Manny at St. Dominic's. He was a bookish guy, tall, thin, with a chip on his bony shoulder. A Jesuit's pet. He disapproved of my dressing like my Mexican friends, even passing as one, thought I was ashamed of being half-Filipino. We were the only Filipinos at school.

The truth is, he may have been born in Quezon City, but he grew up in Fremont and Santa Monica and is as suburban as you get. He was as much a poseur as I was.

One day he gave an oral report on his native country. During the Q-and-A, I pointed out an inaccuracy in the way he pronounced a Tagalog word. People laughed. He reddened and glared at me. A month later he reported that I had turned in a paper written by another classmate, and I got an F.

When Veronica flew back for family visits, she seemed shocked to see me with my Spanish tattoos, the business I'd started training attack dogs, the shaved head. Once, at a restaurant with her mom and dad, I took her aside and showed her my pistol—as if that would impress her. But unlike the other relatives who gave up on me, she still came over to our neighborhood, picked me up, and we'd go surfing together. At Bay Street if we were lazy, or up the coast to Zeros or Topanga if she felt like the drive. An old bond. But she was different now, too. Something about the confidence with which she moved on her board, the swell of her breasts against her black tank top, the beads she let dangle around her wrists and neck even in water, an impervious indifference to the stares of local surfers. We'd come back, shower, and walk to the Rose Café for breakfast. She was a tomboy but nonetheless drew stares, with her long bourbon-colored legs, her pretty half-Asian face with its high cheekbones. The neighborhood may have become trendy, with new ocean-view condos nearby, but the blocks around my place still had black kids selling pot to people in fancy cars. Veronica drew catcalls from the Mexican laborers waiting for work; yet none of it fazed her.

I was surprised when she married Manny. He'd gone to UCLA and worked as a youth counselor while majoring in Social Work. The idea that an awkward man like him could help "at-risk youth" was a joke, I can tell you from my vantage point—they needed the mentoring of someone they could relate to, someone who had gone down that road and been pulled back by a guiding hand. It didn't seem to work out, because not long after they had Emerson, he quit—or lost?—his job to become a stay-at-home dad.

We're keeping Emerson at home for a while, Veronica

told me when he was old enough to enter kindergarten; she worked as the manager of a popular Mexican chain restaurant. We're a bit worried about the other kids, she said.

He's going to have to deal with school sometime, I said.

I know, she said, But he's still a bit behind.

As if he'll ever fully catch up, I thought. But every time I came over, the kid laughed at my face, grabbed his walker, and hurried my way, clattering that metal contraption across the floor and slamming against banged-up furniture and walls in the process.

Tito Tomas! he'd scream, laughing.

Hey, sunshine, let's go out for a walk, I'd say, grabbing him and lifting him into a bear hug.

Veronica had stopped taking Emerson out to the playground, because he couldn't keep up with the energetic activities and ended up alone. And she resented the stares of the mothers and nannies, the other children especially. Manny, to his credit, believed this to be wrong. He insisted on dragging Emerson out to the parks and malls. He insisted that other people were fucked up to stare. They argued over it. She'd search the neighborhood to find him. They screamed at each other in public.

Manny tried to make Emerson use his walker *everywhere*. The neurologists and PTs told them it would keep his muscles stretched. But Emerson refused. He threw tantrums at malls, dropped down to his knees and cried, drawing the stares of passersby who looked at Veronica as if she were abusing her disabled child.

Go on, leave us, I would tell her. Go shopping.

She'd hesitate but walk away, letting me kneel down beside her boy. I'd smell his sweaty, musty hair. I cherished his boy-smell, these sweet moments, the joy and sorrow I drew from these fleeting seconds of male bonding of which I wanted more. I would whisper in his ear, make him laugh, coax him with promises of ice cream—and have him using his walker in no time.

He let me take him to Douglas Park, played on the slides and swings, tossed bread at the ducks in the pond, walked over grass. The park had changed since I was a kid. Gabe and Veronica and I used to wade through dirty pond water, catching tiny frogs and tadpoles in the reeds. Now the pond had been converted into a fancy Japanese water garden, complete with babbling streams, wooden benches, landscaped boulders. Even the ducks looked cleaner. The kid's play area had new bright play equipment, handicap accessible, and the mothers seemed different now, too. Thinner, more stylish.

Manny resented my ease with Emerson. The boy let me take him to the basketball court across the street from St. Dominic's after Sunday mass. Manny watched with jealousy as Emerson used his walker on the crowded court, without shame or self-consciousness, and let the black teenagers lift him up to dunk the ball.

Nothing I did was good enough for that chump. After I got saved and became a youth minister at an evangelical strip-mall church in Culver City—where I ran the boys' club, as well as addiction recovery groups—you'd have thought he'd come round to me. But he never did.

I drove my truck up to their apartment complex and started circling the block, looking for a parking spot on the narrow side streets. I smoldered over exactly how to do what I wanted to do. Remembering my mother's worried face, I thought, Hold on, don't do anything rash, you're risking a lot of hurt and pain here, will let down a lot of people if you get caught breaking probation. They'd put you away for a long time. When you got out, how old would Emerson be? But then I remembered his slit braces in Veronica's hands and that was it.

I pulled into the driveway behind one of their neighbor's cars, blocking it in. I stomped around to their garden apartment and banged on the green door. The front blinds moved, then shut. I banged on the door again. It finally opened.

Manny wore a sling, his face blue and black, a piece of skin torn below his eye, stitched. It looked as if someone had pressed barbed wire into his face.

Veronica's not here, he said.

I want to see Emerson.

He's at your *tita's* place, Manny said. He spoke a bit snidely, as if I should have known.

Get in my car, I said.

What?

We're going for a drive.

He tried to protest so I grabbed his shirt and pulled him out of his apartment. I put him in the truck and we sat there, engine off, windows open. The air smelled of sun-warmed avocados fallen on the grass.

So, Veronica tells me you got yourself beat up by some kid's father, I said.

Manny shook his head. Lips tightened, angry no doubt that Veronica came to me. It wasn't like that, he said.

That was a smart move, I said. Now Emerson will really have his peers' respect.

You don't understand. I couldn't *not* do anything. We tried talking to the teachers, the principal. They said they were investigating, but they need to expel that kid *now*, Tomas, to keep him out of Emerson's *face*.

So you went over to the father and got beat up.

Fuck you, Tomas.

Maybe you lost your cool? Made them defensive.

You've got a lot of nerve, Tomas. This is *my* son we're talking about.

His jaw trembled with anger. I felt hot, my shirt damp against my vinyl seat. The fermenting avocado smell made me feel like hurting someone. But I told myself to hold my temper, let him talk.

I said, Tell me what happened.

And he told me.

That's not a satisfactory explanation, I said.

What the fuck do you want from me?

I plucked one stitch from his face, causing him to kick the dashboard in his struggle. He cursed. I quieted him with a look and said, When Veronica came to me this morning, her face was bruised again. I should *really* hurt you. But I am going to give you an opportunity to redeem yourself. To be a real husband and father.

Manny began to speak but seemed to think better. Then he asked, Where are we going?

Where does Harley Douglas live?

Venice.

Do you know the house?

Yeah, he said after a pause.

We drove down the hill to Main Street and headed south past the arty boutiques and cafés and restaurants. We crossed Rose and headed into Venice. Beyond the older buildings to the west I caught flashes of bright ocean. We crossed over streets that used to be canals nearly a century ago, blocks where amusement park rides and buildings had once stood.

We reached Abbot Kinney, with its more boho shops,

looking a lot like Santa Monica's posh Main Street had when I was a kid. The martial arts studio where I used to study Filipino stick-fighting when we lived in Oakwood, the black neighborhood inland to its north, the old bungalows and cottages ravaged by cool salty nights. But Harley Douglas lived on the ocean side, on the gentrified streets. Many of the weathered buildings had been renovated, or replaced by condos. I noticed a beautiful woman walking a pure white husky, while sipping from a paper coffee cup. The neighborhood is one of the few in Los Angeles where people actually walk.

When we lived near here it was a different place. The old buildings colonied by hippies were falling apart then. Some were empty, condemned. Our house was on its last legs. On stormy evenings, Pacific Ocean winds would blow against the clapboard walls on our creaking block.

Even then, some of the older structures were starting to be torn down and replaced by upscale condos, but in the summer of '94 a gang war broke out between the blacks and Mexicans and the construction stopped.

From the look of things now, real estate had soared again.

That's where they live, Manny said, pointing to a narrow modern structure of steel and wood and glass four stories high.

I parked across the street.

That's a pretty funky house, I said.

He's an architect. Designed it himself.

You got beat up by an architect?

He used to be a military engineer. Apparently he has a black belt.

He's still an architect.

What are we doing here? he asked.

Sit, look, listen, I said. Tell me about the father. Tell me what he looks like. We need to plan.

The house was made of ecologically friendly materials, and utilized solar energy. His first floor was concealed by a shiny hammered metal wall softened by elegant bamboo. Its entrance opened to a narrow alley, but the sound of waves echoed among the buildings. He must have had quite a view. I could see the upper levels above the bamboo. They were walls of glass that revealed glimpses of affluence and style—leather furniture, a drafting table, pieces of skylight and sky.

I made the preparations and dropped Manny at the boys' club. Then I drove back to Venice and parked near the architect's house. I stood and waited in front of a condo complex across the street, smoking. When a man left Harley's house and headed down the sidewalk with a little English bulldog, I followed. He matched Manny's description of the father: shaved head, artsy glasses. When he neared my parked truck, I hurried my step. Perhaps he sensed me coming up, because he turned. One look at me and he got a bit nervous.

Hi, he said. A moment passed. Can I help you?

He wore tortoiseshell glasses, black turtleneck, jeans, and a black-faced Omega watch.

Nice day to walk your dog, I said.

He looked upward as if he hadn't already noticed the overcast sky, the June marine layer, with its thick smell of ocean salt. In the humid air my joints throbbed.

Yeah, sure, he said. He spoke uncertainly, his tone part fear, part annoyance.

Your dog pooped on my lawn, I said.

He seemed relieved—an explanation for my body language. I'm sorry about that, he said.

You're supposed to scoop it up.

Like I said, I'm sorry. It won't happen again. He started to pass.

Get in the truck, I said, pointing.

What?

I pulled out the ice pick, set it against his chest. Like I said, get in the truck.

He noticed the tinted windows. I pressed the point against his nipple, which was visible through his microfiber shirt, and he obeyed.

What do you want from me? he said. You want my wallet?

Put on this bandana. Cover your eyes.

In our family, my grandmother's brothers fought as guerrilla soldiers in the jungled mountains of Laguna and Quezon during the Japanese occupation. Two had been Philippine Scouts and on the American payroll before MacArthur retreated to Australia. I only knew them years later, as old men, drunkards who loved to boast in a mixture of English and Tagalog and Spanish. They visited Los Angeles and stayed with us several times, trying to claim the veterans' benefits they had been promised. I thought they were losers because they kept asking, even though they never got anybody to listen to them. They struck me as dreamers. Then they got me drunk when I was nine. They told me I took after them, the Laurels (that's my mother's maiden name). Indeed, a few years later I grew tall and broad—the conquistador's barrel chest, they called it.

They don't seem like soldiers, I told my mother and her sister. We were visiting them in San Pablo, an old Spanish-Malay city among coconut haciendas south of Manila, and they drank San Miguel beers from a crate on their picnic table. I was at a separate table, where the women sat.

That's only because they're old, Mom said.

What did they do?

Eduardo and Pedro were the worst, she said. They ran the hacienda like gangsters. They once shot a man for looking at their sister the wrong way.

Wow, I said. What else?

She said, One of their brothers—*Tio* Bien, the good one, the gentle doctor—visited the farm one year from Hawaii, where he was living. He hired a skit to travel on the railroad between the farm and the city of Tagkawayan.

What's a skit?

It's like a platform made of bamboo, Mom said. It has wheels and a little lawn mower engine. Boys run them over the train tracks like homemade taxis. Anyway, *Tio* Bien hired one and was riding into town to drink some *halo halo,* when the skit was stopped by bandits. He gave them his watch and money, but they shot him in the kneecaps anyway. Then they left. When he got back to the hacienda, his brothers grew furious. They found out from tenant farmers what village the bandits came from. They rode there on horseback with machine guns from the war. They shot into the thatched *nipa* huts.

Why didn't they find out who did it? I asked. They could have hit anyone. Even a baby.

They weren't thinking about that, Mom said. They were sending the message that this is what happens if someone hurts our family.

I shook my head, furious, bothered. My mother and aunt spoke with disapproving low voices, almost whispers, shaking their heads with shame. But they were also secretly proud, I sensed.

When I got jumped into a Latino gang, my mother and her sister and their brothers may have been disappointed in me. But on a trip I took back to Manila, my grandmother's brother Eduardo took one look at me—the broad muscles, the weight-lifter's shoulders, the tattoos covering my arms and back—and he nodded in approval.

You are a true Laurel, he said.

That night, we got shitfaced on San Miguel gin.

In my church we have an inscription that indicates the bread and wine are not His body and blood, but only symbols, remembrances of the Father. But I have a secret heresy. When I eat from the loaf, when I sip from the cup, I feel in my heart His presence and know I have consumed real flesh and real bodily fluid that is absorbed by my body. It is the Philippine Catholic inside me. I have other secret idolatries. There is a tattoo of the Virgin Mary on my back, from the base of my neck down to the crest of my buttocks; her shoulders spread across my shoulder blades, her feet step on the serpent coiled at my hips. All the other tattoos my congregation knew about, and I removed them by laser—across my arms and shoulders, my neck, my chest. When we went out to the frigid stream for full immersion, I kept two layers of undershirt on so they would not see the Holy Mother beneath.

They would not understand. But about some things I cannot let go.

I took Veronica to my church once. She hadn't been to Mass in years. She said the rituals were meaningless, rote, hierarchical. I wanted to expose the unborn baby to Jesus, and thought our more spirited evangelical service might rekindle the piety of her childhood. But she looked surprised at the Spartan worship space and asked where the altar was. She puzzled at the aluminum chairs we had instead of pews, scanned the floor for kneelers.

When the Christian rock band played and the clapping started, she moved and swayed, even smiled. Her eyes teared during the witnessing, as a man read a letter from an eleven-year-old boy who had written an autobiographical story about hearing his alcoholic father beating his mother through the bedroom wall, then confessed that this boy was his own son. A feeling passed through the crowd like a cool insuck of breath through our bodies. Veronica looked around with surprise.

She seemed impressed when I showed her the boys' club facility and explained our drug rehab programs and outreach ministries.

Afterwards I felt hope as we stepped out onto the crunchy gravel, the strip-mall glass glistening across the boulevard.

What did you think? I asked.

I liked it, she said.

You think you might want to come back?

She seemed sad as she smiled at me. I don't think so, Tomas, she said. She touched my arm, and her fingers lingered.

Well, if you ever change your mind . . .

She looked sorry. As if I had shown her my ugly baby and expected a compliment.

Veronica kept active even during her pregnancy. She continued to wade in the waves and liked to lie out on the beach. She let me feel her sandy abdomen, the growing baby within. We knew it was a boy from the ultrasound, but had no idea there was anything wrong with him. He kicked beneath her warm skin. With my ear against her taut belly button, I could hear sounds of him—or Veronica—moving. Could hear the muted rumble of collapsing waves.

* * *

The boys' club behind the church building used to be a martial arts studio. It still smelled of Japanese floor pads, bare feet, must, and male sweat. It smelled like an old futon. The blindfolded man sniffed at the change in smell, the warmer temperature. He jerked when I shut the metal door and snapped the lock. I sat him on a chair in the center of the room and bound him there.

I'm going to take off your blindfold now, I told him, after I flipped over the only sign with our congregation's name on it.

From behind, I pulled off the bandana. He looked around and said, Where am I?

But I was gone. I was in a hallway behind mirrored one-way glass we had installed to observe the group sessions and recovery groups that met in that room.

I turned to Manny, who sat next to me on an aluminum chair against the wall; watching Harley's father through the one-way glass.

Is that him?

Yeah.

Okay, I said, and pulled the ice pick out of my satchel. Place the tip of the blade on the soft part below the kneecap. Make sure you really punch it through the cartilage. The knee's like tree bark. If you don't get below the surface, the tree doesn't die.

Manny looked at me. You don't actually expect me to do this . . . ?

I do.

He crossed his arms.

Do it for Emerson, I said.

What's all this to you?

In my family—the Laurels—we protect our own, I said.

I held the blade out to him, but he shook his head. I walked into the other room. I knew Manny would be watching from behind the mirrored glass. Harley's father looked up at me.

Who are you? he said.

I kneeled before him, my face close to his own. His chair rattled as his bound hands struggled. I touched his cheek, brushed it softly.

Do you have a son? I asked.

Yes.

Do you love him?

Yes.

I am a father too, I said loudly enough for Manny to hear, and then I reached down and stuck him.

THE HOUR WHEN
THE SHIP COMES IN
BY ROBERT FERRIGNO
Belmont Shore

One good deed . . . One good deed is all it takes to get a man killed. One good deed, one step in front of the other. Yancy staggered down Pomona toward the beach, straightened his shoulders and kept walking. Not far. Pomona ran parallel to Alamitos Bay, close enough to smell the waffle cones at the ice cream parlor on Second Street . . . and the strawberries. He had stopped for a Jamba Juice before they hit the house on Pomona. Mason had complained, eager to get started, but Yancy insisted. A large Strawberry-Kiwi Zinger with protein powder and spirulina. No idea what that shit did, but why take a chance. Full of antioxidants and nutrients specially formulated to increase longevity . . . *live forever*, the sign said. Yancy laughed, and pain shuddered through him.

Beautiful day in Belmont Shore. The yuppie jewel of Long Beach. Late afternoon, the hard chargers on the freeway now, heading home from the job. They spent so much for the Belmont Shore address, but they were hardly ever home. Working late at the job. Cardio classes at the gym. Cursing their way through traffic, radiators boiling over. Spinning the wheel, faster and faster, hamsters in Porsches. Beep-beep.

Three young mothers wheeled their babies down the street. On their way back from the bay. Towels wrapped around their waists, breasts cupped high and tight in their bright bikini tops. Coconut oil glistening. Talk, talk, talk, while their babies lolled in the shade of the strollers, hands next to their sleepy pink faces. Husbands on the way home. Mexican maid cooking dinner. Just enough time for a yoga class.

One of the wives looked at Yancy, saw him watching. She smiled, and Yancy smiled back. He stepped onto the grass, let them pass. Half tempted to bow. Some sweeping flourish. Probably fall on his face. He watched them glide down the sidewalk. The one who had smiled stared at something on the sidewalk. Blood. She looked back at him, hurrying now, and Yancy hurried too. Get to the beach. He wanted to walk on the sand. Listen to the waves. He wanted to walk down the beach until he got to the *Queen Mary*.

Here he was, born and raised in Long Beach and Yancy had never set foot on the *Queen Mary*. Fucker had been docked in Long Beach Harbor for thirty years, but he had always dismissed the idea of visiting. Tourist trap. Floating mall. Overpriced and snooty to boot. Assholes dressed as commodores selling postcards and saltwater taffy. So here he was now . . . at the end of it all, determined to make it aboard. Maybe the guy from the fish-and-chips stand would pipe him aboard. The *Spruce Goose* had been parked right next door when Yancy was a kid. Parked in a huge dome. Awesome fucking airplane. Bigger than the biggest jumbo jet and made out of wood. Yancy used to imagine the *Spruce Goose* busting out of its dome some Halloween night, jumping the *Queen Mary*, the two of them going at it like Godzilla and Mothra. The *Spruce Goose* was long gone. Moved to Oregon or Kansas or some state far away, after flopping with the tourists here. Not enough shit to buy. Just a giant airplane that some guy actually built and flew once, skimming across the waves in Long Beach Harbor. One time, a hearty fuck-you, and then he landed and never flew it again. Yancy had gone to see it three or four times, brought his younger brother James, the two of them standing there for hours just looking at it.

Sirens in the distance as Yancy crossed onto the beach, sand crunching underfoot. Police or ambulance. Headed to the house on Pomona probably. What a mess. He had asked Mason if he was sure about the address. Asked him twice. Mason was sure. Mason was always sure. New guy, PJ, was jumpy. Mason's nephew. Bony kid who talked too much, like he was afraid if he stopped jabbering they would see the fear in his eyes. As if Yancy could miss it.

The beach almost empty this time of day. Just a few wind-surfers making the best of it and families of Mexicans from inland who didn't like mixing with the Anglos sunbathing on the bay. The offshore oil rigs pumped quietly a few thousand yards off the coast, the rigs planted on fake islands painted in pastels of green and pink and blue. They looked like cheap condos out there. Yancy walked along the bike path that wound through the beach, a twisting path to the *Queen Mary*. Couldn't be too far. Couple of miles maybe. He could do that. Good to have goals, that's what that English teacher told him one time. What was his name? Yancy shook his head. Mr. Something . . .

The house on Pomona . . . supposed to be the usual crash and bash. Knock on the door, then bust it open with the swing-arm and rush inside. Mason had bought the swing-arm from some junkie who boosted it out of the back of a SWAT van. Twenty-five-pound steel battering ram. Your tax dollars at work, that's what Mason used to say before he broke down a door. It had only been funny the first time he said it, but that never stopped him. The three of them had clustered around the front door on Pomona, PJ hyperventilating, Yancy trying to calm him down, and Mason rearing back with the swing-arm—here we go, men, your tax dollars at work.

Must have been thirty or forty pigeons on the bike path ahead, pecking away at bread crumbs that some asshole had left. So much for survival of the fittest. Yancy walked right through them, the birds squawking as they gave way, then closing in behind him to return to the bread. Yancy kept moving. Making pretty good progress. The *Queen Mary* visible in the distance, just beyond the pier. His feet hurt. The concrete too hard. Better to feel the sand. Better to be barefoot.

A wino rummaged through a trash can nearby, pulling out half-eaten burgers and loose french fries. Yancy held onto the trash can while he took off his boots. Eight-hundred-dollar Tony Lama lizardskin. Custom-made for Yancy's flat feet. The boots worth every penny. He handed them to the wino.

"I don't shine no shoes," said the wino, a french fry dangling from his mouth. "I got my pride."

"They're for you. Keep them."

The wino didn't react at first, then warily took the boots. He grinned, started to put them on. Stopped. Shook one of them. It made a sound. He turned the boot upside down and blood splashed onto the sand. The wino jumped back, stared at Yancy, backing off now.

Yancy peeled off his socks. One white. One red. Tossed them into the trash can and walked toward the water. The sand warm between his toes. Unsteady now. The sight of blood. It never bothered him . . . unless it was his own.

The house on Pomona was supposed to be fat with coke and cash, but Yancy knew as soon as they got inside that it was a mistake. Three guys sitting on the couch drinking cans of Diet Pepsi and watching tennis on TV. Never met a dope dealer that didn't crave sugar . . . and *tennis?* Give me a fucking break.

Where is it, motherfucker? PJ had shouted, waving his gun. Turn it *over*, motherfucker, or I'll blow your fucking brains out!

Which was *way* too Tarantino, even if it was the right house. Yancy had gone over everything with the kid beforehand. Gone over it ten or twenty times. *Yancy* did the talking. We bust down the door, flash the fake badges, and always speak in a soft, polite manner. Violence, then calm. Violence to get their attention, calm so they did what you wanted them to. After they gave up the dope and money, *then* it was back to the violence. A fast finish and out the door. Last thing Yancy wanted was some doper with a grudge looking for him. Unacceptable. No witnesses was the order of business, except when you broke into the wrong house. Times like today, when it happened, and it *did* happen, you just apologized, put away the badges, said *send a bill to the city,* and hauled ass. No muss, no fuss, no bother. Not today though.

Yancy lurched across the sand, the beach dotted with clumps of brown oil from the offshore rigs. He splashed into the ocean, walked in until it reached mid-calf, then headed north, paralleling the shore, straight for the *Queen Mary.* Cool water, real tingly, a nice little wake-up. He bent down to roll his pants up, lost his footing, and flopped down. Sat there soaking his ass in the ocean. Yancy saw a family of Mexicans eating dinner on a blanket, radio blasting, *niños* playing in the sand. *Mamacita* pointed at Yancy—look at that silly *gringo!*—laughing, and Yancy waved back. He stood up, put his hands on his knees until his head cleared. Walked on.

Soldiered on down the beach. A small plane cruised over-head, trailing a *SECOND ST. SPORTS BAR $2 TEQUILA SHOTS* banner. Yancy kept his eyes on the big boat. Man needed a focus. Something to aim for. *Queen Mary* was the biggest thing in the area.

Getting hard to breathe. Little gurgly sounds every time he took a breath. Tempted to take off his bullet-proof vest, but no telling what that would do. The cinched vest proba-bly the only thing holding him together. Shallow breaths helped. First time in his life he had ever been winded. Yancy lettered in football, baseball, and track in high school. Couple of his records still unbroken at Long Beach Poly. Go Rabbits! Yancy laughed and it hurt worse than ever. He got a scholarship to Cal State, Long Beach, but only lasted a semester. Long enough for Mason to call him *college boy*. Like Yancy was supposed to be ashamed for not moving his lips when he read a newspaper.

Splash splash splash in the shallows. He left a light chum of blood trail in the water. A geezer in plaid Bermuda shorts approached, a sunburned beachcomber working his way along the tideline with a metal detector, moving it back and forth, back and forth. Yancy's uncle did the same thing every weekend after the crowds were gone. All along the beach, head down, earphones cupped in place, oblivious to every-thing but the *beep-beep* that signaled the mother lode. Or a buried beer can. Uncle Dave . . . the treasure hunter. Man had gone to every one of Yancy's football games, cheered himself hoarse, then told him afterwards every mistake he made, every dropped pass, every poorly chosen cutback.

"Any luck?" called Yancy.

The beachcomber lifted one earphone.

"Any luck?" repeated Yancy.

The beachcomber glared at him. Shook his head. Moved on.

Right, pops. Keep your secret stash. Guy probably found a class ring with a glass stone a month ago and now claimed the beach. His old lady was probably glad to get him out of the house, packing him tunafish sandwiches with the crusts cut off. A seagull screamed at Yancy, swooping low. Could be worse. He could be drawing buzzards.

More sirens now. Meat wagons on the way.

Yancy had waved his badge at the yokels watching the tennis match, started to apologize for ruining their front door when PJ barreled over to the couch, started pistol-whipping the biggest one. Yokel went down like a bag of shit.

Yancy had looked over at Mason, like, You brought this asshole to the party, you vouched for him, now jerk his leash. Mason just rolled his eyes.

Maybe if the yokels had taken the beating, things might still have worked out okay, but this buff dude with a Rolex, probably the guy who owned the home, this buff dude grabbed PJ, and just like that, PJ capped him. Just jammed the gun in his face and *pow pow pow*. Guy's head made like a melon. Nothing for Yancy to do at that point except let nature take its course. PJ had his rage on full throttle. No way you could get in the way of that. The other guy on the couch had his hands up, like, Don't shoot, man, I surrender. PJ shot him in the eye. Tapped a couple into the pistol-whipped guy on the floor. You would have thought it was Fourth of July, what with the sound and PJ grinning, bouncing around, stepping on teeth, face sprayed with blood. Yancy turned away, watched the tennis player on TV holding up a gold trophy, his clothes so white . . . Yancy turned at the sound of a toilet flushing. A girl came out of the bathroom.

Yancy stayed in the water as two young men in black suits approached. Bible patrol. They hit the beaches every day, trolling for converts. Or maybe it was easy duty to score points with God. The Bible boys stayed on dry land, stepping back every time the waves rolled in. Doing the hokeypokey. Ugly-ass shoes on the boys. Big black shoes with thick crepe soles. Jesus could walk on water, but they didn't want to put it to the test.

"Could we talk to you for a minute, sir?" asked the one with the dusting of pimples across his cheeks.

"I'm in kind of a hurry."

"Always time to hear the good news," said the other one. The one with the frayed collar and the thin lips. "We just need a few moments. Could change your life."

"My life's already changed."

"Are you all right, sir?" said the one with the pimples.

Yancy walked on. The one with the pimples kept pace for a few steps, then gave up. Other fish in the sea. Yancy was a lost cause. He believed in God . . . *his* God, not theirs. That was the problem. No way God forgave everything you did. What kind of a chump would that make God? You do all kinds of evil shit your whole life, then at the last minute you say you're sorry and the pearly gates swing wide? No way. Heaven would be filled with con men and hustlers if that were the case. No, God was a referee. He kept score, that's it. At the end of the day, you were either in positive or negative territory. God didn't hear sorry. He didn't hear boo-hoo. He just added things up. You had to respect that motherfucker.

He was tired. Now I lay me down to sleep . . . the prayer his mother taught them, him and James . . . Now I lay me down to sleep, I pray the Lord my soul to keep. God bless Mama and James and Yancy. Good luck with that last one. Better to trust putting one foot in front of the other.

Would be nice to call James. He was probably still at work. Welder at the port. Sucking in lead fumes for eighteen dollars an hour and benefits. Rented apartment and a car with rust on the door panels and maybe a movie once a month. Amazing the things that made people happy. Wife and a little girl, Cleo. Another one on the way. Kathy sexy and skinny when he married her, now her hips were spreading like a jumbo jet. Yeah, amazing the things that made people happy. Yancy had gone over there for Christmas, bought too many toys for Cleo. Too many expensive toys. James and Cleo exchanging looks. Yancy making excuses why he had to leave early.

Limping now, he walked under the pier. Concrete piling crusted with barnacles. Cigarette butts floating on the water. Voices from the pier echoed around him. Vietnamese fishermen trying for dinner, casting their lines with easy flicks of their wrists. Skaters and skateboarders rolling. Music, music, music . . . Keep walking. The *Queen Mary* closer now, the railings edged with silver. Three smokestacks stark against the sunset.

Everything would be different if the girl hadn't walked out of the bathroom back at the house on Pomona. She hummed as she closed the door behind her, clutching a baby. Must have been changing it when the killing went down. It . . . he, she, whatever. Yancy didn't know from babies. What he knew was taking down dopers and getting away clean.

Yancy tried to make her disappear, make her go back into the bathroom, pretend she hadn't seen anything. Mason knew better. He had his faults, but he knew what he had to do.

The girl stood there, mouth moving like a fish, no sound coming out. Eyes shifting from the bodies on the floor to

Mason. She half-turned her body as Mason raised his pistol. Half-turned her body, as though that would protect the baby.

Maybe that's why Yancy had done what he did. Stupid thing. No explaining it really. Just as Mason tightened on the trigger, Yancy shot him in the head. He shot PJ too, but not before PJ shot him four times. Kid was quick, you had to give him that. Three of PJ's rounds hit Yancy in the vest, but the impact of the rounds twisted him, and the fourth bullet slipped under his arm, bounced around inside him, tumbling like a load of laundry in a dryer. Good thing PJ liked a 9mm Glock. All the young guys did. That's what they saw in the movies. Yancy preferred a .45. He felt the comforting heft of the .45 in his jacket with every step. Mean gun, no grace to it, but one shot in a vital area and you were dead. Case closed. 9mm had no stopping power. Man could walk forever with a 9mm slug in him. Yancy was proof of that.

The girl was unhurt. Hysterical, of course. She found her voice after he killed Mason and PJ, the girl screaming so loud he could hardly wait to leave.

Funny . . . he had made such rapid progress toward the *Queen Mary* at the beginning, but now he seemed to be moving slower and slower. He walked along the edge of the water, where the sand was hard-packed. He kept walking but didn't seem to be getting any closer. It was like . . . he was being allowed to approach his goal, get it in sight, but there were limitations. Like the *Queen Mary* was off limits. Going to be dark soon. At this rate . . . he was never going to get there.

He just wished he could figure out why he did what he had done at the house on Pomona. Killing Mason . . . how could he explain that? Mason was making the right move. The girl had seen them. Could ID them. Rules were rules. Mason followed the rules . . . it was Yancy who had broken them. PJ was a hothead and Yancy knew he wouldn't work with the kid again, but Mason and he had partnered for three years. Mason had thrown him a party when Yancy killed his twelfth man. His first dozen. Mason made a big deal about it, rented a suite at the Four Seasons and hired a couple of hookers for each of them. Top-quality ladies too. Mason talked too much and stank up the car with fish tacos and jalapeño burritos, but Mason was dependable. Yancy was the one who'd had a change of heart, and that bothered him. It was like his whole life up until now was *wrong* somehow.

The girl didn't remind him of anybody. She wasn't particularly pretty or gentle or sad or any of that other crap that always made the movie bad guy spare her life. And that bit about her trying to protect the baby . . . he didn't even *like* babies, and besides, that was just a reaction on her part. No courage or nobility to it. She probably didn't even know what she was doing. Yancy coughed, spit blood into the water. He was too tired to convince himself, but what he had done in that split second at the house gnawed at him. Throwing away his life, that's what he had done. Nothing wrong with his life . . . nothing . . . and yet he had tossed it aside with the squeeze of a trigger. Blowing away Mason and PJ . . . Now what was he supposed to do? Ask James to get him a job at the port?

Yancy stumbled up onto the dunes. Soft sand with not a speck of oil on it. Sand like sugar, heaps of it . . . and he had a perfect view of the big boat. He sat down. Just a little break. A little rest before starting back up again. He lay back on that pure white sand. Stretched out his arms, scooped them back and forth. Made sand angels. He and James used to do that when they were kids. Spreading their arms wide, the two of them making flapping sounds. Wings big enough to carry them to heaven. Now, though, his sand angel was sloppy and uneven . . . broken somehow. Yancy lay still, arms poked out at a crooked angle. Just a little rest, that's all he needed. He watched the *Queen Mary* floating there in the blazing sunset. Every seam and rivet in sharp focus. Ship of gold. Close enough to touch.

WHAT YOU SEE

BY DIANA WAGMAN
Westchester

It was a street like any other street in Westchester. Small square homes lined up on either side like kindergarteners on their first day of school. Tidy but timid, they were little houses where your neighbors might live, where your mother might live, where you might live if it was all you could afford in Los Angeles. Two bedrooms, one bath, sometimes a small sun porch in the back. On Orange Street it was still 1965. The yuppies hadn't found it and torn up the green lawns to do drought-tolerant landscaping with native plants.

Orange was my childhood street and I was stuck there. I'd inherited the house from my mother and I had nowhere else to go. After living in New York City and other points east, I'd come back to L.A. to take care of her. Not that she needed me; she was dying and there was nothing I could do. But I moved right back into my childhood room. I slept in my twin bed with the brown plaid polyester bedspread. My blue ribbon from freshman football was hanging where I'd stuck it in ninth grade on the bulletin board over my desk next to my picture of Bruce Lee. Everything in my room was the same as I'd left it, but covered in a shroud of dust. It made me sneeze. My mother would call out while she still could: *God bless you.*

Sneeze.

God bless you.

Some days it was our only communication.

Then she died and I stayed in my room and she went to Heaven. At least that's where she had always told me she was going. And I wasn't. She would be singing with the Heavenly Choir and I would be roasting in the flames of Eternal Damnation. If only I had died before I was twelve and got caught jerking off in the Sunday school teacher's car. My mother never forgave me. The Sunday school teacher wouldn't let me back in her class. From puberty on, everyone agreed I was just like my father, the missing felon.

The first few days after she passed away, I watched a lot of TV and didn't eat anything. I wanted to see how long I could go without food. It was just something to do. The commercials made me really hungry. So, after eighty-one hours and twenty-two minutes, I ate. Whatever she had in the house. Cans of peaches and kidney beans. Dried prunes. I even made a devil's food cake from a box mix that had probably been on the shelf since the last time I'd been home. My birthday, three years earlier. We'd had a fight and she'd never made me the cake.

Once I was eating, I started pacing. I made a route from the TV to the kitchen to the back door. Touch the door. Turn around. Kitchen to my mother's room, and touch the headboard on her stripped bed. Turn around. Into the bathroom. Touch the glass poodle on the window ledge. Turn around. Into my room. Touch the empty fish tank, the blue ribbon, and the row of James Bond books. Back to the TV.

The glass poodle broke. Guess I tapped it too hard that time. It fell on the tile floor and shattered. After that I was careful to wear my shoes. Even in the middle of the night. I enjoyed the crunch when I went into the bathroom to pee in the dark. It sounded as if I were walking on potato chips. That made me laugh. I pretended I was an explorer in the

Amazon and I was crushing cockroaches the size of hamsters. I imagined I was king of the world and I had jewels strewn before me wherever I might walk—even to take a shit. Eventually the pieces were all broken down in a fine, annoying grit that stuck to my rubber soles. When I started trailing glass dust all over the house, I cleaned it up.

Cleaning was good. I cleaned a lot. I moved the TV cabinet and cleaned behind it. I found a Christmas card from 1979 when I was six years old. I remember that Christmas. I remember wanting something so badly and praying for it as hard as I could, but what I got was something different. I liked it too, but it wasn't what I'd been asking for. I can't remember what it was, only the want like a tight place in my chest. I pushed the couch to the middle of the room so I could get the dust bunnies along the baseboard. I hoisted the armchair on top of it. That looked pretty good to me, so I climbed up and sat in it. Of course I tipped over and fell. I banged my arm hard on the colonial-style coffee table. As if they had coffee tables in the Colonies.

Immediately, I carried the coffee table out to the curb. That was enough of that. Someone driving by would take it home to his mother and she would be so happy. The front door opened in the house across the street. I didn't know those people. Out came a young black girl, in candy-pink capris and a tight white tank top with glitter in a heart on the front. The neighborhood was mostly black people now. Not that it mattered to me or my mom—even before she was dead.

The girl was carrying her car keys, but she stopped at the door to her little red Chevette. "Sorry about your ma."

She made me notice the flowers in the yard next door and the blue sky.

"She was old," I said. "And sick."

"You puttin' out that little table?"

"I always hated it."

The girl laughed. Her teeth were as white and sparkly as her shirt. She nodded. She knew what I meant.

"Do you live there?" I asked.

"It's my brother's house. I'm just staying with him for a while."

"Welcome to the neighborhood."

She shrugged and her brown shoulders gleamed in the sunshine.

"Wanna come in? Have a drink or something?" I asked.

"I got to go. I'm late for class."

Loyola Marymount University was right nearby. She didn't look like one of those stuck-up Loyola students. Stupid Jesuit school. I'd been destined for it starting at about, oh, maybe two years old, but that was another way I'd disappointed my mother. Too dumb to get into Loyola.

"Not LMU?" I asked her.

"Over to the aviation college. I'm gonna be a flight attendant."

"See the world."

"Exactly."

She got in her car then and drove away and I was glad to know she'd be back. I left the coffee table out, but I pulled it off the sidewalk and onto the edge of my lawn. Just in case she wanted it for her mother. Then I went into the house and sat down on the couch. I could see the table through the big picture window. I could see her brother's house across the street. Later, I'd be busy doing other things and I'd walk through the room and look out the window and see her struggling with it. I'd come out and lift it into her car. Then she'd have to take me over to her mom's with her so I could help her get it in the house. We'd have fun and then she'd be a flight attendant and fly away.

And one day, awhile after that, I'd see her on an airplane. I'd be sitting in first class, in a really nice suit, blue, no, maybe dark charcoal-gray, and I'd be flying on my way to some big deal and there she'd be.

"Would you care for a beverage?"

"Don't you remember me?"

And of course she would and she'd be so impressed and she'd look great in her cute stewardess outfit like a military uniform and we'd go right to the airport bar after and talk and talk and talk. Every tired businessman in his wrinkled old suit that came in would be jealous and looking at me, and she'd be looking at me too.

I practiced walking through the living room and glancing out the window. The phone rang and I lost my concentration and I realized I might actually miss her coming to pick up the table if I wasn't watching every minute. I got the phone out of the kitchen and sat down on the couch with it.

"Hello?"

"Gabe? That you?"

"Yeah," I said.

"How they hangin'?"

"Who is this?"

"Who the fuck do you think it is?"

Guess I was concentrating so hard watching for her to return that I wasn't listening very well. It was Marcus, of course. He was my one buddy left from high school, the only other kid I knew who didn't graduate. He had his own apartment and some kind of import business.

"I got some more work for you."

I didn't want to work right then. I was waiting. If I left and went to his office and did something, I might miss her.

"I need you, Gabe. And don't tell me you don't need the money."

Of course that got me thinking. If I had some money, I could ask her out someplace, not just over to the house. I hadn't showered in a few days or changed my clothes, so I told him I'd be there in a while.

"Hurry," he said. "It's important."

I drove my mother's car over to his office on the south side of the airport. I went past Dockweiler Beach, the noisiest oceanfront in America. I pitied the tourists who parked their RVs down there for some fun in the sun and then had to shout over the planes coming and going all day. When I was a kid there were houses nearby, but the land had been bought up for the airport expansion. Now it was just weeds growing through cracked cement—the roads were there but the houses, the streetlamps, everything else was gone. It was the driveways that gave me the creeps, parking for no place.

Marcus's shop was in an industrial park. Row after row of white industrial buildings, like carryout boxes stacked on a metal shelf. They all looked the same except for the company logos. Marcus's shop was the only one without a sign, just a glass door up three cement steps. I always told him he needed to hang something up.

The same old tired secretary, Kimberly, was sitting behind the desk. Her hair had gotten blonder and more and more like broom straw over the years. She smiled at me and I saw how her maroon lipstick was bleeding up into the wrinkles over her lip.

"Hey, Gabe."

"Hey, Kimberly."

I sat and waited. Actually, it was nice to be someplace other than the house. I'd been to the funeral home, of course, and the funeral, but other than that I hadn't been anywhere. The brown-and-beige-flecked carpeting was soft under my feet. I could feel the glass grit from the broken poodle coming off my soles into the fibers, and I felt bad, but I was glad to be rid of it. Marcus had someone come in and clean anyway. I shuffled my feet back and forth, back and forth. Kimberly looked up at me.

"I like the new carpet."

She nodded and went back to what she was doing. Whatever that was. I sat on the same beige Naugahyde couch Marcus had always had. I think his parents had it back when we were in high school—in the den. I picked up a magazine off the end table. It was about golf. I tossed it back on the table.

"What the hell you got golf magazines for?" I asked Marcus when he came out.

"Come on," he said.

I followed him out the door and around to his little storage unit in the back. The sun glared at me, reprimanded me, and I hadn't done a thing wrong.

"Do you play golf now or what?"

"Pay attention."

"Golf is a loser game."

"Will you shut up?"

He unlocked the garage door and lifted it open. I liked the way it looked flat when it was down and then folded like a paper fan when he opened it. I ran my hand over the part I could reach. You couldn't even tell it would fold.

"Gabe. You with me?"

"Jesus, Marcus. You act like I'm an idiot. "

"This is important."

"My mom died, but I'm just the same."

"Your mom dying's got nothing to do with it. This is all you."

"That's right. One hundred percent prime American man." I laughed. He gave a snort.

Behind some boxes there was a square silver metal suitcase that looked like it held equipment of some kind.

"Grab that," he said. "Put it in your car."

It was lighter than it appeared. I'd expected the weight of a piece of machinery. "What's in here? Hundred-dollar bills?"

"I'm donating to Toys for Tots."

I laughed. Marcus wouldn't donate a rotten egg to his starving mother. I carried the case back around to my car. I opened the trunk.

"Don't put it back there. Put it in the backseat."

"It's a fuckin' suitcase."

"Backseat."

"Yessir." I closed the trunk, walked around, and threw the case on the seat.

"Shit! Be careful."

"It's a metal case."

"I told you it's fragile."

"No, you didn't."

"I did."

"No, I'm sorry, Mr. Big Shot Importer, you did not."

"Then I'm telling you now."

"Then I heard you now."

He handed me a piece of notebook paper with a map drawn on it. It wasn't far away. It was parking lot number 4 in the Ballona Wetlands.

"What am I supposed to do in a parking lot?"

"The guy who wants this will meet you there."

"In a parking lot? This sounds mighty fishy."

"To who?"

"Ballona Wetlands—fishy—get it?"

Marcus shook his head.

"Or should I say *birdy*—it's a bird refuge, after all."

"What the fuck would *birdy* mean?"

"Good point." I started to get in the car, and then I stopped. "It's five minutes away. Why don't you take it yourself? Or get old Kimberly to do it on her lunch hour."

He wasn't smiling. "You want the money or not?"

I shrugged, and then I thought of what fifty bucks would buy me and my pretty brown girl. I felt a burn like hot liquid run down my throat into my chest. And lower.

"Wanna come over later?" I asked Marcus. "I got someone I want you to meet."

"Just get this done. Then we'll see."

"Can you give me some money now? I'm starving. I need to get a burger or something on the way."

"I'll give you twenty now, but don't stop till after you make the drop-off. This has to be there—A.S.A.P."

"A.S.A.P. What are you, some kind of general?" He looked pissed off, and that made me laugh. "And you did not ever tell me before it was fragile. You did not."

He growled. I loved it when he growled. That meant I'd got him good.

I waved goodbye from inside my mother's car. It still smelled like her, that perfume she always wore, and the hairspray. She never got that old-person smell like some people. She just smelled like herself until the day she died, and then she had a weird shit smell cause her bowels sort of let go. There was a used Kleenex in the cup holder. Maybe her last

Kleenex from the last time she drove the car. I didn't like to think what was wadded up inside it. It had bothered me all the way over to Marcus's and I had meant to take it in and throw it away in Kimberly's little metal trash can, but I forgot. It made me mad to see it, so I opened my window and threw it out. I didn't want to litter, but I just couldn't stand seeing that tissue anymore.

This was all I ever did for Marcus, take shit places. Sometimes it was one box, sometimes it was many boxes and I'd get to drive the van. I liked his van; it was more official than Mom's car. Usually I just took the boxes to the airport and waited around while the guy did all the paperwork.

Awhile back I had asked Marcus, "If you're an *im*-porter, how come I'm always taking boxes away? Shouldn't I be picking them up?"

"I use the smart guy for that."

We both laughed at that one. I knew the other guy who worked for him.

This was the first time I'd taken anything to a parking lot. I didn't care what Marcus was into, and I knew I was safe or he wouldn't have asked me, but it was odd. When I stopped for my burger I would open the stupid case and look inside. Maybe I really was Santa Claus delivering toys. Somehow I doubted it.

I headed away from the airport, toward Westchester proper. There was an In-N-Out on Sepulveda, and if it wasn't crowded I could just dip into the drive-thru and be on my way in minutes. I had to eat. It was after noon and I'd had nothing. Goddamn traffic. All around me. Who were all these people? Westchester had been a quiet place when I was a kid. I remember watching the gnats cluster in the sun right in the middle of Lincoln Boulevard. I remember crouching on the sidewalk in front of Baskin-Robbins and feeding ice cream drips to the ants. Mom always ate rainbow sherbet. I always had mint chocolate chip. I should have brought her some sherbet when I first got home and she could still eat. It made me feel sick suddenly that I hadn't. I hadn't brought her anything. I saw my Baskin-Robbins, but it just looked ugly, sandwiched between Starbucks and an expensive juice place. I felt so sad. And old. Thirty-three and I felt like I was a hundred years old. I wasn't hungry anymore. I figured I'd just get on with delivering the stupid old case.

I turned onto a side street, Winsford Avenue, and wound back through the neighborhood toward Lincoln. Winsford wasn't as nice as Orange Street, my street. Nothing looked as nice anymore. The sky was gray and nobody had a green lawn and the goddamn planes kept going overhead.

Then I saw it. I had to turn on 80th to meet up with Lincoln, and there it was: the Collier School of Aviation Technology. Her school. It was right here and I was driving right past and I knew it was another moment of destiny. It was brown cinder block, about three stories high, just a box, but what more did a school need to be? I could see the fluorescent lights on in the upstairs classrooms. That's where she was, sitting under that vibrating, humming, greening light, listening to a lecture or maybe practicing carrying a tray of coffee cups down a turbulent aisle. *Bump. Bump.* Her hip jostling against my shoulder.

"I'm so sorry," she'd say. Then she'd turn and see me. "Oh, it's you."

"I wondered when you'd notice."

I drove into the parking lot. I circled through until I found her Chevette. She really was there. All I had to do was wait. But I had the stupid case to deliver. It was quarter to 2.

Her class was probably over at 2. I couldn't get to the Ballona Wetlands and back in fifteen minutes. I could leave her a note if I had a piece of paper and a pencil, a note that would say, *I was driving by on my way to an important meeting and saw your car. Hope you had fun at school. See you later.* But she didn't even know my name.

I sat in my mom's car thinking about it, trying to decide what to do. She might remember me if I drew a picture of the coffee table, or of the birdbath with the plaster angel in my front yard. But again I'd need a piece of paper and a pencil. I must've sat for a while, because then I saw her. I saw a whole bunch of young stewardesses-to-be coming out of the building. They were walking together and talking and they were all so pretty, and then there she was. Prettiest of all. I saw those pink pants and that bright white white white top. She made me smile.

I got out of the car. "Hey," I called to her.

Of course she looked startled. Who wouldn't? She was not expecting me, her neighbor with the coffee table, her funny-guy neighbor all showered and shaved and standing by her car. She frowned.

"It's me," I said, "the guy from across the street."

"Yeah, I know."

"You comin' over here or what?"

She took a step toward me, then plucked at her girlfriend's sleeve and pulled her over too. They stopped a little ways away. "What are you doing here?"

"I want to be a stewardess too."

"We're called flight attendants."

"Lah dee dah. Well, I'm a goods-and-services transport technician."

"What's that?" It was the girlfriend who asked. Truth is,

I can't even remember what she looked like, I was so blinded by my girl's shining radiance.

"I make deliveries."

They both laughed.

"I was driving by on my way to an appointment—"

"A delivery, you mean."

"And I saw your car. You wanna go with me?"

"On your delivery?"

It was a stroke of genius, thinking of that. I could see she wanted to. She was intrigued. What did I deliver? And where? I was in a service industry just like hers and we were interested in each other's work. Sitting at the kitchen table at night, I'd ask her about the funny passengers she helped and if there were any babies on the flight, and she'd ask me about Roger the airport guy, and Marcus, and Kimberly. We'd talk and tell each other stories over dinner.

"Your chariot awaits," I said to her, and I bowed.

"I'm bringing Chara with me. Okay?"

That was her girlfriend obviously, and I was naturally a little disappointed. "Okay."

Chara got in the backseat. "Ooeee. What's in there? It smells."

"It does not," I said.

"You're not sitting right next to it. It's like Clorox or something. Nasty." She pushed it away from her.

"It's fragile, so be careful."

My girl sat up front. She turned toward me and smiled and her brown eyes were big and happy. They were beautiful eyes with black lashes so long and thick they looked like the bristles in my hairbrush. I wanted to feel them against my cheek; *butterfly kisses*, my mother called them.

"Where we going?" she asked.

"Ballona Wetlands."

"What for?" Chara in the backseat was a complainer, I could tell. "I need to get home."

"Won't take long," I said. "I'm just giving that suitcase to someone. My friend's in the importing business. Stuff from all over the world." I looked at the clock on the dash. It had been quite awhile since I left Marcus. I knew the guy would be there waiting. I hoped he wouldn't be too pissed that I was late.

"What's your name?" I asked her.

"Terrell," she said. "I was named for my dad, Terry, and my aunt, Ellie."

"It's pretty."

"What do they call you?" Chara asked from the backseat.

"Gabe, short for Gabriel."

"A real angel," Terrell said.

"He sure is white," said Chara.

"Nothin' wrong with that."

Right away, Terrell and I were together in the car, a duo. Immediately we were joined and Chara was on her own. I don't know how long they'd been friends. I don't know if they even really liked each other, but I knew Terrell was mine. She was falling toward me. I could feel the pull, like she was the iron shavings in my old science kit and I was the magnet.

She couldn't help turning to me. I was happy. "You're awfully skinny," she said. "You need to eat more."

"After this, I'll take you for a burger or some french fries."

"I'm starving," Chara said.

I wanted to make her get out of the car. I should have, but of course I didn't. We're all so nice to each other, nice and polite, until we're not. Maybe if we were rude in little ways at the very moment we got annoyed, we wouldn't kill each other later. I drove down the hill past LMU and turned left off Lincoln into the Ballona Wetlands Preserve. I saw the wildflowers blooming and the bog smell was pleasant, earthy, and wet, like a mud puddle in the backyard. We bumped along. The road wasn't well paved. Terrell squealed when we bottomed out in a particularly large pothole, and I laughed at her.

"How are you gonna be a stewardess if the bumps bother you so much?"

"Flight attendant." Chara corrected me like a schoolteacher.

Terrell just giggled. "I sure don't like the bumps," she said to me, and me alone.

She had told me a secret. I felt bigger then, like I'd grown six inches taller and thirty pounds heavier and I had hands and feet like a big man. I wanted to touch her shiny shoulder, but I didn't because of Chara.

"There," I said. "There's the parking lot."

My piece of paper said *parking lot 4* and I saw the little wooden sign with the yellow number 4. The sky was like a baby store—pink and blue. The lot was empty. Marcus would kill me.

"There's no one here," Chara said.

"Will you shut up?" I couldn't hold back.

"I'm getting out of this car."

"Don't."

"I refuse to be spoken to like that. I'm gonna call my brother to come get me."

"Stay in the car." This from Terrell. "Please?"

"I don't want to stay with that smelly old thing." She pushed the case hard and it made a thump against the other door.

"Don't touch it!" I shouted.

"What's in it?" she asked.

"I don't know."

"Money. Drugs. You know, Terrell, how they make it smell so the dogs can't sniff it?"

"Chara." Terrell frowned, but her friend was getting hysterical.

"It's not good. It's not safe. Where are we? What are we doing here? I want to go home! You tell him to take me home!"

Terrell turned around and leaned over the seat. "What's the matter? What's wrong with you? Gabe here lives across the street from my brother. He'll take us home, soon as we deliver this."

"Stop the car!" Chara screamed.

She opened her door. I slammed on the brakes and she fell forward onto Terrell's seat. She screamed, and when she came up her nose was bloody. I hadn't meant to stop short, but I didn't want her to fall out onto the street.

"Oh my God," Terrell said.

Chara was scrambling out of the car. She stumbled in the dirt parking lot. She was wearing a little skirt and ridiculous high heels.

"His mother just died!" Terrell called to her. "Wait."

Chara was trying to run away.

"Where is she going?" I couldn't help but ask. We were way back deep into the preserve, surrounded by bog and birds and not much else. A black town car came down the road toward us, moving fast, dust in a plume behind it. I breathed a big sigh of relief. My guy. He was later than I was.

Chara was flagging him down.

"Chara!" I shouted. I had gotten out of the car. "Stop. That's my guy. That's who I'm meeting."

Terrell was out of the car and running toward Chara now. The town car had stopped and I could see the man had rolled down his window. He was big; he looked too big for the town car. He was hunched over the steering wheel so his head wouldn't hit the ceiling. He frowned up at her, at Chara. She was crying and her nose was bleeding and she was begging him to let her in the car, to take her away, to call the police.

"He's got something bad in that case!" she said. "He's a crazy man!"

"What the fuck are you talking about?" I hollered.

Terrell reached her before I did and she pulled on Chara's arm. She was trying to drag her away from the car and apologize to the man at the same time. He seemed amused. He was looking at the two girls, he was looking at my girl and he was smiling.

Couple of silly females, I'd tell him. Chara just fell off her goddamn shoes. Marcus and Terrell and I would laugh about Chara later. I'd sit on that creamy Naugahyde with my arm around her and we'd be drinking a beer and laughing about poor Chara and her stupid shoes.

The guy reached out his window and grabbed Chara's arm with his giant's hand. He started to roll forward. Chara had to run along with him. He sped up. Terrell was running too, trying to peel his fingers from Chara's arm.

I hurried back to my mother's car. I opened the back door and the case fell out onto the ground. It fell hard and I worried about breaking whatever was inside. I picked it up. Something inside had come loose. Something was bumping around in there.

"Here!" I came running toward the town car. "Take it."

Chara was trotting now, and blubbering. On those spike heels she was jogging, but she was getting tired. She stumbled and then she fell and made this horrible choking sound, but he didn't let go, he just dragged her along next to him. Terrell screamed then. A beautiful, high scream, as much like a bird as a woman, in so much pain it hurt my heart to hear it. She put her fists over her eyes.

Good, I thought. *Good. No one should see this. My sweet baby can't see this.* The driver dragged Chara until she stopped flopping, and then he dropped her. She lay there and he backed up and ran right over her. Then forward. There was this popping sound, loud as a firecracker but more hollow and round, and then a scuffling, and when I looked again, Chara's legs were flat, but her arms were clawing in the dirt. I wanted her to die so she'd stop that noise, stop scratching. She was like a fly with its wings plucked off. Terrell had fallen to her knees. I had the case in my hand.

"Here!" I screamed again at the guy. "Here!"

Take this, leave my girl alone. Take this suitcase.

I ran toward him, but he was spinning his car in the dirt, doing a 360, heading for Terrell. She got up. She was no fool, and she started to run. She zig-zagged back and forth so the car couldn't follow her. Made me so proud the way she ran and tried to save herself. She ran like the wind, like a nymph, like an angel. I was coming straight toward the car. I held the case in front of me. He was coming for both of us.

"Stop!" I screamed at him. "Stop!"

I flung the case at the car, but the catch opened in the air, must've come loose when it fell out of the car. A head, a human head, launched out of that suitcase like a sixty-yard pass into the air. I stopped and watched. I saw the face, eyes open, mouth in a sneer; I saw the veins and tendons dangling from the neck as it spun in the air. It went over the fence into the marsh. *Splash.* A blue heron took off and sailed away. The car idled behind me. The suitcase lay open on the dirt. The foam rubber inside was black and shiny—with blood, I suppose. I couldn't tell. Brain fluid. Snot. Tears. I turned to Terrell. *Run*, I mouthed. Keep running. But she was looking at the marsh. She was wondering if she had really seen a man's head fly out of a suitcase or if it had fallen from the sky. Maybe it had come from that plane overhead. Maybe there had been some kind of midair collision and it would start raining body parts and she would have to help out with all the dead and hurt people. Maybe she was on another plane, serving cocktails and making conversation with the passengers. She was anywhere but here.

There was another loud noise and Terrell went forward. I think I saw the bullet enter her back and slip into her heart. I know I felt it. I heard my mother singing. She and Terrell would be great friends, a mother and the daughter that she never had. That was Heaven. It was. And I felt the heat coming for me up through the ground, I heard it rumbling behind me, getting louder and louder. The soles of my shoes were melting, my bones turning into oil and beginning to bubble, and I deserved it because I had started all of this. There was a moment, *BAM*, a flash, as I followed that blue heron and I thought my mother's arms reached for me. I was way up high. I saw it. I saw it all. The Kleenex I'd thrown out the window. My house on Orange Street. The coffee table still on the front lawn. I was sorry. I was so sorry.

ABOUT THE CONTRIBUTORS

Wendy Werris

MICHAEL CONNELLY is the author of seventeen novels, many of which feature LAPD Detective Harry Bosch. He lived in Los Angeles near Mulholland Drive for fourteen years and now splits his time between California and Florida, where he grew up.

ROBERT FERRIGNO is the author of nine thrillers. His most recent book, *Prayers for the Assassin,* was a *New York Times* best-seller. For more information, visit www.prayers-fortheassassin.com and www.robertferrigno.com.

Claudia Kunin

JANET FITCH is the author of the novels *Paint It Black* and *White Oleander.* She is a third-generation resident of Los Angeles, where she lives in the Silverlake district. Currently, Fitch teaches in the Masters of Professional Writing program at the University of Southern California.

Jeff Kreider

DENISE HAMILTON'S crime novels have been short-listed for the Edgar Allen Poe and the Willa Cather awards. A native Angeleno, she is a former reporter for the *Los Angeles Times* and a Fulbright scholar. Visit her at www.denisehamilton.com.

Mario G. Reyes

NAOMI HIRAHARA is the author of the Mas Arai mystery series, featuring a Japanese American gardener and atomic bomb survivor living in Altadena, California. A former editor of *The Rafu Shimpo* daily newspaper in Los Angeles, she has produced more than seven nonfiction books related to Southern California and Asian American history. Her latest novel, *Snakeskin Shamisen,* is an Edgar Award finalist. Her website is www.naomihirahara.com.

Bob Buck

EMORY HOLMES II is a Los Angeles–based writer. His stories have appeared in the *San Francisco Chronicle,* the *Los Angeles Times,* the *Los Angeles Sentinel,* the *New York Amsterdam News, Written By* magazine, and other publications.

Ted Roberts, Los Angeles Times

PATT MORRISON is a veteran *Los Angeles Times* reporter and columnist, host of a daily program on NPR affiliate KPCC, commentator for NPR's *Morning Edition,* and author of a best-selling book on the Los Angeles River [non-fiction, really]. She has been a six-time Emmy-winning host and commentator for a local PBS public affairs program, and host of a nationally syndicated book show.

JIM PASCOE made a name for himself in the noir/crime fiction community as the copublisher of the critically acclaimed indie press UglyTown, which brought out his first two books, *By the Balls: A Bowling Alley Murder Mystery* and *Five Shots and a Funeral.* He is writing a dark manga series called *Undertown,* as well as a number of original comics based on *Hellboy Animated.* He lives in Los Angeles.

Ibarionex R. Perello

GARY PHILLIPS writes about crime, giant three-armed robots, babes with Ph.D.'s in tights, and other such subject matter. He is finishing up a novel set during World War II, coediting the *Darker Mask* anthology of edgy superhero prose stories, and writing a coming-of-age graphic novel about black and Latino teenagers growing up in '80s South Central L.A.

Anne Yard

SCOTT PHILLIPS was born in Wichita, Kansas, and spent many years in Paris before heading to Southern California. After moving, over a twelve- or thirteen-year period, from Studio City to Ventura to Woodland Hills to Koreatown to Pacific Palisades, he eventually gave up and relocated, tail between his legs, to St. Louis, Missouri.

Niles Fuller

NEAL POLLACK'S memoir, *Alternadad*, was published by Pantheon in early 2007. The editor of *Chicago Noir*, Pollack lives in Los Angeles with his family. His website and blog, www.nealpollack.com, are generally informative and amusing.

Brian Orter

CHRISTOPHER RICE is the *New York Times* best-selling author of three novels, mostly recently *Light Before Day*. A Lambda Literary Award–winner, he is also a regular columnist for the *Advocate* and is currently a visiting faculty member at the graduate writing program of Otis College of Art and Design. He lives in West Hollywood. For more information, visit www.christopherricebooks.com.

Carla Roley

BRIAN ASCALON ROLEY, a Los Angeles native, is the author of the novel *American Son*, which received the 2003 Association of Asian American Studies Prose Book Award. It was a *New York Times* Notable Book, one of the *Los Angeles Times'* Best Books of the Year, and a finalist for the Kiriyama Pacific Rim Book Prize. More information can be found at www.brianroley.com.

Maximillian Silver

LIENNA SILVER was born in Russia, and immigrated to the United States before Perestroyka came to the rescue. In Los Angeles, she began translating plays and screenplays, and cowrote a project for British Screen International. Her short stories have received numerous honorary awards, and she is working on a novel about contemporary Russia.

Dan Chavkin

SUSAN STRAIGHT was born in Riverside, where she still lives with her family. She has published six novels. Her latest, *A Million Nightingales* (Pantheon, 2006), set during slavery, is the first of a trilogy about the characters who appear in "The Golden Gopher."

Jerry Bauer

HÉCTOR TOBAR is the son of Guatemalan immigrants and the author of *Translation Nation* and *The Tattooed Soldier*. Born in L.A., he has been editor of the bilingual San Francisco newspaper *El Tecolote* and features editor at the *LA Weekly*, and he has written for the *New Yorker*, the *Nation*, and other publications. He now reports for the *Los Angeles Times* from Mexico City, and is married with three children.

Tod Mesirow

DIANA WAGMAN is the author of three novels and the film *Delivering Milo*. She is the recipient of the 2001 PEN Center USA West Award for Fiction. She teaches in the film department at California State University, Long Beach.

NEW ORLEANS NOIR
edited by Julie Smith
288 pages, a trade paperback original, $14.95

Brand new stories by: Ace Atkins, Laura Lippman, Patty Friedmann, Barbara Hambly, Tim McLoughlin, Olympia Vernon, David Fulmer, Jervey Tervalon, James Nolan, Kalamu ya Salaam, Maureen Tan, Thomas Adcock, Jeri Cain Rossi, Christine Wiltz, Greg Herren, Julie Smith, Eric Overmyer, and Ted O'Brien.

New Orleans Noir is a sparkling collection of tales exploring the city's wasted, gutted neighborhoods, its outwardly gleaming "sliver by the river," its still-raunchy French Quarter, and other hoods so far from the Quarter they might as well be on another continent.

MIAMI NOIR
edited by Les Standiford
356 pages, a trade paperback original, $15.95

Brand new stories by: James W. Hall, Barbara Parker, John Dufresne, Paul Levine, Carolina Garcia-Aguilera, Tom Corcoran, Christine Kling, George Tucker, Kevin Allen, Anthony Dale Gagliano, David Beaty, Vicki Hendricks, John Bond, Preston Allen, Lynne Barrett, Jeffrey Wehr.

"This well-chosen short story collection isn't just a thoughtful compilation of work by South Florida's best and upcoming writers . . . [it] is also a window on a different part of Miami-Dade and its melting pot of cultures." —*South Florida Sun-Sentinel*

BALTIMORE NOIR
edited by Laura Lippman
298 pages, a trade paperback original, $14.95

Brand new stories by: David Simon, Laura Lippman, Tim Cockey, Rob Hiaasen, Robert Ward, Sujata Massey, Jack Bludis, Rafael Alvarez, Marcia Talley, Joseph Wallace, Lisa Respers France, Charlie Stella, Sarah Weinman, Dan Fesperman, Jim Fusilli, and Ben Neihart.

"Mystery fans should relish this taste of Baltimore's seamier side."
—*Publishers Weekly*